CHRISTMAS WISHES & HEARTWARMING KISSES

A SWEET HOLIDAY COLLECTION

SOPHIE MAYS

With
SUNNY BROOKS

CONTENTS

KEY WEST CHRISTMAS

A GIRL'S GUIDE TO CREATING CHRISTMAS

SANTA BABY, MAYBE

SCOTTISH HOLIDAY

INTRODUCTION

This Sweet Romance Christmas Collection includes 6 wonderful, heartwarming holiday books! We hope these stories enliven your spirit, make you smile, and get you decking the halls in no time! Merry Christmas!

In **From New York, With Love** we join Emily and Josh as they confront some of life's trickier decisions. Throw in a Christmas tree farm visit, some warm apple cider, good Southern cooking, and everyone's favorite little town of Magnolia Harbor. Watch the downtown come alive under the twinkling holiday lights and find out if Emily and Josh will be celebrating the New Year alone or together.

In **A Whole Latte Christmas**, Sonia and Aiden connect, miscommunicate and come to know the true spirit of the Christmas season. Sip a warm latte and get snowed in to an adorable town in the Canadian Rockies.

In **A Girl's Guide To Creating Christmas**, single mom Natalie is overwhelmed running her small flower shop. Can her precocious daughter Fiona convince her after-school mentor, Paul, to help her plan a magical Christmas for her mom, and hopefully remind Natalie of the true meaning of the holidays?

In **Key West Christmas**, Josie makes a dramatic life change, but quickly realizes the realities of paradise may be a little more than she bargained for. Can her new friend Nate help her find her holiday spirit in the not-so-snowy Key West, Florida?

In **Santa Baby, Maybe,** Colin and Nora cross paths but never manage to connect; at least, not as much as they'd like to. When an unexpected layoff is thrust upon Colin just weeks before Christmas, his life begins to take some interesting turns. But could the upsetting changes really be a blessing in disguise? And could a woman like Nora ever look at him as more than the nice guy who held the door for her at Starbucks, especially if she found out he was also the mall Santa?

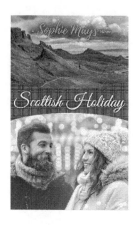

In **Scottish Holiday,** Jillian goes in search of her past and inadvertently finds her future. Venture to the wee Isle of of Lewis off Scotland and help Jillian track down her roots.

FROM NEW YORK, WITH LOVE

A Magnolia Harbor Holiday Novel

Sophie Mays

FROM NEW YORK, WITH LOVE

A Magnolia Harbor Novel

Speaking from personal experience…

One of the hardest things to give up is one's sense of identity. And while having a personal identity is important, it's amazing what can happen when you open yourself up to just being the simple, lovable human you were born being. No pretenses, no politics, just a person open to the world, open to learning, open to new experiences. That is often when true growth is allowed to happen. May each of us have those moments in life where we let down our well-constructed guard and open ourselves up to something new.

And if you do, may you be rewarded with something magical!

Love, Sophie

WELCOME TO SMALL TOWN USA

" *L*adies and gentlemen, we are nearing our destination. Please return your tray tables to their upright and closed position, power down any electronic devices you might be using, and store them under the seat in front of you until we land."

Emily thought that the stewardess had a kind voice, and she definitely loved the slight Southern accent. She grinned as she looked out the window.

"You won't be able to see anything quite yet, hun."

She looked over at the man seated beside her, an easy smile on his face. He was tall, taller than even her father who was over six feet, and built long and lean, with broad shoulders, strong arms, and a sharp jaw line. His weekend rock climbing kept him in incredible shape and had helped her to stay fit as well. Besides, it was kind of a fun date and allowed them to spend even more time together.

His hair was kept short, almost military style. She always wondered what he would look like with shaggy, unkempt hair, but she decided it would just be weird. Since he had kept it that way since she had known him, she was used to it and liked it just the way it was. He was clean shaven and had dark, thick eyebrows, bright blue eyes, and long, dark eyelashes that Emily was perpetually jealous of.

She was crazy about him, and she had secretly screamed like an excited little girl when he had invited her to his hometown for Christmas.

She shot him an animated grin, complete with a little shoulder shimmy. Josh shook his head, chuckling at her goofy mood.

"It's just been forever since I have been on a plane at all. Not to mention been able to go somewhere I've never been to before."

He laughed, and lifted his book off of the tray table, locking it upright again.

She returned her gaze outside, watching the clouds fly by the window, reminding her of mountains and valleys and idyllic places that always seemed like the exact opposite of her hometown of NYC. The sunlight was bright and warmed her face. She closed her eyes, totally content, and excited.

When she opened her eyes, the sunlight reflected her own face back at her. A round faced, moss green eyed woman with a childlike expression plastered on her face. Her light reddish hair was tied up in a messy bun, and she wore simple makeup and some pink lipstick. People often asked her if she dyed her hair, and then followed up with asking her who her stylist was. She loved to respond truthfully that it was natural, after which she almost always got skeptical glares, assuming she was keeping her beauty secret under close wraps. In a city like New York, it was to be expected. The hard edged cynicism was something she was so accustomed to that it just felt like home.

She didn't care, though. Josh thought she was pretty, and his opinion was the only one that mattered.

"The current temperature outside is fifty-seven degrees," the flight attendant said, and there were both whoops and groans from other people on board.

Emily snickered. "The difference between a northerner and a southerner, right?"

Josh nodded his head knowingly. He crossed his arms over his chest, and Emily relished the thought, not for the first time, that he was her boyfriend.

Her face melted into a teasing gaze. "So where does that leave you?" she asked, wiggling her eyebrows questioningly.

Josh considered her words, his eyes softly focused on the tiny fans and lights over their heads.

"Well, I suppose that my natural tendency is to think that fifty-seven is totally normal a week before Christmas. But in the last five years, I've gotten used to the frigid cold of New York. So I'm not sure. I guess a little of both."

Emily leaned her head on his shoulder affectionately, squeezing his forearm with her hand. He placed his hand over hers and gently ran his fingers up and down the back of her hand.

Even though they had been together for almost a year now, Emily still felt the spark of excitement whenever his fingers touched her skin. She was in a perpetual state of infatuation, just like a junior high girl. She was totally okay with it. It had been a long time since she'd lost her heart to someone, and the biggest cynic in the world couldn't convince her that this feeling wasn't well worth the risk.

Soon they were out of the clouds, and the stewardess was coming around to collect the last of the trash from the passengers. In the far off distance Emily had seen the plane passing over green, snow-capped mountains out of the window, a speckling of stretching farm fields, sprawling forests, and now coming into frame, the ocean.

"Wow," she said. "It's so green out there!"

Josh laughed. "Strange for this time of year, right?"

She nodded. It was so beautiful. She loved the city, loved the lights, the sounds, the people everywhere. It always felt so alive to her. She was never bored, and she could have literally anything that she wanted to eat at any time of day. It was ever changing, moving, growing. It felt like the center of the entire world.

But this felt alive too, in a completely different way. It was alien to her. Even though she had traveled to sparsely populated areas before, it still felt like culture shock to see it. Where was all of the concrete? Where were the lights?

She knew that the closest big city to Magnolia Harbor, the name of the town where Josh was from, was about forty-five minutes away, which seemed baffling. What had he done for fun growing up, she sometimes wondered.

"Do you think it will snow for Christmas?" She turned her eyes brightly on him. She couldn't tell which view she liked better; looking at Josh, or looking out of the window.

He shrugged his shoulders. "Not sure. If we get one or two days of real snow a year, it's a good year. And literally, everything closes."

She looked taken aback. "Really? Why?"

Josh leaned closer to her, peering out of the window past her. "Well, since we hardly get any snow, we don't really have the means to deal with it, you know? It's not like in the city where the snow plows come out and save the day by salting the streets. No, we just wait until it melts, which usually isn't very long."

"Huh," Emily said, looking back out the window. "It's just so weird that two hours ago, we were shivering in the snow." She tugged at the scarf around her neck. "I probably won't need this anymore, will I?"

Josh shrugged again. "I guess we will just have to see."

She sat back against the seat. They were almost there. This was really happening. She was really going to be meeting his family.

This was a big step in their relationship. He had met her mom plenty of times, but she was always jetting off with her new boyfriend, or busy with some other obligation. Her mom was like a hummingbird, absolutely terrific, but hard to catch for long periods of time.

This would be the first time Emily had met his parents, not to mention his sister, his brother, and the rest of his extended family.

It was pretty overwhelming.

"Okay, so your Mom's name is Nancy, right?"

Josh smiled, and gave her a look that she took to mean *how many times are you going to ask?*

"I know, I know," she said. "I'm just nervous."

"You are going to be just fine, Em," he said gently, patting her knee, and then just letting his hand rest there.

His affection calmed her racing heart ever so slightly.

"And your Dad is Phil," she continued.

Josh placated her and nodded his head.

"Brother is Kyle, sister is Ava..."

"Yes, and yes," he replied.

She was glad that he was allowing her to talk through her anxiety. He had learned early on that she tended to ramble when she was nervous, and she appreciated the comfortable way he let her.

"I just don't like living inside my head when I'm in freak out mode," she reminded him.

"I know," he said. "It's totally fine."

She exhaled sharply and looked back out of the window.

His parents had been married for almost thirty years, which was amazing in her mind. Each of her parents had been divorced more than once. She wondered what that kind of love was actually like. She liked the idea of it, definitely, but had always wondered if it was actually possible.

Apparently, it was. She would see soon enough, she figured.

"Em," Josh said quietly, inclining his head down to her. "They are going to love you. Trust me. There is nothing to be worried about."

She nodded up at him, but she still felt unsettled.

"I just don't want them to see this city girl who is dating their perfectly charming son. Everything I know about small town living I've learned from bad comedies!"

Josh smirked. "All they are going to see is the wonderful woman who has captured my heart and my soul."

She felt her cheeks flush, and she tried to stifle the massive grinned that wanted to overtake her face. "You are so sweet," she replied.

The plane touched down, and Emily was amazed at the view of the mountains in the distance. There was a layer of fog on the ground as if one of the clouds overhead had followed them down on their descent.

Emily pulled her phone out of her case and turned it on at the same time that Josh did. He opened his text messages.

She felt a pang of anxiety.

"Apparently they are running a few minutes late, but will meet us just outside of baggage claim," Josh said, sending a quick reply.

Emily nodded, feeling the encroaching frog in her throat. She opened the camera app and turned slightly away from Josh. While he was busy scanning work emails, she checked the state of her makeup. Some of her eyeliner had smudged, so she quickly fixed it. Her bun, however, was holding strong, which pleased her.

She pulled her lipstick out of her purse and reapplied.

She caught Josh in the camera looking at her, one eyebrow arched in question.

She closed the camera sheepishly.

He leaned over and kissed her on the cheek before getting to his feet to retrieve their carry-ons.

"You look beautiful, Em. As always. And seriously, there's no need to worry."

She jokingly rolled her eyes, putting her lipstick back in her purse. He was a man. He didn't quite understand a woman's need to be presentable and put together for the first time she was to meet her boyfriend's parents.

Josh helped a sweet old woman seated in front of them collect her bag from overhead, and Emily's heart swelled. He was such a good guy.

They carried their carry-on bags off of the plane, thanking the flight attendants as they passed by them. They stepped out onto the gangway and Emily was pleasantly surprised when there was no rush of icy air to greet them. Instead, it felt like a crisp, fall afternoon. Her spirits lifted, some of the nervousness falling away, as she followed Josh into the airport proper.

There were tons of people traveling, but, then again, it was the holiday season. Every seat at the gate was full, Emily observed, and everyone looked wither excited, flustered, or exhausted. Deck the Halls was playing over the loud speakers overhead, and the small airport was decorated with tinsel, Christmas lights, and ribbons everywhere you looked. Even though there was no snow outside that Emily could see, it still felt cheery and full of the Christmas spirit.

The airport was nothing like La Guardia, which was cavernous in comparison. There were a few shops, a couple restaurants, and less than half the number of gates, but Emily found it charming, even nostalgic. She told Josh it looked like something out of an ABC Family Christmas movie like she used to watch when she was a kid.

Knowing they still had a few minutes, Josh stopped and bought them both coffees at the Starbucks kiosk, and they followed the bright green signs and arrows that led them to baggage claim. She inhaled the friendly, familiar peppermint mocha aroma, comforted immediately by its warm presence in her hands. She tried teasing Josh for ordering an Eggnog Latte, insinuating it was a frou-frou drink for someone who carried himself like a CEO, but he just slurped it happily.

Baggage claim was flooded with people from arriving flights, hurrying to collect their belongings and begin their holidays. She and Josh were no different, but she was thankful that they had packed mostly everything for their weeklong trip in their carry-on bags. They only had to wait for one checked bag containing Christmas gifts and they would be on their way.

Josh towered over a lot of the people in the long, broad room. It was loud, too, with everyone talking over one another, or calling out to others, and the occasional child crying. It was bustling, but Emily didn't mind. It felt like being in any department store this time of year in New York City.

She watched as he scanned the room, and when recognition and delight appeared on his face, she knew that he had found his parents.

A small wave of nausea came over her, but she put on a brave, big smile, and grabbed his hand as they made their way through the crowds toward them. She inadvertently squeezed tightly, and he replied with a reassuring squeeze of his own.

Emily was torn. She wanted to get the waiting over with, meet them and be done with it, yet she also had a strong impulse to turn around, run back through the airport and have the plane take her back home.

"Hi!" she heard in a jubilant tone.

They broke free of the crowd, and Emily found a couple standing near the brochures kiosk.

Immediately, she could see the resemblance between Josh and his parents. It was quite striking.

His dad was as tall as Josh was, and built almost the same way. Even at his age, he appeared to be in fantastic shape. He had dark, slightly receding hair that was flecked with salt and pepper just above his ears. He wore glasses, but still seemed to have the air of youth in his eyes. Dressed smartly, he wore a navy blue North Face jacket and well-worn jeans.

His wife, Josh's mother, was not nearly as tall as her husband and had hair that reminded Emily of honey. It was short, cut just below her ears, and slightly curly. It bounced when she clapped her hands excitedly. She had a gentle face, and Emily could see where Josh got his baby blues from.

She was very pretty and didn't look nearly old enough to be Josh's Mom. She, too, was dressed well, in a pair of cute ankle boots, green skinny jeans, and a black jacket.

As they approached, Josh's Mom threw her arms out wide, almost dancing she was so excited. When he was in reach, she threw her arms around his neck, laughing.

Josh's father looked at Emily with the same elated expression on his face. He stepped forward to her.

"You must be Emily!" he said, and he held out his hand to her.

His demeanor was just as relaxed and easy going as his son's, and immediately she felt at ease. She accepted the handshake, and he enveloped her hand with his other one, heartily shaking it.

"I am. It is very nice to meet you, Mr. Morris."

Mr. Morris shook his head. "Please, call me Phil."

The excited laughter of Josh's Mom was shortly turned on her, and Emily felt Mrs. Morris' arms wrapped around her neck, hugging her.

Emily was totally taken aback. Physical affection, apart from Josh's, was not something that she was used to. Startled, it took her a moment to reciprocate.

"Oh, sweetheart, we are so glad to have you!" Mrs. Morris said from somewhere near her ear.

When she pulled away, she kept her hands on Emily's shoulder, looking her all over.

"Oh, Joshua, she is just as cute as a button!"

Emily smiled at the recognition of her accent. Josh had a slight accent, not having been in the south for five years, the potency of it had worn off. But his mother's accent was thick and pleasing to the ear.

Josh grinned. "She is indeed."

She turned back to Emily, lowering her hands. "We are so pleased that you could join us for Christmas. We have been just dying to meet you."

Emily, feeling sheepish, nodded her head.

Josh disappeared momentarily and returned with their checked bag. "All right, we are good to go," he notified the group.

"Here, let me carry your bag out to the car," Phil said, reaching out for Emily's bag.

"Oh, thank you," she said, surprised. Apparently, chivalry was not dead, and she rather liked it.

"Yes, yes, let's get going! Aunt Mary is back at the house getting dinner ready!" His mother said, and they all turned toward the exit together.

"Is Ava coming over today?" Josh asked.

"She is," Phil answered. "She will be over for dinner."

Josh's face split into a smile again.

Emily sighed, her earlier tension seeping away like snow melting in the spring sunshine. She felt better like the worst was over.

Outside, Emily was surprised at how mild it was. She commented on it, and Josh's mother laughed. "Josh said that it was snowing in New York yesterday, wasn't it?"

"It was," Emily replied.

They walked across the parking lot and located their car. Emily was surprised to see a nice, high-end Subaru waiting for them. She wasn't sure why she had been expecting a station wagon or a pickup truck.

Josh helped his Dad pack the trunk, and they all slid inside the car.

Josh's mom hovered her hands over the vents in the car and looked at her husband. "Hurry up and turn the heat on. It's cold!"

Josh looked over at Emily and made a gesture like he was freezing, rubbing up and down his jacketed arms. Then he reached across the seat and took her hand in his, squeezing it reassuringly.

You did great, he mouthed at her.

Thanks, she mouthed in reply. *I like them!*

That seemed to please him.

The landscape was already far different, made even more apparent as they got outside of the airport. There were no towering skyscrapers, no stand still traffic, and no horns blaring from an obnoxious amount of yellow taxis. It was refreshing to see more green than concrete, and more sky than glass and metal.

They pulled away from the airport, and again, the surroundings changed. Emily gazed outside, fascinated by the lack of anything familiar around. It was both exhilarating and alienating.

His mother turned around in her seat, still grinning at the two of them.

"Welcome to small town USA."

THE MEET & GREET

*E*mily began to relax as they drove along. She was asked about all of the typical things: did they have a nice flight, how her job was going, and if Josh was working himself too hard. Emily was happy to answer all the questions they had for her. Josh's mom had insisted Emily call her Nancy, though she told Josh not to even think about it, and the easy repartee between them all had Emily feeling as if she already knew them.

About an hour after leaving the airport, Nancy said, "Here we are, Magnolia Harbor."

The charming sign on the side of the road looked as if it could have been hand-carved, painted in salt sprayed blue and white. It was like stepping into a different world, Emily thought, or driving straight into a Hallmark movie town.

The main downtown itself, she saw, was a small, two lane road with brick and mortar storefronts. There were flower boxes outside of the windows, happy hand painted signs, and even some swanky little spots that looked newly renovated. There were people walking along the sidewalks, and Emily was convinced that it was as pretty as a postcard.

"Awful busy today," Phil said.

"Yes," Nancy agreed. She turned around and smiled at Emily. "This is Main Street. This is where most of our commerce is. This and a few other side streets just off Main. All of the roads from the harbor lead here, and this is where all of the tourists come in the summer. Granted, most of the year is pretty quiet. Christmas is mostly just the locals. The coast hardly ever has picturesque Christmas snow for Christmas, though we get light dustings, and sometimes we get a full on snow storm."

"And sometimes you can walk around in shorts and flip flops on Christmas Eve," Josh's father interjected.

"True," Nancy continued, "but it certainly isn't the tropical Christmas that Florida has. However, it has its own charm, and we love it just the same."

"Small town America," Josh said and grinned at Emily. He gazed back out the window with the same pleasant look on his face. "It's hard to fully appreciate until you've been away from it for a while."

They turned down another side street and followed some hills further and further up. The trees became sparse and as they rounded a corner, nestled atop a hill, a lovely, two story, white home with sky blue shutters appeared. There was a great green yard surrounding the house, with a few large, ancient oak trees, one with a tire swing attached to a branch as thick around as Josh's waist.

When they pulled into the driveway, she could immediately see why there were so few trees toward the back of the house.

In the early afternoon sun, Emily saw the hills spill down directly to the Atlantic Ocean, facing the harbor of Magnolia Harbor itself. The dark blue and gray waves lapped against the shore in the distance, and she could see a few houses dotted along the landscape, all of which must have spectacular views as well.

They stepped out of the car, and Emily could only stand there, holding onto the car door, looking in awe at her surroundings.

She could smell the salt in the air and felt the wind whipping back the few strands of hair that had come loose from her bun. She inhaled deeply, letting it all sink in.

She could get used to this, she told herself. She needed to vacation outside the city more often.

Josh and his Dad gathered their suitcases from the trunk, and Emily followed Nancy to the front door.

It was the prettiest house that she had ever seen. The front door was inlaid with frosted glass, etched in a lovely, symmetrical almost tear drop pattern. The foyer inside the door opened up into a long hallway that stretched all the way to the back of the house, revealing a wall of windows that gazed out into the harbor. It was full of homey furnishings, mostly made of wood or stone, a round mirror, candles, and what looked like a beautiful hand carved pew that must have been taken from an old church. Burlap and cotton pillows were scattered across it decoratively.

"Hello?" Nancy called as she stepped inside.

There were several distant cries of jubilation in response, followed quickly by a number of people coming around the corner at the end of the hall.

Emily felt a rush of cool air as the door opened behind her, and Josh and his father entered the house.

The group of people took turns tossing their arms around Josh, asking all sorts of questions, all speaking over one another. Emily stood back near the staircase in front of the door and waited patiently for the attention to inevitably turn on her.

She had not prepared for the onslaught of half a dozen people, so when they finally noticed her, she didn't know what to expect. She had expected there to be a lot fewer hugs and a lot more brief acknowledgments. That was what she was used to, after all. Loud acknowledgments, but brief. Not this level of warm familiarity.

She hugged everyone, feeling her eyebrows arching up into her hairline with surprise with every new loving introduction. But despite the initial anxiety that had washed over her, she felt happy. She could not remember that she had ever been welcomed so warmly by anyone.

"Emily, this is Aunt Mary," Josh said, gesturing to a short, plump woman with dark hair that fell to her shoulders, streaked with gray. She beamed at Emily, her cheeks rosy and her blue eyes bright. She waved with both hands. She wore a lovely floral sweater and jeans with a crisp white apron wrapped around her waist.

"And this is Grandma Thora," he continued. The woman who stood beside Mary was even smaller, slight framed, with white hair that was short and styled in a way that Emily thought could only come from a trip to the salon, though was probably just from years of practice. She wore a lovely pair of blue glasses on a chain around her neck. She had on a bright red fleece sweatshirt, a nice pair of slacks, and a wide smile.

He also introduced his Uncle George, who was Mary's husband; his cousin Martha, who was almost eight months pregnant and had soon teetered back to the kitchen; and he introduced his other Aunt Lily.

"And I'm Ava!"

A young woman slightly younger than Emily re-appeared through the crowd. She had been one of the ones who had hugged her already as the group had taken turns jostling for hug position. She had a thin, pretty face, with the same color eyes as Josh. She had thick auburn hair that was tied in a braid that hung over her shoulder. She wore a pretty yellow cardigan with jeans and a floral scarf in her hair.

Emily beamed. "You are Josh's sister."

"Only sister," she teased, and she knuckled Josh in the side. She wasn't even as tall as Josh's shoulder.

"I thought you weren't coming until later," he replied, batting her hand away and rubbing his ribs.

Ava shrugged. "My boss let me go early. Said it would be a shame to waste any time with you now that you are actually back in town."

She turned and pointed to the scarf around Emily's neck. "Cute scarf!"

Emily touched the soft fabric. "Thanks," she replied.

"Come on, let me show you to your room," Nancy said, touching Emily gently on the arm. "Don't worry, I will bring her back down quickly so you can all talk to her."

Those gathered at the foot of the stairs laughed. Josh and Emily followed his Mom up the steps.

"Don't worry, dear," Nancy said, lacing her arm through Emily's. "They won't swarm you like that again."

Emily waved it off as if it was nothing, but relief ran through her none the less.

"We are just all so excited that you are here. Josh has not brought a woman home to meet his family since college. And even then, she still lived sort of local. Plus, she only came for dinner."

They came to the landing, and Emily found another long, narrow hallway with a window at the very end. She could see that instead of a view of the harbor, there was a wonderful view of the surrounding trees that seemed to go on forever.

Dropping her voice, Nancy added, "And don't worry, I don't think that Josh has ever been as serious about a woman as you."

"Mom, come on," Josh piped in, easily able to hear her hushed tone. Though he was scarcely trying to hide his good-natured appreciation of his mom reassuring Emily of his devotion.

"Here we are," she said, opening the first door on the right. "This is Ava's room. I hope you don't mind that the two of you will be sharing a room."

"Of course not," Emily responded. "I have a roommate back in New York. I am used to sharing a small space with someone else."

She walked into the room and was pleased with how pretty everything was. The full sized bed was positioned right in the middle of the room between the two windows on the far wall. There was a shabby chic dresser in a distressed finish along one wall, and a small closet filled the other. A small air mattress was blown up between the bed and the wall, beneath one of the windows.

"Though I definitely don't have a view this amazing from my apartment," Emily said, peering out of the window as she set her purse down on the air mattress.

"Hey, I made the bed for you!" She turned and saw that Ava had snuck into the room and was now standing beside Josh.

Emily shook her head. "No, the air mattress is fine. I would hate to take your bed."

"It used to be my bed. Well, I guess it still sort of is. But I am only staying for the next two nights. I have my own place in town."

Emily glanced at the bed. "No, I couldn't."

"I insist," Ava said as she took Emily's suitcase out of Josh's hands and tossed it on the bed.

"My room is across the hall," Josh said, stepping out of the room and opening the opposing door.

Curiosity overtook her, and she followed him across the hall.

The room was entirely different than his loft in New York City. His apartment was decked out in sleek, modern furnishings, with dark woods, pure whites, muted colors, and polished cement. His room here could only be described as the exact opposite. His bed was solid wood, and it was only a twin sized, which was amusing to her because he was so tall. The wallpaper was like something in a hunting cabin, with ducks, deer, and bears in the pattern. There was a stack of clean quilts stacked on the carved dresser which looked like it had been found in that same cabin in the forest. A shelf ran around the room about a foot from the ceiling, and she saw stuffed animals, toy cars, and even a working toy train up in it.

On the wall were pictures, both framed and apparently cut from magazines. Cars, sports team photos, and even a photo of him, Ava and another boy who Emily assumed was his older brother Kyle. His favorite sports team, the Tar Heels, were proudly represented on a small flag banner that hung above his bed.

Emily leaned against the door frame. "This is not what I expected," she said, smirking.

Josh flopped down on the bed. "Oh? What do you mean by that?"

Emily shrugged. "This feels too…country for you."

Josh grinned. "Nah, I like the rustic, slightly industrial feel. The wood and the steel."

Emily reflected and realized that the more she thought about it, perhaps his apartment was a lot more like this room than she had initially thought, just modernized. While he had a sleek modern dresser in his bedroom, he had a rough cut West Elm wooden coffee table in the living room cut straight from a large slab of tree trunk, and instead of quilts, he had down blankets available in every room. His couch, which was a very modern gray sectional sofa, was surrounded by soft lights with gentle decorating nods to the forest and the ocean, and had a big painting of a harbor hanging over it.

She suddenly felt like she understood him so much better. These things that she had always loved about him, his love of the water and the ocean, made so much more sense seeing them in the context of his youth.

Nancy poked her head into the room. "Josh, I am heading down to help with dinner. You two should join us. I imagine you are starving."

"Yes, ma'am," Josh said, nodding his head.

Nancy and Ava smiled then walked back down the hall.

Emily arched an eyebrow. *Ma'am? Never heard him say that before...*

Emily felt a flush of heat and decided to pull off her scarf and outer sweater. Being inside and out of the wind, she was starting to warm up.

"Warm?" Josh asked as he lifted himself out of bed and followed her back across the hall.

Emily nodded, walking over to her suitcase. She pulled her t-shirt down as she tugged the sweater up over her head. "It's almost thirty degrees warmer here than back home. I'm definitely too warm."

She and Josh made their way downstairs and into the kitchen. It was just as beautiful as the foyer and the rooms upstairs. Large windows spanned the whole far wall overlooking the harbor, and the view flowed unendingly into the living room beyond. The main living room was filled with squishy couches, a large flat screen, and whitewashed bookshelves flanking a blazing fireplace. Josh's father and uncle were in the living room prepping the fireplace.

"Hey, Josh, come here," Phil called. Josh leaned down, kissing Emily on the cheek, before joining the men.

The kitchen was so bright and open, and to her surprise, modern. Much of the decor gave off an antique vibe, but the stove, the fridge, and the wine fridge were all state-of-the-art. The island in the middle of the kitchen was covered in a bright white quartz, and the cabinetry beneath was basically the same bluish-gray of the ocean crashing outside the window.

"Ah, there you are!" Josh's grandmother, Thora, said, coming around the wide kitchen island. "Look at you. Aren't you freezing?"

Grandma Thora rubbed her hands over Emily's bare arms. "Actually, this is perfect. It was snowing when we left!"

Aunt Mary patted the sweater she wore. "We must look out of our minds to you, don't we? All bundled up like this."

The other women in the kitchen laughed, and Emily had to join it.

"I'm pretty sure half of New England would think it was summer in December if they came down here right now. This is definitely what we'd consider t-shirt weather."

Aunt Mary shuddered, "The moment that thermometer hits seventy degrees, I pull out all of my winter clothes, from sweaters to long johns."

The group "hear hear-ed" in knowing agreement.

Emily couldn't help but be amused. "Can I help with anything?"

"Of course," Grandma Thora said, and she guided Emily further into the kitchen. "How do you feel about mixing?"

"I am confident I can do a decent job," she said.

The very pregnant Martha beamed at her, a pristine apron now tied over her huge belly and handed Emily a glass bowl full of butter and sugar.

"Just cream those, dear," Grandma Thora said. "Those are the basis for my famous sugar cookies."

Emily's stomach rumbled.

"Don't worry, dinner will be ready soon," Aunt Mary continued. "I don't know if Nancy told you, but there's a family tradition around here that everyone picks the tree and decorates together, so with Josh only being able to come just before Christmas, it becomes a mad scramble to get everything done in time. But we love our traditions, and Josh, so we don't give him too hard a time about it." She gave Emily a cherubic wink.

Ava leaned on the counter perched on her elbows, a frosted butter knife held casually in her hands. Emily noticed that she had some gingerbread cookies on a cutting board in front of her.

"So Mom tells me that you are a magazine editor," Ava said, her eyes flashing excitedly at the words.

The other women in the kitchen turned their eyes on Emily.

Emily, whose hand was clamped tightly on the wooden spoon mixing her ingredients, nodded her head. "Yep, I am."

"Wow," Aunt Mary said. "That's a pretty fancy job."

Emily shrugged. "I don't know about that."

Grandma Thora squinted at her, and pulled the glasses hanging around her neck up to her eyes, presumably to take a better look. She picked up a platter of finger sandwiches and walked them over to the table in the dining room. "Isn't that something similar to what Josh does?"

Ava shook her head. "No, Nana, he's a manager at one of those super fancy hotels there in Manhattan."

Emily nodded. "That's true. Assistant manager, though with the way he works, I'm sure he'll be manager one day. That's how we met actually."

All of their eyes were on her again. "Really?" Martha gushed.

Emily smiled sheepishly. "Yep..." she kept her eyes on the butter and the sugar in the bowl. "It was almost exactly a year ago. The magazine I work for was attending an event at his hotel, just before Christmas, actually. It was a really upscale affair, and I managed to knock over an entire tray full of champagne..." her cheeks flushed at the memory.

"I would have probably done the same," Ava commented.

"It was pretty embarrassing. Anyhow, my boss somehow got the managers involved, and Josh ended up being the one to help me get everything straightened up."

"And it was love at first sight?" Aunt Mary said, fluttering her eyelashes.

The women all giggled expectantly, wanting to know.

"Something like that," Emily rolled her eyes coyly, but knew she didn't look nearly as cool and unfazed as she wanted. She had been attracted to him from the first moment they spoke. "I did spend the first few hours of knowing him apologizing repeatedly, but after that, we actually started relating about real things."

The group of women threw one another knowing glances and seemed content with knowing that their Josh was well loved.

"Joshua?" Grandma Thora called. "Can you please get this pitcher down for me?"

"Yes, ma'am," she heard him say, and he made his way back into the kitchen.

Emily was slightly thrown off when she heard him said that. She wasn't sure why if it felt bothersome to her or just made her feel strangely awkward. She had never heard him use such formal language with anyone in New York. Wasn't that a super antiquated thing? Did people still actually teach their kids to say that? She knew it was a form of respect, and he obviously cared about his family deeply, and they him. But something about it was still alien to her.

She watched as Josh reached up on top of the cabinets and lowered down a tacky jug that was decorated to resemble Santa's jacket. It was kitschy, and Emily thought it was so ugly that it was almost endearing. Almost.

Grandma Thora seemed pleased, however, and went to the sink to fill it up.

"Now," Martha said, passing a steel bowl across the island to Emily. "Just set this off to the side while I get the other ingredients for the cookies." She lowered her head conspiratorially toward Emily. "But you can't tell anyone this recipe. It's a secret."

"Oh, don't worry," Emily said, "my lips are sealed."

She moved Martha's metal bowl over to her side of the counter, then reached back for the glass bowl with the butter and sugar to continue mixing it. She didn't even make a full rotation before her elbow swung into the metal bowl and it toppled off of the counter onto the floor.

Mortified, Emily stared at the mess that stretched halfway across the kitchen floor.

"Oh no!" she exclaimed, her hands to her cheeks. "Oh, I am so sorry!"

She looked over at the other women in the kitchen, all of whom burst out laughing. Emily just stared at them, startled by their reaction.

Grandma Thora was laughing the hardest of all. "Oh, sweetheart, think nothing of it," she said, coming around to see the damage. "No harm done. We will get it cleaned up in a jiffy."

Emily, her face as red as Ava's fleece, stepped cautiously away, her feet totally covered in the flour.

"Just like when we met, right hun?"

She looked up and saw Josh standing near the dining table, watching her closely. A small smile crept over his face.

She squinted her eyes in embarrassment, but smiled all the same. Within seconds she joined in with the other women in the room cleaning up the spill, chatting, and feeling more comfortable with these very new people than she did with most others in her life.

Dinner was delicious, complete with cheddar biscuits, roasted veggies, a winter squash soup, three kinds of casserole and chocolate bourbon pecan pie for dessert. Everything looked like it was taken out of a magazine, with the sunset streaming through the back windows, flooding the floor with warm pools of light. Emily's little incident with the spilled ingredients didn't stay in anyone's mind for long, though Josh would occasionally look over at her with a small, sly smirk on his face, and she would nudge him with her foot underneath the table and give him a mock growling face.

After dinner, Emily helped Grandma Thora finish the cookies and then helped Ava decorate some gingerbread men. She was pretty sure that they ate more than they decorated, but it was a delicious mistake that she did not regret.

Emily was totally sure that she had not ever celebrated Christmas without snow, or at the very least, slush. Aunt Mary put on a Michael Buble cd, and they spent a good amount of time singing along to the crooner's holiday songs. Josh's dad and uncle talked about which farm was the best to buy the tree from that year, and his Mom brought boxes down from the attic full of lights and garland and ribbons.

With all the cheer and revelry, she found that the lack of snow outside hardly bothered her.

TO THE TREE FARM

*T*he next morning everyone convened early in the kitchen for shrimp and grits, before the rest of the extended family pulled up and signaled that they were ready to go. Emily and Josh each finished their coffee as fast as they could and scrambled into the car alongside Josh's parents and Ava.

The three of them were shoulder to shoulder in the backseat, and Emily imagined that this must have been what it was like for Ava, Josh, and Kyle growing up.

"To the tree farm!" Josh's dad exclaimed as he hit the gas and pulled out onto the main road heading out of town.

"Okay, so we need to lay the ground work for you," Josh said to Emily. "Every year there is a competition as to who can find the fullest and best-looking tree, cut it down, and get it back to the main area fastest. Extra points are given if you are sitting back casually, drinking cider and looking like you've been waiting on the other team for ages."

"Wait, what do you mean, cut it down?" Emily looked completely baffled. "I thought we were going to a place that sells trees. Are we just, going to the forest? Is that even legal?"

The entire car stifled amused and endearing snickers, before Josh's mom interjected.

"No, you're right, we are going to a tree farm. Believe it or not, a good amount of Christmas trees that you see at tree stands around the country, come from this region of the country. So it's a little bit of a sign of pride that we can't just buy a tree when we have every means of just cutting one ourselves. And don't worry, it's perfectly legal." She gave Emily the warmest, most maternal smile Emily had perhaps ever seen.

"You'll see," Josh nudged Emily's shoulder. "It's pretty cool."

After what seemed like several hours, they pulled onto a long dirt road that led to the entrance of the Tree Farm. When they pulled up to the parking area, Emily saw that there was a more of an attraction than just a farm with some trees. There was a hayride in operation, a roaring fire with logs set around it for sitting on, an adorable country store that had a local gingerbread house competition on display, and free hot apple cider and cookies set up for snacking.

Three other cars pulled up next to theirs, and various members of Josh's family piled out. From the car next to them, a tall man, who was built more like a block than Josh, but was roughly their age, jumped out and crashed into Josh. He had dark hair, dark, thick eyebrows, and wore a Tar Heels baseball cap.

He grappled Josh into a headlock, as Josh tried to duck out from underneath it.

The two men play fought and laughed together.

"It's good to see you, little bro," the other man said.

Josh, still happily panting, swung a hand out to try and knock the baseball cap off his brother. "Good to see you too, Kyle."

Kyle turned his blue eyes on Emily. They weren't the exact same color as Josh's; there was more of a green tint to them, but the family resemblance was still there. She had to admit, he was just as good looking as Josh was.

"So this is the woman who stole your heart?" Kyle asked. He held out a large, muscular hand toward her. "Nice to meet you, I'm Kyle."

Emily grinned widely and took his offered hand and shook. "Nice to meet you too. I'm Emily."

"So have they filled you in on the fact that our side of the family is the reigning champions of the tree competition?"

"I've heard a story or two in the 17 hours car ride that we just had," she chuckled.

"Ha, yeah, I imagine. Well in the last few years, my wife Jillian and I have had to join the competition as our own unit, but you guys are in luck, because we already got our tree, so it's going to be Team Morris back together again."

A slight, pretty woman, who had straw colored hair that framed her face nicely, got out of the driver's seat. Emily could see that she had been trying to wrap herself in as much layering as possible before exiting the heated car.

"Hey hun, come over and meet Josh' girlfriend Emily," Kyle boomed.

Jillian came right over to Emily and gave her a hug. "It's so nice to finally meet you, Emily. Josh has told me a lot about you over the last year. We are so excited that you could actually come and visit."

Emily looked surprised, but Jillian filled her in, "I probably talk to Josh more than Kyle does. I've been with Kyle since we were in college, so I've known him forever. Come on, let's get some cider, I'm freezing!"

Emily threw a happy glance over toward Josh, then followed Jillian over toward the refreshment set up.

The next two hours were some of the silliest and most fun that Emily had experienced in as long as she could remember. Everyone congregated around the fire pit, hot apple ciders in hand, and went over the ground rules. Team Miller was made up of Josh's parents, Kyle, Jillian, Ava, Josh, and Emily. Josh's cousin Martha and her husband joined Aunt Mary and Uncle George's team, while the last team was Aunt Lily, her husband, and yet more cousins. Grandma Thora was the designated judge and told everyone that they would find her sitting happily right here where they were going to leave her, enjoying the fire.

On the count of three, the teams each raced off onto the awaiting tree fields. They had the choice of using either a chain saw or a handsaw to cut the trees down and had all agreed that this year they would use hand saws.

Kyle, Ava, and Josh raced up and down the rows of trees, calling to the others to come check out this tree or another. Emily and Jillian walked arm in arm while Jillian filled Emily in on all the family gossip and funny Josh stories. Nancy and Phil strolled behind their children, sipping their cider, guarding the handsaw and sizing up the tree options.

Eventually, an excited yell came from Ava off a few rows over. Team Miller rounded the tree, sizing it up. Emily had to admit that it was a pretty impressive specimen. There was no way a tree like that would have ever fit at one of her homes. Kyle felt that he had a really strong contender as well, and the group made its way over for comparison. After much deliberation, and a little running back and forth between Kyle and Ava's trees, the consensus was that Ava's was the one.

Everyone took turns sawing at the tree. During each person's turn the rest of the group would sing a Christmas song, and when it was done, the person sawing got to hand off to someone else. It made the work so much more fun, and slightly less arduous.

"This is a workout!" Emily huffed from under the tree, sawing her heart out. Laying across the pine scented ground with branches pulling parts of her ponytail out, she was glad they had chosen to sing Let It Snow instead of O Holy Night.

Roughly ten Christmas carols later and the mighty fir tree fell. The group cheered and high-fived as Nancy appeared on the back of a tractor with one of the farm attendants. After her last turn, she had gone to the main barn and asked for the tree sleigh to be pulled around. The timing was right on. The tree was hauled onto the sleigh and zipped back toward the parking area.

When the group got back to the fire pit, they saw the others moseying up as well. Martha and Grandma Thora were sitting in rocking chairs that had been brought over for them, and they were eating cookies with their feet perched up on log ottomans. With the three trees all present and ready for inspection, Grandma Thora got up and walked around each one, inspecting it with a detective's eye. Josh, Martha's husband, and another cousin each held their team's respective tree. Emily thought they all looked like the most impressive Christmas trees that she had ever seen, aside from the giant tree in Rockefeller Center. But it seemed that Grandma Thora had a discerning eye. She noted a slight bald spot on the side of one, an uneven slope to another, and a wonky top branch of the third. All the teams kept shouting in defense of their contestants.

Come on, Nanna, you know this one's the best!

No way, look at the height on ours.

Yeah, but yours is too skinny, ours is perfectly full.

Nanna, you would have totally chosen this tree if you were out there, trust me.

Finally, Grandma Thora stepped back. Emily couldn't be sure, but she thought she saw the older woman throw a quick, sly look in her direction before declaring, "Well, this was a tough one this year to be sure. I don't know, maybe it's that big city lucky charm, but this year's winner is…Team Miller."

A whoop and a holler came from Josh's immediate family, with a few letdown boos from the others, followed by laughter and claps on the back. This was the friendliest competition Emily had ever seen.

"Alright," Josh's dad said to the group, "Winners treat for lunch! Let's go."

With smiles abound, the large group made its way around back behind the main gift shop and front office to find a huge open barn that had been converted into a restaurant. Picnic tables were lined throughout, and heaters were blaring as they walked through the big open barn doors.

The three boys who had stayed behind to get their trees onto their respective cars soon joined the group, and a down-home royal feast was enjoyed by all.

Emily fell asleep on Josh's shoulder during the long car ride home, cloaked in the magical scent of smoky firewood and evergreens.

DAYDREAMING

*B*ack at the house, the tree was shaken out and left to settle, and everyone looked to be taking some time to unwind. Josh asked Emily if she wanted to take a walk outside with him and she heartily agreed.

The backyard was enormous. Emily was surprised to see that the sloping hill that the house was perched on leveled out a little ways down into a big, flat area with perfectly mowed grass. Currently, empty flower beds lined the stairs that led down to it.

They walked further away from the house, and Emily relished the time alone with Josh. She reached up, placed her hand in the crook of his arm, and snuggled in close to him.

"Cold?" he asked.

She shook her head. "Definitely not. It's wonderful out."

He chuckled low in his throat. "Guess I have acclimated to New York a bit because I'm comfortable too."

The ocean looked like a pane of glass, stretched out across the horizon. The sun, which was now behind them, made long shadows from the trees that seemed to stretch on forever.

"So...how are you enjoying all of this?" he asked.

"Oh, it's wonderful," she replied. "Your family is so nice, and are being so welcoming."

Josh looked down at her. "I'm sorry if they have been overwhelming or overbearing or anything."

"Please, I'm from New York," she replied. "I'm used to overbearing."

"Yeah, but aggressive isn't the same as an onslaught of physical affection."

Emily laughed. "That is true. But no, it's been very nice. I just hope they like me as much as I like them."

"I have no doubt," Josh replied.

Emily nudged him. "So you never brought a girl home before?"

Josh's face flushed slightly while he thought about it for a second. "Never did, I guess. Like she said, once in college. I dated in college, but never to where I felt like bringing the person home for a holiday or anything."

"No girlfriend in high school?"

"I was too busy with sports and all of my advanced placement classes to have a girlfriend. There was one girl at church I liked, but we were never more than just friends."

Emily felt a mix of jealousy, curiosity, and understanding. "Whatever happened to her?"

"She was married as soon as she graduated from college," he said, giving her a knowing look. "So no, you don't need to worry about her ever popping back up in my life. We lost contact after we graduated high school, anyway."

"I guess I kind of understand why everyone sort of freaked out that you brought me here then," she continued.

He nodded. "You could say they can see things are pretty serious."

A joyful bliss swept through her like a crashing wave.

They spent a few minutes talking about their afternoon with his family. Emily asked questions about everyone, about their lives, their jobs, their hobbies. She was especially curious about Ava.

"She is just so sweet. Is she seeing anyone?"

Josh shrugged. "I don't know. If she is, she hasn't told any of us about him yet."

"That's too bad," Emily said. "I bet I could set her up with one of our friends back in the city."

Josh shook his head. "I think she would walk all over them," and then he smiled.

Emily had to chuckle in agreement.

"What do you think of Magnolia Harbor so far?" Josh asked.

"It is breathtaking," Emily replied. "I have never been anywhere like it."

Josh sighed. "I totally understand that. That's how I felt when I moved to New York. It was like a totally different planet. Everything was weird, I didn't know where anything was, and no one was nice."

Emily shot him a mocking look of incredulity. Being a native New Yorker, she had to defend her people.

"Not in the same way southern or Midwesterners are," he added as a caveat.

Emily laughed. "Yeah, that's New York for you."

"But I have come to really like the city, I have to say," he continued. He did a full sweep of their surroundings. "It is really nice to be back, though."

Emily could see why he loved it so much.

They started to walk down the stairs to the big open field area.

"We used to play football in this open area every Thanksgiving," Josh said, pointing to the big clearing at the bottom of the hill. "My cousins, brother, dad, uncles…even grandpa would play. It was always a big event. We even had a trophy."

"A trophy? Sounds intense," Emily said.

Josh smiled. He slid his other hand into his pocket. "My dad, my brother and I won two out of every three games. Used to drive my oldest cousin Talon absolutely nuts. He was the QB on his high school team, so he was very touchy about his talent being challenged. And all us cousins were younger than he was and only played in the backyard for fun."

Emily smiled at the rich family dynamic.

"And my high school graduation party was down here," he continued. He swept his hand over the flat ground. "We had a big tent, with lots of tables and chairs, and my dad grilled enough hot dogs and burgers for almost two hundred people."

"Two hundred?" she asked.

He nodded. "Most of our church came, as well as a bunch of my friends and their families. We had a bunch of games of corn hole going on that sort of turned into a tournament, and that night, we lit sparklers and roman candles and played flag football."

He laughed at a sudden memory. "My friend Mike actually caught a ball in mid-air and ended up landing on one of the strings keeping the tent up, pulling it right out of the ground, which caused the tent to start caving in on itself. At the time we were freaking out about it, but looking back, it was just hilarious."

Emily was almost jealous of all of the memories he had here. She never really had a yard growing up, unless she counted going to Central Park to play, or to her grandparents' house, who lived just outside of the city. But his life was so different than hers, and she was grateful that he was sharing as much as he was with her.

"What about the harbor?" Emily asked, gazing into the distance. She could still see the water in the harbor glistening through the trees. "Did you ever spend time there?"

"Oh man, all the time," Josh said. His eyes took on a distant look. "My parents had a fishing boat that we kept docked at the harbor almost all year round. We used to go fishing all day, then clean our fish right there on the dock at the harbor. I think I spent more time on that boat in the summer than I did in my own room."

"Wow," she said.

"I remember this one time when Kyle and I were wandering around the boardwalk looking for some cheap ice cream. It was so hot that we were miserable. Mom and Dad were prepping the boat to go out, but we were boys and got bored really easily. Mom gave us some money and told Kyle to take me to get something cold for all of us. We found a popsicle stand, and the guy working at it was really nice. He handed us all of the popsicles we had ordered, and as we started walking back, a very aggressive seagull appeared on the dock and started taunting Kyle, who was holding the majority of them.

The popsicles were melting fast in the heat, and we kept trying to shoo him away, but that bird was brave and determined. I was laughing so hard the whole time, I almost cried. Finally, Kyle tried to nudge it away with his foot so we could make a run for it when it jumped into the air and snatched one of the popsicles out of his hand and took off with it. Kyle was so freaked out when the bird actually grabbed the popsicle that he ended up dropping two other ones."

"Kyle was shouting and carrying on, and I was just laughing. Then he started yelling at me because he was so annoyed that the bird had won, but I couldn't get control of myself. It was just too funny."

"Oh my gosh," Emily said, and she laughed along with him. "Did you ever get it back?"

"Nah," he said. "But the guy at the stand saw the whole thing and took pity on us, and gave us four free ones. That changed Kyle's tune."

"It sounds like you had such a wonderful childhood..." Emily said thoughtfully.

"I did," Josh replied, just as quietly.

"So did you lived in this house for your whole life?" Emily asked. The idea seemed crazy to her.

"For most of my life," he said. "Mom and Dad bought the house when I was five. We used to live closer to the center of town, closer to where Ava lives now, but Mom loves the harbor, and Dad knew the guy who was selling the house and got it at apparently a really good deal."

She shook her head at the contrast. "When my parents were still married, we moved almost a dozen times when I was growing up. I lived in apartments, condos, and even a townhouse once. But my dad was always working, and my mom was, well, my mom, and she never wanted to stay in one place for very long."

"You'll like this even more. My grandparents grew up in nearby towns, and my parents not only went to the same high school as one another, but have both always lived in this town, aside from a few summers my mom spent away visiting family when she was younger.

They have only owned two homes the entire time they have been married."

"And they never wanted to leave? To live anywhere else?"

Josh shrugged. "I don't see why they would want to. They love Magnolia Harbor. It has always been their home. Plus, they travel when they want to get away, so it's not like they haven't seen the world."

Emily and Josh stood there together, listening to the branches and the leaves as the breeze ran through them.

"I want to move back here eventually," he said. There was a bittersweet tone to his voice, and she wasn't sure if it was sadness or just reflection.

A slow shock jolted through Emily as she let his words seep in.

"Wait…you want to leave New York?"

Josh looked at her. "Not yet, no," he replied, chuckling. "But I definitely don't want to live in the city forever. It's been a nice change of pace, and important for me career-wise, but at the end of the day I really think I would be much happier in a place like this for the rest of my life."

Her heart sunk, then started to race low in her chest. Why was this the first that she had heard of this? She tried to shake it off and swallow her stress, but it was just not going away.

She had never had to question their relationship. From the beginning everything between them had worked so easily, their lives had fallen into sync so well that she had never considered that they had different long term goals or even dreams that the other didn't know about. This was the first time that she had felt surprised in a negative way by Josh, almost as if he were revealing a deep, dark secret that had the potential to change the entire course of her life.

Their conversations had always felt like they both imagined that they would be together forever, living their life in New York, growing old together. Maybe they would get a cute weekend house upstate one day, as a lot of their friends eventually did. That was a New Yorker's version of moving to the country. She had never even considered him wanting anything significantly different.

"What about your job?" she asked, clambering for something to say, trying to sound casual. She wondered if he had always felt this way, and had always planned to leave the city, or if this was an epiphany he was having right this very moment.

He shrugged. "I don't know, I love my job for what it is now, but sometimes I daydream about ways that I could translate my hospitality and managerial experience to open an upscale bed and breakfast or something here. Maybe closer to the harbor, or on Piper Bay, which is that island off over there." He pointed off into the distance. "I know how to manage prestigious clientele, like celebrities and royalty. I imagine that dealing with tourists couldn't be any more difficult. In reality, it would probably be a walk in the park compared to the intensity of Manhattan."

"You are probably right," she replied, somewhat reluctantly.

"You okay?" He looked down now to peer into her face.

She waved his concern away. "Of course," she said, putting on a tight smile. "You just never have told me that you wanted to move back here."

"Yeah, I guess I haven't. I do love the city, and I am so glad that I moved there because it led me to you," Josh said, turning to her and taking her hands in his ôwn.

She stepped onto her tiptoes and gave him a kiss. It made her feel slightly less shell-shocked, knowing that he cared as much as he did. She knew he had just been speaking casually from his heart, not trying to drop a bomb on her. Nonetheless, his comment had rocked her foundation a bit.

"Come on, we should probably get back for lunch," Josh said, took her hand tightly in his own.

Emily's thoughts bounced around inside her head as they walked back toward the house. What surprised her the most was her reaction. Her job and entire persona in New York was based around her ability to put out fires all day long, to not freak out or overreact to hardly anything. When it came to work, she was an ace at dealing with potentially cataclysmic last minute changes and deadline-looming drama, so the idea that a simple comment could unnerve her so much was both shocking and unsettling.

I must really be madly in love with this guy to be this freaked out at the idea of him leaving, she thought as they made their way across the field. She never really imagined her life without him in it. So, did that mean that she wanted to marry him? None of their peers ever seemed to get married, or even talk about it. They talked about their careers, travel plans, but never weddings. The topic wasn't even part of the realm of dialogue, even though they were all well within marrying age.

Did other people their age get married in places outside of New York? Everyone she knew just basically dated forever, or until they broke up. The idea of breaking up with Josh seemed unthinkable, but the idea of leaving her entire world seemed completely preposterous as well. Maybe if it was to Los Angeles or London for work or something, but otherwise she was pretty sure that she wouldn't be open to living anywhere else. Even if she went to one of those other major cities, her thought was that it would only be temporary.

All of these questions were more loaded than she was prepared to answer tonight. Emily looked around as they continued walking, Josh reflecting on another story from his childhood, but she wasn't really listening. Try though she did, everywhere she looked now took on a different hue. What in the world did people even *do* in a town like this, aside from celebrating holidays together, or visiting for a wistful getaway weekend? She wondered where the closest artisanal coffee shop was, and if there were any good ramen places nearby. She had everything at her fingertips in the Big Apple.

New York was her *home.* Could she abandon the only place that she had ever known for love? It seemed, somehow, farfetched. She had been raised to believe that she was the only person she could truly rely on and that giving up your own dreams for someone else was met with heartbreak and disappointment more often than not. She wasn't a cynic about love by any means, but she had always assumed that she would meet someone who wanted exactly what she wanted out of life, and therefore, there would be no major compromises, and nothing to later regret if things didn't work out.

A fresh wave of uneasiness passed over her, and she tried to nod pleasantly as Josh continued to talk.

The area was absolutely beautiful, she knew that. She loved the charm of it all so far. It didn't even feel real. She wasn't sure she had heard a siren at all since she had landed.

"Josh, I was wondering if –"

But she was cut off when the front door of the house opened, and a Josh' brother Kyle stepped outside.

"Hey, there are you are! Dad just got the tree set up in the stand, and it's finally straight. Apparently, Nana is insisting that we all go in and help decorate it right now. I was sent out to come find you."

Josh smiled at Emily. "You ready?"

"Ready as ever!'

Kyle nodded. "Oh, and we grabbed a couple of pizzas on our way over. Figured everyone would need some grub, so hope you're hungry."

Emily grabbed her stomach, "That sounds great, I'm starving."

"Did you get it from that place, *Vita?*" Josh asked as they climbed the stairs back up to the porch.

"Yeah," Kyle said. "According to Ava, apparently the guy who owns it makes a killer pizza. Actually spent time in Italy learning to cook."

"That's awesome," Emily said.

Little things like that helped her to like the idea of living in a small town. It definitely was not New York City, but maybe they weren't as cut off from the outside world as she had originally thought.

Emily pushing aside her thoughts from the previous conversation for now. She told herself that she was going to enjoy her time here, and then if they needed to evaluate their relationship when they got back to New York, then they would deal with it there. For now, she would keep the conversation out of sight, out of mind. At least that was what she told herself.

The three of them made their way inside and into the bustle of the tree decorating cheer.

CHRISTMAS EVE

*T*he days had been quickly filled with family time. Dinners and lunches had been planned at everyone's houses on various nights, and between eating and socializing, Emily felt like the days had flown by. There were even more cousins than she had met the first night, and everyone wanted a chance to visit with Josh and his new girlfriend. They met new babies, looked through old photo albums, and played board games with a near constant rotation of people. Emily had never experienced anything like it. It was both so simple, and yet a totally jam-packed exciting time.

Dawn came early through the large window on Christmas Eve morning. Emily laid awake in her room, listening to the even breathing of Ava lying on the air mattress beside her bed.

It was hard to believe that she was not in New York for the holiday. But she had to admit, this year, she almost felt like a child again. There was so much Christmas cheer, so much laughter, and so much joy everywhere. It reminded her of when she was young, and when her parents were still together.

Christmas had not been the same since her parents had divorced. She either spent Christmas with her dad in his cramped apartment in Brooklyn, watching him as he worked on his next architectural design, or with her mom in the city, either attending charity galas or getting to know her mom's newest boyfriend.

The family that Josh had is what she had always wished for in a family. Stable, well connected, always together. She imagined it was partially a result of no one moving out of the town.

Was that a good thing? She couldn't imagine people not wanting to explore further than their own town. There was so much opportunity elsewhere, great jobs that could not be possible in such a small place like this. Not leaving the city was different, it was like a million towns and boroughs all in one. You could move from Manhattan to Brooklyn and never see your old neighbors again.

She gazed up at the ceiling and sighed heavily.

If things were to turn out with Josh, and that was a big *if*, because they had not even discussed marriage really, then what would happen to her job? Everything in her life revolved around her work, and she always thought it would be that way.

Had she wanted to be a wife and mother? The words sounded weird floating through her head. Yeah, eventually, she admitted. But that always seemed to be a thing that would happen down the road somehow.

*But I'm not getting any younger...*she thought. *How much longer am I going to wait to make this decision?*

Most of her friends were not married, so she didn't feel that pressure at all. But in the last few years, she had started to hear whispers and uncertainties about being single, though they were always quickly brushed off and laughed about.

She and Josh hadn't really discussed marriage much, perhaps mostly because she had told him from the very beginning that she wanted to take their relationship slow. She explained that her parent's relationship had ended poorly and that she was very cautious about finding a man who would not leave her in the same way. Plus, she had dated a string of people prior to meeting Josh who just ended up being complete duds, and she was hesitant to have her heart hurt again.

She didn't mention that aspect to Josh. But she was glad when he had completely understood and had respected her wishes. They had tried to take it slow, but quickly found themselves inseparable. He really was her rock and her confidant, and it didn't hurt that she still thought he was as sexy as they day she met him. The times that the subject of marriage did come up, it was always treated jokingly. Like the time in Central Park where Josh pointed to an elderly couple and said, "Are we going to just end up with four teacup dogs that we roll around in strollers when we are an old married couple like them?"

She rubbed her palms over her eyes and raked her fingers through her hair, trying to clear her mind and think happy Christmas thoughts. Eventually, she drew herself out of bed and padded down the hall to the bathroom for a shower. The house was still quiet, and she was glad that she was able to try and wash away some of the frustrations and disquiet with hot water. She stood under the steamy spray for a long time, trying not to think about Josh leaving New York. She hated the idea, hated it to her very core. But what was the alternative? Move to the middle of podunk with him?

She wasn't sure she could do that, either.

Ava had gotten up and left by the time Emily went back to their room, so she dressed quickly. The smell of bacon and biscuits drifted up the stairs to her, and she hungrily followed the aroma. She found Josh downstairs in the kitchen.

Josh offered her a cup of coffee, which she eagerly accepted.

"Splash of milk and two teaspoons of sugar," he said, and winked at her as he took a sip of his own.

She kissed him on the cheek before joining him in enjoying hers.

"No long sleeves again?" Nancy said from the stove, giving Emily an up and down glance. She grinned. "Well, I hope you brought some with you. It is supposed to get cold tonight for the light show."

"The light show?" Emily asked.

Josh beamed. "It's a yearly tradition in town. On Christmas Eve, all of the stores and restaurants close at noon, and at eight o'clock in the evening, there is a grand light show all over town, all synchronized with music and everything."

"That sounds amazing," Emily said.

Josh grinned. "I was hoping to take you down into town this morning to explore a little bit before the shops all closed up."

"I would love that," she said.

"Give you two a little privacy," Nancy continued. She walked over to the island where a few potatoes were waiting to be sliced. She picked up the knife and began to cut them up. "Figured you would enjoy a closer look at our sleepy little town."

"I definitely would," Emily agreed.

Josh borrowed his Dad's car for their trip around town, and soon the two of them were winding along quiet side streets, looking at all of the decorations on the houses. Emily was astounded by the beauty of some of the properties, and the size of the yards that some had. It was stunning, and when Josh told her that most of these houses cost less than her apartment in New York, she ogled at him.

"You can't be serious!" she said. She had never been much good with money, but she just could not believe that actual full houses outside of the city were so inexpensive. Or maybe it was just that her apartment was that pricey. "Is living in New York really that overpriced?"

"Oh yeah," he said, nodding his head. "Why else do you think I am so enticed to come back here?"

"I totally get it," she agreed, looking out of the windows.

She started to fall in love with some of the cottages, all different shades of pastels and grays and whites. They were all so pretty and had so much character. She wondered what it would be like if she and Josh were to purchase one together. She looked over at Josh and noticed that his hair looked a little shaggy for the first time since she had known him. She realized that he looked at ease in a way that she had never seen. The corner of her mouth drew into an impish smirk at how cute he looked. Then another adorable place caught her eye.

"Oh, I like that one," she said, pointing to a pretty blue and white cottage, with a large front porch that wrapped around to the back of the house.

"I have always loved that house," he commented, and her heart soared at the fantasy of house shopping together.

There was something fun about looking at and comparing houses with him. A lot more fun than picking a cookie cutter condo in the middle of Flushing or Queens.

And the sheer amount of land everywhere was something she couldn't get over. She loved the trees, and the green everywhere she looked. Some homes even had access to lakes and rivers that dotted the landscape, and she imagined little girls and boys running and playing, while she worked studiously from her laptop on the porch, reapplying sunscreen as needed.

They found a parking spot at the very north part of Main Street, and Emily was shocked to see just how busy it was. There were people coming and going from every shop, with boxes and bags and wrapping paper in hand. Many of them would greet others as they walked by, and Emily quickly realized that pretty much everyone in town must know one other.

"Where should we go first?" Emily asked.

Josh shrugged his shoulders, his hands in the pocket of his green Columbia jacket. She had purchased that for him for his birthday a few months before. She loved him in green. "I figured that you could just wander in to which ever places struck your fancy."

Pleased with the idea, Emily decided to peek into the first shop. It was an antique shop, and Josh knew the owner. Apparently, they had gone to church together.

"He was in my Sunday School class when he was just this high," the antique shop owner said, holding a hand to her hip.

Emily let out an endearing giggle as Josh bowed his head sheepishly.

And so it continued up and down the street. They would find a shop that would make Emily gasp over something or other, and they would walk inside to explore.

She was excited to see that every shop was decorated for Christmas. Most of them had trees in the corner, and more than half of them had classical Christmas music playing in the background. It was all so warm and inviting, she felt like she was in an old Christmas movie.

She found a home décor shop full of accessories and instantly fell in love with the nautical themed pillows and dish sets. She insisted that all she wanted was for Josh to buy her the adorable octopus silverware for her birthday next year. They went into a jewelry store, where she found some very pretty crystal necklaces, a gorgeous rose gold watch, and the prettiest ring that she had ever seen. The center was a soft pink morganite stone set in a halo of moissanite, which created a diamond like glow around it.

"Those are stones that are found in meteors, the moissanite," the woman behind the counter told them.

"Really?" Josh asked, immediately more interested. "How cool."

"And they cost the fraction of a diamond."

"They are just as beautiful," Emily commented, as she gazed at the ring in the cabinet.

Next Josh took her across the street to a little restaurant that she had seen earlier called *Vita*.

"Hey, this is where we got the pizza last night, right?" she asked.

"It is. And I wanted to take a peek inside. How does lunch sound?"

"If it is as good as the pizza, then definitely," she replied.

They walked in and found the place packed, but a man with dark hair and a closely trimmed beard appeared. He was almost as tall as Josh and was clad in a black t-shirt with a white apron tied around his waist.

"Hey, guys, good afternoon," the man said, coming forward to greet them. He held out his hand to Josh, and then to Emily. "My name is Michael. Allow me to be the first to welcome you to my restaurant."

"Wow," Josh said. "Then you're the one who is engaged to my sister's boss."

"Who is your sister?" Michael inquired, his hands on his waist.

"Ava Morris."

"Ava!" Michael said. "Yes! She is the sweetest girl, isn't she? And my fiancée would be totally lost without her."

This town keeps getting smaller and smaller, Emily thought. But rather than feeling smothered, she found that she rather liked that everyone knew each other, and somehow, it was all connected.

45

"And you are?" Michael asked.

"I'm Josh, and this is my girlfriend, Emily," Josh introduced them.

"Wonderful to have you both," Michael said. "Let me find you guys a seat."

He crossed over to the hostess stand and perused their seating chart. "Ah, here we are. Let's get you a table back here."

Emily liked that this Michael always seemed to be smiling. It was definitely one of the reasons that she loved Josh.

Maybe there was something in the water here, she mused. It was something that everyone back in New York could do with having a dose of.

"We had your pizza last night," Josh told him. "It was out of this world. And I live in New York."

"The city?" Michael asked as he handed them their menus once they were seated. Josh and Emily both nodded.

"Well, that's quite the compliment. Thank you very much."

"It's the truth," Josh continued.

Michael grinned. "I lived in New York for a while, cooked in some incredible restaurants."

Emily's ears perked up. "Really?"

"Oh yeah," Michael continued. "It was both great, and a learning experience, more about myself than the food though. Well, you guys probably know what it's like. I pretty much worked all the time, at full capacity. And I loved it, the busyness, the pace, the energy; but I also found that when I wasn't working, there was nothing left of me to give. Eventually, I got really burnt out on it, but the blessing was that I learned a lot about myself. I knew I loved to cook, I loved to succeed and be around people, but once I was able to slow down, I remembered that I loved living life too. Does that make sense?"

Emily and Josh both nodded, fully pulled in to his story.

"Anyhow, I have to say I have the best of both worlds now, I work hard, I relax hard, and I'm part of an incredible community. So, in the end, I don't think I would have changed anything because I can't imagine not ending up where I am now."

Josh shook his head, feeling what in sync with Michael.

"But you guys came for food, not philosophy, so let's get you fed." He offered them a wide, inviting grin. "It's great meeting you guys. My waitress Hannah will be over to serve you shortly."

They thanked him, and he stepped away, back to the front.

"This has got to be one of the busiest days of the year, and he is personally greeting his guests?" Josh observed. "That is impressive."

"And chatting with them. If it is the same Michael your sister was talking about the other night, he absolutely loves his job and all of his customers. He thrives on the busyness."

Josh nodded his head. "It's admirable. And wow, I could totally relate to his story."

Then he turned his eyes on her.

"What?" she asked.

Josh searched her face, and she saw his eyebrow corner twitch. "Something has been on your mind since the other day."

Emily felt her cheeks flush, and she ducked her head to pretend to scan the menu.

"I'm fine," she said dismissively. "Everything is fine."

She could feel his eyes on the top of her head as she scanned the page with the tip of her finger.

"Oh, they have tortellini," she said. "In a pesto sauce! I wonder if it is as good as Michelangelo's..." she said.

"Emily," Josh said.

No. Not here, not now.

She did not think she could handle this conversation right now. She did not want to start an argument on Christmas Eve, or worse, start crying in front of all of these people

"Hmmm, what do you think," she continued, hoping that he would just drop it. Hoping he would see that she did not want to discuss it right now. "Should we get something to split? I don't want to ruin our dinner later on."

He reached across the table and took her hand in his.

"Emily," he repeated, barely above a murmur.

She couldn't help it. He had locked eyes with her. He knew her too well.

"I just..." she began. She swallowed, wishing that their waitress would come with some glasses of water. "I just feel a little overwhelmed right now."

He seemed to understand. "I know it is a lot of pressure to meet pretty much my entire family in a matter of a few days."

She nodded. That definitely was part of it, but she couldn't get his words out of her head from the other night, and everything that Michael had just said added to her chaotic inner dialogue.

Everything about Josh fit perfectly into the surroundings. And it somehow made her feel like maybe she didn't fit in. She and Josh fit perfectly in New York, but what if she wasn't right for Magnolia Harbor Josh, or even Magnolia Harbor?

"I'm sorry," she said quietly. "I guess this is all just so different for me. I'm just so out of my element, and I'm not sure if that's a good or a bad thing anymore."

"That's totally fine. I know exactly how you feel," he reassured her. "That is how I felt when I first moved to New York. Everything was strange. I didn't fit in. Nothing made sense. I began to question everything. And I definitely longed for the familiar."

She stared back at him now. "That's...that's exactly it." Though she had to admit to herself, that wasn't completely exactly it. She knew that at some point she needed to give words to the truth that he might move here and she didn't know if she could do that with him.

"Don't worry, Em," he said gently. "I am here with you, by your side the whole way. Just like all the rock climbs we've been on, we can do anything as long as we're in it together, right? Trust me. I'm not going anywhere."

How did he know that that was exactly what she needed him to say? It made her heart constrict, and then melt.

"I love you," she said, very simply, feeling her eyes grow misty. "More than you will probably ever know."

"Nonsense," he said, and he reached over to touch her cheek with his fingers. "I need you more than you need me. And I love you more than the moon loves the stars."

Her eyes grew mistier still, and she only managed to not get choked up because that was the moment the waitress finally arrived with their waters. The cheerful woman lightened the mood and allowed them to start bantering about silly, easy stuff again.

Their lunch was exquisite. Emily felt sated, both physically and emotionally, knowing that she was letting her fear get the better of her. Knowing that Josh loved her so much and was perfectly at ease with her fluttering, she was able to relax a little. They always had a mantra when they went rock climbing, that however scary the climb looked, or however technically impossible the route felt, they would figure it out and get through it as long as they worked together. Together, they unstoppable. Remembering that, she did not feel quite so alone anymore.

After lunch, they walked back across the street to a small, white washed building with a big cupcake logo on the front in a pretty pink and blue font.

"This is where Ava works," Josh said. "Mom ordered a couple of cakes and asked us to pick them up before the shops all closed."

Emily walked inside and immediately was overcome by the intoxicating smell of powdered sugar, cookie dough, and coffee.

"Oh, it smells heavenly in here," Emily said.

"Doesn't it, though?"

Ava stood behind the counter, leaning casually against it.

"Hey," Josh said. "Do you guys have Mom's order?"

"Right here," Ava said, and she reached under the counter and produced a couple of boxes.

"And Nana is okay with the extra baked goods?"

Ava shrugged. "She likes Hope. Says her stuff is the real deal."

He turned to Emily to explain, "For as long as I can remember, if anyone dared bring in outside desserts for the holidays, Grandma Thora use to treat it like a personal assault. People had to smuggle in pies like contraband. So being able to bring these are high remarks."

Josh returned his attention to Ava, "Speaking of Hope, where is she? I was hoping to meet her."

"Just left with her son Rylan a little while ago. They were going to get dinner ready at her house."

"Smart. You going to be home for dinner?"

"I'm just going to lock up here in about a half hour. We've had all of our holiday orders picked up already and Hope said it was fine to close early," Ava replied, checking her watch.

"Good," Emily said. "I would not be nearly as fun without you."

"Well, thank you. At least someone in this family appreciates my contribution!" Ava grinned.

She looked over at Josh. "Oh! And are you ready for tonight?"

Josh shot his sister a look, and Emily turned from Ava to Josh expectantly.

Ava shook her head and waved reassuringly. "No, no, nothing exciting, Josh just loves the light show. He has insisted that we all say nothing about it so that you get to feel the magic of the entire event." She teased Josh, "I think he is building up too much hype if you ask me."

Josh cocked a crooked smile at Emily. "It's my favorite Christmas thing. You will love it. You'll see."

"I believe it," Emily replied.

Josh picked up the boxes from the counter.

"All right, well, Ava, we will see you back at Mom and Dad's. I'll try not to eat all of the gingerbread cookies."

Ava waved dismissively. "Go ahead. I have decorated so many of those in the last few weeks that I am pretty sure my hands are going to fall off."

THE LIGHT SHOW

They met up with the rest of Josh's family back at his parents' house. The temperature had dropped even lower, and everyone was collecting all of their winter gear for the evening outing, with jackets and hats and gloves. Emily just laughed. Even with the chillier evening, all she took was a sweater, a light scarf, and a winter hat.

Josh promised that they had extra gloves if she needed it.

They all shared a light meal, with Grandma Thora promising the main dinner would be served once they returned from the light show. This didn't surprise anyone, and Emily discovered it was a pretty consistent tradition. She snuck a cup of coffee before they left to tide her over and warm her bones from the impending chill.

The sun set before seven, and they all climbed into the cars and started down to town again. Emily and Josh rode with his parents, and the group sang along in loud, mostly out of tune voices to a myriad of Christmas songs.

Josh kept looking over at Emily, with an almost childlike excitement on his face. She was happy too. This would be the first Christmas they had ever spent together. There was something incredibly magical about that.

Main Street was totally packed with people. They had to park off of a side street and walk some distance, but even from a few blocks away she could hear the music and the chatter of a gathering of people.

They walked around the corner, and Emily realized that they were at the far end of Main Street which opened up into the town green and the harbor. It was the opposite side from where she and Josh had been earlier that day. There were people everywhere, on the sidewalks, seated on benches near the shops, and even mingling in the street.

They passed between some police road blocks, preventing anyone from driving through the center of the village.

The air temperature had definitely dropped, and Emily was glad that she had taken her hat. She felt extra cheery and cute decked out with her dark jacket and jeans. Everyone else around her looked as if they were expecting a blizzard.

The best thing about it all was that Emily realized she felt like she was home. The people standing shoulder to shoulder was a pleasant change from all of the emptiness and space between people and houses the last few days, but somehow, it felt even better than in the middle of the city. She didn't feel like she had to hold her purse close to her chest or to cling to Josh for protection. Everyone near her had a friendly comment or a merry Christmas to share. It felt like a big family of strangers, who, if given the chance, wouldn't stay strangers for long.

It was like the best of both of the worlds, bustling activity combined with friendly, neighborliness.

Overhead, strung between the buildings, were thousands of Christmas lights. None of them were lit, but everyone was standing below them expectantly. They crisscrossed and wound through one another, reminding Emily of a million tiny icicles sparkling over their heads.

Josh's family all scattered to talk with various people, and Josh offered Emily his arm. They walked along a part of the street which was a little less populated.

Ahead of them was a little white pop-up tent with a long, white table beneath it. There were several tall coffee carafes, a number of tin foil covered plates, and a few smiling people standing behind the tables handing out paper cups and plates to passersby.

"Want something warm to drink?" Josh asked.

Emily, feeling the tips of her fingers starting to numb a bit, nodded her head.

They approached the table, arm in arm, and the kindly looking man behind the table looked up.

"Well, look who it is!" the man said.

Josh grinned and nodded. "Hello, sir. It's good to see you."

The man beamed. "It is wonderful to see you as well, my boy."

Josh looked down at Emily. "Emily, this is Pastor Alan. Pastor, this is my girlfriend, Emily."

Pastor Alan looked like what Emily expected every pastor should look like. Kind, gentle, and wise, with a youthful, inviting smile.

"Emily, it is lovely to meet you," Pastor Alan said, and the two shook hands.

"Likewise," she replied.

Pastor Alan looked up at Josh. "It is nice to see you back in town. How is life in the big city?"

Josh shrugged his shoulders. "Busy, for sure. I do love my job, though. I'm always meeting new people from all over the world, and I've learned that I'm capable of working harder than I ever thought possible."

"Wonderful," Pastor Alan said. Then he looked over at Emily. "So how long have you two been together?"

"About a year," Josh replied.

Pastor Close had a gleam in his eye as he looked at Emily. "You should know that this fine man is unlike many others. I have known him since he was just a boy, and he has always been thoughtful, intelligent, and compassionate."

Emily gazed up into Josh's reddening face, giving his arm a squeeze.

"He is a very good man," she replied. "That was one of the first things that drew me to him."

Josh told Pastor Alan all about the church that he had been

attending since he had moved to New York, and Emily listened intently. She had been going with him for the last six months or so, whenever she was able to get away from work. She always knew that Josh's faith was an important part of his life, but to see it in person with others around made her heart swell.

When she and Josh left to go back to New York, she knew that their lives would continue on the way it had. They would be back at their jobs, working non-stop, flopping onto the couch at the end of their long days, trying to hang out with friends when they could. But now, for some reason, that made her sad. They would keep moving, changing, and growing of course, but there was an urgent pace to their life in the city that didn't allow for the type of things she had experienced since being in Magnolia Harbor. Here they got to really spend time together, and with the people, they came into contact with. She finally truly got the meaning of the phrase "being in the moment." When they spent time with his family, there was no rush to it, the got to bond on a deeper level by just being in one another's company, having animated discussions, playing card games, and just being a family. It felt so special to be a part of all of these wonderful traditions in Josh's family, and by extension, being part of the town.

There was something appealing about having constants in your life, something Emily had never really known. It gave her a feeling of stability that was surprisingly comfortable. New York was the exact opposite. Everything was always changing. Even her favorite restaurants were always changing, since many of them didn't stay in business for very long. The styles changed, her neighbors changed, even her co-workers changed almost monthly.

She never dreamed that she would want life to be any different.

Looking around, she wondered how long she would be able to enjoy so much inconsistency. Her mom was the epitome of inconsistent, and she was very New York, but she never seemed truly content, almost as if her constant going was intended to fill the void of not having anything meaningful when she stopped. She thought about her childhood and the stress she often felt growing up. She wore it like a badge of honor, the way most of her peers did. They considered themselves worldly and street smart, but she also noticed that a lot of her friends took anti-anxiety medication like it was part of the food pyramid. Would she want to raise kids in that sort of high-stress environment? Or was there another option where you could still have a life you loved and yet, provide something better for your kids?

As if to answer her questions, she saw a few kids run by, glow sticks clasped tightly in their small hands as they waved them over their heads. It was completely safe for them to run about in the street here, knowing that everyone knew everyone.

"Here you go, Emily."

She jumped at being jolted out of her own thoughts and refocused her attention to Pastor Alan.

"I'm sorry. Did I interrupt an important thought?"

She smiled and shook her head. "Oh, no. I just was daydreaming a little."

He smiled, almost as if he knew what she was thinking. "Happens to me all the time. Here. Have a hot chocolate."

Emily took the hot, steaming beverage gratefully. "Thank you very much."

"You are very welcome," he said.

Josh promised to swing by the church again before he and Emily left town, and then the two of them turned away from the table to allow someone else a chance to have some cocoa.

"He is a really nice guy," Emily commented.

Josh grinned behind his cocoa cup. "He is. He's really funny, too. He was a huge help to me when I was in college."

They turned and faced all of the lights. Emily could see the excitement building in the air. The crowd was almost buzzing with anticipation.

Emily chewed on her lip. She wanted to be in the moment and pay attention to the light show, but her mind couldn't stop turning over and over, grappling with the flood of mixed emotions. The brief conversation with the Italian restaurant owner, Michael, replayed in her head. So much of her identity was wrapped up in being a New Yorker, being a city girl, pursuing her career and being successful at whatever she did. She thrived on the competition, or so she thought. It was a rat race in some ways, but everyone around her justified it.

As she looked around at people and children enjoying one another's company, she didn't see the competition, she saw camaraderie and joy. People actually *living* their lives, however simple she may have thought those lives were a mere week ago. She felt as though she was on the outside looking in, at the people in the streets of Magnolia Harbor and at herself in Manhattan; suddenly she felt ashamed of herself for being so shortsighted and critical.

All of her life she had never even considered living any other place, and she almost pitied the rest of the world for not living the life she did. Now as she looked at it, perhaps it was she all along that deserved to be pitied. She never really knew that a place like Magnolia Harbor actually existed outside of movies, and until this week, she didn't understand what life in a small town had to offer. Almost like a light bulb popping on, she got it now. It wasn't easy to explain, but she just got it.

Josh looked down at his watch. "It is ten to eight. Sometimes they start a little early. That would be great. I'm actually starting to get hungry again."

Ten minutes. For some reason, she felt like she had to get all of this off of her chest and she couldn't wait any longer. She knew that she had promised herself that she would wait until they got back to the city before bringing any of this up, but she wasn't sure that she could get through the rest of the trip without getting all of her thoughts out of her head.

She looked around, looking for signs that it was not the right time.

Was Christmas Eve the right time to bring up stuff like this? Was there ever a good time?

"Josh?" she asked, and she reached up, grabbing the elbow of his jacket, tugging on it gently.

"Yeah?" he asked, lowering his cocoa, just about to take another sip.

Emily's was still untouched.

"Can we talk for a second?"

She watched some concern flashed across his face, and then he nodded his head. "Is everything okay?"

Emily sighed. "Yes, I think. I just..."

She glanced around and saw that if they were to walk just a short distance back down the road, they would be out of earshot.

She took his hand and pulled him away from the crowds.

"Is this about earlier?" Josh asked. "I could tell that there was more bothering you than what you let on."

Now that he was standing there in front of her, waiting for her to tell him what was on her mind, she didn't know quite what to say or where to start.

So she just decided to tell him everything.

"You said something the other day that caught me off guard a little, in several ways," she began. She was picking at a corner of her sweater sleeve. "The other day, when we were outside walking around the yard, you said how you eventually planned to move back here one day."

Josh's cocked his head listening, but she sensed his shoulders sag slightly.

"Please let me finish," Emily insisted. "When you said that, I was surprised. You had never said anything like that to me. I mean, I knew that this was where you were from and that you loved it here, but it never crossed my mind that you would ever want to leave New York."

She swallowed. It hurt to say all of this, but it was a painful release, allowing her to feel as if she could breathe again.

"And the idea of you leaving New York," she hesitated, "The idea of you leaving *me*, it just, it caught me off guard. The idea of us breaking up just seemed unfathomable. I guess I had always thought that we would stay together forever. I definitely never had intended to leave you for any reason, even though I know I haven't ever really talked about getting married or anything. And I think it's always been pretty obvious that I never planned to leave the New York. But if your desire to move home was strong enough, and if I found that I couldn't leave the city, what did that mean? Where did that leave us?"

He looked like he wanted to interject, but she just kept going; the floodgate was open, and she needed to just let everything she had been bottling up out.

"I don't know why I just assumed that we would always be together, living in New York like we are now. Maybe it was naive, or maybe I wasn't paying enough attention to things you said. I don't know what it was, but hearing this new piece of information threw me completely off balance."

She felt tears welling up in her eyes. "Because it wasn't something I could talk you out of, or would want to talk you out of. I could hear in your voice how much you knew that this was going to be the right thing for you, and I realized that I love you too much to ever want you to sacrifice something that meaningful, even if it was for us to stay together. You know that whole, if you love something, set it free thing? Well, I get it now. I don't like it, but I get it," she said, her lips beginning to tremble.

"So this trip has been absolutely perfect in so many ways, but also a huge mind scramble for me. I have never known anything aside from my current life, and in some ways, I guess I feel like it identifies me, or has informed who I am. I'm embarrassed to say it, but I think it's true. My job, my city, my friend group, my identity is so much more wrapped up in those things than I realized. It is my life, and it always has been. And coming to terms with that reality brought up a whole load of other questions about what it is I truly want in life, what's important to me deep down, and scariest of all, whether I was willing to make sacrifices for another person, knowing that there are no sure things in this life." She had regained some of her composure and was just speaking from her heart now, as best she could.

"I didn't think that I would ever be able to be happy anywhere but in my world. But when you said that you wanted to come back here, I also realized that the last thing that I wanted to happen was for us to break up. The thought of not having you in my life…how could that version of my life ever be happy either? So I began to try and open my eyes, to look beyond the idea of Magnolia Harbor as just a pretty place to visit, to try and see if it through unjaded eyes."

She wiped a stray, chilly tear off of her cheek. "I have been being won over by your hometown since the moment we touched down here. I can see why you love it here so much. And strangely enough, I can also see why no one ever leaves. The views are stunning, the town is charming, and the sheer amount of land that comes with houses is just insane."

Josh laughed softly as she chuckled through her tears. "And it isn't just that. Your family is so wonderful. They are so unlike my own family. I have never known what it is like to have a stable family who cares about more than just their jobs or their own interests. My Mom, I love her, but she never would have prepared a room like your Mom did for me. And your Dad…showing me how to play cards like that, only one day after knowing me? My Dad would never have done that. He was always too caught up in his work."

She laughed, but it was sort of hollow, maybe a little depressed. "Maybe I am just jealous of the family that I don't have, of the stability that I never understood. Like I told you, I moved apartments so much as a kid that nowhere ever felt like home. My apartment right now is the first place that I have lived in that has felt like home. And I share it with a girl that isn't really even much of a friend."

She looked around her. "This place…it just feels too good to be true, you know? I grew up with the grit and grime and glamor of the big city. This all just feels too soft and delicate for someone who feels as hardened as I do. And I want to believe that living in the city is really all that it is cracked up to be. A week ago, I would have argued to death with you that New York is the best place in the world to live."

Josh squinted at her, taking in everything she was saying.

"Now, I don't really think so," she said quietly, looking off into the distance.

She turned her eyes to Josh, who looked like he was eagerly, yet patiently waiting for his turn to talk, but she was not done yet. She took a deep breath and spoke with a slightly lighter, happier tone.

"The idea terrifies me, and I need you to know this. I am starting to really like the idea of moving here one day, I mean if that's something that you wanted me to do with you." She crinkled her nose, "I want to explore all that this little town has to offer and all the other little towns nearby. I want to go to the harbor and spend the day by the ocean. I want to play in the one day of snow here, and enjoy the warmer weather the rest of the year."

She took a step toward him took his hands in her own. "Josh, I want you to know how much I love you. Life was never as good when we've been apart previously, and all of this has just made me realize it that much more. I know that I've been so wishy-washy about marriage and our long terms plans, and I am grateful that you just went with it. But I don't think that I can see the rest of my life without you in it. Being here with you, really thinking about what I want in my life, it has just made all of these dreams that I didn't know I had come to the surface."

She shook her head. "If I am not making myself clear, I just want you to know that I will do anything to make sure we stay together. Even if it means that I have to leave the city, to leave everything that I've ever known, and move to a tiny, sleepy oceanside town."

Josh, who had been searching her face the entire time she spoke, suddenly scooped her up into his arms and spun her around in the air.

When he finished twirling her, he slowly lowered her to the ground and planted her with a long, firm kiss.

"Emily, there's no one in this world for me other than you. You are my best friend and the person whose face I look forward to seeing at the end of every day. I wouldn't dream of moving anywhere in the world if you weren't by my side." He ran his fingers through her hair, tucking her long bangs behind her ear.

"I am so sorry that you've been going through all of this alone all week. But I guess I'm somewhat glad for it too. You know how I always say how much I appreciate rain storms. One of my favorite things about them is that even when you can't see it, I like to believe that there's a rainbow out there afterward. I don't know if this is quite the same, but maybe I can bring a little rainbow to your thunderstorm of a week…"

Josh began rifling through his jacket pocket.

"What are you doing?" she asked, wondering if he had gotten her a snack from the concession stand when she wasn't looking.

He put a finger up with one hand while his other tried to make navigate past the gloves hanging out of his pocket and the hand warmers buried within. Finally, he pulled out a small, maroon velvet box from his jacket.

He got down on one knee in front of her, in the middle of Main Street, as her hand flew to her mouth in shock.

When he cracked the box open it revealed the same ring that she had mooned over at the jewelry shop earlier in the day.

"Josh…" she breathed, and the tears came fresh and fast.

"The moment I saw that ring, I knew it was a sign. It is one of a kind, just like you."

At that exact same moment, Dance of the Sugarplum Fairy floated across the breeze, the light show over their head began twinkling and dancing across the sky.

"Emily, I want you to know that I want to spend the rest of my life with you, too. So why don't we make it easier? Will you marry me?"

Without a second thought, she threw her arms around his neck and held him tightly, laughing into his shoulder. The sounds of her happiness and tears were drowned out by the lights and music overhead.

He was finally was able to hear the mumbled yes that she was yelling into his shoulder. A firework exploded over the harbor, and they both turned to look. Emily tried to tame down her hair and used the sleeve of her sweater to wipe her eyes. Josh took her hand and slid the ring onto her trembling finger, both of them laughing as he tried multiple times before succeeding.

With another kiss, he pulled her in close to his side, and they watched the dazzling light show overhead. Emily gazed at the ring and held it high overhead where it sparkled brightly amidst the holiday display. She saw now and understood in her heart that she was part of a larger tapestry than she had ever imagined was possible. Her gorgeously perfect ring shone above the sea of the community before her, and now more than ever, she couldn't wait to see where the next part of their lives lead.

ACKNOWLEDGMENTS

This book was such a fun trip down memory lane in so many ways, from my time in New York, to cutting down a Christmas tree for the first time. While this story was purely fictional, I loved tapping in to those memories, emotions, and times. I hope you enjoyed reading it!

A WHOLE LATTE CHRISTMAS

A Heartwarming Small Town Holiday Romance

A **Sophie Mays** Novel

A Whole Latte Christmas

To my mom,
We all made fun of you when you bought your first overpriced espresso
machine. Many years and thousands of tiny, lovely shared moments
around that machine later, you've proven, yet again, that moms always
do know best.
Love You

FOREWORD

The Canadian Rockies hold a special place in my heart because my family enjoyed many Christmas vacations there. If you even get the chance to visit Jasper, Lake Louise, Canmore, Banff or any of the other spectacular towns in that region, I would highly recommend it. In the meantime, pull up an armchair, grab a cup of hot mocha and cozy up with A Whole Latte Christmas! Enjoy!

CHAPTER 1

a soft skitter of snowflakes shimmered through the air as the two female figures made their way through the low-limbed trees. The pine needles shuddered off their icy coats, spraying the girls in a fine mist.

Sonia grabbed her sister's sled and hefted it under her arm along with her own.

"It's fine, Yvette. I'll just carry it."

"Thanks, Sis. You're the best," Yvette said as she ran ahead and jumped awkwardly into a particularly high snow drift.

Sonia shook her head as she lugged the sleds through the snow. "You're an idiot you know!" she called after her sister. Though they were barely four years apart, Sonia's sister Yvette played the little sister role to a 'T.' No matter that Yvette's left arm was bound up in a bright blue cast from a recent break, her fearless nature could hardly be suppressed.

Sonia had spent her life in the role of the responsible one, if only by sheer proximity to Yvette. It was only this past year when Sonia left to teach English abroad that suddenly had Sonia looking like the mischievous, unpredictable one. In truth, Sonia was practical, but plenty adventurous. However, it was an attribute that didn't tend to shine through the way it did with her sister. Still, the two had plenty of fun together, especially during their yearly "Kick-off to Winter" sled run.

From the time they were children, Sonia and Yvette would trudge out to the hill near their grandmother's house every single day they could leading up to Christmas. On the first day, they would stand at the top of the slope, declare the beginning of "Official Winter" with a unison cry, then take off down the hillside at warp speed. The winner of the race was treated to her sled being hefted back home. Once they got there, she was also awarded hot chocolate topped with homemade marshmallow in the biggest mug their grandmother owned. The mug was sculptured in the likeness of a giant snowman, and was downright ridiculous, but boy did it hold a lot of hot chocolate.

Sonia took a deep breath. The cold air filled her lungs. It stung her nose and made her eyes water, but it didn't bother her. To her, this was what started Christmas vacation: sledding down the hill and playing like she was a kid again.

"Sonia," Yvette said, standing with her good hand on her hip. "You're so slow! Come on!"

"Oh, we'll see who is slow when we get on the sleds," Sonia said. "Then you'll be begging me to slow down!"

Yvette laughed. "I don't think so! I'm going to be a lot faster this year. My cast makes me streamlined."

"That won't change anything," Sonia said as they reached the peak of the hill.

"Give me my sled," Yvette taunted.

Sonia reluctantly handed it over. "Don't start until I'm ready."

"Okay, old lady," Yvette said, flopping down onto her stomach. There were a few other people out enjoying the snow covering the picturesque town's best sledding spot. The hill was a straight shot over the smooth snow ending at the edge of the mostly iced-over pond. They weren't the only ones racing down the hill, and peals of laughter, followed by snow-drift wipe outs could be witnessed on either side of them.

"Ready!" Yvette's voice echoed through the woods.

"Set, go!" Sonia called, pushing off. She flew down the hill, a smile pasted on her face. She loved the feeling of flying. As she reached the end of the hill, she looked back and saw Yvette a few feet behind her. Sonia jumped up and struck a victory pose.

"Oh, stop it!" Yvette said. "That was just because I couldn't push off correctly. Let's do it again! I'll totally get you this time."

"Go ahead and try," Sonia said.

After their second race and another clear victory for Sonia, they decided they should go down the hill holding hands. Yvette howled as they tried to cling on for dear life. As seemed to happen almost every time they attempted this, their sleds ended up crashing into each other halfway down. The two flew off their sleds and rolled over like ragdolls to the bottom of the hill.

Sonia was laughing so hard her stomach hurt. "Are you alright?" she asked her sister, happy tears stiffening in the creases of her eyes.

Yvette sat up and attempted to brush the snow out of her eyes with her snow-encrusted cast. She ran the edge of the cast across her tongue, trying to dislodge the long brown hair stuck in her mouth. Sonia lay in the snow trying to catch her breath. She looked up at the brilliant white clouds waltzing across the crisp blue sky and was glad to be home.

Just then, a sharp shriek ripped through the air.

Sonia's head shot up instantly. She looked at her sister just as a second scream rang out. This one was the sound of someone calling for help.

Sonia jumped to her feet, steadied herself on the uneven hill and searched for the source of the noise. Her eyes scanned the pond. She quickly located the little girl flailing around beyond the icy edge where the water hadn't fully frozen over yet. Before she even thought about what she was doing, she ran to the edge and dove into the water, swimming the few short strokes out to the small child. She scooped the girl up under her arm and swam back, already feeling the icy water soaking through her multiple layers of clothing. Sonia felt several pairs of hands pulling the girl out of her arms. Then she was hoisted out onto the ice. She could hear the barking orders of someone speaking insistently into the phone. Moments later she was wrapped in layers of jackets.

Her sister's arms flung around her adding warmth to her frozen cheeks. Yvette's words repeatedly whispered, "You're gonna be okay. The ambulance is pulling up now. Just lean into me, and we're going to get you out of these wet clothes as soon as we can."

Her words were reassuring and gave Sonia something to focus on through the shiver overtaking her body. Her sister's tight arms wrapped around her helped keep Sonia's body from shaking. Sonia tried to open her eyes and locate the child who she could hear coughing up water. She saw the flashes of people standing around, and a man kneeling a few feet from her, ripping off the little girl's outer jacket and bundling the tiny figure in his own.

She rasped to her sister through chattering teeth, "I'm okay. How's the little girl?" Her voice was barely audible. Her sister shushed her and told her everything was fine. Sonia thought that Yvette's work as a ski instructor on the nearby mountain had prepared her well for this kind of situation.

Moments later she was lifted by two more sets of arms onto a gurney. Before she knew it, her jackets were being stripped off, and a rush of warm air from the back of the Ambulance began pricking her skin. Sonia rolled into the layers of warm blankets and closed her eyes.

CHAPTER 2

$\mathcal{T}$wo hours later, Sonia sat on the edge of a hospital bed, a paper cup of warm tea cupped in both hands. She was dressed in the oversized gray sweatpants and a dusty pink sweatshirt that one of the EMT's had in his gym bag.

"That's the beauty of a small town, huh?" came the voice of her sister as she entered the room. Sonia cocked her head, questioning.

"Friends of friends of friends. You don't get to borrow fine duds like that just by being any old person," Yvette motioned to Sonia's outfit and crooked a smile at her sister.

Yvette lifted herself up onto the squeaky plastic mattress next to Sonia. "They didn't have anything healthy, so you got Twizzlers." She handed Sonia the slim red pack of licorice. As Sonia reached for it, Yvette pulled it back and popped her lightly on the head with it. "I'm proud of you for doing what you did...but please try never to do that again." She pointed the Twizzlers at Sonia like a teacher reprimanding her pupil. Sonia smiled and grabbed the crinkled package from her sister's hand.

"I definitely won't be doing any recreational ice swimming anytime soon. I can at least promise you that." Sonia set down her weak, watery tea and went to work opening the candy wrapper. "Did you find out what room the little girl is in?"

"Yeah," Yvette replied, "351, up on the third floor. She's in the pediatric unit. She's doing fine, but they just want to keep her there a little while longer."

"They delivered my discharge papers, so I'm going to go up and check on her I think."

"Well, if you're feeling okay, I want to go check on that EMT, if you know what I mean," Yvette started winking with an overly dramatic face.

Sonia rolled her eyes. "I don't know if you heard me earlier, but just in case you didn't, you're an idiot." She chuckled at her ridiculously goofy younger sister.

"Nah, he's actually super nice. I know him from the mountain. I'm going to thank him for letting you borrow his sweats and figure out how to get them back to him. And maybe if he's lucky, I'll let him sign my cast."

Sonia shook her head. "Lucky guy. Okay, well I'll go up and peek in on the little girl. Then meet you downstairs in about 25 minutes so we can go home. Sound good?"

"It's a plan," Yvette agreed.

The girls walked to the elevator together and Yvette kissed her sister's messy-haired head before splitting off to find her EMT friend.

The elevator binged and let Sonia out on the third floor. She shuffled in her hospital issued slipper socks, which were barely more than beige tubes with dots of puffy paint for traction. She certainly wasn't going to win any beauty awards, she mused, that was for sure. Sonia took in the brightly colored hallways that lead her down a corridor and into the pediatric section. There wasn't much activity on the floor, and she watched as a nurse exited a room up ahead on the left. Sonia's feet shuffled toward the only room with activity. When she got to the door, she popped her head around the corner to be as unobtrusive as possible. She jumped in surprise to find herself face to chest with a large body. She tried to jerk her head up to get her bearings on what had just happened, but she was virtually enveloped by the man's body. When she was finally able to back up enough to focus, she was still less than a foot away from the startled face of the stranger.

Without warning, he reached out and grasped her shoulders. Sonia's eyes widened and she froze up.

"Thank you!" he expelled with such gratitude that she quickly understood who he was. "I have no idea how you...just, thank you."

The guy was a little older than Sonia, with thick brown hair that hadn't been highlighted by the sunshine in quite awhile. She couldn't tell the exact color of his eyes, but they were staring at her with such appreciative intensity that she had to look away, slightly embarrassed.

Realizing how forward he was being, the man let go of Sonia's arms and took a step back. "Sorry, it's been such a crazy day, and I haven't wanted to leave Jada's bedside. But I was intending to come down and find you."

"Oh, that's alright," Sonia started, a little discombobulated, "I'm totally fine. How is she? She's your...daughter?"

"What? Oh, no, not my daughter. My niece, she's my brother's daughter," he motioned into the room where Sonia could see a man and a woman playing with the little girl in her bed. "I was just taking her out for a playdate today and...well, it's safe to say that I may be officially the world's worst uncle." His hands rubbed his eyes and down his face as he said this. The man had obviously been pretty shaken by the experience. "Just for the record, it isn't an excuse by any means, but I was watching her. It just happened so fast and..."

Sonia decided to cut him off. "As long as she's okay, everything's alright," she gave him a smile that she hoped would make him feel a little comforted.

"Please, let me pay you. You just saved my niece's life. I have. . ." the man began to fumble through his pockets, but Sonia shook her head.

"No thank you. I don't need anything. Everyone is okay, and that's all that matters."

"I know this is so awkward, but I'm just at a loss right now. Please let me repay you." The man was holding out a couple $20 bills, but Sonia continued to decline.

"At least let me take you out for coffee!" he finally offered.

Sonia pivoted back on her heel and took a good look at the man. His hair looked wild from where he had run his worried hand through it earlier, and his face was stubbly but kind.

"Okay," Sonia said, "I can do that."

He shook his head in gratitude and pulled his phone out from his back pocket. "Great, thank you. That makes me feel at least the tiniest bit better." They exchanged info and Sonia excused herself, her socked feet sounding like Velcro as she padded back down the hall and away from him.

"Interesting," she thought. She was truly relieved to find out the little girl was safe, and the coffee date was an unexpected twist. Then she rolled around the uncle's name in her head. Aiden.

Sonia made her way downstairs hoping that she would quickly find Yvette and get whisked back to the comfort of her grandmother's house.

CHAPTER 3

*O*ver the next few days, Sonia texted on and off with Aiden. Their texts were brief and mainly had to do with setting up their date. Sometimes he would send her funny little quips that made her laugh. She wasn't sure if he was crazy, or just had a good sense of humor and a lot of time on his hands.

"Who are you texting with?" Yvette asked, trying to peer over Sonia's shoulder.

"That guy. The uncle of the little girl," Sonia attempted to hide her phone by tossing it onto the couch. "No big deal."

"What is he saying?" Yvette squinted suspiciously at Sonia. Sonia knew her sister was already deciding whether to deem this a fateful encounter. Either that or figuring out how to deconstruct this guy before he could cause any damage. Yvette had two modes, romantic and skeptic, and it just depended on how things were going in her own life as to how she would react to Sonia's.

"I'm going out to drink coffee with him," Sonia finally answered her sister.

"Do you like him?" Yvette asked, leaning closer to her sister.

Sonia shook her head. "I don't even know him! And besides, you know better than anyone that I am taking no new applicants in the dating department. I am so over it. Fresh start, no drama remember? That's one of the reasons I left, and that's my mantra in coming home." Sonia pulled on her gloves and grabbed her scarf off the hook, "Besides, he just wants to thank me for saving his niece."

As Sonia drove through the town, she took in all that she had missed for the last year. The Canadian Rockies were so stunningly picture perfect this time of year that she often thought it looked even better than the brochures put out by the tourist board. The towering trees with their see through branches shot skyward as if pointing to the evening sky. Sonia passed a family of elk grazing passively on a small cropping of grass poking through the frosty ground. And off in the distance, she could see the towering mountains that cradled her hometown in the safety of their walls.

Sonia's car carefully crunched along in the snow as she looked for a parking spot. Evergreen Valley was a quaint place with a downtown that resembled a postcard. They had a decent amount of visitors and tourists pass through who were drawn to the area because of the nearby resort. However, there were very few people out in the evenings when the temperatures dropped, and people retreated the warmth of their cozy fireplaces.

She was supposed to meet Aiden at a coffee shop called the Artist's Corner, just a block off of Main Street. She had never heard of it so she assumed it must be new. Sonia spotted a parking place and pulled in. She shut off the car and tucked the keys in her pocket.

When she stepped into the coffee shop, she instantly stopped and took it in. The decor was eclectic, to say the least, though also very inviting. One wall was a giant chalkboard, while another was a cluster of repositionable canvases. The other areas were painted a beautiful purple, offset by a creamy, mellow white. It was pretty appealing, she thought. The chalkboard had a few scribblings in one corner where people had signed their names, but otherwise, the interactive walls were pretty much untouched. Sonia looked around and saw that Aiden was the only person in the shop.

"This place is so neat," she said with genuine enthusiasm. Looking behind the service counter, she didn't see anyone. "Where are the owners?"

"I'm the owner," Aiden said.

"You own this place?" Sonia asked. She looked around at the walls with new admiration. "What a cool idea!"

Aiden had a little smile on his face. "Thanks. I liked the idea of letting the customers be involved. I'm not the best artist by any means. My own painting abilities are a work-in-progress, but I don't mind. I like the idea that you don't need to be perfect at something to do it. Plus, we have great coffee." He leaned back against the counter. "I have a mantra that I live by. Sometimes coffee is just coffee...but sometimes, the right coffee can change your life." He grinned at her.

He motioned around at the empty café. "Unfortunately, it's been a pretty rough start. In case it wasn't apparent, I'm open right now."

Sonia instantly felt bad for him. She knew that feeling of putting your heart into something only to find yourself let down. She was always thankful that she had faith to help her through those times.

He shrugged and made light of the situation. "What would you like to drink tonight, Madam?" Aiden offered.

Sonia smiled and went up to the counter while Aiden went behind it. She surveyed the menu. "I'll have a vanilla chai latte. Believe it or not, I've never had one before, but it always sounds delicious."

"Excellent choice. I shall have an almond milk latte myself. Would you care to take a seat while I whip up your order?"

"Actually, I'm kind of interested in seeing how you make a latte." Sonia pointed behind the counter. "May I?"

Aiden nodded as he grabbed a cup and turned on the machine.

"Why do you think business is so slow?" Sonia asked.

Aiden shrugged. "Believe me; I've been asking myself the same question. Logistically everything is solid. I did a ton of research and have a business background from school. But there's just something missing."

She watched as the dark aromatic espresso poured out of the shiny chambers into his cup. "On one hand, I know that setting up a slightly non-traditional coffee shop in Evergreen was a gamble, but I don't know how to explain it other than that I felt like it was where I needed to be. Anyhow, I've tried advertising, but again, I can't help but think that there's something missing. There's a spark that I haven't figured out how to light. And whether I want to admit it or not, I can't keep chipping out money if nothing is coming in."

His eyes had sunk a bit as he grated fresh nutmeg over top her chai. She could tell the problem was weighing on him heavily.

Sonia nodded, rolling his words around in her head.

"Maybe we just need to figure out a way to get the word out," she perked.

In an attempt to change the subject, he let out a small whistle.

The tapping of tiny nails came into earshot as a minuscule dog rounded the corner. The dog was decked out in the most absurdly cute frou-frou winter outfit that Sonia had ever seen.

"Are you kidding me?" she looked up at Aiden as she tried to suppress the giant grin overtaking her face.

He scooped up the small pup. "This…is the cafe's official mascot. Meet Pepper."

He took the dogs miniature paw and shook hands with Sonia. The brightly colored doggy sweater was a marvel in and of its own right, and Pepper herself was downright adorable. Pepper cocked her head, inspecting Sonia.

Sensing Sonia's inspection of Pepper's wardrobe, he explained, "When I was traveling for work, I ended up in South America. I befriended a local kid who insisted that I needed a companion. There are so many dogs that need homes there that when he brought me Pepper and told me she needed a family, I couldn't say no. However, I didn't realize I'd be moving to the tundra at some point, so Pepper and I have had to figure out how to adapt." He looked at Sonia and knew what she was thinking. "I don't know what to tell you; she has a mind of her own. I bring her to the dog store, and she picks out what she wants. I've tried more subdued fashion choices, but she won't have it. I wake up to find them in shreds." Sonia suppressed a snicker.

Aiden shrugged and placed the dog back on the floor where Sonia now noticed a small dog bed.

At a loss for words and trying hard not to fixate on the hilariously dressed animal, Sonia ripped her attention away and tried to think of something else to talk about.

"Can you show me how the rest of the machines work?" Sonia asked.

He motioned her over, and she joined him at the frother. As he explained his process for making his specialty drinks, he grabbed a metal container and helped guide her hand in the smooth, consistent motion that kept the milk from overheating.

"If you pay the right amount of attention you can get the perfect foam," he turned a stainless steel handle to off with his free hand and the milk steamer sputtered to a stop. "And if you do..." he grabbed a cup and elegantly poured the milk in this way and that. Sonia leaned into his demonstration. "...If you do, you may be lucky enough to get...something, like...this," he set the metal container down and handed her the ceramic mug.

Her eyes widened as she saw that he had somehow managed to create a beautiful, scripty heart design out of the foam.

"How...?" she looked up at him with her jaw dropped. She was as impressed as a child at a magic show.

"I know that no latte art can adequately describe my thanks, but truly, from the bottom of my heart, thank you for saving my niece. She means the world to me and I truly do think that you're a hero."

Sonia opened her mouth to respond but simply gazed at him for a second before shutting it. Words would only ruin that perfect compliment, so she let the moment just be.

Aiden took in a big, slightly self-conscious breath and let it out audibly.

He handed Sonia her drink. "So here you go. The world's best vanilla chai latte! Named so because it was made with extra appreciation and love," he smirked, and an adorable dimple creased his half smile.

Sonia took a sip.

Looking on expectantly, Aiden asked, "What do ya think?"

The exotic flavor was warm and comforting like hot chocolate, yet much lighter, almost invigorating. It was spicy and creamy, with the scent of cardamom and nutmeg swirling into her nose. She discreetly licked her lips. "I like it. Do you know that I'm always nervous to try something new?"

"I find that kind of hard to believe. You strike me as the bold and fearless type."

She spit out a laugh, "Hardly!"

"Well I would bank money on the fact that anyone who rushes headfirst into a frozen pond without a second thought, at the very least, isn't a blushing flower," he challenged.

Sonia made a cute gesture of agreement. "I didn't say I was shy…I guess it's more that I'm cautious about giving new things a chance," she scrunched her nose and looked up at him. "I like what I like."

He accepted her admission with a warm smile of his own. "No doubt," he replied.

Aiden turned off the last machine and motioned to the front door. "I don't think I'm going to get any customers tonight. Do you want to take a walk down the street? Pepper needs to go for a walk anyway. Did you bring a scarf?"

"Yep," Sonia said, pulling her scarf out from under her jacket's collar. "I think a walk would be nice." She pulled her hood up and looped her scarf loosely over her mouth.

"I love the snow," she commented as they stepped outside. Sonia looked down the street and smiled. The light poles were lit up with Christmas shapes and day old snow lay along their path.

Sonia stood into the covered brick entryway and watched as Aiden locked up the café. "Ready?" he asked.

Sonia nodded, her eyes lit up with holiday spirit. "I love Christmastime here," she said. "It's perfect."

They descended the large cobblestone steps that lead to the sidewalk and Aiden reached down, gently taking Sonia's hand. A shiver swept over her. She felt the warmth of his hand even through the glove and her heart unexpectedly began to sing.

"These steps ice over and are not to be trusted," he cautioned as he helped her down.

As they started along the well-trodden path Sonia wished she didn't have to remove her hand, but self-consciously slipped it away and into her coat pocket.

"So how is it that you ended up here," Aiden asked as they walked along the cobblestone side street.

"Me? Oh, I'm from here." Sonia replied, slightly taken aback. She'd never been mistaken for a visitor before.

He gave her an odd side glance. "Well I know I don't run the most popular establishment, but how have we never crossed paths if you're from here? I mean, the town's not that big."

"That is true; there's not too much that goes on around here without someone or other knowing about it. I actually just got back," she told him. "I grew up here and always loved it, but I just needed a change. I took a job teaching abroad, so I've been gone for the last year. I just got back in time for the holidays."

He started to speak, thought about it, then casually asked, "So are you going back soon?

She scanned the tumbled pavers that formed the bumpy path they were walking along. Then her eyes raised up to the antique style lamppost strewn with golden garland and strung with holiday lights.

"No, I ended my contract. It was a great experience, but I was ready to be home. I know where I belong and I was ready to get back here."

A light smile flashed across his face, "Yeah, it's a special place."

She looked at him covertly out of the corner of her eyes as they walked silently for a few minutes.

She really did love her family and the town she was from. It had been hard growing up in a place that relied so heavily on its seasons to fill out the small population. Maybe hard with the wrong word, but she had fallen prey more times than she'd like to admit to developing feelings for someone who up and left once the winter or summer season was over.

"How did you end up here?" she asked back.

"Well, that is an interesting story. Hm, or maybe it's not that interesting at all," he reasoned. "Growing up my family moved a lot. My mom was in the military and my dad was a consultant, so my brother and I never really had an official hometown as it were. That's not to say we moved as much as some people do, but it was enough to never feel completely settled. My grandfather had retired up here after my grandmother passed away and occasionally invited my brother and I up to visit. Once I was out on my own, I guess I just took up where my parents left off. I took a job that had me constantly traveling. My brother followed my mom into the military and even though we were never in the same place, we've always stayed close. A few years back he got injured, and the only person with a stable home was my grandfather. So my brother came here to recuperate, and at the same time, he was able to help my grandfather out. I guess there's magic in the air here because next thing I knew he was married and had a kid on the way! It blew my mind; I never thought I'd see the day when my brother settled down. But honestly, I've never seen him happier."

They crunched along the path as he continued, "Then some stuff happened to me, and I just realized that I didn't want to live the rest of my life with no one close to me. My soul started to feel sort of hollow. I don't really know how to describe it."

He placed his hand on the curve of her back and helped guide her around a corner. She was enraptured by his story and the smooth honied way he spoke.

He went on, "For some reason, the idea of losing my brother struck a chord with me, and after a little soul-searching and a lot of prayer, it hit me that I needed to be close to him. Long story short, I wrapped up my affairs, moved here and the mess of coffee and pie you just saw was created!" he said with a cute, self-deprecating tone.

"How about here?" he asked, motioning to a bench overlooking the town green and the skating pond. Her eyes sparkled up at him, the chill nipping at them.

"I love this spot," she said.

"Me too. It's become one of my favorite places to sit and think about things. Plus, Pepper is pretty fond of the dog run."

"It can be good people watching too," Sonia chimed in. "Especially when the little kids are out on the pond learning to skate."

As Pepper ran around the dog area, Sonia couldn't help but feel a comfortable warmth overtake her. After being away from this place, the scene was idyllic. There was something so simple, yet spectacular, about life in this small town. She appreciated the chance to take it in.

They sat there a long while, talking and watching Pepper fight with the snow piles that were seemingly threatening her. Eventually, the chill started to set in, which always indicated to Sonia that it was getting late as the temperature made a discernible drop.

Pepper lead them for about a block before deciding she was too tired to go on and dramatically collapsed at Aiden's feet.

"This is how she tells me she's ready to be carried," he said. "Subtle, isn't it?" Sonia laughed as he scooped up the tiny pooch.

They reached the end of the lighted street and paused in front of the Artist's Corner. Sonia felt a few snowflakes fall and land on her cheek. She smiled up into the dark star-lit sky.

"I should probably get back now," Sonia said. "Thanks for showing me your café. I think it's terrific."

"I appreciate that. I'm glad you came," he said warmly. "As you may be able to tell, you were beyond the highlight of my night."

Sonia blushed. He had a certain charm about him; she had to give him that.

Stopping at the bottom of the steps that lead to the coffee shop door, Sonia bent down to pet Pepper.

"Maybe," he stopped himself, choosing his words cautiously, "Maybe you can stop by some time. Or, we could go do something, if you're not busy."

She didn't answer immediately, then stood up and replied, "I think we could arrange that. I've had a really nice night." She smiled at him with a feeling of pure sincerity.

She saw him make a micro-movement towards her. With the realization that he might kiss her, she backed up slightly and hurriedly said, "My sister's going be waiting up for me, so I should get going." She quickly leaned down again and rustled Pepper's ears.

"And you," she said, "You are nothing short of a tiny puffball, and I think I love you." Pepper cocked her furry head in recognition and gave Sonia an appreciative snarfle.

CHAPTER 4

"*S*onia," Grandma said at breakfast the next morning. "I just got a phone call, and Margaret has had a bad fall. Her daughter is in charge of the youth choir, but she needs to be with Margaret right now while she is in the hospital. They are supposed to put on the program for the church on Christmas Eve. I told Grace that you would be the perfect one to take over her position."

"Me?" Sonia said, her eyes opening wide.

"Yes, Sonia. You have that lovely singing voice, you have the background for it and you are so good with children."

"I believe they have mostly prepared already," Sonia's grandma continued. "They only have the one performance, and they have a few practices scheduled before then. Grace said you could ask a girl named Rebecca if you needed any help knowing what to do."

Sonia took a deep breath. She didn't have any good reason not to do it, aside from basic nerves. Plus she was always saying how a person should serve whenever they got the opportunity. She mulled it over for a minute before replying.

"Okay, Grandma. You can tell Grace I'll do it."

Grandma smiled and patted Sonia's hand. "I knew you wouldn't turn down this opportunity. You'll barely have to do a thing. I'll go call Grace right now."

"Can you ask her what songs they are singing, so I can at least be familiar with them?" Sonia asked. Her grandma agreed and left the room.

Sonia spent the afternoon inside. She was getting a bit of a runny nose and wanted to ward it off by drinking lots of hot tea and playing Scrabble. Sonia and Yvette switched off playing against their grandmother. Their mom joined in after she had finished some work, and the four women spent a pleasant afternoon having quality family time. No matter how hard they tried, though, Grandma was still the reigning champion.

A light snow fell as the day progressed and soon the girls were asked to go out and shovel the driveway.

Sonia got dressed in her slightly damp snow gear and walked out into the snow. Her sister was busy pulling out the shovels and wasn't paying attention for once. Sonia grabbed a small handful of snow and stuffed it down the back of Yvette's snowsuit. Sonia laughed and ran away when her sister sprang into revenge mode.

"That's for trying to cheat at Scrabble!" Sonia yelled, taking refuge behind a tree in the yard.

"Two letter words count!" Yvette shouted back while scooping up an armload of snow into her casted arm. "It's not my fault if you don't bother to read the Scrabble Dictionary!"

Sonia was laughing so hard it hurt. She always felt a sense of accomplishment when she managed to get one up on her sister.

"Come on," Sonia called out. "Truce!"

"There is no truce until I get you back," Yvette said.

Sonia finally agreed to stand still while her sister threw one and only one snowball at her. It smashed into Sonia's eye, and she quickly cleaned the wet stuff away.

"Come on," she said to Yvette. "Let's get this driveway done."

As the girls began to shovel, it became apparent that Yvette's one good arm wasn't up to the challenge of wielding the large plastic shovel.

"Change of plan," Sonia proposed. "I'll shovel the drive, and you get started on building a snowman. This yard is in desperate need of some holiday cheer. I think we've been slacking this year."

"Let's make it a girl," Yvette declared. "We can put my extra purple scarf on it so that it's clearly a snowwoman."

"Alright then, snowwoman. Let's do it."

The previous few years had been tumultuous for their family, with their father leaving and their grandfather passing away. But the women had rallied together and weathered the changes well. Sonia, her mother, and sister had moved in with her grandmother, and the foursome had seamlessly pushed forward without complaint. Which was why a snowwoman seemed particularly apt this year; a snowy matriarch standing proudly to spread holiday cheer.

"You start forming the big ball while I shovel," Sonia said. "I'll pile the driveway snow for the smaller ones."

"Let's see who can do it faster!" Yvette called out, as always, making everything into a competition.

When she went back inside with her sister two hours later, Sonia was ready to go into hibernation. She always forgot how tired she got after playing in the snow. Once she had cleaned up, she climbed into her warm and cozy bed and told her mom to wake her up when dinner was ready. Then, Sonia began drifting off to sleep. Just as Sonia's eyes were firmly shut, her phone vibrated loudly on the nightstand.

Sonia startled up and glanced sleepily at the screen. It was a text, and it was from Aiden. Her stomach dropped, then filled with nervous butterflies.

Sonia cautiously opened it, as though afraid of what the message may say. In fact, she realized that she was afraid of what it might say. It was likely something charming or witty, and the idea of it made her nervous. She had not felt the way she had last night about someone in a very long time, and she really, really didn't want to.

When she was about to return home from her teaching job, she had given herself a stern talking. She had decided that she didn't want to date anyone for a very long time. She just wanted to be with her family and figure out what she was supposed to do next with her life. She had been hurt and let down in the past, and it felt not only safer, but smarter, to simply cocoon herself off from that happening again.

"Had a great time last night. What did you do today?" Sonia took a deep breath. Just picturing him on the other end of the phone, sitting there with Pepper on his lap texting her, gave her nervous flutters.

No, this wasn't good at all.

Before she could stop herself, she had responded. Ten minutes later they had a date set up for the following day.

Sonia turned her phone off and rolled over in her bed. She placed a large pillow over her face to try and tone down the huge smile plastered on it.

CHAPTER 5

*O*ne week and several casual dates later, Sonia asked Aiden if he wanted to go to the Winter Carnival. It was at the ski village located in the next town over, and she completely sold him on the idea that it was an absolute must do activity if he'd never been.

Sonia drove over with her sister, who was working at the booth that the ski school was sponsoring. She hugged her sister goodbye and went to the arched entryway of the festival to wait for Aiden.

When she saw him, her face lit up with a smile that matched his. Aiden walked over and kissed her on the cheek.

Outstretching a hand to lead the way through the entry he said, "Shall we?"

They made their way through the festival, stopping at the various booths to see all the local artisanal goods. They sampled chocolates and got their pictures taken at a photo booth with some goofy props. Sonia chuckled at the printed photo strip before slipping it into her jacket pocket. The four shots showed Aiden in a felt Christmas tree hat, while she donned a halo.

"I'm glad they gave us a duplicate set," he said, "so I don't have to fight you for those."

They got to the carnival ride section and got in line for the Crazy

Himalaya. It whipped them around, smashing Sonia into Aiden with the centrifugal force. The adrenaline heightened the mood even more, and the two of them were cracking up the whole time.

Since Aiden wasn't from the region, Sonia felt compelled to introduce him to some of the local fare. They got Beavertails & frozen Maple syrup on a stick.

"So basically this is a funnel cake, or actually it's more of an elephant ear, right?"

"Well if you're going to get technical about it," Sonia replied, "a Beavertail is essentially fried dough, but it's made with an extra dash of Canadian kindness, so it's a little bit different. Plus, it has a waffle pattern, so as you can imagine it taste nothing like an elephant ear."

Aiden grinned and bit into his powdered sugar dusted confection.

They walked around more and eventually found Yvette at the ski school booth.

"Hey!" Yvette exclaimed. "Get on over here you two crazy kids. Do you want to try your hand at our makeshift carnival game?"

Yvette leaned in conspiratorially, "Actually we need you to look like you're having a lot of fun so that it brings the crowds. Apparently, we didn't know what we were up against." She motioned to the super professional set-ups on either side of their comparatively small booth.

After playing for a good ten minutes, a small crowd started to gather with people getting in on the action. Yvette relented, "Ok, you guys have done your part. Here, you won two tickets to the ice skating rink. Free ice-skates on behalf of the ski school. Do me proud," she smiled and handed over the red paper tickets.

Sonia looked at Aiden, "You up for some ice skating?"

"I never turn down hard-won tickets to ice-skating," he replied, "… but I'm going to warn you, it's been a while."

"Well, you are in luck because you are in the company of the Evergreen Valley junior ice pond skating champion…" Then she mumbled a year that he couldn't understand.

She could see him trying to do the math from the numbers that he thought he could make out from what she had said.

"You were the ice pond skating champion when you were…Five?"

"Listen," she said, "it was very tough competition, and I earned that crown fair and square."

Now he looked even more confused. "There was a crown?"

"Ok, there are some people that may say that it is more like a beauty pageant on ice skates, but I am not one of those people. So we will just let it be, and you can simply know that you are in the hands of a professional."

He let out a decent laugh and threw his hands up relentingly.

"I have complete faith in your abilities," he said, "and worst-case scenario, at least I taught you how to run the machines at the cafe if I don't make it out in one piece."

She looked up at him with a mischievous grin.

They laced up their skates and tiptoed their way cautiously onto the ice. It was a man-made skating rink, but it was very much in the fashion of a hometown skating pond. It was smoothed by hand and definitely did not have a Zamboni's glassy finish.

They both wobbled a little on the thickly bladed skates, but Sonia quickly gained her composure and started to slide across the ice. Aiden tried nobly, but it took him several more minutes to get his bearings and figure out how to stand up properly. Finally, the two of them were skating in unison, the holiday songs floating through the air and a light snow falling from the starry sky.

A slow song came on, and Aiden slipped his hand into Sonia's. She looked at their laced fingers as a small smile crept across her face.

"I think speed may have been the only thing keeping me upright," he said cutely without looking at her, "so I need this for safety reasons."

"Ah," she replied.

They skated hand in hand as the song played. As they skated in the wide looping circle, their stride got in sync and soon they were gliding along like pros.

As the song neared it's end, the next song started to play over top of it. A considerably more upbeat tempo begin.

Let's hear those sleigh bells jingle and ring ting tingling toooo. Come on it's lovely weather for a sleigh ride together with you...

Both Sonia and Aiden quickened their pace to keep up with the flow of skaters gliding to the music. As they rounded the corner on the backside of the rink, Sonia felt Aiden starting to lose his balance. She gripped his arm tightly for support, but before she knew it, he had wobbled so much that the two of them went flying into the snow drift off to the side. The rush of cold snow up the back of her jacket made her shriek. Then she started laughing hysterically.

Through their tangled legs and arms, she could hear Aiden apologizing. "I am so sorry! So, so, so sorry!"

Still in hysterics, Sonia laid where she was in the snow, tears of laughter freezing across her face. She felt Aiden roll up on his shoulder trying to disentangle their skate blades. As she lay there, he propped up on his elbow, blocking the overhead lights from her view. She peered into his eyes and tried to catch her breath from laughing.

"I cannot believe I did that while skating with the Evergreen ice pond skating queen. That is so embarrassing..." He grinned down at her teasingly.

This sent her into a new fit of giggles, though she decided that he deserved to be pelted with some snow for the slight against her well-deserved title. She grabbed a handful of snow and smashed it gently, but firmly into his face. This sent yet another wave of glee through her. She was pretty sure she was punchy from laughing so much.

"You didn't..." he admonished. Looking at her only inches away, his mouth aghast. "You are so going to get it," he threatened through his own laughter.

They wrestled for superiority while he tried to get a handful of snow. With their skate blades still being entangled, however, they didn't get very far. Finally, both of them flopped back, completely exhausted from the effort, but glowing with the bliss of playfulness. He turned his head toward her. She could feel his breath condensing on her cheeks, and it felt as if they were sharing the same air, breathing together. His arm was draped over her waist, and the feelings that shot through her core were so electric that she thought she would just pass out. Her eyes scanned his face, taking in every inch of it. Then slowly, but before she could even understand or argue, he was kissing her. It was slow and warm, and she felt as if the icicles caked into her hair had all melted away. All she knew in the world was what was happening at that very second. She kissed him back with a dizzying passion. She fluttered open her eyes to see his face backlit by the most magical night sky, with gentle sparkling snowflakes being illuminated by the floodlights overhead. She closed back her eyes and just melted into the scene. For a moment she thought she was either asleep or in a dream, and she was certain that she could lay there for a million more hours.

Shhhhk. The sound of a skate blade skidding up beside them awakened her from her fantasy. It was one of the people from the skating concession, an older lady in her 60's who looked like she could give anyone a run from for their money on the side of a mountain.

"You two okay?" she asked. "I saw you go down, but you've been down here a while, so I just wanted to check on you."

Blushing and embarrassed, the two of them sat up and worked overtime to disentangle their skates.

"Totally fine," Aiden said. "It was my fault. I'm a novice, and this was one of my first lessons. I think I need to invest in a 10-pack."

The lady reached a hand and helped each of them up before giving them a wry smirk and skating off.

"Stick to the outskirts of the rink," she called behind her. "The landings are softer."

The duo decided that they had proven themselves enough on the rink to deserve a hot chocolate. Sonia could barely look at Aiden after what had happened. She felt like her face was in a permanent state of flush, and she was sure he could see it if she were to look at him straight on. They found a bench and sipped their whipped cream topped hot cocoa.

"Not quite Artist's Corner caliber," she assessed about the hot chocolate, "but it hits the spot."

They looked out at the people milling happily around them. The ski village was alive with the energy of the season.

"Maybe you could set up set up a coffee kiosk at next year's festival," she thought aloud.

He was looking off far in the distance with a dreamy sort of stare. "I really hope so. That's a good idea. I hope I can make it that long."

She listened intently to his response, a tightness creeping into her chest.

He still wasn't looking at her when he said, "I can't imagine having to leave all of this."

He glanced sidelong at her. "It would be great if a lot of this was still happening this time next year."

She realized the sweetness of his words, but couldn't help feeling a ripple of doubt starting to weave its way into her internal dialogue.

The sheer bliss she was feeling just moments before began to turn into a mild anxiety. She sat on the bench and began fidgeting with the paper cup holder, avoiding looking at him as much as possible. Sonia realized that what Aiden was saying wasn't ill-intentioned, but his words rung in her ears with the truth of her biggest fear. There was no certainty that he would be here a year from now. Nothing was keeping him here in all reality. He loved his family, but this was a whim, something he had never attempted in his life. It wasn't his home.

She knew that the silence had gone on a little too long, so she offered up something. "I hadn't even asked where Pepper was tonight. She must be flipping out without you."

"Oh no, she's being dogsat by Jada, and there is nothing Pepper likes more than a play date over at Jada's house. She is in doggy heaven, I assure you."

Sonia forced an appreciative smile in response. She knew it was unfounded, but her anxiety was growing, and she realized that need to remove herself from the situation as quickly as she could. The stress was overtaking her, and she just needed to sort things out. But not in front of Aiden.

"I know this sounds kind of pathetic," she finally managed, "but I am so exhausted from today and kind of feel like passing out. Would it be awful if we called it a night?"

She still refused to meet his eyes, feeling a little dramatic but also like she might cry if she looked at him.

He could sense the shift in mood and being the gentleman that she could tell he was, he tried to make it seem less awkward than it was.

"Yeah, that's probably a good idea. I have to be up early to walk Pepper and open the shop. If ever there will be a busy week at the café, it will be this week, right? Or so I'm praying."

He stood up and took her hand to help her up as well. They walked to the front entrance, and she told him good night.

"I'm just going to go see how long Yvette will be, so you don't have to wait with me."

He took the hint, and though she could sense his air of disappointment, he graciously kissed the top of her hand and said good night. She swallowed thickly as she watched him walk away towards the parking lot.

This felt awful, she admitted to herself. Sonia's experiences with disappointment and heartbreak had been bad enough that she never wanted to experience either again. Yet in this attempt to avoid future pain, she felt almost worse. She reasoned with herself that at least now she was strong and confident. She had a knowing certainty that having her heart broken by Aiden would crush her, and she was terrified to set herself up for that. Something this intense could only go one of two ways, she decided. What were the chances that this virtual stranger who she met under extraordinary circumstances, this charming and easy-going man, with his handsome face and infectious smile…what were the chances that this was her soulmate? The gamble on that just seemed too great.

Sonia measured her breathing until she felt calm and walked slowly back to wait until Yvette's shift was over.

CHAPTER 6

*T*he next day, Sonia convinced her sister that they should build a snowman for their snowwoman. This was secretly Sonia's way of avoiding going to the big hill again, sensing that, given the timing, she may run into Aiden walking Pepper.

"Sonia!" Yvette complained. "We've only gone to the hill three times this season! We're breaking our tradition! I don't get it, why don't you want to go?"

"We'll go tomorrow," Sonia promised. "I think my muscles are still sore from all that skating." This was clearly an exaggeration, but Sonia had not told her sister the full story of the previous night's ice skating adventures.

Sonia needed some serious time by herself with her Bible and journal before she would be able to see Aiden again.

Sonia looked at her sister who was making a one-winged snow angel.

"I'm getting cold actually," Yvette said. "Do you want to go inside?"

"Shocking! I don't see how rolling around in a pile of snow wearing your thinnest winter jacket could make you cold...But sure, let's go in. What do you want to do instead?" Sonia asked.

"We haven't done our Christmas cookies yet!"

Sonia placed a hand on her stomach as she thought of eating clumps of cookie dough. "Yep, food always wins out. Let's go bake some Christmas treats!"

The girls tugged off their snow gear and scrambled into the kitchen. As they began searching through the cupboards, they realized that they were missing quite a few ingredients.

"Go ask Grandma if she bought the chocolate chips," Sonia said. "I'll keep looking."

A minute later Yvette skidded back into the kitchen on socked feet and told Sonia just what she feared.

"She gave me ten dollars so we can buy chocolate chips. She said we need to get some more mints for her mint bowl, too."

"She said its mistletoe season and she doesn't want one of her granddaughters going around town with stinky breath," Yvette guffawed.

The girls trekked over to the local grocery store, and they got the supplies they needed. That afternoon, they baked up three different kinds of cookies, including sugar cookies to decorate, and fudge, which needed to set.

"We should probably test one of each kind," Yvette suggested with an impish smile.

Sonia laughed. "You would suggest that." But knowing perfectly well that she intended to eat her fair share of their efforts.

The girls sat down with tall glasses of milk and ate their Christmas cookies.

"Tomorrow," Yvette said, "we can make chocolate covered pretzels."

"We better not eat everything," Sonia said. "You know Grandma likes us to give some to the neighbors."

"The neighbors can bake their own cookies," Yvette complained.

"Hey, where's your Christmas spirit?" Sonia asked. Yvette threw her sister a wink.

After dinner, Sonia retreated to the room she shared with her sister.

She knew that Yvette would be watching TV for the next hour and she could have time to spend with God.

Sonia opened her Bible to Genesis chapter twenty-six where she had been reading about the history of the beginning of the world. She read two chapters, but didn't feel any more settled about her Aiden situation than she had felt when she began reading. Sonia sighed and began writing out her prayer to God.

"God, I am super confused and frustrated right now. I really like Aiden. He's amazing. He's funny, kind, respectful, he makes me laugh, and I feel like I can talk to him about anything. . ."

Sonia paused for a moment and smiled at her memory of him. "The problem is that I can't tell the future, and the idea of him leaving Evergreen if his business doesn't work out, it just feels too vulnerable. I want someone to love me because we are right for each other, not because I'm convenient. I don't want to be the novel girlfriend experience on his cozy little small town adventure. It's so hard to listen to common sense because it feels like there is this strong connection between us, but I can't help thinking that that's just the weakness of human nature taking over."

As Sonia closed her eyes and murmured the words, a conclusion settled over her.

"I know," she wrote, "that I don't want to be with Aiden if he isn't serious about creating a home and a life here. I know that this is where I belong, so it's up to him to know if it's the right place for him. I will give it a little time to see if he can show me where he really stands on the issue."

"But in the meantime...Please, keep him away from me." Sonia laughed at what she had just written and scribbled it out. "Help me enjoy this time with my family. I don't want to worry about running into him. I just want to go sledding with Yvette and feel normal."

"Okay," Sonia spoke aloud, "I'll go sledding. It doesn't serve my purpose if I'm not spending time with the people I love doing what we love together. Thank you, God."

Sonia zipped her journal shut and set both the journal and her Bible on the nightstand. She snuggled down between the sheets and closed her eyes. Her sister always teased her for going to sleep so early, but Sonia didn't care.

Yvette came in a while later.

"We're going sledding tomorrow, right?" she whispered.

Sonia nodded sleepily as Yvette turned off the light and crawled in the bed across from her sister. "Good night."

"Good night," Sonia murmured.

CHAPTER 7

*W*hen morning broke, Sonia awoke feeling at peace. She knew that they would have to get out to the hill early if they wanted to go. Choir practice was at four o'clock that afternoon, and Sonia needed some time to look over the songs first and prepare a few things. She felt fairly comfortable that she had everything in order, but she just wanted to be sure.

"Ready?" Sonia chirped as her sister sleepily ate breakfast.

"You're too happy in the morning," Yvette said.

"Me?" Sonia struck a glamorous pose. "Never."

"Quiet down," their mom said as she rinsed off her dirty dishes.

Sonia apologized and curled up on the couch with a book while she waited for Yvette to finish up. She hadn't returned Aiden's text's other than one quick "Just got super busy. Touch base with you soon." Now it was itching at her, distracting her from reading. If she did see him, would she have to explain her completely unnatural exit the other night? Or the terse text? Should she reply right now just in case? Sonia shook her head. She was already playing head games with herself, which was something she hated.

Half an hour later, Yvette was chugging toward the front door. Sonia grabbed their sleds from the shed, and they hurried through the snow. Sonia found herself already smiling in anticipation of sledding down the hill.

"I hope we can put in overtime today," Yvette said.

Sonia smiled. "Don't worry. I am not planning on going for a swim in the pond, so we should be able to get a few extra runs in."

The girls reached the top of the hill, and Sonia let Yvette call the race. They swooped down, and Yvette had an early morning victory.

Yvette started dancing. "I told you I was going to beat you. Okay, we can go home."

"Okay, let's go," Sonia said, testing her.

"No, no!" Yvette protested. "I was just kidding. Geesh."

The girls joked with one another as they began walking back up to the top. For some reason, Sonia got the odd sensation that someone was watching her. She looked around at each person within eyesight until finally, near the back of a house, she spotted Aiden. Sonia's stomach tightened. She suddenly felt very conscious of every movement she had made since arriving.

"Come on, slowpoke," Yvette called from farther up the hill. Sonia broke eye contact with Aiden and raced up the mound after her sister. She knew she should say something to him, but then her ego got the better of her. If he wanted to talk, he could come start a conversation.

"You won't win again," Sonia said. She fully intended to push off with all of her strength, but she was distracted. When Yvette called the race, Sonia's foot fumbled and her push was weak. This time, Yvette was nearly glowing.

"It's like you forgot how to start," she teased. "That was awful!"

They went back up the hill, and Sonia glanced to her left. Aiden was definitely closer, and his eyes were trained on her. She had come here to hang out with her sister, and she was trying with all her willpower not to be distracted from that.

Sonia won the next three races, so Yvette suggested they both ride on the same sled. They ended up tumbling down the hillside and into a ball of giggles.

"Hey," Aiden said as Sonia began going up the hill again.

Sonia stopped and turned back to him. "Hi," she said, trying to keep the excitement out of her voice.

"How have you been?" Aiden asked. Sonia turned and looked at her sister who was climbing up the hill alone. Yvette called a "hello" out to Aiden and kept walking.

"I'm all right," Sonia said. "Where's Pepper?"

Aiden looked around. Just then the tiny pup bounded out from behind a snowdrift. Dressed in a colorful snowflake patterned puffy jacket, Pepper barked at Sonia, then launched herself into a soft pile of snow. Sonia raised her eyebrows.

"She likes to play hide and seek," Aiden shrugged.

Sonia tried to stifle a giggle, then looked back at Yvette. Yvette was talking to a young girl that didn't have a sled. Yvette ran back down to Sonia and Aiden.

"Sonia, I just made a little friend. She's never sledded before. I'm not even joking, like never in her life. I'm going to give her a quick crash course. Can I use your sled? "

"Of course," Sonia said, happily handing over her sled. She knew a perfect excuse when she was handed one. When her sister was out of earshot, Sonia turned back to Aiden.

She wanted to apologize for leaving so abruptly the other night, and for not responding to his texts, even though she knew that she had needed to take the space.

"I want to say that I'm sorry…" she started.

He hushed her and shook his head, "You don't need to say anything. We all have our reasons for doing what we do."

"We're getting close to Christmas. Are you guys all ready?" he asked, making the conversation comfortable. Sonia appreciated the gesture.

"I think so! We still have a little more baking to do, but we've decorated and are having family time, which is what we like to do." Sonia was feeling energized now. "Do you have any family traditions for Christmas?" Sonia asked.

Aiden smiled. "Well, I haven't been here that long, so I guess we are sort of working on some new traditions. But when I was a kid, we had some. No matter where we were in the world, my brother and I would wake up at the crack of dawn. My mom said we couldn't wake her up earlier than 6:00, so we were always right there at their bedroom door at 6:01. My dad would go down the stairs, and turn on the lights. Then he would always tell us that it looked like we had been bad because Santa had only left coal for us. We would protest, and then we would all come tumbling down the stairs." Aiden laughed. "Every year, he said the same thing." They both breathed in the happiness from his memory. "What about your family?" he asked.

"My sister and I have an annual tradition that we try to sled every single day in the weeks leading up to Christmas. And we do our Christmas baking."

Sonia was enjoying conversing with Aiden so much that she wanted to keep it going a little longer. "When I was little, my mom would give me ten dollars to buy her a present. My grandma would take me shopping. When I found something that cost about $30 that I wanted to give my mom, my grandma chipped in the rest of the money. When my mom opened the present, her mouth fell open. She would say 'you got this for $10?'"

Aiden laughed. "Well, I was the younger brother, and I totally looked up to my older brother. When I was six years old, I wanted to give him a present, but I didn't have any money. So I picked a bunch of different things from my room, mostly things he had given me before, and wrapped them up."

Sonia laughed. "Oh, Yvette has done the same to me. It's really cute when kids just want to show you love."

"I agree," Aiden said, pointing at Yvette who was letting the younger girl ride down the hill between her legs. "Looks like your sister is taking after you; fearless yet sweet."

At the compliment, Sonia felt her cheeks redden slightly.

Taking a breath, Aiden suggested, "If you're up for it, I would really like to go out with you again."

Sonia turned her eyes to focus on Aiden.

"Maybe tonight?" Aiden suggested.

She immediately shook her head. "I already have a commitment."

Sonia sensed how her words had sounded. He had gone out of his way to ask her out again, even though she had distanced herself and she had shot him down.

She quickly scrambled to clarify. "I told my grandma that I would take over the choir practice."

"You're leading the choir?" Aiden asked.

Sonia shrugged and confessed her own surprise at the news. "I certainly wasn't planning on it, but the woman in charge of the choir had a family emergency, and they just needed someone to help keep things in order. I was asked to do it. So now the fate of the Christmas Eve performance is the responsibility of yours truly."

"No way!" Aiden said. "My sister-in-law already has tickets to that!"

First Sonia's eyes lit up, then she looked at him a little embarrassed, "Oh great, now you will get to see first hand if I totally mess up the recital!"

"It will be perfect, I'm sure," he said with a kind twinkle in his eye.

With that little boost of confidence, she confided, "It's strange because my favorite part of Christmas has always been Christmas Eve when we go and watch the youth performance. And now I'm in charge of it!"

He smiled at her, a touch proudly, "I think you are going to do great. I bet it will be the most unforgettable performance they've ever had."

Sonia's nose crinkled bashfully. "Listen, as soon as I can sort a few things out, I'd really like it if we could do something."

At that, Pepper came flying out from behind a fallen log. She jumped around maniacally for a minute until she flopped down at their feet, seemingly expired. The pup wriggled around in a gleeful backbend in the snow, then froze her position looking happily up at them with her tongue out the side of her mouth. They both chuckled.

"Well I'm going to take that as a sign that she is both happy at the idea of seeing you again, and she's ready to be brought inside."

Aiden reached down and dusted off the bright pink and blue jacket that Pepper had covered in snow. "When it's a good time for you, let me know. I'll be here." He gave her a sweet, crooked smile and walked away.

Sonia's breath caught in her throat. She wanted to call him back, but she knew that she still needed time. If it was right, she had to trust that it would all fall into place.

CHAPTER 8

*T*hat afternoon, Sonia practiced the songs for the choir, looking up and listening to the ones she didn't know. Her grandma had an old piano in the living room, and Sonia tried to play out the harmonies. Unfortunately, the piano didn't sound particularly good. Sonia worked to tune it, but it was still a bit off when Yvette came in and began plunking away on the keys.

Sonia covered her ears. "Yvette, you need to take lessons. Desperately," Sonia said.

"I don't see why you never teach me," her sister harassed.

Sonia looked at her sister bemused. "Because, my darling sister, you have the patience of a third grader when it comes to things that you can't master in ten minutes. And there is a lot to learn if you ever want to play like I do."

Yvette banged out a made-up tune on the keys with her one hand. "I think I'm pretty good. Prodigies don't need lessons."

Sonia looked at the time. "I'm going to tell Mom I'm going to the church now."

"I'll tell her for you. But can you take her car?" Yvette asked. "I have to go out later, and I want to take ours."

"Sure," Sonia replied as she grabbed the keys off the wall.

"See you later!" Yvette called, as she drug her hand down the length of the piano in a noisy parting gesture.

Sonia had driven the same way to church for her entire life and knew the route by heart. On a whim, she decided to take a different way so that she could pass by the Artist's Corner. The street was filled with cars, but she couldn't see inside the café to see how many people were inside. Sonia debated running in for a drink. On one hand, she wanted to stop by and support the café, but she didn't want to confuse Aiden by making him think she was only coming in so she could see him.

Sonia shook her head and kept driving. She arrived at the church a few minutes later. She pulled her hair back into a ponytail and tugged her scarf up over her face. Sonia stepped inside the church and saw the youth milling around. The youngest were eleven, and the oldest were seniors in high school.

"Hello!" Sonia said, clapping her hands to get their attention. They were teenagers, though, and it took a little more than that to draw them out of their conversations. Sonia looked around the auditorium and whistled.

The teenagers stopped and looked at her. "I'm Sonia," she said. "I'm going to be taking over the position of choir director." Sonia shed her scarf and jacket. The heat seemed to be working on overdrive. She wished she hadn't worn a sweater.

"I have the list of songs that you've been practicing. Now, where do the altos stand? Everyone else, file into place as well."

The teens started wandering into some semblance of order. Sonia held up a set of sheet music that she had found on the auditorium's first bench. She studied the notes. By the time she put the papers down, the teenagers were more or less in line.

"Which section is the altos?" Sonia asked. A group raised their hands. "Alright, perfect," Sonia said. She worked for the next two hours on preparing the teens to give the church an excellent performance. It was hard work keeping the teenagers on task, and by six o'clock, Sonia was pretty much wiped out. She made sure that all of the teenagers were out of the church, then took her phone to call the lady who was supposed to lock up. The woman said she would be by in the next ten minutes, but that Sonia could go ahead and leave.

Sonia hurried to her car to escape the cold. Once she was in the safety of her car she checked her phone's messages. Her mom had called three times, and Sonia instantly became worried. What had happened? Was Grandma all right?

Sonia called her mother back, jiggling her leg up and down as the phone rang. Her mom answered on the third ring.

"Sonia!" she said. "Where are you?"

"I'm- I went to choir practice."

"With my car? You didn't ask permission!"

"Sorry," Sonia said, feeling like she was in high school again. "I thought you knew I had choir practice tonight. And Yvette said she would tell you I was leaving with your car. Where is she? Why didn't she tell you?"

"Why didn't you just tell me yourself? It would have taken maybe two minutes."

"I know. I should have told you, but I thought Yvette would. I didn't think there would be a problem. Didn't Grandma mention where I went? She knew I had choir practice tonight."

"Your Grandma is the reason I am calling you," her mom stormed. "She went to the store an hour ago. She was just going to pick up some chocolate, and she hasn't come back yet. I called her, but she's not answering. I'm worried, and I want to go to the store after her."

"I'll go," Sonia said. "I'm near her favorite store anyway."

"Call me when you find her," Sonia's mom said with an audible note of worry in her voice.

Sonia hung up and quickly drove over to the market. She reached the store and saw her grandmother's car parked along the street. Sonia searched for a parking spot, found one, and rushed inside. For all of the fear that had been rushing through her body, Sonia didn't know whether she could believe her eyes when she saw her grandma calmly talking to an employee of the store. When Sonia realized that her grandma was all right, she approached the two.

"Sonia!" Grandma said. "What are you doing here?"

"I came to check on you. We were worried! Mom called and said you hadn't come back, and you weren't answering your calls."

Grandma smiled and squeezed her granddaughter's arm. She turned back to the store employee. "I think I will be fine now that Sonia is here. Thank you so much for your help."

"My pleasure," the woman said.

"Merry Christmas!" Grandma called out.

Sonia led her grandma to the door. "Didn't you buy anything?" she asked when she realized her grandma didn't have a bag in her hand.

"I sure did," Grandma said. "I left the bag in my car when I came back inside. You see, when I got in my car to leave, it started making strange noises and was sputtering like it was going to die. So I came back inside the store to ask for help. I know something is wrong with that old vehicle. It's been around longer than you have."

Sonia laughed. "Grandma, everything you own is older than me."

Grandma chuckled. "Well, it appears I forgot to charge my phone again, and it wasn't working either. Then I got to talking with the store clerk and lost track of time. Why don't you call your mother and tell her everything is alright? Did you come in the car?"

"Yes," Sonia said. "I parked it right there. How about I take you home, and we will figure out about a mechanic later."

"I don't want a poor mechanic to work on my car tomorrow," Grandma said. "They need to enjoy their Christmas Eve. We can worry about it after Christmas."

Sonia put an arm around her grandma to help her through the slippery parking lot. When they got inside the car, Sonia quickly called her mother and told her that they would be home soon. As Sonia started up the car, she got an idea.

"Grandma, would you like some coffee or hot cocoa to warm you up?"

Grandma smiled. "I can never turn down a mug of hot cocoa, but we should really get home so your mother won't worry anymore."

"I'm just going to make a quick stop," Sonia said, driving slowly down the side street of the little town. She pulled into another parking spot and told her grandma to wait in the car. Then, Sonia went inside the Artist's Corner to give it some business.

Aiden was sitting behind the counter, and he smiled with surprise when he saw her.

"Do you need something to warm you up?" he asked.

"Yes, I'll take two cups of hot cocoa."

She watched as Aiden quickly grated a bar of dark chocolate and whipped up two cups of amazing smelling hot cocoa. He handed her the cups and tried to refuse the payment.

"Please," Sonia said, "I am here to help support you and spread the news about your café, starting with my grandma." Aiden smiled.

Sonia started to leave, before stopping and turning back slightly.

"Thank you for warming up my day," she said, a pink flush sneaking into her cheeks. She quickly turned back around and pushed open the door.

Stepping outside with the two steaming cups in her hand, she scurried back into the warm car. She handed her grandma one of the cups and set the other in her cup holder to cool off as she drove.

"What is that place?" Grandma asked. "It must be new. I've never seen it before."

"Yes," Sonia smiled, "it's new. It's a terrific coffee place. One day when it's a little less hectic, I'll have to take you inside."

Her grandma sipped her drink and mused, "Mmmm, I'm looking forward to it!"

CHAPTER 9

*S*onia dressed nicely on Christmas Eve. Combing her hair back off her face, she surveyed herself in the mirror. She felt respectable, but pretty; the perfect combination for a Christmas Eve choir director. She was in high spirits and felt like nothing could dampen her mood. The choir was supposed to perform at five o'clock. Afterward, she would come back to her grandma's house with her family and celebrate the evening by reading the story of Christ's birth.

When she arrived early at the church, something instantly felt wrong. She stepped into the church, but no blast of warm air greeted her.

"Oh no!" Sonia murmured. She walked deeper into the church, and the cold air did not cease surrounding her. She took off her scarf and tried to find someone who could help her. Maybe they only turned on the heat when people were going to be there, she mused.

"Sonia," one of the teenagers came up to her. "What are we going to do? It's super cold in here!"

One of the younger girls began to cry. "This was supposed to be a perfect night," she warbled, "I can't believe everything is ruined."

"Hold on," Sonia said. "Everyone needs to calm down. We are going to get to the bottom of this."

"But, Sonia," another girl said, "there is no way I can wear my Mary costume if it's this cold. I'll freeze!"

Voices of concern and a chorus of teenage white noise rose up.

"Guys!" Sonia shouted out, getting them to be quiet. "I said we are going to solve this, but you guys need to remember right now that this performance is not about you or you or you." She pointed at different students. "This is about celebrating the birth of Jesus. You are only thinking about yourselves. You need to be remembering that Christmas is not about us. It is about Jesus. Now, I want you guys to come up with some solutions while I go see if the heat simply needs to be turned on."

Sonia began walking around the church looking for one of those electricity boxes. She felt desperate to find a solution.

"Excuse me," a man said, rushing to catch up with her. "I've just been down in the basement to read the settings. I'm the building's superintendent, by the way. It seems as though the heater is completely broken. Apparently, it became overloaded yesterday when it was trying to pump extra heat, and now, it's refusing to pump any."

Sonia nodded. "Okay, so heat is not a possibility at all tonight?"

"Not unless you want me to try to call someone who knows heating systems."

Sonia shook her head. "No, it's Christmas Eve. We'll be okay. We just need to come up with a plan. Are there many guests here yet?"

The man shrugged. "I don't know. I've been down in the basement, and the kids told me to find you here."

Sonia's nose was frozen from not wearing a scarf. "Okay," she said, glancing at her watch.

They were supposed to start the program in less than twenty minutes. Why was this happening now? And when she was in charge, no less!

"Just give me a minute to think," Sonia said. The janitor walked away, and Sonia quietly prayed.

"God, please help us out here. We really want to put on a beautiful program for You, but it seems like that just isn't going to happen now."

Sonia felt like she should go back down the hallway and into the worship center.

Her inner voice protested. "What am I going to tell them? I don't know what to say," Sonia whispered. Yet, she felt compelled to go into the worship center. So, with heavy feet, Sonia plodded back down the hallway, trying to think of how she could phrase telling the people that they were not going to be able to put on the Christmas program.

Sonia stepped in through a side door at the front of the worship center. A few people turned to look at her. They were all bundled up and shivering. Sonia looked out over the crowd. Where was her mom? Maybe her mom would have a good idea. Suddenly, Sonia's eyes landed on Aiden. Her heart jumped as all the pieces fell into place. Sonia rushed over to where he was sitting with his family, bouncing his niece on his knee.

"Can I talk to you for a few minutes?" Sonia asked.

Aiden nodded and deposited his niece with his sister-in-law. Aiden followed Sonia out of the worship center and into the entrance.

"Something's happened with the heat?" Aiden concluded.

Sonia nodded. "Could you tell?" she asked with a bit of sarcasm.

"I don't know," Aiden teased, "maybe the icicles hanging off the man to my right's mustache was a good hint. Look, if you're going to ask me if I'm secretly a handyman, the answer is no. I don't know anything about this sort of thing."

"Neither do I," Sonia said, "but I didn't want to ask you that."

"You wanted to ask me to do a solo," Aiden suggested.

Sonia laughed. "No! Now, would you listen for half a second? I thought since the heat is off here, that we could have the performance at the Artist's Corner. It would be perfect! The spectators wouldn't freeze, and people would get to know your café."

Sonia bit her lip. "What do you think?"

Aiden was slowly nodding his head. He finally grinned at her. "I think you are a genius. It's a great idea!"

Sonia gave a little squeal then covered her mouth. "You'll do it?"

"I'll do it," Aiden nodded. "I don't know if there will be sitting room for everyone, but we'll see what we can do. I'll go over there now and get everything ready."

He embraced her in a hurried manner. As he rushed out the front door, Sonia paused a second. She now knew that she needed to have a serious talk with the man who was weighing so heavily on her heart.

Sonia hurried back into the worship center and up to the stage. She nodded toward the sound booth to make sure the microphone was on. She was given a go signal, and she spoke to the crowd of people who were looking to her with hopeful eyes.

"Because the heat is out in the church, we are going to hold the program at the Artist's Corner. It's a new café that opened up this summer, and it's at the very end of Second, one block off of Main Street. Because parking is limited, I will ask that you walk down if possible. If you are disabled or have trouble walking, we will be saving those parking spots for you. Thank you!"

Sonia bounded down the stairs and out a side door to where the teenagers were waiting. "Did you hear that?" she asked. The teens nodded.

"Everyone should have all their props with them!" Sonia yelled over the noise. "Don't leave anything behind! We are going to lock up the church!"

The teens were excited as they started their walk down the street. It was perhaps a three block walk, and Sonia felt like a shepherd as she herded them along and kept them from getting distracted by the store lights.

"Let's beat your families there!" Sonia called out as motivation. That made the choir begin running forward. Sonia chased after them, laughing as a few snowflakes fell from the sky. They reached the café, and the teenagers were temporarily distracted. A few went over to the chalkboard and began writing messages. Some asked where the paintbrushes were.

"Guys," Sonia said, smiling quickly at Aiden who was arranging chairs. "You will have time to try out those things afterward. Let's get ready, because everyone will be here in just a few minutes."

The teenagers excitedly followed her directions as she explained where to put the props. Aiden went over to the chalkboard and quickly drew a Christmas tree. He drew a miniature manger scene underneath.

"There!" he said. "Just like Christmas 2000 years ago."

The students all laughed, and Sonia gave Aiden a stern look. "Don't distract these youth from their directions," she commanded. Aiden laughed and went back to arranging the chairs and bringing benches out from the back.

Five minutes later, the occupants of Evergreen Valley began pouring through the doors. Soon children were all sitting on laps, and everyone was crowded in. There really was not enough room, and the fire code was beyond stretched at that point, but Sonia could not stop smiling.

The youth started to sing. Their voices rose up in perfect harmony, and Sonia closed her eyes to let the sound wash over her. The scent of cinnamon danced through the air, mixing in with the music.

Sonia wanted to cry; it was all so beautiful. She hadn't been planning on directing the choir, and she certainly hadn't planned on meeting a man who made her heart go crazy. Even so, she couldn't imagine a more perfect Christmas. When the choir had finished their entire performance, the space erupted in loud clapping and cheers. Sonia turned and caught Aiden's eye. Her heart swelled with such intensity that she wanted to rush across the room and into his arms.

She swallowed down the feeling as best she could and took a step toward him, but she only got a foot before she was swept up in the collective arms of the elated teenage choir.

"Eggnog all around!" she heard her tenor cry. And another wave of Christmas cheer washed over the crowd.

CHAPTER 10

$\mathcal{E}$veryone from the church began lining up to order warm drinks and treats. Sonia saw Aiden running around like crazy; then she remembered her lesson on how to work the machines. Sonia washed her hands and moved through the crowd until she was behind the counter.

"I've got the orders," Sonia said. Aiden smiled at her as Sonia took orders and got the pastries, cookies, and Christmas treats into bags. Aiden prepared the coffees, and Sonia made the hot chocolate orders. They were able to quickly satiate the droves of church members. Some left the café right away, but others stayed behind. Every one of the customers, it seemed, made comments on how good everything was.

Aiden handed out the paintbrushes and paint, and the teenagers went to work on the canvas. Sonia saw Yvette detailing the Christmas tree drawing with elaborate hand-drawn ornaments.

Finally, Sonia's mothers turn in line came. "I can see that if we want to drive you home tonight, we may need to wait much longer," Mom smiled, cocking an eyebrow at her daughter.

Sonia looked concerned. "I'm sorry! I hadn't even thought about that. I just wanted to help Aiden out. Do you think Grandma is getting tired?"

Mom shook her head. "I think your grandma is spryer than I am. Anyway, I should probably order and not hold up the line. That will be four hot chocolates, one of those for my hard working daughter, and four chocolate chip cookies."

Sonia smiled as she punched in the order. "Thanks, Mom." She squeezed her mom's hand across the counter, then dove back into taking orders.

Almost an hour later, the line was gone. They had run out of most of the baked goods, and Aiden was making a list of things he needed to buy. Sonia sat on a stool behind the counter and sipped her somewhat still warm hot chocolate. Aiden finally came and sat beside her.

"Tired?" he asked.

Sonia nodded. "Who knew taking orders could be so exhausting?"

"I know. But listen, do you hear that?" Aiden said, motioning to the room. Talk was swirling around the café, people laughing and chatting away while they sipped their drinks and enjoyed the atmosphere.

"I don't even need to count the money you took in to know it is basically more than I have made my entire time in business. I think my little cafe might just make it after all." He looked around at the packed room. "And even if it doesn't, I at the very least know where home is now. Sometimes I marvel when I realize that when you trust God, He finds a way to bring you exactly what you need...when you are ready for it." When he said that, his eyes fell on Sonia.

Sonia searched his face, awestruck at his words.

The sound of someone clearing their throat interrupted Sonia's trance. Startled, she looked up to find her grandma at the counter. Sonia jumped off the stool to attention.

"Would you like to order something, Grandma?" Sonia asked.

"No, thank you, I am quite full of hot chocolate, thank you. I just thought I would come over and say hello. Your mother was telling me that Aiden Moran is the owner of this café. How are you, Aiden?"

Aiden gave Sonia's grandma a kiss on the cheek and a gentle embrace over the counter. "I am doing just fine, ma'am."

"I am so glad to see men like you being entrepreneurs. Taking an idea you love and following it will make you happy, young man."

Aiden smiled. "Sonia, did I ever tell you about when I first met this young man?"

Sonia shook her head. Her grandma had never mentioned Aiden, although Aiden had indicated that he somewhat knew Sonia's grandmother.

"Well, Sonia, you know how I am about my charities. I always visit the soup kitchen at least once a month, and this young man was serving there." Sonia tried to keep her look of surprise to herself as she turned to Aiden. "Yes, and you should have seen how he worked." Her grandmother began describing the scene. "He was whirling around that place, serving this person and that person. Maybe he just seemed fast, because you know I have slowed down a good bit. But he was smiling just as he was smiling tonight. He wasn't receiving money or compensation for his work, but he was helping everyone out, happy as could be."

"That's a great story, Grandma." Sonia's felt lighter than she had in years. The last thread of worry she had been holding onto rushed away. Sonia couldn't stop the smile that spread across her face.

After a few more minutes of chatting, Sonia's grandma went back to the table with her mother and sister. Sonia turned to Aiden, her heart beating fast. They were sitting so close that their knees touched.

She didn't know what to say, but she hoped her smile said everything. Aiden gently reached out and took her hand just like he had their first evening together. This time, neither one was wearing gloves. Sonia felt the heat from his hands even more intensely. He gently stroked her palm with his thumb.

"Thank you for your help tonight," Aiden said. He looked down at her hand held in his. "I can't imagine a more perfect Christmas Eve."

"Me either," she whispered. "Crisis and all."

"So," Aiden began, his eyes lifting to meet hers, a smirk crossing his face, "are you finally going to be my girlfriend?"

Sonia looked up immediately to see if he was serious or if he was teasing her. His face was teasing, but she could see that his sentiment was completely serious.

She opened her mouth to answer, but got caught up in his gaze; his words circling in her head.

Aiden broke in before she could answer. "How about just for today. I don't mind. You can break my heart in two days. But this day, and being with you right now, is just so perfect, that it feels necessary."

With that said, Pepper bounded around the corner and began pawing at the stools Aiden and Sonia were teetering on. Aiden reached down and scooped Pepper up with his free hand.

"Okay, I take that back. Now it's a perfect Christmas moment." Aiden lifted Pepper to his face, and the dog proceeded to lick his face in loving appreciation.

Sonia tightened her grip on his hand. "Yes!" she exclaimed, looking around to see if she was being too loud. "Yes, I would love to be your girlfriend."

"Do you hear that Pepper?," Aiden said. "She said yes!"

Sonia giggled and pulled Aiden toward her. She wasb't brave enough to kiss him yet in front of so many people, but she had to embrace this amazing human who had come into her life and turned it upside down.

"So," Aiden laughed, pulling back from her, "I think this is maybe the hundredth time I have asked, but will you go out on a date with me?"

Sonia took his hand in both of hers as she gave her answer. "Yes, I will. The day after tomorrow?"

"I would love to," Aiden said.

Sonia really wanted to kiss him. She looked at his lips then smiled up into his eyes. Aiden leaned forward and kissed Sonia's cheek, then he lifted her hands to his mouth and gave them each a kiss. Pepper laid across his lap, apparently able to sleep through the pounding sound of her heart.

"Merry Christmas," Aiden whispered gently.

"Merry Christmas," she replied just as softly.

They sat behind the counter, hands entwined, until Sonia's mother said they should go home.

Sonia hugged Aiden and gave him a quick kiss on the cheek before she rushed out into the snow, where a glowing moon was smiling down upon her.

EPILOGUE

*A*fter her family woke up early to do their stockings and have breakfast, Sonia went back to bed for much of Christmas day. She was completely wiped out from the night before, and the emotional roller coaster of the past few weeks.

By evening, they had exchanged presents, listened to carolers and she had wished Aiden a Merry Christmas. Christmas was cozy and warm, everything she had wished for.

ONE WEEK LATER

Sonia worked quickly on the machine as she raced to get her project done before Aiden's arrival. She had been practicing all week. They had been joking all week that today was going to be their official one-week dating anniversary and she was excited to surprise him. The machine whirred to a stop. Sonia cocked her head with scrutiny, inspecting the finished product.

The front door chimed. Sonia jumped, then shrugged her shoulders and conceded, "Well, it is what it is."

Pepper's tiny nails pitter-pattered across the floor and over to her. The dog's fur-lined jacket had her looking as cute as ever.

"Hey!" Aiden boomed as he entered the café. Sonia ran out to meet him, and Aiden dipped her into a full-on Hollywood movie kiss.

"You're here early," he said, then he drew in a sniff. "Do you have the machines going already?"

Sonia whirled around and picked up her coffee artwork, presenting it to Aiden. "Happy anniversary!" she exclaimed.

"It's an almond milk latte!… And check that out," she proclaimed proudly, pointing at the foam design while keeping a straight face.

His eyes opened wide as he took in the worst latte art he had ever seen. Aiden searched for words. His mouth moved around forming shapes as he looked for the right response.

"It's… incredible," he finally decided on. "I have never seen latte art quite like that. I think it's the best one of those that I have ever seen…"

She beamed up at him and held his face for a minute, before completely losing her composure and cracking up.

"It is so awful!" she exploded, tears pouring from her face with laughter. "It's supposed to be a heart, but honestly, if you can even tell it's coffee I'd be impressed."

Aiden joined in on her laughter, then took an appreciative sip.

"Well it tastes great, and that's what really matters!" He flashed her his broad, authentic smile.

"I heard somewhere once that sometimes coffee is just coffee…but sometimes, the right coffee can change your life," she said, looking up at him with an impish grin.

Before she could say anything else, she felt Aiden's fingers lace through the back of her hair as he pulled her to him. As his passionate kiss and secure embrace ignited her heart, her spirit swelled with the hope of a new love. She looked into his eyes and knew that he was here to stay. Slowly her arms raised up and wrapped around his neck, as a final thought danced through her head. *And to you, a happy New Year…*

ACKNOWLEDGMENTS

To my latte loving sisterhood: My-my, Ani, Cristi, Caroline, Amelia and the original coffee maven, my mom...I love our spunky caffeinated spirits and send you each many latte's of appreciation for being my wonderful confidants, muses and partners in crime. I love you each more than a triple shot with a chocolate chip cookie on the side.

To the makers of Teeccino: When I've not been able to drink coffee, you have saved my sanity. Thank you for creating a wonderful and healthy coffee alternative, that I'm always excited to drink. May I spread the word of your glory and soon be able to find you in drive-thrus across America!

To the ever lovely Laurel: Your spirit permeates this story. Thank you for infusing it with your genuine soul.

To the guys (my dad & Drake): Thank you both for supporting me and helping to make my dreams a come true. There are no two finer gents.

To Caroline: Thank you for talking me through the late nights on this one. You were the world's best "injun-spiration".

To my mother-in-law Julia: Yet again, your advice and feedback were paramount! Thank you for all the support and patience you give me. Don't stay away too long…we need you here!

To Lincoln & Avery: You have inspired more coffee drinking in me that I ever thought necessary. I wouldn't trade the two of you for the world.

KEY WEST CHRISTMAS

A Whimsical Holiday Romance

Sophie Mays

Key West Christmas

To the Florida Keys~
You are like nowhere else on Earth

FOREWARD

AUTHOR'S NOTE ABOUT DIALOGUE:
The character of Esterline is originally from Haiti. Please note that an apostrophe (') indicates where an H-sound has been removed.

Example: She flew down here at the drop of a hat.
Would be written: She flew down 'ere at the drop of a 'at.

Being from Florida where we have a large Haitian population, this way of voicing her dialogue felt natural to the character. However, I wanted to give you forewarning about it so as not to interrupt your flow of reading. I hope you enjoy Key West Christmas!

CHAPTER 1

"*M*om, didn't you hear anything I just said?" Josie set down a box next to the front door, trying to keep her phone sandwiched between her shoulder and ear.

Their condo—no, it was just *his* condo, now—hardly looked any different with Josie's things packed away. The furniture was all his, to begin with. Mike had been living here for five years already when he asked Josie to move in. They'd only been dating for ten months at that point, and she was relatively new to the city. Now, several years later, Josie realized that she hadn't ever really lived here like she was planning to stay.

"I'm hearing every word, honey, and I still think you need to think about this. I mean, what's so wrong with a man who works too much? Would you rather have a man that works too little? It just means he's willing to support you, support a family. It's a good thing."

Sometimes, it was a real Olympic sport trying to keep her temper under control when on the phone to her mom, Lucia. As Italian as she was, Lucia was even more stubborn than most mothers about the value of the traditional family. She herself had stayed home all her life to raising six children.

"Mom, you need to get out of Connecticut every once in a while."

It was the least angry thing Josie could think to say, and probably the most true. Josie was holding the phone with her shoulder while she folded the last of her clothes into a big plastic storage box, so her patience was already rather frayed. In an effort to shift the subject, Josie tried to avert attention to one of her sisters. "Mom, Susan keeps trying to get you up to Michigan to visit her and the kids, you should go, for once. It's not good for you, staying at home all the time alone."

The conversation had been flipped, and Lucia's displeasure was now audible. She huffed into the phone, and Josie could see her putting her hands on her hips. "Now you know I'm not here alone. The church ladies come by practically every day and we read our Bibles together—"

"I meant go out and do something fun, Mom," Josie interrupted, smiling.

"Now, that's not funny, young lady. I guess that means you haven't been reading your Bible lately?"

Josie thought of Mike's bookshelf out in the living room. He had a collection of James Patterson and an assortment of reference material for his legal practice. There was a whole second bookshelf in his office stuffed to overflowing with notebooks, papers, files, and binders, but the one out in the living room was more for leisure reads. Josie had found a little space to put her handful of favorite books, and her dusty old Bible that her parents had given her when she graduated high school. It hadn't been opened in almost ten years.

Her mother sighed over the phone. "Your father would be heartbroken, Josie."

"Dad had a beer almost every night of his life and put money on the Patriots every week. I don't think he'd mind."

"Josie Ward, your father was a good, Christian man. Shame on you."

Josie had to suppress a laugh. Angus Ward had been a jolly, fun-loving father, but if he ever made it to church, it was at the behest of his well-meaning wife. At nearly a hundred pounds overweight, with the drinking, and the smoking, his massive coronary attack had only been a surprise at the moment it happened.

In his memory, Lucia seemed to have chosen to remember only the things about her husband that would improve his chances of avoiding damnation. Josie let the subject drop.

"Anyway... I have a company moving my things tonight. They'll be here any minute, and I still have so much left to pack..."

Her sentence trailed off. She didn't really want her mother to know that she hardly owned a thing in the world besides her clothes and a few odds and ends. Lucia had strict opinions about living a sparse lifestyle—to hear her tell it, a house wasn't a home unless it was crammed full of the material proof that people lived there.

On that note, Josie walked out to the living room to fetch the armful of books off the shelf. Along with the heavy leather-bound Bible were Jane Austen, Jodi Picoult, and the first few Janet Evanovich novels. *All J's*, Josie thought absently as she stacked them in a second box sitting open on the living room floor.

"Honey, I really think you need to stop for a moment," her mother whined through the phone. She sounded desperate. Maybe she'd heard her daughter stacking the books into the box. "Michael is such a nice man, I'd hate to see you walk out on him for such a little thing."

Josie sunk onto the living room sofa and put her head in her hands. A little thing? It was hard for Lucia to understand—her idea of a problem was the roof caving in or someone taking their children out of Sunday school. Angus had been a loving man to his wife and kids, so much so that Josie doubted Lucia even understood that anything different existed.

But Mike was different. He was a good guy, and good-looking. He had a great job, and rarely bothered Josie about anything she wanted to do. From Lucia's perspective, no doubt he seemed like an excellent husband, but Josie needed someone to bother her every now and then. She needed someone who cared enough to meddle. She needed someone to be there with her in the evenings, and not endlessly buried under a pile of legal documents in their office.

Mike wasn't even here trying to stop her leaving. Their fight had been short and seemed more like a courtroom debate than a tearful lover's quarrel. Josie had tried to talk to him, to reach him somehow.

All Mike had wanted to do was tidy up the issue so they could get back to life as usual.

"It's not a little problem, Mom," Josie said finally.

"But honey," Lucia said, in a small voice. "You're turning thirty next year... you can't be so picky about men anymore."

Josie clenched the phone in her fist as if she was attempting to crush it. She counted to ten inside her head. At times like this, it was hard to recall that her mother meant the best.

Yes, Josie Anne Ward was twenty-nine, but that hardly seemed like a death sentence. She was healthy, and she liked to run every day before work. If left to its own devices, her long, raven hair was wildly curly, as if it had forgotten that the year was no longer 1989. Josie had become an expert at a young age in taming her wild mane into respectable hairdos. Her looks seemed to alternate between both of her parents, but her fair Irish skin and bright green eyes were definitely inherited from her father's side. Though her complexion was dusted with a bit of a tan—it's hard to live in Virginia and not get a little sun. Thankfully though, she wasn't breaking out in wrinkles or age spots, and overall she felt healthy and youthful.

"My flight leaves in four hours, and I'm going to be on it," she said firmly. Her mother sighed, exasperated, a sound of defeat. The battle had finally been won, it seemed.

"And you're leaving right before the holidays! Who will you spend Christmas with?"

"I don't know."

"And what about your job? The last I heard, you were putting in for a transfer—"

"I got the transfer, Mom, it's all settled," Josie answered, shutting the book box and unrolling the screeching tape across the flaps. She worked as a travel agent, and her company Go-To Travel had offices all over the east coast. "I start work on Monday."

"Today's Saturday, Jojo, you won't have any time to settle in and relax."

The time was 10:23. The movers were scheduled for ten, which meant they were late and Josie was running on borrowed time to stay on track. She wanted to be at the airport two hours early because even though it was just barely December, she knew it was a wreck of a time to be traveling.

"Don't worry about me, Mom. I'm sure I'll be doing plenty of relaxing when I get there. At least I won't need my cold-weather clothes for a while."

CHAPTER 2

$\mathcal{T}$he first blast of muggy, thick Florida air that Josie got was a warning draft. It wafted through the airlock when she was climbing off the plane and onto the enclosed walkway; the chill of the plane instantly melting off her. Then, a burst of air conditioning swept over her again, but it didn't erase the little seed of nerves that was growing in her stomach.

Key West, Florida was a tourist haven. No doubt about that. Even if she'd been a layperson just strolling through, the huge variety of visitors—from European couples speaking German, to single American businessmen, to huge families from Brazil all speaking Portuguese at once—would have tipped her off. But Josie worked in the industry, and she'd seen the numbers firsthand. She'd booked many a trip to the Keys over the years. This was just the first one she'd made for herself.

Her Delta flight had been right on time, which (the Captain had announced with a chuckle) was a record for this time of year. Josie had stuffed her purse into her carry-on to avoid another checked bag, and now that she was out in the terminal she retrieved it and dug out her cell phone. Her mother wasn't exactly tech-savvy, but Josie sent her a short message of 'I'm in Key West. I'll call you when I get to the house.'

The only missed calls were from Lucia and Josie's sister, Maria. Mike hadn't tried to get a hold of her. Josie couldn't even claim to be surprised.

As Josie made her way through the airport, the sound of Bing Crosby singing Mele Kalikimaka floated through the air. For the first time, she heard the song differently. Catching glimpses out the window, she saw blowing palms and not one snowflake in sight. Yet the airport was decked out in holiday style, with shimmering light displays and a grand Christmas tree decorated from top to bottom in a combination of traditional ornaments, pure white sandollars, and colorfully painted starfish. Josie had spent collective months of her career arranging vacations to Florida, calling Floridian hotels, campgrounds, scuba shops, cruise lines, restaurants. A part of her felt like she was already acquainted with the culture of Florida life. But she'd never actually been here in person.

When the sliding doors outside Key West International opened and Josie stepped out into the sweltering, almost solidly-humid air, she had a flighty moment of panicked doubt. What had she gotten herself into?

Taxis thronged the airport, but Josie had to fight to get one that wasn't already waiting for a passenger who'd called ahead. She felt silly for not considering that—she'd always taken the bus line to work back in Richmond, or caught a ride with Mike on his way to the office. By the time she climbed with her luggage into a cab, she had sweated through the light fabric of her blouse and her hair was going haywire.

"'Ere for a while?" the driver asked pleasantly with a light Jamaican accent. He'd kindly helped her load her bags into the trunk, and it was only when they were both in the A/C shelter of the taxi that he struck up a conversation. Josie sighed; judging from the logjam of taxis, vans, and cars waiting to get out of the arrivals platform, her fare was going to be painful.

"Just moved here," she replied. The cabbie laughed delightedly, flashing white teeth against his dark skin.

"A newcomer, then! You 'ave family 'ere?"

"No, no family in Florida. They're all up in the New England area."

The cab was inching forward at a respectable rate. Her driver nodded sagely. "Just gettin' out o' the cold weather, then?" He made a shivering sound. "I lived in New York for five years, and I'm not goin' back to anywhere with snow."

Snow. It hadn't snowed very much in Richmond, Virginia this year and taking in a white Christmas was one of her favorite holiday traditions. "Yeah, it gets cold up there. My mom lives in Connecticut, and she says they've already got a foot of snow, and it's not even Christmas yet."

"Well, don't you worry about snow here. You came at the perfect time! We're 'aving a *heat* wave right now!" He emphasized the word heat and laughed again. Traffic was breaking up, and their taxi eased through the exit gate and onto the road. "The only ice you're gonna find here is in your drink, I promise."

Josie couldn't help but laugh with him, and watched the palm trees cruise past. This was definitely a different world from the one she was used to.

"Mrs. Dupart?" Josie asked hopefully.

The number wasn't visible on the house, but the neighbors on the left had pointed her in the right direction when Josie wandered up to the wrong place. With her big suitcase and duffel bag hanging off her shoulder, she felt ready to faint, struggling to breathe in the thick afternoon air.

The elderly Haitian lady that answered the door smiled a big, toothy grin and opened the door wide. "You must be Josie Ward. Come in 'ere, you look ready to fall over, dear."

Josie was ready to fall over. She staggered in the front door of the pristine white two-story, into a neat, breezy foyer. Mrs. Dupart motioned for her to set the luggage down by the stairs, and led her into the kitchen.

"What you need is something to cool off, and I'm not takin' no for an answer. And call me Esterline, my dear, Mrs. Dupart is what the tax man calls me." She laughed and dug through the pale wood cupboards for glasses. Josie took a seat at the high kitchen table; it was cooler inside, but not by much. Mrs. Dupart—Esterline—didn't seem to care for A/C.

Her new landlady was a short little bundle of energy, dressed in colorful capris and a matching sleeveless blouse. Her hair wasn't visible—a white fringed scarf was wrapped around her head and knotted in the front. Josie, whose thick dark curls were wilting and clinging in the heat to her neck and back, was starting to think a head scarf wasn't a bad idea.

"So I 'ave the guest house ready," Esterline was saying. She'd pulled out two glasses and clinked ice into each. Josie recalled the taxi driver's word and smiled. "We'll let you cool off a little, and then I'll help you carry your things out."

"Oh, you don't have to," Josie protested at once. Esterline seemed sturdy enough, but Josie couldn't stomach the thought of letting a little old grandmother carry her luggage. "It's only out back, right?"

"Yes, about fifty feet from the back porch," Esterline agreed. "Lemonade? I 'ave iced tea, too, if you like."

"Lemonade would be lovely," Josie answered, and accepted a glass. She sipped and looked around Esterline Dupart's kitchen; it looked like an island version of her own mother's cooking space, packed full of bowls and measuring cups, a hanging basket of fruit in the big window over the sink. Herbs grew in little pots on the window sill, and pictures of about a dozen laughing children covered the fridge.

"Your family?" she asked.

"My grandchildren," Esterline took the seat across from Josie. "My oldest son lives in Haiti with 'is wife and 'is daughters. My 'usband's there, too. We run a shipping business based in Port-au-Prince. 'E spends 'alf the year there, 'alf the year 'ere. My other son and my daughter live in Orlando, so I don' see them often enough, but," she sighed and shrugged her shoulders, "you do what you can do."

Josie nodded. She understood perfectly.

It was a relief to find that she got on so well with Esterline; they sat together for half the afternoon, chatting and telling stories. Josie felt more like a guest than a renter, and it was balmy island twilight before she picked up her bags again to cart them across the back lawn to the prim little guest bungalow.

"It's perfect," she said, and meant it. The miniature house was exactly what she'd had in mind when she booked the lease with Esterline. It was a studio-style layout, with enormous windows in the front and back, and a skylight in the roof to let the Florida sunshine in. Brightly patterned curtains hung around the sleeping area, and the house came already furnished. Absolutely perfect.

"Well, come in the mornin', and I'll make you some breakfast," Esterline told her, handing her the key. "I suppose I ought to let you settle in a bit. Just let me know if you need anything."

With a wave, Esterline let herself out, and Josie was alone.

A shiver went down her spine, despite the heat. She'd never been alone. Ever really. Before Mike, she'd had a roommate, and before the roommate, she'd lived in a college dorm. Prior to that she'd lived in a house with two parents and five siblings running around. At her age, it felt a little strange to realize that she'd never lived by herself before.

She unpacked some of her clothes. The boxes from Richmond were due to arrive tomorrow, but they didn't contain anything vital. All her summer clothes and work clothes were with her, and she set about putting them away in the small closet and dresser. Now that she was left to her own devices, the world seemed quiet, and a little empty. Lonesome. She had made the decision to leave Mike so abruptly. True, it had been eating away at her for a long time, and she had tried so many things to fix the gaping inadequacies of their relationship, but as she sat here now, alone in a foreign place, she couldn't help but think that maybe she'd been a bit rash.

Josie shook her head. It was just nerves. She was just anxious and in a new place. She was bound to have some reservations about such a major life change. It would be fine, she told herself.

It had been a long, hot day, and Josie felt coated in a film of sweat. In addition to a slow paddle fan overhead, there was a more powerful looking oscillating fan in the corner. She gratefully turned it on, letting it blow straight on her for a solid 60 seconds before moving on. She'd have to see about getting an A/C unit for the window, or something. In the meantime, she headed to the bathroom for a long, cool shower. Nothing like a shower after an exciting day.

The moment she turned off the water and stepped out, Josie already felt drenched with sweat again as moisture beaded and dripped down her skin. Her hair was always a pain—she had so much of it—but now it seemed too humid for anything to dry. It certainly didn't feel like December here. More like August.

Movement caught her eye in the mirror, and she caught sight of the wall behind her. At first, she didn't register what she was seeing. A large black splotch, skittering along the wall.

Josie's stomach dropped into her feet as she shrieked.

CHAPTER 3

*T*here was a crowd on the street, causing Nate Richardson to slow, curious.

It was Saturday, so he'd left the scuba shop for a couple of hours to hunt up some dinner before it was time to start the night dives. It was always tourist season in the Keys, but the holidays drew a commotion of internationals and continental Americans eager to try everything. His appointment book was packed from now until March.

He decided to cut through the neighborhood on foot when the red-blue strobe of police cruisers caught his eye. They were parked outside Esterline Dupart's house. Worried, Nate headed toward the on-looking crowd of neighbors.

All seemed well, however, and he could see Esterline herself was safe, speaking with an officer who was nodding and visibly sweating in his uniform.

To his surprise, Nate saw a young woman nearby, wrapped in a bathrobe with sopping wet hair. She looked mortified. Her face was bright red, and she was speaking to a second officer.

"What happened?" he asked Martha Pageotte, who lived across the street and happened to be standing nearby. She sighed and rolled her eyes.

"Miss Esterline has herself a new renter, and I don't think the girl has ever seen a cockroach before."

Nate chuckled. Newbies could eventually handle the heat, and the tropical atmosphere was never hard to get used to. But if there was one thing that got the same reaction out of each and every newcomer to the Florida Keys, it was their state bird, the flying cockroach.

"I could hear her screaming across the way," Martha went on, eyebrows raised and a small smile on her face. "She sure has got some lungs on her—no wonder Esterline thought she was being murdered."

Nate watched the woman. He thought he could hear her apologizing to the cops all the way across the lawn.

"I hope she doesn't have too hard a time," he sighed, turning away. He had a business to get back to, and he doubted a crowd was appreciated. "It'll be worse in the summer," he chuckled half to himself as he walked away.

The day after next, on his way to The Dive Bar, Nate stopped at the store and picked up a welcome basket. It wasn't the usual sort of welcoming items, but he had a feeling his gifts would be more appreciated than candles or scented soaps.

He'd lived in Key West for seven years. His former life as an investment banker in Chicago had been fine. It had been the life he thought he wanted, but after several years the beyond fast-paced life had finally started taking its toll. Until the day he'd taken a vacation to South Florida, and never looked back. He realized that he didn't want to waste his life away doing something he didn't enjoy or living somewhere that didn't make him happy. The laid-back life of renting out surf and dive gear on the beach was the dream he hadn't realized he had. His friends who had come down to visit said they didn't even recognize him at first, but they were all envious. So while Nate wasn't a Key West native Floridian, it hadn't been near long enough to forget that it all took some getting used to.

He stopped at Esterline's front door to say hello, and after promising to stop in for a chat sometime, she waved him around to the guest house in the back. It was seven in the morning, and the sun was hot already, making the air feel like steam off a tea kettle. Nate lived much of the year in shorts and tank tops, and today was no exception. With the current heat wave passing through, it was going to be another steamer.

He knocked on the door of Esterline's guest house.

"Oh—hello," she said. Her face flipped from eager to confused when she caught sight of Nate standing on her welcome mat. She'd probably expected Esterline. Her gaze dropped to the basket in his hands.

"Hi! Nate Richardson." He held the little basket in one hand and held the other out for her to shake. "I live nearby, and I thought I'd stop in to welcome you to the Keys."

"Josie Ward," she replied, smiling hesitantly. He caught her looking over his worn board shorts and his ratty flip-flops. His sun-bleached hair had been brown, once, but fell over his ears in a wheat-colored mop now. She took the basket he offered and looked inside. "Oh! Thank you!"

He'd bought her several cans of Raid and a variety of roach traps. There were also some less thematic things, like a frozen Key Lime Pie on a stick and a voucher for snorkeling from his shop. The basket had been a whimsical touch on Nate's part; he could have brought it all over in a shopping bag, but this had more of a personal touch.

It was clear that she wasn't from around here. Her pale skin was a little tan, but not Florida-tan. Her dark hair hung in long wavy curls, and she was dressed in sweltering business casual, complete with a knit fabric blazer and black pencil skirt. He could see that she was sweating already.

"Off to work?"

"Yes, I was just about to leave," she admitted, still holding the basket. "I've been trying to figure out the bus schedule all morning. I think my line comes to the bus stop down the street at seven-thirty…"

"Wearing that?" Nate wished he hadn't said it, but it was too late. She frowned.

"What's wrong with this?"

Might as well be honest, now. "Those buses are pretty stuffy. You might want to try on something cooler." He shrugged, hoping to diffuse the tension.

Her face darkened a little further, and she set a hand on the door. "Well, thank you, again—this is very nice of you. I have to get going, but... I didn't even think to buy my own."

"You'll be glad to have it." Nate could take a hint. He waved and turned to leave. "If you ever want to go diving, I'll be on the beach. I run a rental shop down there."

"Maybe," she answered, and closed the door.

Nate walked back around Esterline's house with a spring in his step. She was a little prickly, but he liked that.

CHAPTER 4

y the time Josie arrived at the Key West office, it was 9:05 am. She had been scheduled to start at 9:00. She'd left the house early, trying to make a good impression on her first day.

On top of that, she felt like she was melting. The bus had been hardly air-conditioned, and once it was crammed with people, Josie felt like she was in an oven. She'd sweated through her blouse; the blazer had come off while she was waiting at the bus stop. Her hair was bedraggled and limp, not to mention damp with perspiration, and the small amount of makeup she'd put on this morning was blurred and smeared most unprofessionally.

The route hadn't been as direct as the guide seemed to suggest, but Josie had no other way to get to work on such short notice. She'd called to explain why she was late, but her explanation only sounded like an excuse, even to her own ears. She hated being late in and of itself. But showing up at the office five minutes late and looking like she'd slept on the street in her work clothes, was almost enough to send her packing for Connecticut, right then and there.

Her new boss, Mr. Trevor, met with her when she came in. If she had to guess his age, she'd say at least sixty-five, with suspenders and a neat tie. About her height and probably near twice her weight, he had the air of a man who'd been doing his job a long time and knew how he liked things run. Mr. Trevor didn't seem like a bad sort of manager, but Josie could see in his spectacled eyes that he didn't think much of someone who arrived late on their very first day.

"It might be a good idea to work out some alternate transportation, Miss Ward," he told her finally. "Welcome to Key West. If you have any questions, myself or Hannah would be happy to help."

Her job here in Florida was virtually the same that she'd had back in Richmond; Josie could have wept with relief. She'd thrown her life into a spin cycle with leaving Mike and moving here to Key West. But arranging vacation packages—that was something she knew how to do.

After settling into her desk in the small office, Josie retreated to the restroom and emerged fifteen minutes later with her make-up repaired and her clothes as straightened as she could make them. She had a mental count of things to pick up, and water-resistant mascara had just made the list.

Aside from Mr. Trevor and Hannah the receptionist, she had two co-workers, both agents like herself that spent most of the day on the phone. There was a tangible air of uncertainty between them all; their desks were at different corners of the small office, but no one even tried to communicate for most of the morning. It wasn't until afternoon, when Josie was glowing from a second successful package arrangement that she struck up a conversation.

Her two fellow agents, Marcus and Dana, had been working at Go-To Travel for three and six years, respectively, and hadn't had a new co-worker in all that time. Josie had stepped in to fill the desk of a long-time agent who'd retired this year, and as a result, no one in the suite seemed really sure how to manage a newcomer. But once the ice was broken, Dana proved eager to talk nonstop, and Marcus loved to narrate his work day.

By five o'clock, Josie had fallen happily into a routine at the Go-To Travel Key West office; after the cockroach incident Saturday night and her disastrous arrival this morning, that was exactly what she needed. Something—anything—to go right.

"You're here in time to help us with all the New Year's trips," Dana told her. "I was afraid Marcus and I would have to handle them all. Ugh."

"Miss Ward! A moment?"

It was Mr. Trevor. Josie had been on her way out the door with Dana. She waved good-bye to her new co-worker and inched towards Mr. Trevor's office.

"Um… yes?"

He smiled up at her from his computer screen. "I'm looking at your numbers. I have to say, I'm impressed. You seemed to be having a rough time this morning. Do you have a way to get home?"

"Eh…" Josie shrugged, resigned. "The… um… bus."

Mr. Trevor winced in sympathy, with a hearty chuckle. "Let me call you a taxi for today. On the company."

Back at her little bungalow, Josie breathed a sigh and took off her heels. If only she could afford to take a taxi every day. She might have to buy a car, at this rate—she didn't know if she could handle the bus every Monday through Friday.

The basket that man had brought by—Nate?—still stood on the dinette where she'd left it. Josie stood by the door, thinking, for about a minute straight. She set down her purse and picking up a red can of Raid.

Nerves firing with terror, she moved through the house, room by room, and looked in all the corners and under the furniture. She scanned the ceilings and checked around the windows. Her search uncovered three more roaches, but these were tiny compared to the monster that had snuck into her bathroom. She ended up using half of the first can just in that half-hour alone. The Raid seemed to work, and she unwrapped the roach traps and set those in the kitchen and the bathroom and under her bed.

The bugs had frightened her so much, that Josie actually forgot to turn the fan on until after she'd changed into a light summer dress. She washed her face and put her hair up in a ponytail. It hardly seemed any cooler, since the air on her neck was also warm. There was just no way to win, here.

With a sigh, Josie slipped on a pair of sandals and crossed the lawn to go visit Esterline. The friendly old lady had made her promise to come and tell her about her first day at work.

CHAPTER 5

onday, Tuesday, and Wednesday all went by without Josie Ward making an appearance at the beach. Nate was disappointed, but not too surprised. She didn't seem to be the surfing and diving type.

Business at The Dive Bar was booming, as usual. The heat wave had finally started to dissipate, making way for the pleasant winter weather that had locals wearing sweaters and visitors flocking to the Keys in droves, with temperatures hovering between 65 to 78 degrees on average.

Nate employed two local kids to help run things, and all three of them were on hand for the weekday afternoons, renting out and receiving gear, cleaning used equipment, printing forms, filling out paperwork, and trying to keep anyone from drowning. He didn't really have time to be worrying about Josie Ward, but he found his thoughts drifting her way at odd times and wondered if she was doing all right.

Of course, Esterline would take care of her. The poor lady got terribly lonely in the months her husband spent in Haiti, and Nate always thought it was a shame that she should have to live in that house alone when she loved to chat and fuss over others. It was a good arrangement on all sides, so there was no reason for him to be concerned.

Regardless of this, Thursday evening found him walking over to Esterline's. He'd promised to stop by for a visit, anyway, so now was a better time than tomorrow. Esterline went out with her church group a couple nights a week, but Nate wasn't sure which; he'd find out when he got there, at least.

Tonight seemed to be a meeting night, because when Nate knocked on the door of the Dupart house, no one answered. If Esterline had been on the same side of town, Nate was convinced she would have heard someone coming to visit. She had to be out, then.

He stepped around the corner of the wrapped porch and peered at the guest house in the back. Lights were on inside, although the sun wasn't quite set.

He stepped off the porch and walked toward the guest house. If Josie was in, maybe she could use a friendly face.

When he knocked, he caught her face looking through one of the big windows to see who was there. Nate waved, smiling, and she disappeared from the window and opened the door seconds later. She gave him a small, nervous smile, and he saw that she'd adopted a shorts and tank top mentality.

"Hi!" she greeted. "Thanks again for the bug spray. It's come in handy a few times."

Nate laughed. "I figured it would."

"Esterline's at her church group—"

"I thought she might be," Nate admitted. He ran a hand through his shaggy hair. "Actually, I was thinking you might come out with me. I could show you a little of Key West."

Her green eyes widened. "Oh! That would be… I'd really like to, but I have work in the morning."

"I didn't mean tonight," Nate said quickly. That wasn't entirely true; if she'd been willing to go out tonight, that would have been just fine. "Maybe you'd like to come out with me on Saturday. I can take you down to the beach by the reefs. I know the guy who owns the shop, so I think I can get us a discount." He added the last part teasingly, but he wasn't sure Josie caught it. From the way she looked at him, Nate suspected she might not have gotten the joke.

"That sounds like fun," she agreed finally. There was something hesitant—anxious, even—about her manner and her tone. Nate smiled again, trying to reassure her.

"So I'll see you Saturday afternoon? Can I come by and pick you up here?"

"Yeah! I'll be here."

"Okay," Nate put his hands in his pockets. It had been years since he felt like such an awkward kid. "I'll, uh… I'll see you Saturday, then. Tell Esterline I said hello."

He turned and nearly fled. Josie was pretty and a bit of a mystery, but she was sure difficult to talk to. People on the Keys weren't usually so high-strung. Everybody was so relaxed here, even the tourists were usually pretty casual by the time they got to his dive shop. Nate had forgotten that anything except a Margaritaville state of mind even existed.

Saturday came, surely as it had last week and the weeks before. Of course, it turned up as one of the busier days they'd had in the season, but Andy and Benjamin swore up and down that they could handle the shop long enough for Nate to romance a lady. Nate had rolled his eyes, but not corrected them; after that his assistants were relentless in their teasing.

Esterline was home this time, and was rocking in her rocker on the porch when Nate arrived to pick up Josie. He'd driven instead of walking. It was hell to find a parking spot, but he had a feeling Josie would appreciate the transport. He parked the car in front of the house and crossed the lawn with a friendly wave to Esterline, who grinned knowingly and waved back.

Josie answered on the second knock, as if she'd been just beside the door.

Some kind of greeting had been on the tip of his tongue, but words slipped out the side of his head when Nate laid eyes on her. She was wearing a white crop top with high-waisted denim shorts. She looked like an old navy pin-up girl, complete with red flats on her feet and her black hair tied up at the back of her head.

"Wow," he murmured.

"What?" she asked. She looked confused; maybe she really hadn't heard him. He shook off his momentary fluster.

"Ready?" Nate asked brightly. He was glad he'd at least opted to go home and change. He couldn't help but feel a little tattered compared to her style.

"Yeah!" She picked up her bag off the floor and some sort of white cover-up off a coat peg and followed him out, locking the door behind herself. "So where are we headed?"

"Down by the beach," Nate answered.

"Don't be out late, you kids," Esterline called from the porch with another grin.

"We won't," they said in unison.

Nate could see he'd chosen right bring the car; Josie seemed relieved. "Not used to walking everywhere?" He tried not to stare as they pulled away from the curb.

"Not really," she admitted. "I moved here from Richmond, and I always took the bus or the subway there. But your bus lines aren't as reliable here. I was late to work on Monday."

Nate winced. "You have to add an extra hour on to any kind of public transit. It's hard to guess how many tourists will be on the bus at any given time, and they can get pretty far behind schedule."

"If that's not an understatement, I don't know what is," Josie agreed.

"So what'd you move for?" Nate asked. He was only trying to make conversation—and stop staring at her —but Josie seemed uncomfortable with the question. She twisted her mouth, thinking, as if not sure how to answer. "You're not in witness protection, are you?" he cautioned.

She laughed and shook her head. "No, nothing like that. I just transferred down here from Richmond. I'm a travel agent—I work with Go-To Travel."

"Ah, I see. So if you think about it, you're the one that makes the buses so crowded." He chuckled at the look she got on her face.

"Well, if that's how you want to look at it. I've never actually been to the Keys before now. I can't tell you how many trips I've planned for people to come here, but I've never visited, myself."

"So why move here?" They were coming up on the beachfront now, which was where traffic was at its worst. Nate headed for a parking lot nearby where he knew he could park for free.

Josie sighed and shrugged her shoulders. "I guess... Well, I wanted to move away from Richmond, and this transfer was open, so I took it. I thought it would be nice to try something new, you know?"

"I know how that is. I used to live in Chicago before this."

"That's a long way away! How'd you end up here?"

They'd pulled through the ticket booth of the parking lot, and Nate rolled down the window. "Hi, Ernie."

"Oh, hey Nate," said the attendant, a middle-aged Cuban with dark glasses and a thick mustache. He raised the barrier with a smile and a wave. "Go on in, man."

"No fee?" Josie asked, raising an eyebrow.

Nate shrugged his own shoulders innocently. "I give him a bit of a... local's discount, I guess, at my shop."

"Huh," she nodded. "You didn't answer me about moving here, though."

"Oh, yeah. Well, I was living in Chicago—I used to work in banking up there, and I didn't do half bad, really. Things were going all right, but I felt like I was married to my job. I came down here on a vacation and I just couldn't leave. So I moved down here and when I could, I bought a gear rental shop on the beach. That was about seven years ago, and so far, so good."

They pulled into an empty spot and turned off the car.

"You know," Nate pointed out as he locked the car. "You didn't answer me, either."

"Yeah, I did."

"No, I asked why you moved, but you didn't really tell me why," he argued amiably. "I moved down here because I love it here. You said, you'd never been here before you moved, which is a pretty gutsy thing to do, if you ask me. It makes me wonder what was so bad about Richmond that you had to leave."

Josie pulled her white shawl over her shoulders; probably for the better. She was going to burn up like bread in a toaster under this sun, and Nate wasn't going to be able to stop staring at her. "You have sunscreen, right?"

"I put some on before I left," she answered, pulling a pair of sunglasses out of her purse. "Why?"

"You have some with you? You aren't used to this sun. You'll need to put more on later."

Josie pulled out a bottle from her bag. 50 SPF. At least she was prepared some of the time.

"Anyway, back to my question." Nate was having a hard time concentrating with this woman. He got distracted with every little thing she did. "You sort of just told me how you got here. I wanted to know why you wanted to leave."

"Oh," Josie said softly. Behind her sunglasses, it was hard to tell what was going on in the silence that followed. The two of them walked along the sidewalk, past shops and umbrella-filled café patios. Gleaming white and brightly-colored buildings lined the road, and people packed in as if no one in Key West actually owned a car. Finally, Josie sighed.

"I just broke up with my boyfriend," she admitted finally.

"Oh—sorry," Nate said quickly. "I didn't mean to pry into something you didn't want to talk about—"

"It's okay, actually," Josie waved him off. "It wasn't a bad break-up. When all was said and done, I just needed some new surroundings."

"I think you did that pretty well," Nate chuckled. He was leading her towards the marina that stood like a forest of boat masts just off shore. "There's no place in America quite like Key West. Hey, do you mind a bit of a change in plans?"

"What did you have in mind?"

"When I asked you out, I thought you might like to come diving with me, but it looks like a good day to go for a sail. What do you say?"

Honestly, she looked too pretty to ask her to change, and Nate wasn't going to pass an opportunity to silently gloat to his friends at the pier. Josie's face lit up behind the sunglasses.

"You mean sail boating? I've never been before. That sounds great!"

When Nate had bought their fare and led her to the right dock, it quickly became clear that Josie had never been anywhere near a boat before. She wasn't savvy with the sailing terminology, but on top of that her balance seemed almost debilitating and upsettingly unstable. Nate sat her down before she could tip over the side, and convinced her to put extra sunscreen on her nose and forehead before they set out.

"So you don't have any family down here?" she asked when they'd steered out into open water. The sun was brilliant over the sea to the west as sunset approached, and the crew loosened the big white sail and caught a southerly wind out around the cape.

"Nope," Nate answered. "No family. I had a girlfriend for a while, and I still talk to her family sometimes. I just have my dad and my brother left, and we all live in different states."

"So what do you do around Christmas?" She watched him, hopeful. The question seemed intimate, even though she had to speak up a bit, over the wind and the waves. He thought about it a minute, but nothing really came to mind.

"Same thing as I always do, I guess," Nate replied. "I go to work, relax in the evenings. I *do* put up some lights on a palm tree in my front yard around December."

She laughed, but it seemed sad. Josie sighed. "I was afraid you were going to say that."

"Why? You wanted a white Christmas?"

Josie didn't answer, but her silence gave her away. Nate looked out over the ocean. No, they didn't get white Christmases here in Florida. He hadn't even seen snow since he got off the plane all those years ago. He'd missed it a little at first, but over time the memory of cold had become just that—a memory. Life in the Keys had erased the longing for brisk winter air and fresh snow as time went by.

"There's plenty to do around here for the holidays," Nate said finally. Josie looked at him doubtfully, bouncing a little as the boat crested a wake. She was awfully cute when she looked at him like that, even with a white sheen of sunblock on her nose.

"Like what?"

"Lots of things." Now that she mentioned it, he had a hard time pinning anything down. There were a couple parades, right? Several neighborhoods put on enormous light displays, and it seemed like this time of year he couldn't walk down the street without seeing a tropical Santa Claus in a window or a Christmas palm tree strewn with lights. Nate just hadn't really thought of it until now.

"Tell you what," Nate took her small, soft hand in his big, rough, tanned one. "I'll scare up some holiday cheer for you. What do you say?"

Josie still looked doubtful. "That's kind of you, but I don't want to make you feel like you have to—"

"I know I don't have to," Nate pointed out.

Josie raised her eyebrows and set her mouth stubbornly. "We only just met, and you're offering to make some Christmas spirit for me? That seems too generous."

Nate laughed. "You really haven't been in the Keys very long."

"What does that mean?"

"I just *want* to," he insisted. "Not because I'm trying to get something out of you. I just want to. Because I like you, and maybe because I could use some holiday cheer, myself."

Josie reddened a little under the sunscreen. "Well, I guess you're not terrible."

It was Nate's turn to wonder if she was joking; her laugh a moment later answered that question. He shook his head.

"One of these days, we'll get on the same page about the jokes."

161

CHAPTER 6

*A*ll the sunscreen in the world didn't seem up to the task of protecting Josie's delicate office-pale skin. When she arrived at work Monday, it was with a fading sunburn that itched and seethed under her blouse. She'd put enough sunscreen on her face to dodge lobster-red, but she was still tender pink across the cheekbones and brow. Maybe she should have slathered sunscreen from head to toe.

Burn or no burn, she had had a wonderful time with Nate Saturday evening. After they had watched the sun set over the ocean from the sailboat, he'd walked her through downtown Key West and showed her the highlights. After a margarita from a street-side cart, they'd wandered through a small outdoor dance party. Josie wasn't usually the type to jump in and dance, but Nate coaxed her onto the floor for two songs, and by the third, she couldn't recall why she'd been hesitant in the first place.

Drunk wasn't how she'd describe it, but they'd been a little tipsy after the drinks, and eventually they walked down by the marina and sat on the docks for a while as the moon rose in a white half-circle over the calm sea. The scene had been almost magical, as she thought back to it. The cross island breeze had blown like satin across her skin and Nate looked as handsome as ever as they held hands and looked out over the glowing ocean. The weather had gotten noticeably cooler, especially at night, and Josie felt like Fall was in there air...even though it was the thick of winter everywhere else in the world.

When they'd sobered a little, Nate drove her home. They'd shared a nervous kiss before Josie climbed out of the car, said goodnight, and she'd gone in to shower and sleep. There hadn't even been a single cockroach that night.

She was still moony about it two days later. Esterline had wanted every single detail of the whole date, which meant that Sunday afternoon was spent reliving the whole outing in happy chatter. She sat on the porch with her landlady, iced tea in hand, and giggled for hours about Nate and sailing and, as Esterline put it, 'that fine hair of his'.

In fact, concentrating on work was a little tough, especially when she remembered the feel of that hair through her fingers when they'd kissed... She could even forgive the ever-present flip-flops, at this rate.

"What?" Josie winced at her own clueless tone. "I'm sorry, sir, could you repeat that? I'm afraid I missed those dates."

Not a client, thankfully. She was on the line with Southwest Airlines, and the man on the other end was not happy about having to repeat the flight days. She copied them down this time and thanked him. He hung up without a reply.

"Have a nice day," Josie muttered.

"What's the matter, Jos?" Dana asked from across the room. "Is Southwest giving you attitude?"

Josie laughed, and Marcus gave her a sympathetic frown. This time of year, all the airlines were a bit touchy. No one knew it better than the travel agents.

"Just don't try to book with Doubletree today," Marcus warned. "They've had me on hold for like half an hour. The last girl said their systems were down."

Josie and Dana groaned.

By the time she was on the bus home three hours later, hotels with trippy reservation books and airlines with snippy customer service reps had worn down the lingering magic of her date with Nate. In contrast to the freshness of the island air, the heat on the bus was oppressive, as usual, and the people-mover was packed with laughing, screaming children. Josie climbed off a stop early—she couldn't bear the noise for another minute.

Her shoes were sturdy low heels today, so walking an extra six blocks wasn't the worst thing that could happen. She carried her suit jacket over her arm and her purse over the other and started off towards Esterline's.

From inside her purse, Josie's phone sang out a chirpy tune. After a minute of rummaging, she pulled it out; it was her mother calling. *Well, this should be good...* Josie thought, hitting the answer key.

"Hi, mom."

"Hi, Jojo. I just wanted to call and see how your first week was—I had a bit of a busy weekend at church, or I would have called you yesterday. I didn't catch you at work, did I?"

"No, I'm just on my way home. It's been going great. My job is fine—it's just the same thing I was doing before, really." Josie hesitated. "And I met someone really nice."

"Already?" Lucia half-shrieked. She couldn't have sounded more pleased if Josie admitted to winning the lottery. "Well, tell me about him!"

Josie laughed and went into the full report of her date with Nate, their sailboat ride, her sunburn, the dancing. She left out the margaritas —her mother only approved of the communion wine and the sherry she used for cooking.

"And then he took me home, and dropped me off," Josie finished. Her mother made a suspicious noise, and Josie could see her face. "Oh, fine. We kissed, and that was it."

"You sure?"

"Mom, come on," Josie rolled her eyes. "I'm sure. Are you going to tell me about your weekend at the church, or what?"

"I was just helping them fundraise for the Salvation Army," Lucia answered. "I spent most of Sunday over at St. Joseph's. They're getting all the decorations put up, and I stayed to see the tree lit up. Do you have a tree? Are you going to put lights on a palm tree this year or something?"

The vision of her hometown awash in decorations hit a little close to her heartstrings, and Josie felt her throat shut. She coughed to clear it. "Maybe. We'll see. I just got here, I don't really know what I'm doing yet. Maybe I'll help Esterline with whatever she's doing. She seems so lonely here without her family."

"She sounds lovely, Jojo. I'm glad you're settled in."

"I'm getting there." Five more blocks just to get to her own bus stop, and then another street length after that. Josie had definitely not yet nailed how to dress properly for long walks under the intense Florida sunshine. Ocean breeze or no ocean breeze, someone was going to find her empty clothes and shoes with no trace of Josie but a pool of sweat on the sidewalk. "I have to admit, I've been a little down," she finally confessed to her mother. "Maybe it's just breaking up with Mike…"

Lucia clucked her tongue sympathetically. "I'm sorry to hear that, dear. Maybe, if you called him—"

"No, Mom," Josie said quickly. "No. I'm not going back to Mike. I'm just feeling… I guess I miss home, a little. Christmas is coming. Mike never wanted to do anything except put up a tree and call it good. I mean, we exchanged presents, but he was never really into the holiday season, and now that I'm down here, it doesn't even feel like December."

Lucia was quiet for a minute. "Well, there's always room here for you, if you want it."

Josie's heart twisted. Truthfully, she'd looked for an opening in Connecticut before anywhere else. Go-To Travel didn't have an office in Connecticut. The closest opening was in Massachusetts, and she wasn't up for that commute on a daily basis.

The call of home and family was almost overwhelming. Josie fought off dreams of climbing off an airplane to the sight of falling snow. Meeting her mother at the airport, going home, baking cookies and volunteering at St. Joseph's together. It was nearly enough to make her forget her ten years with Go-To Travel, the oasis of Key West, and even the alluring Nate Richardson.

"Thanks, Mom, but I can't just pack up and leave and quit my job,"

Josie said at last. "I'll visit soon. I promise. But I'm not ready to leave everything and move back to Connecticut."

Lucia sighed. "I know, you have to live your own life. That's what your father was always telling me about all you kids. I just miss you, is all."

"I miss you, too, Mom," Josie said, and it was the straightest truth she'd spoken all day. "I'll call you back later, okay? I'm just getting back to my house."

"Okay, Jojo. You call me soon. Love you."

"Love you, too." The phone went silent, and Josie put it away in her bag. She bit her lip and continued on towards Esterline's pristine white house, under the palm trees and the dazzling Florida sun that was now casting pink in the late afternoon. She didn't want to drop everything and go home, she reminded herself. She had her own life to live. She was an adult, doing just fine on her own.

When she arrived at Esterline's, it was to find Nate and her landlady sitting out on the porch laughing together.

"Listen to this devil!" Esterline said with a smile. "It 'asn't even been three whole days and 'e wants to take you out again."

"If you want to," Nate added quickly, pushing his sun-gold hair out of his eyes. "I don't want Esterline to think I'm trying to kidnap you."

Her spirits had jumped already, just by seeing him. Josie nodded quickly. "Yeah! I'd love to—here, I just need to set my things down and change into something lighter. Give me five minutes."

Josie hustled to the guest house. She let herself in, closed the door, and quickly flung open her closet. She wished she had another outfit as good as the crop-top and shorts. She felt lucky to fit into that one. She hadn't gone running in weeks, what with the move and all else. She had a couple of sundresses and shorts and blouses. Josie shut the curtains and threw off her business clothes.

Flats, whatever else she wore, she had to wear flats. Her heels were definitely retired for the day.

Where were they going? Josie bopped her head against the wall gently. She should have asked before she stripped her clothes off. Nate had mentioned diving, but it was getting late for that, wasn't it?

Indecisive, Josie threw together an outfit of a flowy green skirt and white tank top. Simple always worked, she reasoned.

She pulled on sandals and grabbed her bag; the clock on the wall said she'd only been seven minutes.

Nate was waiting out front for her and gave a small wave. She shivered at the sight of him; he hadn't been too impressive at first, with his beach-bum appearance, but his strong, toned body and that great hair were winning Josie over at lightning speed.

"I'll see you when I get home, Esterline," Josie waved as she and Nate headed off on foot down the street.

"Don't worry about me, darling," Esterline waved back, sitting on her porch swing. "I'll be fine. You two 'ave fun, now."

"So," Josie turned to Nate. He offered his arm; she looped her hand through it comfortably. "So, where are we going?"

"Well, I happen to know of a great place for dinner," he said with a grin. He hadn't shaved today, Josie noticed. His beard grew in a little darker than his hair. "But beyond that, it's a surprise."

"I guess I'll just have to trust you, then," Josie sighed.

No one could say that Nate didn't have a touch for surprises. They headed through Key West, and he brought her to a little café named Gemma's, which was a hole-in-the-wall situated a street over from Main. As soon as Josie walked in, it felt like she'd stepped into the set of a Christmas movie. Fake snow dusted the floor, and tinsel was strung everywhere. A big decorated pine tree took up more than its share of space in the crowded dining area. Delighted, she let Nate lead her to a table with Holly trimming and a red tablecloth.

"They do this every year," Nate explained. "Sure beats the heck out of takeout."

It sure did. Gemma's offered a full Christmas-dinner-for-two option on the menu, complete with steaming oven-roasted turkey and cranberry sauce. The diner was crowded, and most tables seemed to be enjoying the holiday special. There was a contented murmur throughout the building. Happily, Josie noticed that floating lightly in the background was the sound of a stereo playing Christmas tunes.

"This is great," Josie told him, and she really meant it. The food was phenomenal, and she had never imagined that a place like this existed in Key West. "I'm surprised there isn't a line out the door."

"Shh," Nate told her in a whisper. "You're a local now, so you have to keep the secret." He winked across the table.

A cozy warmth spread through her limbs as Josie officially ate too much. She didn't think she had room left, but when the server brought around apple pie, complete with a vanilla ice cream snowman on the side, she and Nate had to share a piece. That was definitely where they drew the glutinous line, though. They split the check between them and staggered back out into the evening air.

"Now I know what a turkey feels like," Nate cheerfully complained as he led them along.

"Where to next? Walk on the beach?" They were strolling along hand-in-hand, and Nate was nudging them in the general direction of the ocean. It didn't occur to Josie that trusting him so easily was strange; Nate had an easy, relaxed air that was powerfully contagious.

"Not a walk," he replied. He pointed. "A ride."

Josie stared, and then had to giggle. He was pointing at a trolley, a big open-air vehicle that was already filling with people. "What's this?"

"The holiday light tour," he explained as they got in line to buy tickets. "I've never done it before, actually. It's—"

"More of a tourist thing?" Josie finished, smirking.

"More or less."

It was another half hour before the tour was set to leave, but Nate and Josie nabbed seats on the trolley. It was more of beach-mobile than a traditional streetcar, Josie realized, with big, sand-friendly wheels under the wooden frame and brightly-painted benches. Strings of lights were crisscrossed all over it, making the trolley a show in and of itself.

By the time the tour started, the trolley was packed.

"Hello, and welcome to the Key West Christmas Light Tour," the guide announced over the speakers. "Now, don't forget, ladies and gentlemen, that some of our tour travels through residential areas, so please, no yelling or rowdy behavior, this is Christmas, after all…"

He ran through a short list of precautions, and the cart rumbled into motion.

Josie found herself forgetting that just hours ago, she'd been dreaming of running home. It was still relatively warm compared to what she was used to, but there was something unavoidably festive about the massive holiday light displays. They rolled past entire houses strung over with white lights and 'Merry Christmas' signs. A good number of Key West residents and businesses participated, some even putting together displays out on private sections of the beach. It was an hour-long ride, and by the end of it, Josie found that 'Rockin' Around the Christmas Tree' and 'Frosty the Snowman' were just as prone to getting stuck in one's head, whether you were surrounded by snow or sand.

CHAPTER 7

"*I*t's no trouble, Esterline, don't be silly."

Josie set the ladder up at the corner of the porch. Esterline hovered below, wearing turquoise and white today. Another gorgeous Key West Wednesday. Josie had come home from work to find Esterline puttering around with a ladder out front. Everything became clear when she saw the jumbled boxes of Christmas lights open on the lawn.

"I am still able to climb a ladder, Miss Josie," Esterline had insisted, hands on hips. But in the end, Josie had convinced her to accept some help. Josie couldn't very well let a sixty-year-old woman climb up and down a ladder all evening. And so, here Josie was, in shorts and an old t-shirt, sitting on the top of the ladder (which specifically had a DO NOT SIT placard) untangling a string of multicolor LED's.

It wasn't such a hard job, really. She found untangling the light strings almost cathartic after awhile. Thankfully the nails to hang the lights from were still hammered into the house. The Duparts left the nails in because, as Esterline put it, twenty different nail holes looked worse than one nail.

"We could just wait for Nate to come by," Esterline said finally. "You're going to fall off that ladder, sitting on it like that."

"I don't think Nate is coming by," Josie said absently, looping lights in and out of each other. "He didn't mention stopping by today. How did these get tied up like this?"

"Well, I 'ope 'e stops by this weekend," Esterline said, grinning wickedly. "I thought 'e might volunteer to 'elp me pick up my Christmas tree."

"Well, I can help with that, Esterline," Josie said; her eyes still didn't stray from the strand of lights, which was gradually coming apart. "I may not be a bodybuilder, but I can pick up a tree. Ha! Got it."

"'Ere's the next strand. But you don't 'ave a car, my dear."

"You have a car."

Esterline put a hand over her heart. "You can't mean my 'usband's Bug? Oh, girl. 'E'd 'ave a stroke if 'e knew I put a tree on 'is car. 'E spends more time polishing it than driving it."

Josie strung the lights up and climbed down the ladder. She moved it six feet over and clambered back up. "Not the Bug, then," she chuckled, "but I'd hate to ask Nate. We haven't even been dating a whole week. I can't be asking him to run errands already."

Esterline was feeding lights up the ladder to Josie now. "'E don't mind. Men need to feel useful. They like being told what to do."

Josie laughed. "I know at least a few men who would disagree with you, Miss Esterline."

When the first row of lights circled the house, Josie climbed onto the roof of the first story to wire up the second story, despite Esterline's protests. She took off her shoes so she could grip the roof with her bare feet and worked away in the refreshing evening air. There was a terrifying moment when a huge wasp came buzzing past her head and nearly caused Josie to plummet onto the lawn—Esterline told her to come down after that, but Josie threw up the rest of the lights before slipping back inside through the upstairs window.

By now, twilight had fallen. Esterline plugged in the light strands. The two women stood out in the street, arms crossed, taking in their handiwork.

It was perfect. Snow or no snow, the house made a festive picture, with all the Christmas lights sparkling against the white paint and the porch light's welcoming glow.

"Definitely worth falling off the roof for," she told Esterline.

"Who fell off the roof?" Nate walked up the lawn, admiring the house. He was carrying a carton of milk—no, not milk. Josie looked closer and realized it was egg nog.

"No one, thank you very much." Josie leaned up and kissed him on the cheek. "I see you went shopping."

"Well, it's not Christmas without a little holiday oil for the gears," he chuckled.

Esterline's porch was quickly becoming Josie's favorite place. With a glass of eggnog apiece, she and Nate and Esterline sat on the wicker rocking chairs while night fell over Key West, telling stories and admiring the glow. Several neighbors lit up their houses, as well, and the street was awash in glimmering brilliance.

"Now, about my Christmas tree," Esterline began, hazel eyes sparkling.

CHAPTER 8

"Thank you, ma'am, sir. And how was your dive?"

Nate accepted the gear back from the last group of the day. Night dives were later tonight, but regular hours were just about up. He listened to the woman and her husband excitedly relay everything they'd seen on the reef. Though in some ways he'd acquired a local's cynicism when it came to the overflowing tourist population, he also loved seeing satisfied customers. He took genuine pleasure in helping people to see that the ocean was even more beautiful than they imagined.

"Ah! I thought that was the last of it!" Benjamin accepted the final two sets of gear and lugged them into the back for sanitizing. Nate took the deposit return slip into the closet that served as an office, to file with the day's records.

"I'll help you in a minute, let me just get this all squared away."

"You don't have time for that," Andy called from up front. "You have to go meet your lady friend, right? It's almost romancing hour."

Nate threw a wadded-up piece of scrap paper through the doorway. "Quiet, you."

"Hey, if you'd seen her, you wouldn't tease," Benjamin called from the storeroom. "I saw the two of them downtown on Monday, and she is fi-i-ine."

"You're both fired," Nate told them, but the threat was empty. Both boys laughed.

"You better be careful," Andy teased. "You're getting old, Nate. All the hot ones want a younger model."

Nate rolled his eyes. What really made him feel old was when his two teenage assistants had to explain apps on the iPhone, or help him install new accounting software on their dinosaur of a computer. Trying to taunt him about women didn't excite that fluttery panic feeling in his gut—after all, they might know computers, but romance didn't change, and he'd had far more time to learn than these two. No matter how many times they reminded him that thirty-two wasn't twenty-one.

"Why don't you let me worry about that? I need this shop ready for night rentals in two hours."

"You're letting me take a lot of night shifts lately," Andy replied, grinning through the office door.

Nate didn't have a ready answer to that. He frowned at the books he was updating, even though the numbers gave him no cause for consternation. Business was booming. But that was, in part, because before Josie came, he'd practically lived at the shop. Was he going to start losing money with all the time devoted to her? Would it come down to his livelihood or Josie?

It had happened before. When he'd bought The Dive Bar, he'd been dating a nice girl from Miami. Though they lived over three hours apart, they got along well, like salt and pepper. That is until Nate had taken over the business, and she'd suddenly found that his trips up to Miami to visit her were growing too few and far between.

They'd broken up six months after he'd put his signature on the lease for The Dive Bar. Nate had been disappointed, but being single freed up the time he needed to pour into his dream of life by the open ocean.

What about Josie? She was much closer, close enough to visit on the way home from work. But was that going to be a boon or a curse?

It was so very easy to wander over to her little guest house behind Esterline's place, instead of working the long hours that had gotten him this far. Not once had Nate ever thought of being at The Dive Bar as work. Not until he had one other place that drew his attention.

Josie was struggling with a feeling of newness, of displacement. And Nate wanted her to feel at home here—maybe for reasons that weren't entirely altruistic. But he had a life here to live himself. At some point, he'd have to stop living on Esterline's lawn and let Josie make her own way.

At some point. It was a broad time frame. His brain wrestled with his emotions for a few minutes.

"I'll be in most of the weekend," he said finally.

CHAPTER 9

*M*eanwhile, Josie was in the middle of her own pitfalls at work. She'd had a slow week. Marcus and Dana had been able to make up time for the rough Monday, but Josie was having a string of crummy clients and long hold times. Even hotels and airlines that usually pulled through were proving unreliable. To a degree, that was to be expected around mid-December, but by Friday, Josie was lagging behind her coworkers.

"Sir, if I could—"

Click. *He hung up on me*, Josie thought, stunned. Although, the longer she sat there thinking about it, the less it surprised her. He'd been a jerk right from the start.

She set the phone down and rubbed her temples with her fingertips. Her headset was digging into her skull, and her brain was ringing with hold music and dial tones. She looked at the clock. 6:52 pm. She was almost two hours overtime; Marcus had left shortly after five, and Dana had slipped out while Josie had been bickering with a representative from the Hilton. Mr. Trevor had left for the weekend, and Josie could hear Hannah packing up her things to head out.

With a sigh, she hung up her headset and started making notes.

When she got back in the office Monday, she'd have to pick up where she left off. Maybe Monday would bring her better luck.

"You heading out, Josie?" Hannah asked sweetly. She didn't have to say the subtext. *Are you heading out so I can leave, too?*

"Out for the weekend," Josie agreed. She swung her purse onto her shoulder. Just as she pushed her chair under the desk, her phone jangled from inside the bag. Not wanting to make Hannah wait, Josie followed Hannah out into the office building hallway before fishing it out. It wasn't a call, just a text. It was from Nate; she smiled and opened it.

Mind if Esterline lets me in your house? I have a surprise!

Josie stopped in the middle of the hallway. A surprise? What kind of surprise needed him to be inside her studio cottage while she wasn't home? Josie had a laundry list of ideas, but the top choices weren't likely to get approval from Esterline. Unless Nate just wanted to rob her blind, but she had a hard time believing that. Esterline liked him too much, and that old lady was sharp.

Sure. I'll be home in about an hour.

Then again, knowing the bus lines here in Key West, it could well be more than that. Josie let herself out into the early evening air, wondering how well the air conditioning would work in an affordable used car.

Her curiosity grew at an exponential rate during her bus ride home. Her fellow passengers weren't so rowdy today, so Josie stayed on until the stop at the end of Esterline's street, trying all the while to figure what surprise Nate might have cooked up. He was proving to be a resourceful planner.

He met her out front of Esterline's house with the lady herself, who insisted Josie come inside right away. It turned out, Nate had delivered the Christmas tree from the farm and set it up in the corner; though it was undecorated, as of yet. Josie wondered if he'd brought her a tree. She had no idea where he'd put a tree in the guest house, though.

It was an agonizing hour of small talk and discussing every detail of her day at work before Josie managed to beg off with Nate to the back cottage. Usually, if she was eager to be alone, it was in respect of the overwhelming need to take a shower at the end of the day. But this Friday hadn't been as humid as the days before it, and Josie had forgotten her slightly damp clothes by the time she was unlocking the door to her cottage. Nate stood behind her as the door swung open.

Josie almost dropped her bag in shock.

Her cabin had been decked out in holiday style. Red bows and strands of garland were festooned along the tropical shades and bamboo blinds. A brightly-patterned blanket showing reindeer and snowflakes was thrown over Josie's small couch. There was a smell of cinnamon and pine, and Josie realized there were several lit candles adorning the kitchen table next to a shiny thermos and two matching red mugs. A smooth, deep voice swirled through the background singing, *I'm dreaming of a white Christmas...just like the ones I use to know-*

And best of all, a miniature Christmas tree sat by the front window, possibly the only place in the entire guest house where it wasn't underfoot.

"How did you do this?" Josie asked, breathless. She was floored, and there was no way to disguise it. She stared at Nate in wonder. He put his hands in his pockets and shrugged.

"I had some stuff lying around." He led her over to the couch; Josie hadn't noticed at first, but on the living room table was stacked several DVD's: *Jingle All the Way, White Christmas, A Christmas Story.* She laughed.

"I guess we're having a movie night?"

"That was the plan," he agreed, leaning forward and kissing her forehead. It was a good plan.

"I have one last thing before we settle in," Nate continued as he positioned Josie in the middle of the living room. She started to look up and around to see if he had dangled mistletoe. Nate stood across from her expectantly, then she heard a small beep as he pressed a remote he had hidden in his pocket. As the overhead fan started to turn, glimmering snowflakes began showering down from atop the fan blades. The snowy spectacle didn't last long, but it was spectacular. As Josie stood there amidst the falling confetti snow, she couldn't help but laugh into giggles, lifting her hands to catch it as she would in real life. Nate also seemed to enjoy his impromptu handiwork, smiling at her reaction, and at the fact that it had actually worked.

They both stood there until the last snowflake had made it's way gracefully to the ground. "I promise I'll clean this all up," he assured her. "That's part of the package." He gave her an almost shy smirk as he picked a glittery snowflake out of her hair.

Well into the night, they lazed around together on Josie's loveseat, hands wrapped around ceramic red mugs, sipping hot chocolate poured from the thermos. The temperature had dropped into the sixties, so Nate had opened all the windows, allowing the brisk night air to make its way through the tiny house. Bundled up under the blanket, warmed by one another and the steamy beverage, Josie couldn't imagine being any cozier.

Nate stayed for hours, and eventually, Josie found herself drifting to sleep on his shoulder.

"Thank you for all this," she said sleepily. She wanted to say it before she drifted off for the night. "This... this is more than anyone's ever done for me. It means a lot."

Nate wrapped his arms around her. "Never? Not even your ex?"

Josie shrugged. Her long week and their pleasant evening together had dulled the memory of Mike and his long office hours. It didn't hurt so much anymore. "Never. See, Mike... he didn't really care for holidays. I guess he just didn't really care for anything except work."

Nate was quiet, at that. Josie was too tired to notice. "It seemed like he would spend days there. It's been a long time since I really did anything at all for Christmas, but here, it's not even snowy..." she yawned. "I'm falling asleep, though. I don't think I'll make it through another movie."

"I should get going, anyway," Nate said. Josie sat up and turned off the DVD player, and the credits of Jingle All the Way vanished. The lights on the tree Nate had set up gave off a halo glow, and the candles they'd lit had the air smelling of cinnamon sticks and forest pine. Nate got up, and Josie pulled herself to her feet to follow.

"Good night," Josie said shyly, smiling up at him through the soft lights. Nate paused on her front step, hesitant. It looked like he was on the verge of saying something.

Finally, he leaned over and kissed her gently. It wasn't passionate or sweeping, just a sweet, intimate touch of lips that widened Josie's goofy, tired grin.

"See you later?" she asked.

Nate nodded. "Yeah. Have a good night, Josie. Happy holidays."

CHAPTER 10

I t had been five days since their movie night, and Josie hadn't heard from Nate once.

She didn't know what to make of it. Their date on Friday had been wonderful, or so she'd thought. They'd had a cozy evening watching Christmas movies and enjoying the decorations he'd snuck in, laughing together and enjoying each other's company. Josie had been on many worse dates in her lifetime, and few better.

So she was at a loss to explain the radio silence. Twice, she shot a text his way. Saturday morning she'd sent him a short good morning, to which he had never responded. Wary, she'd tried again Monday night. Nothing, nothing. It reminded her so strongly of the years of solitude with Mike that she was having a hard time keeping her mind on work.

The week was crawling by. Josie kept typing up then deleting new messages to send him, and once her finger even hovered dangerously over the call button. Did she want to get a hold of him? It was a struggle to remind herself that this was surely coincidence. He was busy, that was all. Not avoiding her.

Why would he be avoiding her? She hadn't done anything.

In fact, the most egregious mistake she had made thus far was overthinking the whole situation. Her sales had already taken a chip lately—she left work on Wednesday barely caught up to office standards. Mr. Trevor nodded grimly to her as she left the office of Go-To Travel. As if she didn't have enough to turn over in her head.

Usually, she went home straight after work, but today Josie stepped out into the Florida sunshine and looked around. The bus stop was to her left. She strolled down the sidewalk to her right, towards downtown.

Since arriving, Josie had been too busy to explore Key West, except with Nate. Afraid of the bugs and intimidated by the heat, most of her time was spent either with Esterline or at home with a book. She put on her sunglasses and took her time walking down Main Street.

Key West was a new place, truly. It was like nowhere Josie had ever lived, and definitely like nowhere she'd visited before. The strangeness of it all had overwhelmed her at first. She forced herself to slow down and take it in. She bought a lemonade from a stand by the road, and sat alone by the ocean.

It wasn't a bad place, Josie decided. True, it sure didn't feel like December up north, but Key West wasn't all humidity and giant flying cockroaches. Ever since the initial heat wave had passed, the days had gotten progressively cooler. No one would mistake it for the thick of winter, but the pleasant mix of warm sun rays and crisp ocean air blowing across the island was invigorating and, if she were to really admit it, perfect. She loved that the people were relaxed here, too. And they were kind. Although she was beginning to understand the local's endless impatience with their vacationing guests.

Even if Nate didn't call her back, it was still a beautiful city.

Josie walked to the downtown bus stop. Time to get home, get a shower, and call it a day. Refresh and get ready to hit the phones tomorrow with renewed energy.

While she waited, Josie eyed the flyers tacked up in the announcement boards, covered with glass to protect the papers from the odd tropical storm. There was a Christmas Carol Concert coming up next week, the day before Christmas Eve. She wondered if Nate would be talking to her in time to attend.

Below that, an announcement caught Josie's eye. A lighted boat parade?

She read it through as the bus was pulling up. That sounded interesting; she filed away the dates and times in her head and danced off to catch a seat before her line took off.

When her phone rang that night, Josie forgot how worried she'd been and suddenly realized she was miffed, flat-out annoyed. What did he think this was, just leaving her hanging for a week and now ringing her up like nothing had happened?

"Hello?"

"Hi, Josie!"

She could hear the smile in his voice. Josie's temper flickered out like a candle in a sudden draft. All the things she had in mind to tell him hung back, as if suddenly shy.

"Hey, Nate," she replied finally. "How've you been?"

"I'm fine, I've just been at the shop." Of course. Josie swallowed past a dry lump in her throat. Work. Did all men retreat to their jobs, eventually? Was it pandemic?

"That's okay. I was starting to wonder why you didn't answer my messages, though." She winced. To her own ears, she sounded like a petty teen. "I know you're busy," she added, "I mean, you don't have to call me every day. It... It's okay." She buried her face in her free hand. None of this actually sounded any better.

Nate took a little while answering. "I've been slammed over the weekend," he explained eventually. "By the time I got your message, I thought it was too late to answer. And then I was back in the water early for morning dives."

She could tell he was trying to both find the most kind excuse he could, but was also genuinely happy to be talking to her. She decided to get over her ego and move past it, for now at least.

"Of course," Josie agreed quickly. Too quickly. "Hey! Um... I saw this flier today, and since you have been coming up with all the ideas, I thought maybe I could... throw one on the table. There's this light boat parade—have you heard of it?"

Nate chuckled, loosening something in Josie's chest that she hadn't realized was clenched tight. "Of course. It goes right past my shop. I could bring you down here to watch it, if you like."

"Yeah! That sounds great! When?"

"I could give you directions to come down tomorrow. It's right between regular dive hours and night diving, so the timing couldn't be better."

Josie wrote down the directions Nate gave. Tomorrow at dusk, on the other side of Key West from where she'd visited so far.

They had been dating since she arrived in Key West, practically down to the day, and for the first time Josie felt a flutter of nerves.

CHAPTER 11

*J*osie took another look around the marina; she hadn't been to this side of the island before. Nate said his shop was on the shore near the north boat ramp. That was only partially helpful. First, Josie had a hell of a time trying to figure out which ramp was the north one—none of the signs said north, south, or any direction in between.

When she was fairly sure she was on the right track, there was still the issue of making her way from one end of the docks to the other. The beach was crowded with hundreds of people who'd all shown up to watch the lighted boats sail past. The parade was set to start in less than an hour, and Josie was still making her way along, looking for the sign that read The Dive Bar.

She actually heard Nate's voice over the clamor before she saw the sign. His shop-front could really use a fresh coat of paint, but was charming in its own way. Josie pushed her way through the crowd and waved. Nate smiled and waved back, then turned to finish up with the two customers he was helping.

There wasn't another place to wait, except in the middle of the thronging crowd, so Josie snugged herself up beside the wall of The Dive Bar, just at the end of the counter, to wait.

You couldn't help but people watch in a crowd like this. Couples—lots of couples, of all ages—walked together holding hands. Moms and Dads struggled to herd their children, and every now and then an infant wailed fussily. Groups of friends laughed and joked as they walked by. Josie saw many a Santa hat, and more than one of Rudolph's red nose.

Her heart squeezed a little. She appreciated all Nate had done, but there was something here that touched her even more deeply than Christmas meals and lighted trees.

"Hey!" Speak of the devil. Josie peered around the counter to see Nate leaning over from his side. "I'm about done here—give me another minute and I'll be right out."

"Okay." She swooped in and stole a kiss, laughing, before Nate retreated back into the depths of his shop with a handful of loose papers and receipts. True to his word, barely five minutes clocked by before he slipped out of a door in the back and took her hand.

"Where are we going?" Josie asked over the noise.

"Right here."

"What?"

He led her to the back of the shop; a ladder leaned against the edge of the roof. Smiling, Josie let herself be helped up, onto the roof of his rental shop. The roof was tilted slightly, but with a little balance, they climbed up and into view of the surprise he'd set out—a bottle of wine and two glasses, balancing on a tray he'd leveraged against the roof's tilt.

"VIP service," Josie remarked, approving. Nate bowed his head in acceptance.

Their view was breathtaking. From the roof, they perched together up out of the crowded pier as an announcer in the marina welcomed one and all to the Key West Annual Lighted Boat Parade. Josie and Nate sat together on one side of the table and watched as a line of brightly-lit sailboats and schooners and yachts glided past.

But it was the crowd that Josie had her eye on, no matter how hard she tried to enjoy the show. The families, most especially. Enjoying the experience together. Enjoying Christmas together.

A tear glistened in her eye, and Josie swiped it away as discreetly as she could.

"What's wrong?" he asked. Josie smiled and shook her head.

"It's nothing," she lied. The lie was so bald-faced, she sighed and shrugged her shoulders. " It's just... I thought it was the Christmas spirit I was missing. And now, looking at all this, I'm not so sure, anymore."

Nate sat there, relaxed in his shorts and a powder blue long-sleeved t-shirt. But she noticed a cautious stillness overtake him.

"Is it me?" he finally asked.

"No!" Josie answered at once—that was true, absolutely. "You've been incredible. I've never met...anyone like you. Anyone who would go out of his way like this for me," she motioned to the romantic make-shift setup.

"But it's not enough." The statement was, in part, a question. Josie shook her head.

"It's not like that, Nate. It's not about you."

"I think maybe it is," he replied gently. He wasn't angry, and he was accusing. There was sadness in his voice now, and it was worse than if he'd yelled. "Maybe you just need more than I can give."

"What do you mean?" It was Josie's turn to be tense and wary. Nate rubbed the back of his neck and sighed.

"I mean, maybe there isn't anything I can do to make you comfortable here," he said.

Josie's throat had gone dry. The noise of the crowd and the end of the parade had faded into a pulsing background cacophony, shutting them up in their own little world above. She felt trapped, cornered by what he was saying. Cornered by the possibility that it was all true.

"Do you think... that I don't care about you?" she asked finally.

Nate shook his head. "No... I don't think that. But I think that what you're looking for is something more than I can give you."

"What do you think I'm looking for?" Josie found herself asking. "It's not like I'm looking for a wedding ring, or children, or any of that. It's only been a few weeks. I—" Her world was spinning, and it had nothing to do with the wine. "I think I'm going to head home."

Nate didn't stop her. Josie climbed off the roof and stumbled back into the crowd of parade-goers.

What more could she possibly want? After all he'd done. Nate had been everything good and generous and gentlemanly. He'd done more for her in two weeks than Mike had bothered in any single year, possibly all the years they'd been together. What more could she possibly want?

But there was a corner of her that whispered the truth. Nate was right. There was some unsettled need in her, and until she could figure out what it was, no person was going to be able to be fully let in. Was it home she wanted? Snow? To go back to a world she knew?

She had walked through the marina, and made her way home. The night was cool with a gusty breeze, and she even found herself rubbing the chill off her arms once or twice. Crickets and cicadas buzzed through the night, and cars cruised past, full of teenagers and tourists. Families.

Esterline wasn't outside when Josie walked past the house and she didn't feel like seeking her out. Heart aching, she crossed straight to the guest house in the back and let herself inside.

It was dark, of course, but Josie didn't flip the lights on. She plugged in the string LEDs that Nate had set up for her, and soon her studio living space was awash in a soft, hazy light. She sighed and rubbed at her eyes.

Her boxes from Richmond had been sitting in the back of her living room for a week, now, and she opened the top box. This was the one where she'd piled her books, and she dug through carefully until she found the one she was looking for.

Sniffling, Josie settled on the couch and opened her Bible for the first time in years. The pages were thin and a little bit brittle, but they still smelled new and fresh, just like the day it had been given to her.

In the quiet of her little guest house, Josie paged through her Bible under the Christmas lights. The moon moved overhead, hours passed, and midnight found her snuggled into the blanket Nate had given her, Bible still open on her lap.

CHAPTER 12

*W*hen Nate stopped by Esterline's, he couldn't remember ever seeing the little old lady ever give him such a stern look. In fact, he couldn't remember her ever giving anyone such a stern look.

"Is Josie home?" he asked hopefully. He felt like he was back in middle school, asking a girl's parents over the phone if she could talk right now. "She's at work," Esterline answered, putting her hands on her hips. "Not that it's any of your business."

Nate's heart sank. He felt bad enough without Esterline guilting him on top of everything else. "Esterline, I just came by to make sure that she's all right. I messaged her a couple of times, and she said she got home fine, but that's not really what I was worried about."

Esterline raised both of her eyebrows. Today, she was dressed in white pants and loose pink blouse, with a matching white scarf and sandals. She looked too grandmotherly to be so skeptical.

"Well, if I 'adn't 'eard it with my own ears, I wouldn't 'ave believed it," she replied stiffly. "You, Mr. Richardson, askin' a girl how she is through a phone? Why 'aven't you come by to see 'er?"

Nate sighed, shoulders sagging. "It's a long story, Miss Esterline. Do you know when Josie is coming home?"

"A long story, hmm?" Esterline opened her door wider. "Well, I can't say I know when Miss Josie will be 'ome, but why don't you come in and tell me more? I can't get a word out of 'er about it."

Relieved, Nate walked into the Dupart house and followed Esterline through to the kitchen. She waved him at the table and opened the fridge. She poured him and herself a glass of lemonade without asking; it looked like he didn't get the privilege of choosing for himself today.

"Now," Esterline took a seat across her kitchen table from him. "Let's 'ear it."

There wasn't as much to tell as Nate thought. It felt as though he and Josie had at least half a dictionary filled with stories already. But he went through their short romance and his attempts to bring some Christmas down to Key West for her, and finally, his fears that nothing would be enough to make her feel at home, or make her want to stay. Esterline wasn't the best listener—she had a tendency to interrupt and talk over him. Somehow he managed to say what he meant to, and at the end the two of them sat together in silence, sipping lemonade.

"She's a sweet girl, but I think she's a little confused, 'erself," Esterline said at last. "She flew down 'ere at the drop of a 'at, all by 'erself. She doesn't 'ave any family 'ere, and not many friends just yet. It's 'ard to be in a new place alone."

Nate turned his glass around in his hands. "That's why I was trying to give her a good Christmas."

Esterline rolled her eyes. "And it was out of the goodness of your 'eart, was it?"

Nate reddened under his tan. "Now, I don't know what you mean."

"Only that she's a pretty girl, and that's enough to catch any man's eye," Esterline replied.

"I don't only like her because she's pretty," Nate argued. "She's fun, and smart, and… different."

"Oh, different," Esterline rolled her eyes again. "You redecorated her house because she's different?"

Nate frowned. "Now you're just being difficult."

"Well, she's upset, that much I know," Esterline admitted finally.

She seemed to have decided that Nate had jumped through enough hoops. "She stays later at work than usual, and slips in when I'm not looking. She doesn't 'ave much to say when we visit. There's something on 'er mind, and it's bothering 'er. I don't know if it's you that she's upset over."

Nate frowned and rested his chin on his hand. "I don't know if it is, either. I think maybe she's just really, really missing home. There's not much anyone can do about homesickness."

"Hmm," Esterline twisted her lips as she thought. She clinked the ice around her glass, wondering. "It was 'ard moving 'ere from Haiti," she said absently. "I 'ad Moliere, and we started a family, and that 'elped me stay busy."

A twinge of something unexpected shivered up from Nate's gut at that. Josie wasn't looking to start a family. She'd said as much, hadn't she? The last time the subject had come up with a woman, he'd nearly run for the hills. This time, he realized, the idea was intimidating, but not entirely unpleasant. Strange. Maybe he'd finally grown up.

Esterline was still thinking out loud. "I remember back then I used to send letters to my mother. Things weren't so fast as they are today."

In Nate's head, a light bulb went on. Stunned, he just sat there for stretching minutes, turning the idea over. "Hey, Esterline..."

She paused, and caught the look on his face. "What?" she asked suspiciously.

"I think I might have an idea. But I'm going to need your help."

CHAPTER 13

*I*t was Friday, and Josie hadn't seen Nate in a week. He'd texted her to make sure she arrived home in one piece; she assured him she was all right. She didn't see him over the weekend. She spent hours of overtime hiding at work, burying herself in the phone lines. In a week, she'd flipped her floundering numbers upside down and Mr. Trevor was smiling and waving at her again.

She knew she was transparent. Dana and Marcus had asked, on the Monday following her parade date with Nate, what had happened to make her look so glum. Nothing, she insisted. Just stuff on her mind. Nothing to worry about. And Josie had put on her headphones and answered no further inquiries.

Sooner or later, though, she had to go back to Esterline's guest house. Mr. Trevor didn't like her enough to let her sleep on the office floor. And today was Friday, which meant she was stuck, stranded with no Go-To Travel to distract her all weekend. Even three days before Christmas, she wasn't permitted to come in on Saturday.

And so Josie found herself back at her front door, unlocking it and letting herself back into the little Christmas haven Nate had made for her. Her heart ached at the sight of it all, though her mood couldn't have been less festive.

Josie stripped off her work clothes and dropped them in the clothes hamper. The cockroach traps that Nate had given her were working magic; she hadn't seen a single roach since she put them out. The bathroom was safe—she double-checked the shower and corners to be certain before turning the water on.

The day washed off easily. Josie had the water set much cooler than she'd ever had it in Richmond, and it felt wonderful. Now, if only her thoughts washed away so easily. That would be really useful.

When she was submitting the paperwork to transfer to Key West, Josie had been sure that what she needed most was a change of scenery. But now that she was here, and the scenery couldn't be more different, she found that maybe a change to something new wasn't quite what she had needed.

With the water off, Josie stepped out of the shower to dry her hair as best she could. It took half an hour or more before she'd begin to feel actually dry. The humid air locked in the moisture like a sauna, and she'd be dripping water for what felt like forever. She turned on the oscillating fan and sat in front of it in her bathrobe; that was the only thing that seemed to help at all.

Her phone buzzed where she'd left it on the table. Josie reached for it without looking. "Hello?"

"Hi, Josie?"

It was Nate. Her heart spurred to second gear and she tried to sound normal. "Hi. What's up?"

"I hadn't heard from you since last weekend. I thought you might be lonely, and that would be a shame. Especially considering it's Christmas, and all."

Her loneliness was a living, pulsing thing in her chest. Josie shrugged her shoulders, then recalled that he couldn't see it through the phone, and answered, "I'm all right. After what you said at the marina, I figured you weren't going to waste your time anymore."

"That's not what I meant, Josie," Nate told her.

She knew that. Just the memory still had her a bit defensive, but that was better than the loneliness. Much better. "I know you didn't mean that. Look, I think you're right."

"I shouldn't have said all that, Josie—"

"No, you were right," she insisted. "I moved here on a whim, and there is something missing that you can't replace, and I should have known it. Christmas isn't just about decorations and eggnog—although, you do an impressive job with both." She had to give him that. She went on, "It's about family. And I miss mine."

Nate was quiet until now. "Are you saying that you want to move back north?"

Josie sighed. "I've been thinking about it. I don't know. It sure would be a hassle with work, but... I just miss my family."

There was a knock outside. Josie tugged her bathrobe closer.

"Is that you at my door?"

"Nope." But there was a devilish grin in his voice, making Josie wonder. She stood up and crossed to the door; for a moment she thought it might have been a good idea to look first, but by that time her hand was on the doorknob. She pulled it open.

Her knees almost melted.

"Mom?" Josie dropped the phone.

"Hi darling!" Lucia Ward opened her arms and folded Josie in a hug. "It's so warm here! Do you have air conditioning inside? Did I catch you at a bad time?"

"No! What?! No, Mom, this is the perfect time!" Josie hugged her mother tightly, afraid she might not be real. The phone was still on the floor, but Nate himself stepped through the door and picked it up from underfoot. Josie's green eyes were welling with tears, but she could still see him smiling, triumphant.

"Did you...?" she directed at Nate, her face still in pure wonderment and confusion.

"This young man and your landlady called me," Lucia explained, stepping back and setting a hand on Nate's arm. She beamed at Josie. "Such nice people—you told me they were, of course, but they were so nice over the phone."

Josie reeled. "Wait... are you saying they got you to come visit me?"

Lucia nodded. "Of course, Jojo. They called me—I didn't know you listed me as your emergency contact. That's very sweet of you. Anyway, they called, and told me everything, and even picked me up from the airport."

Josie was staring at Nate. "Thank you. I... I can hardly believe this."

She moved toward him as he opened his arms. Josie stepped into them and buried her face in his neck.

"Jojo?" he muttered.

She leaned back and looked at him. "What, don't you like it?"

"Like it? It's the cutest thing I've ever heard. I'm never calling you Josie again."

EPILOGUE

$\mathcal{I}$t was the best Christmas Josie'd had in years. Esterline wouldn't hear of anything other than having Lucia stay in a guest bedroom in the house. The three days before Christmas were spent cooking, decorating the bare tree in the Dupart house, and sitting out on the porch while evening ripened to sweet nightfall. Esterline's husband, Moliere, had come home for the holiday and the house was alive with shared stories and merriment.

Christmas morning, Nate arrived early and stole more than one laughing kiss from Josie beneath a spring of mistletoe that he kept handy to hold over her head. It was sixty-seven degrees with ninety-two percent humidity when they sat down to their Christmas brunch. Esterline and Nate were both clad in sweaters due to the winter temperatures. Lucia and Josie were dressed light and airy, as though the first day of Spring had arrived. Lucia could hardly believe that Josie liked it here so much, but the smile on her daughter's face spoke volumes.

To her own surprise, Josie realized that she did like it. In this very different, but very lovely new town, she had quickly found a place of belonging where her friends were more interested in long evenings chatting on the porch rather that hiding away behind their desks. A place where humor and optimism seemed to shine through even the scariest experiences. And a place where Christmas spirit was created from the hearts and souls of the people. No one here needed a snowfall to remind them of the joy the holiday season brought. They brought joy to their colorful island home and the holiday spirit burst forth just as triumphantly as any white Christmas she'd ever been part of.

The change to move here had been radical and rash, but soon Josie found herself thinking that maybe, deep down, she knew what she was doing all along.

Later that afternoon, Esterline and Moliere decided to teach Lucia to play cribbage, allowing Josie and Nate to sneak away for awhile.

Josie lead him through the Dupart house and back to her little cottage. As they walked in, she raised her hand and pressed the button on a remote that she' had stationed by the front door. Speakers crackled alive and the sound of Jimmy Buffet welcomed itself into the room. He was singing his own unique brand of Christmas songs and Nate busted out into a hearty laugh. Josie then went around and opened all the windows in her apartment.

When Nate unwrapped the present that Josie had gotten for him, he let out a booming laugh as he looked to Josie for explanation. The towering stack of CD's had every tropical Christmas album that Josie could find. In a soft cooler next to the stack sat two travel tumblers with snowflakes etched into them.

"So I've been thinking about it and I really love a traditional white Christmas, like the ones I grew up with."

Nate's brow furled ever so slightly, but he said nothing.

Josie's eyes darted up at him mischievously, "But...Sometimes, you come to a place in your life where you realize that it's time for some new traditions." Her smirk grew deeper as she tried not to break out into a full on grin. "And on the tails of your inspiring holiday romance, I've decided to plan a few things to show you just how great a Key West Christmas can be."

She walked to the kitchen where a bright red thermos was sitting and picked it up.

"Shall we?" she asked, as she motioned toward the door.

"Field trip?" Nate queried with a wry smile.

"Yep."

When they walked around to the front, Nate saw two beach cruiser bicycles standing at the ready.

"I have Elves," she said, as she threw a wink his way.

Josie threw her thermos and cooler into the front basket of one, then threw her head back to Nate. "You coming?"

He bounded over to his bike and stood in wait. "After you."

They rode through the small streets past the quint, brightly colored Key West style bungalows. Occasionally a rooster would cross their path and cluck at them. They wound their way down to the small private beach that Josie had learned about from her co-workers. She pulled up to a stop, wheeled her bike up against a rustling palm tree and told Nate in her practiced too-cool-for-school way, "Locals only beach."

When they got to the sand, Josie threw down a blanket that she had rolled up in the bottom of her bike basket. She pulled a few supplies out of her bag, plugged the travel speakers into her iPod and queued up Frosty The Snowman. As the sleigh bells jingled in the background, Nate got the picture and the two of them set to work.

On their knees and with bucket loads of water, they finally managed to create their sandy snowman. It wasn't quite as large as Josie had envisioned in her head, but as she thought back to her childhood she remembered that even with a real snowman, that is usually the case. As the two fell back into the soft blanket, Josie sat up and reached back into the cooler. She took out the thermos and the two cups she brought. She clinked some ice into them, which had managed to stay solid due to proper packaging, and she poured over the thick creamy liquid. The scent of peppermint traveled along to Nate's nose. She handed him a glass and raised hers in a toast.

"To a new year, a new home, new friends, and...to new traditions. I hope we create many more together." And with that she clinked Nate's glass and tried to take a sip of her drink, but only got so far before Nate set down his cup and tackled her onto the blanket. His face nuzzled into her long hair and he kissed her temple, her neck, her nose. She felt both smothered and elated by the barrage of kisses he was showering her with. She laughed from her toes, her ribs aching with happiness. She felt like she was being bowled over by puppies, but she couldn't be happier. After he'd felt like he'd adequately showed his appreciation of her declaration, he sat back up, took her hand to get her upright as well, grabbed his glass back up into the air and looked her lovingly in the eye as he declared, "To new traditions!" They clinked and drank their Iced Peppermint Mochas as the ocean breeze blew and white sand danced between their toes.

"Did you see that?" Nate exclaimed, pointing out at the turquoise ocean. "A Key West Reign-dolphin!"

And Josie was pretty sure he was right.

ACKNOWLEDGMENTS

I have so much appreciation for my incredible family and friends. I could not imagine life without each and every one of you!

To my home state of Florida: What a complex history we have. I think it's a rite of passage to dislike where you're from when you are young, but I am not too proud to admit that I love you now more than I ever thought possible. You're quirky and weird and beautiful and diverse. Thank you for being my home. I owe a lot of who I am to your unique influence.

To my parents: For all the incredible the trips to the Keys, thank you. Mom, the time we spent doing crosswords, testing out every local Key Lime pie and bike riding all around town was life changing. It is still one of my favorite memories. Dad, your breathtaking images from those trips will be in galleries one day...Oh wait, they already are! I am so proud of you both and I love you to the moon and back.

To my favorite Florida girls: If only I could write a book about our antics. I wouldn't want to be from any other place, and I wouldn't have wanted to grow up (or grow old) with any other ladies. I love you all unlimitedly.

To Lincoln and Avery: Lincoln, you are wise beyond your years and you make every single day special. Avery, your fearless nature and bustling energy keeps me on my toes, but makes me constantly smile as well. You are the dynamic duo that makes my world turn.

To Emily: Your creativity has been an inspiration! Thank you so much for all your help.

To Drake: What would I do without you? Have a lot less fun, that's for sure. Thank you for always providing your opinion...the world is a better place because of it.

To my mother-in-law Julia: Thank you for letting me call you at crazy hours to get your opinion on cover art, and every other little thing you get roped into. Even when you are far away, know that you are missed and loved.

A GIRL'S GUIDE TO CREATING CHRISTMAS

A Story of Hope, Holidays & Second Chances

with Sunny Brooks

Sophie Mays

A
Girl's Guide
To Creating Christmas

This book is dedicated to all the people out there, who have suffered loss, missed a turn in life, or found themselves overwhelmed and overworked. It is also dedicated to all the folks who go a little above and beyond to make someone else's life special, or simply a little easier.

If you are in a place where you are unsure how to move forward, I just want to remind you that you never alone and there is untapped possibility ahead. The world is brimming with good people dealing with hard circumstances; but you are not alone, you are not an island, and all is never lost. I am proud of each and every person who welcomes another day, even when yesterday was a rough one. I am thankful for every person who brings sunshine and brightness to others regardless of whether they have to or not. And I am proud of all the people who know that sometimes it's okay just to stay in bed and eat a pint of ice cream with the covers over your head; you are giving yourself a break, and that is something each one of us deserves.

If you know someone who is trying to do it all: be a parent, run a business, volunteer, make dinner after working a full day, get in shape, walk the dog, pay bills, spend time with friends and family...and on top of it all they are also trying to be a functioning human being: give them a hug, tell them you see all they are trying to do & let them know they are appreciated.

If there is someone who you see trying to make your life a little brighter, even if it's through small actions, remember to thank them. They believe in you, and that's a wonderful thing.

Thank you for picking up this book and giving this overworked, underslept author the ability to live her dream. This book is dedicated to you!

~

CHAPTER 1

*C*himing bells above the Potted Shed Boutique's front door announced the sixth customer within fifteen minutes.

Andy Williams crooned "Let It Snow," pouring out of the overhead speakers to get customers in the Christmas mood. But Natalie was in anything but the Christmas spirit.

"Can you get that, Emma?" Natalie called from her overstuffed, cramped office in the back of her floral boutique.

Turning her attention back to her caller she pasted a smile on her face, forcing it out into her voice.

"No, of course, we'll be just fine. I'm so excited for you, Keri. What a sweet and romantic Christmas present."

She listened as her close friend chattered.

"Well of course not. Just make sure you take plenty of pictures and bring her something special back... yes, of course, she'll be fine, Keri. She's only seven. They pop back from disappointment so easily."

She listened a little longer before replying once more. "She'll be too busy with unwrapping Christmas gifts to care where we're at... okay, sweetie. Give Jon my love for me, won't you?"

She listened as her friend chattered on, rolling her eyes and staring at the computer screen. She really was happy for her dear friend, but that did not make her problems any easier.

"Yes, I'll make sure she opens your gift on Christmas first. I'll let her know that her Aunt Keri sent it with love. Bye-bye, now."

She clicked her cell phone off and tossed it onto the table. Plopping her head down on her desk, Natalie groaned into her crossed arms and wished a little magical elf would take away all of her problems.

Several minutes later, Emma pranced into the office wearing an elf hat and bells jingling on her shoes.

Natalie groaned at the irony of it.

"Sales are really picking up," Emma chirped, flopping onto the bean bag chair sitting across from Natalie's desk. "We have orders to deliver for five weddings this month and two funerals. That's on top of all of our Christmas and regular orders. The last customer placed an order for ten of your vintage specials!"

"Mmm," Natalie grumbled, staring at her computer screen and pecking away.

"I thought you'd be excited! That's an easy two grand you just earned."

Natalie's vintage special included orchids, eucalyptus, and hydrangea with Limonium white flowers interspersed in the bouquet. They were one of her best sellers, and she charged two hundred per basket.

"How are we supposed to keep up at this rate? There's only so much the two of us can do."

"You need to hire a third hand. I don't know why you won't listen to me."

"Because, you have no idea what you're talking about. It's not that simple, Emma."

"Why're you such a Grinch? It's the most beautiful time of the year. Time for eggnog, secret Santas, gifts, decorations, Christmas parties and music, and—"

"And disappointing little seven-year-old girls," Natalie remarked somberly, pushing her glasses up on top of her head.

"Aww, what happened now?" Emma empathized.

Emma had filled in for Natalie when she couldn't take her daughter, Fiona, to see the lighting of the Macy's great tree. The little girl had been delighted in the experience and had not stopped talking about the ride on the pink pig for days. But nothing could take away the sadness glinting in her eyes over the fact that the experience was not shared with her mother.

Natalie had been meeting with a potential investor seeking to expand her business. To ease the little girl's frustrations she promised to give her the Christmas of a lifetime in New York. That was the only thing that had soothed Fiona's disappointments.

"I can't take her to New York." Natalie rolled back in her chair, preparing for the outburst she knew was coming.

"What! But you promised her," Emma declared, standing up and planting her fists on her hips.

"You think I don't know that? It's not like I want to disappoint her."

"Then why are you?" Emma argued back.

"Because Keri canceled," Natalie explained. "It seems Jon surprised her with an early Christmas gift. They'll be in the South of France celebrating this year."

Natalie had planned to visit her old college roommate and long-time friend, Keri, in New York for Christmas. The two of them were going to give Fiona the Christmas of a lifetime. But unbeknownst to them, Keri's fiancé Jon had different plans.

"She's gonna be devastated. What're you gonna do?" Emma asked, plunking back down on the bean bag.

"I don't know. I'll figure something out. It may have been for the best anyway."

"How's that?"

"Look at all the orders we're getting around here, Em. There's no way I could keep up if I took a vacation. Besides, we need all the sales we can get if I plan to expand."

"But at what expense, Nat? You're making up excuses. That little girl deserves the best Christmas that you can give her. Not to mention, so do you. You need a break from this shop. If you close it for just a few days, the world is not going to fall apart."

"Maybe not the world at large, but our little world would. I can't afford to lose customers to some of the larger floral shops. I've worked hard for what I've built and I'm on the edge of something right now, Emma. I've gotta give it my all."

"You've got to give Fiona your all. She deserves a Christmas with her mother, and not sporadic trips with her mother's assistant. Nor does she deserve to be thrust on that Paul fella. You know, I know you think highly of him, but what do you really know about him?"

"Fiona's crazy about him. If he wasn't good for her, she'd let me know by now. I get good vibes from him, and he's great with the kids. I've watched him with them and he's an excellent mentor for her."

Natalie had enrolled Fiona in a mentoring program the year before, thinking she could benefit from a male role model in her life. She seemed to thrive under Paul's watchful eye, and Natalie trusted him. It wasn't like Fiona didn't have any time with her mother at all. The shop was closed on Sundays, and she left no later than seven-thirty at night Monday through Wednesday.

"I still think she needs time with her mother."

"Her mother does spend time with her," Natalie argued, frowning at her assistant. "But, her mother also has to make a living. It's not easy being a single parent and business owner, you know."

"Hey, I never said it was," Emma argued back, holding her hands out in front of her. "But if you're a business owner, you need to make sure it benefits the both of you. And from what I can tell, it's not. You've got your priorities all out of order."

The bells chimed once more announcing the arrival of a new customer.

"Well, you just worry about yours. Sounds like we got another customer, and I don't pay you to warm my bean bag chairs all day," Natalie stated, pointing at her office door.

"Scrooge!" Emma huffed, making a beeline for the front of the shop.

Natalie dropped her face into her hands, resting her elbows on her black glass desktop. Emma's words pierced her heart. That's exactly how she referred to her own father. Now here she was, acting just like him.

No one else could speak the truth so bluntly to her. Emma had come to work for Natalie three years prior when she had first enrolled at Georgia State University. The young college student had become like a little sister to her over the years. That's why she knew the words Emma spoke, were spoken in love.

She didn't want to be married to her business. But what other options did she have?

Fiona's father, Dan had been killed by a drunk driver when Fiona was just two years old. The only memories her daughter had of the man whom she resembled to a T, were the ones Natalie shared with her. Natalie had the joy of raising her beautiful, sweet, precocious daughter, and she cherished it more than Fiona could ever know. Yet, it was a constant challenge to make it all work, especially when it came to finances.

Her little flower shop she had opened just before Dan's death was just now starting to flourish all these years later. But with its growth came the trial of long days and nights, often hiring a babysitter if she wasn't able to leave her with Fiona's mentor Paul.

"What am I gonna do?" Natalie groaned in the empty room, shaking her head in her hands from side-to-side. Christmas was a mere three weeks away, and she had nothing special planned for her daughter. They hadn't even purchased a Christmas tree.

"Three more weeks 'till the trip, Mom!" Fiona beamed while finishing her homework at the kitchen table.

Natalie's spoon hovered over the pot she had been stirring. The sinking sensation in her heart had become all too common. She knew this wasn't good for either of them. More often than not, Natalie felt like she had to disappoint her daughter these days.

"Mooom?" Fiona called, looking up from her homework.

Natalie straightened her back and turned around with a smile. Her daughter had noticed her silence.

"Fiona, honey, I've got some news."

The little girl's pen dropped onto her book with a dull thud. The gleam that had previously been in her eyes was replaced with a look of wariness.

Natalie sat the soup spoon on the dishcloth and walked around the aisle to sit with her daughter at the table.

"It seems that Keri's fiancé, Jon, bought her a really nice Christmas present."

The look of wariness turned to confusion.

"Mom, does this present mean we won't be going to New York?"

Natalie slowly nodded her head and pressed her lips together. "I'm afraid so. She'll be in the South of France. That's her gift from Jon."

She had not come up with an idea of how to make it up to Fiona. She'd hoped she would have a little more time before breaking the news to her. After all, she'd only learned about the change of plans today.

"Well, we can still go can't we," Fiona pouted. "We can make an adventure of it!" The spark and glow returned as instantaneously as it had been lost.

Natalie had entertained similar thoughts earlier but shook her head side-to-side now. "I thought about that honey. But I don't think that would be a good idea. I've never been before and I don't think the first time we go needs to be just the two of us. We'll plan for it another time, I promise."

"But, Mooom, you said we'd go. You're always making promises you don't keep. It's not fair," Fiona sulked.

"I know and I'm really sorry about that, but I'm working on a plan to change all of that. You just have to be patient with me, sweetie."

"I don't wanna be patient, Mom! I'm only seven. I want Christmas!" Fiona shouted in an attitude that was uncharacteristic of her.

Jumping from the table, she ran to her bedroom and slammed the door. Natalie sat staring after her daughter in shock. She had never behaved that way before, and she wasn't certain how to fix it.

A scorching smell suddenly took over the kitchen, accompanied by the smoke alarm. Jumping up from the table, Natalie ran into the kitchen and removed the pot from the stove.

"Oh goodness!" she grumbled, removing the lid and seeing the mess she had created. "Can I get anything right?" she asked aloud, staring up at the ceiling.

Dumping the soup down the garbage disposal, Natalie grabbed the house phone and ordered pizza delivery for dinner.

After cleaning her mess, she returned to the kitchen table and began packing up Fiona's homework. The writing in Fiona's math notebook drew Natalie's attention when she realized it wasn't her math homework, but a letter instead.

Dear Santa,

My Mom works so hard every day for me and for her. She's really tired at the end of every day. I know if my Daddy were here and not in Heaven, she wouldn't work so hard. All I want for Christmas Santa is some time with my Mom. She needs a vacation. Can you please give us that kind of Christmas, Santa? Pretty please? I've been a really good girl all year, and so has Mom.

Signed,

Fiona Noelle Justice

CHAPTER 2

Giggles filled the room as Paul scooped Fiona up in his arms, helping her make the basket.

"No fair!" Brock, one of the middle-schoolers called out.

"What, the fact that a seven-year-old girl just dunked on you?" Paul teased as he set Fiona down.

She bounced the rebounded basketball and shot a saucy grin at the boy.

The game ended, and the other middle-school boys trotted off, teasing their friend. Paul stretched out his large hand, and Fiona placed her smaller one into it.

"Thanks for that, Fi."

"You're welcome," she grinned up at him.

They headed off to the arts and crafts room. That was the deal. If she'd allow him to play basketball with the boys for a half an hour, the two of them would spend the rest of the day creating snowflakes to hang in her mother's floral shop.

Fiona had arrived in the center's van that afternoon wearing a sullen expression. Paul wondered if something had happened in school, but she didn't seem to want to talk about it. She had instantly wanted to go to arts and crafts to create snowflakes. However, Paul had already promised Brock, Wright, Frankie, and a few of the other middle school boys that he would play basketball.

Determined to pull her out of her somber mood, he had made the deal with her. Despite the fact the boys did not agree with her playing, she had been pulled into the game at the end, to shoot the winning shot. With Paul's assistance, of course.

Paul took mentoring seriously. When Allen Copeland, the center's director, first paired him up with Fiona a year ago, he thought the man had made a mistake. Paul had only mentored boys previously. And while he agreed with Allen's initiative that the children needed more positive male role models in their lives, he did not see how his mentorship of a girl would be beneficial to her or him. What was he supposed to do? With the boys, he could play ball, check out boxing matches and car shows, talk trash, and so much more. He could teach them about being a hard-working, stand-up man like his father had taught him. But what could he teach a girl?

Yet, when Allen challenged him to think outside the box, he couldn't back down. He was never one to shy away from a challenge. Now he was glad that he hadn't turned Allen's suggestion down. He absolutely adored Fiona and often thought if he were ever to have a child, he would want a daughter just like her. Their partnership had been good for him and her both.

Paul cut the tip of his paper at an angle while watching Fiona fold her paper in thirds. He could tell she had a lot on her mind. Her eyes were squinted, while her tongue was stuck out slightly between her lips. Little fingers gripped the paper tightly, intent on getting the snowflake just right.

The bright little girl was always happy, but today a somber expression came upon her face as she settled in with Paul in the room. Her dimples had yet to make an appearance, and the twinkle in her eyes was missing.

Paul nodded at Tina, another mentor, as she escorted two other little girls into the room, and sat at a different table.

"That snowflake's sure taking a lot of concentration," Paul observed in an attempt to draw her out.

Fiona only nodded her head and finished her last fold, before picking up her scissors.

"So, are you counting down the days until your trip to New York?" Paul cut away from the sides of the paper, expecting his question to get her to open up.

"We're not going," she replied glumly.

Paul cut the shape at the wrong angle and mangled his poor little snowflake, which caused Fiona to collapse into a fit of giggles.

"Oh, so you think that's funny, huh?" he said, aiming his scissors at her snowflake.

Fiona shrieked and jumped from the table. Paul placed his scissors on the table and used his fingers to imitate the shearing action, chasing her around the room.

Tina smiled at the both of them, shaking her head, while the other girls continued to chat quietly amongst themselves.

After two laps around the room, they both settled back at the table, where Fiona continued working on her snowflake. Paul grabbed another piece of paper and began re-creating a new masterpiece.

"So, why aren't you going?" he asked, returning back to the subject. He knew she needed to discuss it to make her feel better.

"Mom said Aunt Keri canceled, because of some stupid Christmas gift."

"Your mom's sister received a gift that canceled Christmas?"

"No, silly! Christmas isn't canceled. Mom's friend, my Auntie Keri, her fiancé's taking her to France for Christmas. So we can't go to New York," she patiently explained.

"So, what are you two doing for Christmas?"

"Nothing," she continued snipping away at her snowflake.

"Nothing? Who does nothing for Christmas?" As soon as he'd spoken the words, Paul wished he could pull them back into his mouth.

The sad look that crossed her face pierced his heart.

"What will you be doing for Christmas?" she asked in a petulant tone.

"Uh, well, I, uh… see I've got—"

"See, you're not having Christmas either? What's wrong with adults? Christmas is the most important time of the year."

"Oh yeah?" he challenged back. Not because he wanted to challenge her, he simply wanted to hear her theory.

"Uh-huh. My Grandma Pat said that's a time to celebrate the birth of our Savior. She says the day Jesus was born is a time for us to rejoice. It's about love, forgiveness, and family," Fiona pronounced in a matter-of-fact way.

"Your Grandma Pat is a very smart woman. Is that your Mom's mother?"

"No. She's my Dad's Mom. And her and Grampa Gene live in Montana."

"Well, why aren't you spending Christmas with them?"

"Cuz, they're visiting Carson. That's my Uncle Sid and Aunt Lainey's new baby in California."

"Oh, I see," Paul stated, nodding his head and whittling away at his snowflake. It saddened him to think this little girl would be all alone on Christmas, just her and her mother. Natalie was a nice enough lady. Pretty definitely, but a bit overworked if he said so himself.

"So, why are you not having Christmas?" Natalie turned the tables on him.

Paul smiled, thinking the little girl was very observant for her age. She wouldn't let him switch gears so easily.

He shrugged his shoulders. "Well, my parents live in Switzerland, and both of my brothers and my sister will be spending time with their own families. I'll go to my cabin in North Georgia and relax for a few days."

Fiona thought for a minute, then looked at Paul with a serious expression. "Well, maybe you can help Mom and me this year."

"I'd do anything to help you, Fiona. Just name it," Paul offered with a sparkle in his eyes. He wanted to bring Christmas cheer to this little girl. He couldn't think of another person who deserved it more.

"Great! Here's the plan!" Fiona leaned across the table, and cupping her hands around Paul's ear, she began to whisper the details of her plan.

Although Paul's face lit up with glee, as he internalized what she said, he couldn't help but wonder what he had signed himself up for. He wasn't sure that Fiona's mother, Natalie, would go for any of it. But he did not have the heart to disappoint this particular little girl. She'd had enough disappointments over her lifetime, and he simply refused to add to it, especially during this particular time of year.

CHAPTER 3

"Sorry, I'm late again," Natalie gushed on a rushed breath of air. She had swept into the room, bringing the chill with her.

Fiona looked up from the shoebox she had just secured with a ribbon and ran to her mother.

Wrapping her arms tightly around Natalie's waist, Fiona shut her eyes, smiling as Natalie ran her fingers through her long, curly locks.

"Hi honey, how was your day at school?" Fiona greeted, kneeling down to rub noses with her daughter.

"It was great, Mom! I got an 'A' on my math and spelling tests today!"

"Well, that's just wonderful! I'm going to have to hire you at the shop sooner than I thought with all that brainpower you've got," Natalie teased, tousling her daughter's hair.

Fiona giggled. "I've got a surprise for you and Miss Emma, Mom. Well, actually it's for the shop, but you get to enjoy it."

Fiona pulled Natalie's hand as the two of them walked to the table. She grabbed the shoebox and thrust it into her mother's hands.

Natalie shook the box and pressed her ear against it to listen.

With a smile of delight, she said "Hmm, I wonder what's in here. Must be something special to be wrapped so prettily."

The shoebox was metallic blue, secured with a white bow, sprinkled with sparkling silver glitter.

"Open it!"

"Are you sure I don't need to wait until I'm with Miss Emma?" Natalie teased with a smile.

"No, Mom! Open it!" Fiona pressed her hands together in glee.

"Okay, if you insist," Natalie remarked, setting the box on the table and untying the simple bow.

Pulling one snowflake out after another, she marveled at the six-pointed paper snowflakes gathered in the box. Some were sprinkled with silver glitter, while others were not. She was fascinated with the intricate details of each snowflake.

"These are absolutely beautiful, Fi! Where'd you get these from?"

"Mr. Paul helped me make them," Fiona shared, pointing at Paul standing in another corner of the room with his arms crossed over his chest.

Paul took that as his cue to intrude upon the moment, and began to walk over to them.

"You two must have been working on these for weeks."

"No, we actually just started today. It was a project Fiona wanted to take on, and she insisted we do this for your shop," Paul explained.

"You did these all today?" Natalie asked in bewilderment.

"Yeah, we've had several hours to work on them," Paul replied.

"Oh, I'm so sorry about that," Natalie stated, pressing her hand against her chest. "Um, honey, can you please go get your things, while I speak with Mr. Paul for a moment," she expressed, turning to her daughter with loving eyes.

"Okay, Mom!" Fiona skipped away to do what her mother asked.

Turning back to Paul, she released a sigh. "I apologize for being so late over this last week. But, things have just been busy at the shop, and I haven't been able to get away. With the holiday season approaching it's just...madness. My orders have ramped up, and there's just me and one other person running things. I know that Fiona's been spending a lot of time with you lately, but is it possible that she could remain in your care few more days in the week, and a little later than normal? I know I usually pick her up by five. But I just can't take a break from the shop to pick her up and bring her back. It's just been so crazy, and I can't believe—"

Natalie absently rubbed at her temples before running her hands back through her hair, externalizing her stress.

"Say no more, it's my pleasure," Paul stated, holding up a hand to cut her outburst short.

"I'll pay you—"

"There's no need to pay me. I'll do it. Fiona's a delight, and I don't mind helping you two through the holiday season."

"That'll be great. Now, it'll be every day at least until eight. I know that usually you aren't here on Wednesdays and Mondays. But, she hasn't quite connected with Tina and the other mentors the way she has with you. I know it's asking a bit much, but do you think it'd be possible to—"

He held his hand up once more to stem the flow of her words. "She may have to accompany me to work on a few of those days, but Miss Fiona is no problem at all," he smiled at her, as he crossed his arms over his chest.

Natalie's eyes traveled from his soft, piercing eyes to the thick waves of his bulging biceps. She imagined that his role as what she assumed to be a fitness coach allowed him the flexibility to take Fiona with him. Momentarily lost in thought, she wondered how many hours he had to spend in the gym to get the tone achieved in his body.

"Okay?"

"Um, huh? I'm sorry, my mind is a million miles away, and I was thinking of some things I need to take care of," Natalie stated breathlessly.

"I said I can pick her up from the shop on Saturdays since the center doesn't open until noon. That should make things a bit easier for you. Are you sure you're okay?" Paul asked, placing a hand against her forehead. "You look a little feverish."

Natalie gulped and flinched at his touch. It felt as if a slight jolt of electricity had run through her. She tried to recollect her composure while wondering why his simple touch had that effect on her.

Paul's eyebrow furrowed in concern; her movement did not go unnoticed by him.

"I'm ready, Mom," Fiona announced, breaking the tension of the moment.

"Okay, honey. Well, um, Paul, thanks again for all of your help. And yeah, sure, that offer, uh, that offer will be just fine. Do you know where my shop's located?"

"Nope, but I'm sure I won't have any trouble finding it."

"Okay, thanks again. Sweetie, say bye to Mr. Paul. We've gotta get home," Natalie stated, grasping hold of her daughter's hand and rushing towards the door.

"Mom, slow down, what's the matter?" Fiona asked, waving goodbye to Paul as they hurried towards the door.

"Nothing, honey, Mom's just got a lot to do tonight."

"Hey, why don't I walk you two to the car. It's dark outside and Allen and his wife Deborah, are about to lock this place up anyway. We were the last two remaining."

"Um, we'll be fine, Paul," Natalie stated, attempting to leave his presence as quickly as possible.

"Mom, you always said we have to be safe in the dark. Doesn't that go for Mr. Paul, too? Doesn't he need a buddy to walk outside with?" Fiona asked, pulling on Natalie's hand to slow her down.

Natalie groaned internally as she saw Paul grab his coat and head their way.

"You're right, sweetie, I did." She looked at Paul and smiled apologetically as the three of them made their way to the center's front doors.

It was funny how she had never paid much attention to him before. She couldn't deny he was an extremely attractive man. Yet, Natalie didn't have time for that at this point in her life. It was a struggle just to make time for Fiona after her endless days and evenings at the shop. She refused to compromise another moment of time with her daughter, for the idea of dating. Not that he had asked her. Not even that he had expressed any mutual interest in her, but the idea kept sneaking up inside of her head.

"Miss Fiona, you have a magical night, Princess, your chariot awaits," Paul stated, opening the unlocked rear door of Natalie's, black Honda CR-V.

"Paul, you're so silly!" Fiona exclaimed, strapping into her seatbelt.

Natalie stared at him over the top of the vehicle and smiled, as she mouthed the words "thank you."

He simply nodded, waited for her to get in, then crossed the parking lot to his own vehicle. Natalie drove away with a small smile fighting to break free while girlhood thoughts of kings, queens, and princesses danced in her head.

"Why are you freaking out about this thing?"

"Emma, you don't get it. He's a PE coach," Natalie huffed into the phone, as she walked to her bedroom from the kitchen, armed with a mug of tea.

She had planned to settle down on her laptop and pay some invoices. But after looking at the computer screen for a good ten minutes and getting no work done, she knew she needed to talk about her distraction. She had put Fiona to bed half an hour earlier, and after checking in on her, she knew it was safe to talk on the phone.

"So, what's that got to do with anything?"

"We have nothing in common. I have to think about Fi's future. If and that's a big 'if' I decide to have a relationship, it has to be with someone I can build a future with. They have to be financially stable, and I just don't think Paul can offer me that."

Emma blew a frustrated breath into the phone. "Look, you can't be picky when it comes to love, Nat."

"Whoa! Back your horses up, sugar. Who said anything about love? Anyway, I think we're getting in way over our heads. I don't even know if the guy even finds me attractive. He hasn't expressed it if he has."

"Then, why don't you tell him how you're feeling?" Emma encouraged.

"You're a hopeless romantic, you know that? Besides, I'm not having feelings. It was just the strangest thing that when he touched me, an electric jolt surged through me. Or something like that."

"Mmm, I'm willing to bet he felt the same thing you did. Nat, it's the twenty-first century. There's surely nothing wrong with a woman approaching a man first and making the first move."

"I don't have moves, Emma! You know what? Just forget I said anything. I just couldn't get it off my mind and needed to talk with someone about it. I thought I could talk to you, but you're trying to marry me off for love's sake," Natalie complained.

"I just think that you might be in for a Christmas miracle, and there's nothing wrong with being open to it," Emma continued.

"You know what? I think that's enough for the night. It's time for me and you both to get off this phone. I'll see you in the morning," Natalie stated, clicking the red icon to end the call, without waiting for Emma to say goodbye.

After another fruitless fifteen minutes of trying to pay invoices, Natalie slammed her laptop closed and placed it in her work bag. She stood up and started back toward the living room.

"Mom?"

Natalie quickly turned to her daughter's bedroom. Pushing the door open, she walked to her bed and sat down beside her.

"What's wrong, baby? Did you have a bad dream?"

Fiona shook her head back and forth on the pillow.

"Then what's wrong? I thought you were asleep."

"Mom, do you believe in Christmas miracles?" Fiona asked, sitting up on her elbows in bed. Her large, round, hazel eyes sparkled in the darkened room, with the night light casting a glow around them.

"Why, yes, honey, I do. Why'd you ask that?" Natalie thought back on her and Emma's recent conversation. Irony? She wasn't sure, but she shook her head before allowing any ideas to form.

"Just wondering. Mom, if Santa brought you a great big surprise, would you be mad?"

Not sure where this conversation was heading, Natalie knew it was time to stop the conversation. She didn't want her daughter to experience any further disappointments than she already had.

"No, I wouldn't be mad. But, I'll be mad if you don't go to sleep. We'll both be late for school and work in the morning. Goodnight, honey," Natalie stated, leaning in to kiss her daughter's forehead.

"G'nite, Mom," Fiona whispered, lying back against the pillow, closing her eyes with a slight smile on her face.

Natalie returned to her own room, wondering what that conversation had been about. Her concern only lasted momentarily as her thoughts returned to Paul. She lay in bed, staring at the ceiling, wondering if he were the reason her daughter had begun believing in Christmas magic. From the little she knew of the man over the last year, he appeared to be genuine in his love for children, and very nice. But he lacked the ambition she wanted in a partner. Natalie needed someone whose zest to succeed matched her own the way Dan's had.

Thinking back to her late husband brought on a flood of tears, spilling from her eyes for the first time in a long time. She wondered if she would experience that type of love ever again. She knew her heart had grown lonely through the years, and she had attempted to bury the emptiness and heartache with long hours building her business. Yet, she had lost Natalie-the-woman somewhere along the way. She wondered what that would feel like again...to be loved and held by a man.

CHAPTER 4

$\mathcal{W}$ith only two weeks left until Christmas, special operation "Perfect Christmas" was, in effect, thanks to special agent Fiona and special agent, Paul.

"Well hello, Miss Fiona," Renée Underwood, Paul's secretary greeted the little girl.

"Hi, Mrs. Renée," Fiona greeted, removing her jacket and handing it to the grandmotherly looking woman.

"Look what I've brought for you today." Opening her desk drawer she removed a large multicolored lollipop and handed it to Fiona.

Paul smiled, watching Fiona's eyes grow large as an expression of joy took over her face.

"What do you say, Fi?" he asked, opening his office door.

"Thank you, Mrs. Renée," Fiona stated, hurriedly removing the plastic wrapping of the lollipop to get her first taste of the fruity treat.

Paul paced back and forth in his office and made a few business calls to check on sales, before settling down in his chair.

Fiona knew she was expected to finish her homework during that time, and she took advantage of it. Once Paul finished his calls, they would both need their complete attention focused on the most important business of all.

"Alright, are you ready?" Paul asked, firing up his desktop.

"Yes," Fiona replied, dutifully removing her green spiraled notebook and purple pencil from her backpack.

"So, what's first on the agenda today?" he asked, with a serious expression in his eyes. He knew that this was important to Fiona. He had not lied when he said he would do anything to help her. Not certain when it had begun, but Paul realized that he cared about Fiona very much; more than he ever thought possible. When the holidays were over, and life went back to normal, he would miss these extra hours he spent with her.

While he was disappointed that her mother couldn't find the time to spend with her, he was glad that he was blessed enough to be the one to fill in temporarily. Not that he blamed Natalie much. He knew that it took a lot to make a business successful. He admired her courage to do it, especially while raising her daughter alone. Not for the first time in the last few weeks, his mind wandered. He had begun to wonder what it would be like to have a family of his own.

"You're not paying any attention," Fiona exclaimed in exasperation.

"Sorry, you're right. Now where were we?" Paul asked, refocusing his attention with a hint of a smile.

"Paul, if we're gonna get this right, you're gonna have to focus!" Fiona scolded.

He pursed his lips to keep from laughing. Nodding his head, he encouraged her to read her list.

"Okay, so, we've called Emma, and she's taken the order for the flowers," Fiona read.

"Are you sure they'll be ready in time?"

Fiona visibly bristled at his teasing statement. "I told you, Mom and Miss Emma always get their orders right and on time."

He nodded his head once more. "Duly noted. I've hired the landscapers who will take care of all the lighting in the cabin."

"Good. Did you send the menu out yet?" Fiona frowned, biting down on her bottom lip and studying her list.

"Check."

"Bought the decorations?"

"Check."

"Created the Christmas music list on Spotify?"

He smirked once more, recalling the memorable night he had last night, working at home and making the Christmas playlist. He had to admit, some of the songs made him feel like he was growing a soft spot for all this holiday magic. He had never been one for romance, preferring to date openly. But last night some of the songs had him thinking of curling up by the fireplace at his cabin with a certain someone. The startling part was that it was Natalie's face that kept popping up whenever he had those thoughts.

"Earth to Paul...Earth to Paul," Fiona called, tapping her pencil against the arm of her chair.

"Oh, sorry. Yes, I've got the music list created."

"Good. So, we still need to buy the Christmas tree and wrap gifts. Did you get the wrapping paper and bows?"

"Uh, no, I forgot—"

"Paaaaul, we don't have much time. Christmas is only two weeks away!" Fiona exclaimed, slapping her forehead.

He could no longer contain his laughter. It bubbled up and outwards in an uncontrollable expression of joy. This little girl who had always been so filled with joy was completely taken over by these Christmas plans.

"What's so funny?"

"You. I need you to relax. Everything's going to be just fine. This will be the best Christmas ever, for both you and your mom."

"Promise?"

Touching his thumb and pinky finger together, while holding the other three fingers upright, he promised. "Scout's honor."

"Okay, I'll hold you to that," Fiona stated.

"Good, because we've got a change of plans."

"Oh yeah? What's that?" she asked, setting the notebook and pencil on his desk.

"Grab your jacket. You're going with me to pick out a tree!" Paul stated, scooting his desk chair back and standing up.

He walked to the coat rack in the corner of his office and grabbed his suede, caramel trench coat.

"Yes!" Fiona exclaimed, doing a fist pump, before grabbing her jacket.

An hour later a bundled up Fiona and Paul found themselves wrapped in blankets and sitting on bales of hay inside of a wagon at Yule Forest. Paul inhaled the scent of the pine trees lining both sides of the trail they traversed. It smelled like Christmas, and he couldn't help but smile.

His original intention had been to come pick up a tree, and head back to the office. However, once Fiona spotted the wagon pulling loads of people, there was no denying her. She had pleaded and practically insisted upon a hayride. And as much as he knew he needed to get her back to the office, he could not tell her no.

His heart pounded thunderously in his chest when he said yes, and her face lit up with glee. He couldn't help but think he'd do anything a thousand times over to keep that look on her face. Although he had always been fond of Fiona, she had claimed a special place in his heart when she had been faced with the possibility of no Christmas.

Paul had even called upon his family for a few special requests. His desire to give this particular beautiful, overworked single mother, and her bright, beautiful child the best Christmas either of them had ever experienced was starting to preoccupy his thoughts more than he intended. He had even begun to think of ways to help Natalie grow her business. It would mean more time with her daughter, which was all that Fiona wanted.

As they scaled up the hill towards the end of their trip, the children on board the wagon began to moan and groan with disappointment.

"Just one more time, pullleez," Fiona begged the driver, who smiled warmly at her, as Paul helped her down from the wagon.

"Well, that's up to your father, young lady. If he chooses to let you ride again, I'd be much obliged."

Fiona turned sad, hazel eyes on Paul. "Pulleeez," she pleaded, both hands clasped in front of her.

He had not even had a chance to deny the fact that he was not her father. Then he noticed she never corrected the driver herself. The only thing he knew was that there was no way he could tell her no.

"We really need to get back. Your mom's going to—"

"Mom won't mind. Pulleez," she started up once again with the sorrowful eyes.

A mother jumped down from the wagon and grabbed her toddler in her arms. "Looks like she's got you wrapped around her finger, Dad. It's Christmas…you can't deny her another ride," she teased, winking at Paul.

Hanging his head, Paul could not resist the slight tugging on his hand as Fiona led him back to the wagon.

"Alright. This is the last time, and then we have to cut a tree. Is that understood young lady?"

"Yes!" she shrieked.

"Nope, it's too short," Fiona said, shaking her head and striking out what Paul thought must be the seventeenth tree they'd considered.

"Too fat, too short, too tall, too thin, too green, do you happen to have an idea of the perfect tree in your head?" Paul asked, trudging behind Fiona in the Christmas tree patch.

"Yep! And it's right there!" Fiona's finger led the way as she raced off towards a towering evergreen.

Paul smiled and nodded his head appreciatively. Grabbing the tag that hung from the tree, he identified it as a Carolina Sapphire, standing approximately twelve feet tall.

"It smells beautiful!" Fiona inhaled deeply with her eyes closed as if it enhanced the smell.

Paul followed suit, noting the lemon and mint scented aroma. "It does. I think your mom just might like this tree," Paul noted, fingering the lacy, blue-green foliage, which still held its woody, spherical cones.

"Good job, Fi!" Paul exclaimed, high-fiving her.

"You and your daughter have a good eye for trees," noted an attendant who came to stand beside them, saw in hand.

"She's uh—"

"Hey, we get to cut that ourselves, Mister?" Fiona interrupted, squeezing Paul's hand.

He looked down into her little face and saw something that triggered his heartstrings. No words could express what he knew was in her heart. She just wanted for a moment to pretend she had a father. And Paul wanted to give her that moment. As he watched her smile up at the attendant, it hit him that he wished he could give that to her for a lifetime.

Paul's truck was loaded down with the gigantic Christmas tree, decorations, and wrapping paper and bows, which Fiona happily checked off the to-do list. They pulled into the parking lot of his office building, which shared space with the recreation center.

Before Paul could even come around to her side, Fiona had grabbed the thermos of hot chocolate, opened the door, and hopped down.

"That was the best—"

"Excuse me! Where have you been?" An angry Natalie demanded, crossing the parking lot to confront Paul.

"I was out doing a little holiday shopping," he explained, pointing over his shoulder to the bed of his truck.

"I asked you to watch my daughter a few extra hours, and you're out gallivanting across town with her? I've been calling you and you didn't even answer your phone. Do you know I've been scared out of my mind?"

"I'm uh...I'm sorry, I didn't—"

"Mom, we were out buying a tree for Paul, and I got to ride the hayride, and—"

"Fiona! Please grab your backpack and get in the car now!" she demanded in an angry tone.

Paul reached out his hand to touch Natalie's wrist, but she backed up away from him.

"Look, I apologize for not getting her back on time. I really tried to stick to a schedule, but she wanted—"

"She wanted?...She wanted? Paul, Fiona is a seven-year-old girl. She doesn't get to make decisions for herself. That's why I asked you to watch her for me because she needs a responsible adult around when I can't be. Obviously, I was mistaken to think that you were the one who I could trust. Surely, you're not blaming your irresponsible actions on my daughter!" Natalie snapped, crossing her arms in front of her.

"Look, I said that I apologize. Perhaps, it wasn't the best judgment to stay out as long as we did. And as far as my phone is concerned, my battery died a while ago and I forgot my charger," he said, throwing his arms up in the air.

"Another irresponsible thing on your list. You need to grow up, Paul, and not make excuses for yourself."

"And you need to take time out to spend with your daughter, instead of making your business the most important thing in your world. Maybe, if you made time for her you wouldn't have to ask an irresponsible adult to be a parent for you!" he shouted back.

He had been attempting to hold in his frustration, but this woman was coming at him with full guns blazing.

"Really? You? You're going to judge me? You, the unambitious, know-nothing-about-business, gym rat? When you walk a day in my shoes, then you come back and talk to me!" Natalie raged, before stalking away to her car.

Paul could not utter another word. He had not meant to stoop to that level. He just felt the need to defend himself against her senseless attacks. He couldn't understand what had her so up in arms. After all, she had been the one to approach him about watching Fiona, not the other way around. Although of course, he had benefited from the time spent with her as well. He simply wished he could remove the look of hurt in her eyes, as she leaned forward from the back seat watching the exchange between him and her mother.

CHAPTER 5

For the rest of the weekend, Natalie guiltily replayed her interaction with Paul. She hadn't meant to spew such mean things at him, and he hadn't deserved her lowly attack on his character. Friday had been a really tough day and to top it off, she had received the discouraging news that her investors had backed out. With one phone call, all of her plans about growing her business had fallen through, and she was back at step one. That meant no extra time with Fiona.

As much as she loved her business, Fiona was her first love, despite the things Paul had said. And Natalie just didn't know how much longer her business could hold out if she had to keep running it the way she had...the only way she knew how. There was no way she could go another year like this previous one, where she was working around the clock and barely had time for her daughter, let alone herself.

Paul's words, although hurtful had been truthful. She did need to spend more time with Fiona, and not make her small child feel as if the shop was more important. After she had received the news about the investors that Friday afternoon, Emma suggested Natalie leave early to spend the day with Fiona. She had taken her up on the suggestion.

After frantically calling Paul's cell phone and receiving no response, and then being told by the center director that he had not been there that day, she had panicked. It had been a two and a half hour wait before he pulled in. One of the teens had told her that he had seen Fiona get into Paul's truck with him earlier. With only that string of hope, she had waited in the parking lot for his return. Whether she could rationalize it or not, Natalie still had deep-rooted fears about the people she loved driving off to do some mundane errand and never coming home.

Her worry and frustration had boiled over and spilled out on Paul when he arrived. The result was that Fiona had sulked around at the shop all day Saturday, only speaking to Emma. Mother and daughter had both remained in their bedrooms avoiding each other on Sunday, only speaking when absolutely necessary.

Now that Monday had arrived, Fiona was once more at the shop with Natalie and Emma. She had refused to allow her to return to the center. It was more out of embarrassment than anything else. She couldn't bear to face Paul after her outburst on Friday.

"Fi, have you done your homework?" Natalie asked for the third time, seeing Fiona sitting in the window seat staring out the shop windows.

Fiona refused to answer verbally and simply nodded her head.

"I've got some work for you to do in my office if you'd like to help me," Natalie offered.

"No thanks. I'm gonna work with Emma on some arrangements," Fiona stated, hopping up off the seat and walking towards where Emma worked at a bench.

Emma turned towards Natalie and shrugged her shoulders. When Fiona busied herself with filling the vases with little pebbles, Emma turned back to Natalie.

"Call him," she mouthed.

Fiona squinted her eyes, crossed her arms, and shook her head. She refused to apologize, because, in her mind, she had not done any wrong. Paul should have called and informed her of their whereabouts.

Natalie returned to her office and slammed the door behind her.

Slumping into her chair, she placed her forehead in one hand and fiddled with her mouse with the other.

Spreadsheets opened up on the screen, and she stared sightlessly at them. She wanted nothing to do with work at the moment. Why couldn't she just escape and do something fun with Fiona? Wasn't that one of the perks of owning your own business? Perhaps she would take Fiona to buy a tree for Christmas. They could spend the evening decorating it, and watch some old movies, Natalie mused.

Jumping up from her seat she rushed back to the front of the shop.

"Hey, Fi! How about you and I go out and purchase a Christmas tree? We don't have one at home, and I thought we could decorate it tonight and watch some old Christmas movies," Natalie suggested.

Fiona looked over her shoulder at Natalie and shook her head.

"Come on, give me a chance! Why're you being so stubborn about this, Fi?"

"You didn't have to be so mean to him. You never listened! You never listen anymore. He was worried the whole day you'd be upset, and he wanted to bring me back. I was the one who wanted to do all those things. I just wanted to have a fun day doing Christmas stuff like my friends at school! I just wanted one day to pretend I was having Christmas fun with my dad!" Fiona shouted, and ran to the back of the shop.

Emma's shoulders drooped, as she watched Fiona squirrel away in the rear of the shop.

"Well, you handled that one well," Emma remarked, with a raised eyebrow.

"You know, I could do without your sarcasm for once," Natalie retorted.

"She does have a point you know. You don't listen. Look, Nat," Emma stated when Natalie dropped her head in sorrow. "I get that it's hard on you. But it's hard on that kid, too. She doesn't remember her dad, and her mom is busy making a living and doesn't have a lot of spare time. She was finding a little bit of joy this holiday season, hanging with Paul. And you've taken that away from her, too. I mean, don't get me wrong, he should have called first, but nobody's perfect.

All of us make mistakes from time to time. Just because you can't be with her the way you want and you're feeling guilty about it, don't punish her."

"Em, I'm not punishing her. I just have to make sure she's in good hands," Natalie argued back.

"And you know darn well she is. He's built a good relationship with her over the last year. You've bragged about that countless times. Just because he said something that you're afraid to deal with doesn't mean you get to punish him or her. Besides, I personally think the real reason you're pushing him away, is because you're afraid you like him," Emma stated, sticking her tongue out like a little kid and turning back to her arrangements.

"Not hardly!" Natalie retorted and stomped out of the shop.

Fiona sat in the shop's back garden, kneeling beside the rose bushes. She held one in her hand, which she was picking petals from.

Fiona knew better than to pick her mother's roses, but Natalie knew this was not the time to chastise her for that. Instead, she cautiously approached her daughter.

"Fi, I'm sorry for how I reacted on Friday. It's just that…it's just that I was so worried about you. I'd received some unexpected news about the business, so I left here hoping to spend a little time with you. It caught me off guard when you weren't at the center, and I couldn't reach Paul. I was scared and didn't know what to think. You know you're my favorite girl right?"

Fiona nodded her head and continued plucking petals.

Natalie sat on the bench beside the rose bush next to her daughter's kneeling frame. Gathering Fiona's long, brown hair into a bunch, she began to plait it into a French braid.

"It's my duty to make sure that you're safe at all times. I was entrusted with only one of you, and I have to do my job well. It's what your dad would have wanted. It's what God expects of me. Can you understand that?"

Fiona once more nodded her head and held the rose to her nose to sniff the remaining petals.

"Look, I know you miss not having a dad. Your father was a great guy, and he would have been so proud of you. But you can't go around pretending that Paul is your dad, either."

"Why? He doesn't mind!" Fiona defended, hopping up, causing the half-finished braid to unravel.

"How do you know that?"

"Because I just know," Fiona huffed.

"Sweetie, Paul's a very nice man. But honey, I'm sure there's someone very special in his life. One day he'll get married and have a family of his own, and he won't have a lot of time for all of the kids at the center anymore," Natalie explained.

"He'll always have time for me, Mom," Fiona disputed.

"Sweetie," Natalie stated, reaching out to caress her daughter's face, "I don't want you to get hurt."

"You don't know Paul, Mom. If you did, you'd know he'd never hurt me."

Natalie couldn't afford to say another word after hearing the conviction in her daughter's voice. She wavered in her decision to take Fiona back to the center. But before she did, she would have to talk to Paul and ask him to stop encouraging her childish fantasies.

"Okay, honey. I believe you. But in the meantime, why don't we go out and pick out a tree for the house?"

"Can Paul come?"

"Excuse me?" Natalie asked, her eyebrow arching.

"He's the best tree chopper in the world! Besides, he and I have an eye for the best trees. The man at the tree farm said so!" Fiona declared as if that made it fact.

"He may have to work, honey. We can't just interrupt his life and expect him to come running," Natalie patiently explained.

"Just call him, Mom. He won't mind, I promise. Puh-leeze," Fiona begged.

Natalie considered Fiona's plea momentarily. Weighing the pros and cons, she decided to make that call. She would have to swallow her pride and apologize for her behavior. If he were unable to make it that would work out in Natalie's favor. If he did come, it would provide her the opportunity to warn him about encouraging Fiona's imagination. Either way, she would win brownie points with her daughter, and get back in her good graces, Natalie figured.

Natalie stood from the bench and looked at Fiona's fawn-like eyes. They were hopeful and faith-filled.

This jerk better not let my daughter down, Natalie fumed inwardly.

"I told you he's the best tree chopper, Mom," Fiona declared, standing close to Natalie.

"Yes, you did," Natalie remarked broadly with a smile, rubbing her daughter's soft hair.

"And I told *you* that you have the best eye for trees," Paul added, smiling over his shoulder at Fiona.

Natalie had swallowed her pride and called Paul offering an apology. Fiona insisting they return to the same place Paul had taken her, and he had agreed to drive south and meet them at Yule Forest.

"Yes, you did!" Fiona smiled proudly before turning to her mother. "Mom, can we please go see the animals, since we can't do the hayride?"

"No, ma'am. I told you earlier that we were here for one reason and one reason only," Natalie stated, standing firm in her decision to not take a hayride, or allow Fiona to spend time at the petting zoo.

"But, Mooom, it's Christmas," Fiona whined.

"Yeah, Mom, it's Christmas," Paul stated, taking Fiona's side. He stood and wiped his hands together, removing dust that clung to them from handling the tree.

Natalie frowned, not liking the turn this was taking. She did not give her daughter whatever she wanted just to assuage her guilt for not being available all the time. But it seemed as if this was something Paul did.

"Paul, I don't give Fiona whatever she wants, just because she begs, and put on that cute pouty face," Natalie said, softly pinching her daughter's cheek and kissing her on the forehead. "My final answer is no."

"That's your final answer?" Paul asked, with a smirk on his face.

Not sure what he was up to, she narrowed her eyes and tilted her head slightly. "My final answer."

"Well, it's getting late. I guess I'd better follow you two back home so we can get this tree set up," Paul replied, pulling his coat sleeve up and looking at his watch.

"Yeah, we've got an early morning tomorrow, kiddo." Natalie placed Fiona's hat back on her head and kneeled down to close the top two buttons on her coat.

Noticing the look of sadness in her daughter's eyes, she said, "Hey, what's wrong? We'll get decorations tomorrow and decorate this tree. But tonight, we've gotta go honey."

Fiona nodded her head and looked to Paul.

"Hey, isn't the Grant Park Coffeehouse near you?"

"Yeah," Natalie answered in a hesitant manner. "Why?"

"Oh, no reason. I just thought I'd drop by and get some apple cider. I haven't had any in a while, and they have the best."

"Mom, can we please go, too?" Fiona asked, perking back up.

"Honey, I just told you—"

"But please? Misty always gives me the candy cane with my hot chocolate. And you said you loved their apple cider, too," the little girl reasoned.

Biting back a sigh, Natalie rolled her eyes and muttered, "Sure." She completely missed the wink exchanged between Paul and Fiona. "But we can't stay out too late!" she warned them both.

CHAPTER 6

The days were ticking by faster than Paul or Fiona could mark them off the calendar. Natalie had agreed that he could once again watch Fiona. For his part, he consented to keep his phone with him and always let her know where they were whenever they weren't at the center. That was somewhat of a challenge. Fiona had convinced him that they could not always let Natalie know where they were, or it would spoil the plan; especially when they shopped for gifts.

Now that all of the presents had been purchased, and the decorations were in place, he still wasn't certain how to convince Natalie to visit his cabin for Christmas. Their conversations had picked up in pace, and become a bit easier over the last week, yet, they still mainly focused on discussing Fiona's school performance and how she interacted with the other kids at the center. Sometimes they would get off on a tangent and find themselves talking or laughing over shared commonalities.

In those moments, Paul felt himself bonding with Natalie. He wasn't sure if it was the shared interest in Fiona's well-being, or something special. He was certainly attracted to her physically, though he didn't quite understand the intense spiritual draw that he felt as well. It was as if he could see beyond the closed-off woman who was working so hard to do what she felt needed to be done. He could sense that she had swallowed and buried so much hurt and pain to manage it. It was as if her mind was working a million miles a minute all the time just trying to make everything work. But the rare moments where they got to just talk and just "be" he saw the happy, hopeful, fun-loving woman that he believed she truly was. The woman that she either had forgotten she was, or had decided she was no longer allowed to be. Whatever it was, he admitted to himself that he liked it. He liked her. Her spirit, her vitality, her humor, and her honest heart. If only he could convince her to spend time at the cabin, perhaps he could help her break down some of those walls and get to know the real her better.

"Hey there, kiddo!" Natalie greeted when Fiona burst through the shop doors.

Paul stood back as Natalie picked Fiona up in her arms hugging her close. She inhaled the scent of her daughter's hair and pressed a kiss to it. Something tugged at his heart as he watched mother and daughter express their love for one another.

"So, how was your day?" he asked Natalie when Fiona jumped down and ran to the back office.

"Busy, but that's always good. We've finally got everything set for the holiday deliveries. Emma's taking off to spend time with her family starting tomorrow and won't be back until Tuesday."

Paul noticed the hint of sadness in her voice and had the impulse to do something to eliminate it.

"What do you have planned?"

"Oh, Fi and I will cook on Christmas Eve and open gifts on Christmas day. That's about it. Later that day I'll probably sketch out some new ideas for my business while she plays with her toys. What about you?" she asked, grabbing a spray bottle and spritzing the counters to wash them off.

"Same as you. Probably work on a few things I've got planned for the New Year. That's about it," he remarked, attempting to force a little sadness into his words as well.

He smiled inwardly when he realized it worked. She stopped wiping the counter and looked up at him in disbelief.

"What about family? Don't you have any? Aren't you spending it with them?"

He shrugged his shoulders in a nonchalant manner. "I'm the only single one out the group. Everyone else is married with kids and live in different states. My parents live in Switzerland, so it's just me. What about you? Don't you have family?"

"Well, err, I…uh…well, my father doesn't really believe in Christmas. He's kind of a Scrooge. He owns a bar down in Florida, and that's where he spends his days. My mom, she's off gallivanting the world with her newest millionaire husband."

"Oh."

"Yeah, that's a story for another day." Natalie stared beyond his shoulder, before continuing. "I miss those Christmases of long ago, sitting around a fire telling stories on Christmas Eve. Cooking in the kitchen with my mom, aunts, and grandmother. Opening presents with my cousins on Christmas day," Natalie reminisced.

"That sounds similar to my Christmases. Didn't you have any siblings?"

"No, I'm an only child. When my grandmother died when I was thirteen, Christmas died with her. My parents divorced the next year, and I alternated between living with my mom and dad."

"Wow! That must've been hard. We had Christmas every year as a family until I went off to college. Once I graduated, my parents moved to Switzerland, my mother's homeland. Then I just kinda had Christmas with friends and sometimes with my sister and her family, or one of my brothers. Except for the last two years," Paul explained.

"What happened the last two years?"

"Work. You know how that is," he mumbled. "What've you got planned tonight?"

"Nothing. I thought Fiona and I would head home, grab some pizza, and watch a movie."

"That sounds like a boring night," he teased.

"Why, do you have something better in mind?" she quipped playfully back at him.

"As a matter-of-fact, I do." Natalie raised her eyebrows slightly as he went on. "You see, I need a little Christmas in my life, and I was wondering if two beautiful ladies would join me tonight for a visit to a very special place," he invited, with a charming smile.

"And that would be?"

"Atlanta Botanical Gardens," he replied.

"Yippee!" shouted a little voice, from the back.

Paul fought back a smile while watching Natalie's raised eyebrow turn into concern.

"Young lady, are you back there eavesdropping?"

"No, ma'am."

"You know how I feel about eavesdropping right?" Natalie called out once more.

"It isn't polite," Fiona yelled back.

"Good." Natalie chuckled lightly without letting her daughter see; then she looked thoughtfully between Paul and Fiona taking a minute to think. She turned toward the back where Fiona was and said in a matter-of-fact tone, "Well, now that you're abreast of what's going on, grab your jacket. I guess we'll escort Mr. Paul to the Atlanta Botanical Gardens."

It had been such a long time since the Natalie and Fiona had visited the gardens together. Though Natalie realized that she had never visited it at Christmastime, even before she had Fiona. Garden Lights, Holiday Nights was an amazing event hosted annually by the Atlanta Botanical Gardens.

"What a fantastic place this transitions into at night. I never could have imagined," Natalie said dreamily to Paul. She looked around in wonder, taking in the lights strung busily overhead, making it look as if the entire world was encased in a soft glow.

"Oh wow! Mom, look. Isn't she beautiful?" Fiona exclaimed,

gawking at a twenty-five foot sculpted foliage of a goddess in thoughtful repose.

"Yes, she's even more beautiful with the lights than she is all year round," Natalie marveled. This piece was the star of the garden's exhibit, and Natalie had seen her in countless brochures and advertisements. As they made their way deeper in, the duo looked like fairies fluttering from exhibit to exhibit, pointing and reacting with glee.

Paul watched the two take in the twinkling ambiance and was thankful that he had the opportunity to experience this with them. Coming here had been one of his favorite wintertime experiences as a little kid. Sharing it with his family had been incredibly special, but tonight's experience almost seemed enchanted.

When he first brought the idea up to Fiona, she had assured him that her mother would love it. Anything related to gardens struck a special chord with Natalie. Paul could now tell that was true just by the way her eyes lit up as they toured the gardens.

"Have you guys never been here during the holiday season before?" he asked, pushing his hands deeper into his pockets to ward off the desire to grab her hand in his.

"No. It's a busy season for me, and unfortunately I just never made time," Natalie replied, unable to turn her gaze from the mystical lady before her.

The sculptured foliage shaped in the form of a woman sported tresses highlighted by turquoise, violet, and white lights. The sound of the water cascading through her hands, and the waterfalls in front of her, added to the serenity of the garden.

"Christmas is such a magical and beautiful season. I wish everyone had the chance to be fully immersed in it. Not to mention it's all about our Lord and about love, isn't it? It's the perfect time to be with family and friends. People have commercialized the season so much, we've become infatuated with how many sales we can make, and how business is doing, and all these otherworldly ideas. But it's a time we're supposed to open ourselves up to life, right?"

Natalie smiled shyly up at Paul, before turning away to gape at the beauty of the gardens once more.

He felt a bit embarrassed, not sure what had come over him, causing him to wax philosophical.

Natalie looked up at Paul and whispered. "You're absolutely right."

He stared at her lips, not quite hearing the words. He couldn't help but wonder if they were as soft as they appeared to be. He wanted to know if they tasted like the light vanilla scent that tended to cling to her at all times. Paul found himself searching her eyes, wondering what she was thinking. As the seconds ticked, he realized that she too had difficulty tearing her gaze away from him.

"Mom, Paul, let's go see the carolers!" Fiona exclaimed, pulling both of their hands in the opposite direction.

And just like that, the moment was gone, and they were both thrust back into reality.

They continued to tour the grounds and enjoy the starlit night with the other visitors. By the time they made their way to where the carolers stood serenading, they could both tell Fiona was sleepy.

"Honey, we'll leave after the carolers finish," Natalie stated.

"Mm-hmm," she murmured sleepily with a lovely smile lighting up her face.

Fiona sat on a small wall in the Orchid Display House as they listened to the small group crooning "Silent Night."

Despite the fact that she wore a coat, the high notes of the carolers and the nearness of Paul, caused a shiver to run through Natalie.

Not waiting for an invitation, Paul curled his arm around her shoulders and drew her in close. Looking up at him, she saw the enticement in his eyes. The musical sounds of the carolers faded to the background, along with the whispered voices of the other visitors.

He's right, she thought, there's definitely something magical about this season. And this moment.

As if pulled by two invisible strings that could not be controlled, they drew near to one another. Natalie's senses heightened causing her to notice every little nuance of the moment. From the way her heart thudded in her chest, to the slight flare of his nostrils, she knew this was a once in a lifetime moment. One of those moments that alter the course of your life forever. While she didn't exactly know what that meant, suddenly she no longer wanted to live on the outskirts of life anymore. She wanted to dance closer to the edge, and taste what really "living" had to offer. She tilted her head up towards his and shut her eyes.

The vibrato of a high note from "Oh Holy Night," wrapped around Natalie like a warm blanket. The softness of Paul's lips against hers melted away the chill she felt earlier. His arm dropped from her shoulder to fall gently around her waist, pulling her into him.

The slight stirring of the air around them brought with it the scent of the orchids and the fruity, spicy, amber notes of Paul's cologne.

"Mm," she murmured softly, lifting her hand to rest on the nape of his neck. Just as simple as it had begun, the kiss ended.

They eventually made their way back to their cars and spoke nothing of the moment other than a potent, lingering look into one another's eyes as they left.

Thinking back on it, Paul felt a small sense of victory. Looking into Natalie's eyes after kissing her, there had been no regrets. No censure or apologies had been lurking behind her eyes. Rather, he thought he saw curiosity.

He followed her back to her house and helped put Fiona to bed. They sat in the living room enjoying a quick cup of tea.

"I'm glad you didn't shut me out," he confessed.

"You thought I would?"

He nodded. "You're very protective of Fiona and your relationship with her. You just seem very guarded when it comes to your private life, and I wasn't sure if you were open to sharing it with anyone."

"I'm not sure that I still am," she acknowledged. "I don't know, maybe it's the holiday season like you said. Perhaps, it was just the special feeling of the night," she shrugged. "I haven't had time to explore sharing my private life with anyone, between Fiona and my business."

Paul leaned forward and sat his tea cup on the table in front of them. "What's that sadness I see in your eyes all the time?"

"I just wish it were easier you know? I mean, I love my business and enjoy what I do. It's so fulfilling, creating beautiful works of art with something as natural as flowers and greenery. But, it demands so much of my time, that I don't have enough to give my first love."

"Fiona? She's a very understanding child you know. And you've done an excellent job raising her alone," Paul conceded.

"I know. It's just that sometimes it feels unfair. If she isn't at the center, she's with a babysitter. Now that her Christmas has been ruined, I feel like the worst mother ever," Natalie confided.

"Hey, don't be so hard on yourself. It's hard on her, but she gets that it's hard on you, too."

"I just wish there was some way that I could make it up to her."

Paul sat in silence for a while, watching her mull over her thoughts.

"Why don't the two of you escape for the holiday?"

With her elbow propped on the back of the couch, Natalie rested her chin in her palm and stared at him. "Where?"

"I have a cabin in the mountains. You two can use it. There's whitewater rafting, hiking, museums, theaters, and all types of fun things that I know Fi would love."

He saw the glint of excitement in her eyes, which quickly dulled.

"I can't do that."

"Why not?"

"Paul, you've already done so much for us. I could never ask that of you."

"You're not asking, I'm offering. Besides, that's my Christmas gift to you and Fi."

He watched her closely as she seemed to consider the idea. Standing up preparing to leave, he reached for her hand and pulled her up beside him.

"I tell you what, think about it awhile. Pray on it and let me know your final decision. You have until tomorrow this time," he smiled, winking at her.

"That's no time at all," she disputed.

"I know. If I give you too much time, you might change your mind. Remember, you're doing this for Fiona. The business will continue on. You'll come back refreshed with new ideas and energy. I promise."

"Well, if that's the case, I'm sold! We're going!" She giggled loudly, before pressing a hand to her mouth, not wanting to wake Fiona.

"Great!" Paul pulled her close to him and shared another secret, sweet kiss with her, before leaving for the night.

CHAPTER 7

"You really don't have to drive us up there you know," Natalie stated, setting her rolling bag in the back of her CR-V.

"I thought it would be easier than trying to give you directions. It can be pretty confusing up in the mountains where my cabin is located. Plus there's snow up there this time of year, and the roads can be a bit treacherous."

Paul shoved two more bags in alongside the three that were already in there. The back was crammed with wrapped presents that Natalie had purchased for Fiona.

"Road trip!" The seven-year-old shouted, running down the front steps to the curb where he and Natalie stood.

"Do, you have your tablet and headset, little munchkin?" he asked, turning to Fiona.

She nodded and winked at him, before jumping into the car.

"What about you?" he asked Natalie, eyeing her carefully.

She nodded grimly. "Yeah, I guess so."

"Come on, the two of you are gonna have fun," he stated, opening the passenger door for her.

"I'm just worried about the business."

"You're closed. What is it that you're worried about? Someone's going to die, and emergency funeral flowers can't be ordered?" he joked.

Natalie glared at him, before swatting at him. "You're not funny, Paul."

"Okay, but seriously. Everything's going to be just fine."

After he went to the driver's side and settled in, she turned to him in worry again.

"How are you going to get back?"

"I told you, I've got a little car that I keep up there. I can drive it back, no problem."

"Maybe, you should stay one night to rest up before hitting the road," she suggested nervously, as she bit her fingernails.

"Mm, we'll see," Paul remarked, trying to hide the pleasure in his voice at her invitation.

Driving up the long road leading to the cabin's drive, Paul glanced over at Natalie. She had fallen asleep on the two-hour drive. Despite her protests that she would be just fine driving herself, he knew she had been tired. The extended holiday hours had turned into a couple of late nights closing the shop at ten, and opening up again at seven.

Paul spoke to Fiona in a conspiratorial whisper. "Hey, little one, we're almost here…think we should wake her yet?"

"Wow!" Fiona exclaimed, sitting up in the back seat.

He looked back at her a couple of times to appreciate the scenery from her eyes.

Her mouth dropped in awe, and her eyes filled with glee as they approached the cabin.

"We did a great job didn't we, munchkin?"

"Yeah!" Fiona whispered in amazement. "Look at the lights and the reindeer," she whispered, pointing at the roof.

As they rolled up the drive, he reached over and gently shook Natalie awake.

She rubbed her hands through her hair and murmured softly before opening her eyes. He stopped the vehicle at the foot of the driveway and turned to face her.

Natalie's eyes grew wide, as she sat forward in her seat, holding onto the dashboard with one hand. Speechless she looked at Paul and then back at the cabin a couple of times.

"So, do you like it?"

"Paul! It's beautiful! Where'd all of this come from?" she asked, waving her hand around.

Sleeping through their ascent through the mountains, she hadn't seen the snow blanketing everything. He watched her as she took in the tall mountain ranges around them covered in snow, and the garland, lights, and wreaths that highlighted the season all around the pine log cabin.

"Oh just a couple elves," he laughed, turning to look at Fiona.

"But how? When?"

"Come on, let's go inside, and then we can answer a few questions," he stated, pulling to the top of the driveway and parking.

Fiona ran to the nativity scene and kneeled down in front of it. Paul and Natalie came up behind her, his hand resting on her shoulder.

"So, whaddya think, sport?"

Her large, doe eyes glistened with tears when she looked up at Paul and her mother. She had shared with Paul how much she loved to see the mangers at the churches in the Grant Park area of Atlanta where she and her mother resided.

Paul had added this personal touch for Fiona. His heart burst with joy when she jumped from her knees and threw her arms around his waist.

"Thanks!" she murmured against his coat.

"Any time, Fi. Any time." Paul looked at Natalie, whose hazel eyes reflected a similar sheen as her daughter's.

"Alright, let's get you two inside," he announced breaking the moment. The last thing he wanted was for the two of them to burst into tears on him.

"Alright," Natalie murmured absentmindedly.

Paul noticed she had not moved from her spot. Instead, she took in the large picturesque windows all around the two story cabin. He could tell it was not what she had expected when he offered use of it.

Grabbing her by one hand and Fiona by the other, he escorted them inside.

"Does this belong to your parents'?" she asked, as they entered the spacious living room. Turning in circles, she attempted to take it all in at once.

A wreath made of pinecones nestled in a spray of fresh pine and cranberries rested on the log mantle over the stone fireplace. Two stockings hung, with Fiona and Natalie's names scripted in glittery, cursive font.

Beautifully wrapped gifts lay on the hearth. Paul sat on one of two large leather couches that flanked the fireplace. A wooden table sat between them decorated with acorns and pine, and three-tiered glasses with candles.

All of that, however, paled in comparison to the twelve foot tall Christmas tree, decorated with natural pinecones hanging from simple golden bows. A gold ribbon with white snowflakes imprinted on it curled around the tree. Presents circled underneath stacked four deep in some spots.

"It's breathtaking," she admired, walking around the room, touching the garland, white roses, and poinsettias.

"Where's my room, Paul?" Fiona asked, making her way towards the circular staircase.

"Follow me, my lady," he smiled, lowering his arm for her to take.

"Wait! You two slow down right this moment," Natalie demanded, scowling at them.

"Is there a problem?"

"Who's all of this for? I thought you weren't celebrating Christmas? Are you expecting company with all of these decorations and gifts?" She exhaled in exasperation.

Paul guiltily turned to Fiona, and they wore a look of doom.

"I think we're busted, kid."

Fiona shrugged. "Hey, you're the adult. You're supposed to be the responsible one. I was just being a good little girl and obeying your orders. I'm running to find my room now. Bye-bye," she declared.

Paul's mouth dropped in shock. "You little—"

"Paul!" Natalie cut him off, forcing him to turn back to her.

One hand in his pocket and the other scratching the back of his neck, he dropped his head in shame.

"I'm waiting," she persisted.

"Okay, come here and sit with me and I'll explain everything."

He pulled her onto the couch and described Fiona's plan to give Natalie the perfect Christmas.

"She wanted you to have a traditional Christmas since you work so hard and hadn't had one in a long time. Fiona wrote out this elaborate plan on what that would look like for you, and created a checklist. And she made sure we stuck to it, in case you were wondering. I was in charge of creating a timeline for us to focus on and make it so we could accomplish everything in time for Christmas."

"But you didn't know that I would come," she argued.

"You're right. And up until the other day, I still wasn't sure how to convince you. Now here we are on Christmas Eve, and I'd have to say...mission accomplished...almost."

"What do you mean 'almost'?" she stared at him in confusion.

"Well, if I said another word I'd spoil the surprise."

"Whose cabin is this? Who bought all of this stuff to decorate?"

He reached up to brush a lock of stray hair from her eyes.

"It's mine, and I bought it all."

"But how?"

It was his turn to look confused. "What do you mean how?"

"You're a coach! How can you afford all of this? I mean don't you coach PE? Or work at a gym or something?"

"No," he said, slowly shaking his head and narrowing his eyes. "What gave you that idea?"

"You're always in sweats and t-shirts, or shorts and t-shirts," she shook her head back and forth, lifting her eyebrow as if it should be clear to him. "You're always playing sports with the kids at the center, and I've seen you coaching them at basketball tons of times. Which you're mighty good at, I should mention."

"Thanks," he laughed.

She loved the sound of it, although she wasn't certain what was funny.

"I wear that clothing because it's appropriate attire for hanging out with kids. And you're right, we're usually playing sports or building something with our hands. It would hardly be realistic for me to be there in the suits and ties I wear most days. Nat, I own my own business. Spirit Performance, Inc."

"Wait…what? You own the company that sells all of those workout outfits and DVDs for pregnant ladies and new moms?"

"Yeah."

She placed a hand to her head and laughed slightly. "No freaking way! Why didn't I recognize you?"

"Because I'm not big on publicity for myself. It's all about my company. You don't see me in the ads, the dvds or any of that. I don't like a lot of attention drawn to myself."

"What made you come up with that concept?"

"My sister's first pregnancy. She struggled with comfortable clothing to wear throughout her pregnancy, and she's a huge fitness fan. So I designed a little something for her, and she had a seamstress pull it together. My brother-in-law, Jonathan, had the ingenious idea to make my own company around it. He's in marketing…so it just kinda worked," Paul explained as if the idea was simple enough to understand.

"Wow! I don't know what to say. I feel like such a fool!" she admitted.

"Why?"

"Because I judged you and basically informed you that you could never understand what it's like to be in business on your own. And here you are the owner of one of the fastest growing small companies in the southeast," she held her face in her hands, fighting off the blush of embarrassment.

"Hey, don't do that…come here," he said, pulling her closer and looking into her eyes. "You had no way of knowing. Don't beat yourself up. I was still irresponsible in the way that I took off with Fiona that day. I deserved all of that."

"No, you didn't."

His head leaned towards hers ready to claim her mouth in another kiss. He had thought of nothing else since the last time he kissed her.

Just as their lips neared one another, they heard a loud noise outside.

"Is that the sound of car doors slamming?" Natalie asked, jerking her head up and pulling back.

"They're here!" Fiona announced at the same time, running down the stairs.

"Yep! That would be part two of your surprise," Paul replied nervously, getting up from his seat on the couch.

"I don't understand."

"You will in just a moment," he said, making his way to stand beside Fiona who opened the door.

Over the next few minutes, Natalie was overwhelmed by a flood of people entering the house. Paul introduced his very pregnant sister, Nina, her husband, Jonathan, and their two boys Jacob and Jesse. Next was his oldest brother, Rick and his wife Aimee, with their two daughters Jolene, Deanna, and their sons, Alex, Derek, and Mitchell. Finally, his brother Steve and his wife, Lauren, and their new baby, Angelica.

"Where's mom and dad?"

"Steve's picking them up from the airport in a couple of hours," Nina announced.

"Well, come on boys, let's get the luggage from the cars," Rick pronounced.

"Yeah, I've gotta unpack Natalie's, too," Paul answered.

"Hold up just a moment, Paul. You've got some explaining to do," Natalie countered, with a slight tilt of her eyebrow.

"Pssh, let them leave. We've got lots to talk about," Nina declared, propping her feet up on an ottoman and rubbing her belly.

"Yes, we do have lots to catch up on," Aimee stated as she sat beside Lauren.

"I…I just don't understand what's going on. I mean Paul told me that Fiona, that's my daughter, she came up with a plan to give me this great Christmas. But I don't know how we got to this," Natalie stated, extending her arms with a flourish of her hands to indicate the ladies and the cabin.

"Rick and Nina got a call from Paul, and then I called Lauren, while Rick called mom and dad," Aimee stated.

"You see it's been a long time since we Winters have had a family Christmas," Lauren stated, her shiny, jet black bobbed haircut bouncing as she spoke.

"So, when Paul called and said that he wanted us to get together again at his cabin, we all got excited about the idea. He said he had a special friend that deserved a beautiful Christmas and that her daughter needed a little help pulling it all together," Aimee explained.

"We're just so excited that Paul's not only showing interest in one particular lady, but that he's actually willing to let us meet you. We couldn't miss the chance. And I for one, was definitely ready to meet the indomitable Miss Fiona who's so captured my brother's heart," Nina giggled.

"Yeah, he absolutely adores your daughter," Lauren interjected.

Paul walked in the house, his arms laden with luggage, and breathed a sigh of relief seeing Natalie surrounded by his sister and sisters-in-law.

He disappeared into the kitchen, while his nephews helped Rick and Jonathan unpack luggage and put gifts underneath the tree.

The first chance Natalie got she escaped the ladies and came into the large kitchen where Paul chopped chives.

"I'm so thankful, but why did you do all of this?" Natalie asked.

"Because, I admire you, Nat. I've watched how hard you've worked on your shop and trying to raise Fi. You've done a wonderful job with her by the way. But you're that little girl's hero, and she wanted to give you this and so much more. Seems as if you were lacking in family, and I've got plenty to share," he pronounced, scraping the chives off the chopping block into a bowl with chopped celery and cilantro.

He smiled at her and walked closer. "Please tell me you aren't mad at me."

She smiled back at him and looked down at her feet. "How could I be mad at you, Paul?"

"Good. Besides, I couldn't think of a better way to celebrate this holiday than by being with two of the most beautiful girls in the world," he said, grabbing her hands in his own.

"Hmph! I recall a time when you used to say that to your sister and me," came a soft, angelic voice.

"Mom!" Paul turned releasing Natalie's hands and swooped a petite, blond woman in a hug.

"Okay, that's enough you can put me down now," she chuckled.

Paul did as his mother requested and kissed her cheek.

A booming voice interrupted the two. "Get your hands off my woman, man!" Declared a tall, barrel chested man. Natalie presumed this was Paul's dad, as he was his doppelganger.

The only difference were the lines on the outside of his eyes, and the sprinkling of white tinting the older man's hair.

"Dad! It's good to see you old man!"

"We'll see who's old when I whoop your butt in a game of basketball tomorrow."

"You'll have to forgive these two animals. I'm Mila Winters, Paul's mom, and this brute, unfortunately, is my husband, Charles Winters, Paul's dad."

Natalie reached a hand out to shake Mila's but was surprised by the strength of her embrace, when Mila pulled her into a tight hug.

"I'm Na—" she began only to be cut off by Paul's father.

"You didn't tell us Natalie was this beautiful!" the large man remarked, pulling her in for a hug.

The rest of the family gathered in the kitchen, as it came to the children's attention that their grandparents were present.

"And this beautiful young lady! You must be Fiona," Charles greeted, kneeling down before her.

"Fiona Noelle Justice," she declared proudly.

"Well, such a beautiful name for such a beautiful young lady," he replied.

"I would like to say thank you, Fiona," Mila greeted, standing beside her husband.

"What'd I do?" Fiona asked in confusion, looking first to the adults and then the children around her.

"You're responsible for bringing this family together again. It's because of your very unselfish wish for your mom that Paul thought to have us all share this Christmas with one another."

"It is?" she asked, with a wide, toothy smile.

"Yes, it is. And I hear that ole Saint Nick is very proud of you," Charles stated, rubbing his knuckles against her nose.

"Well, I sure hope so! Because kids get a tough break trying to make adults act right," she announced with a huff, causing everyone else to laugh.

"I would say that it's time to get tomorrow's Christmas dinner in the oven," Mila stated, breaking up the group by shoo-ing them away.

"But Mom, you just got here. You need to rest up awhile," Nina argued.

"Don't you know your mother doesn't know the meaning of the word rest?" Charles laughed in a booming voice.

"That's for sure," Aimee stated, smiling at her mother-in-law.

"You guys go rest. Mom and I can handle this," Paul declared, pulling an apron from the cabinet for his mom.

"No, not this year, dear. Paul, you go out there with your dad and brothers. We, women, will hold down the kitchen," Mila professed.

Lauren giggled before explaining, "Mom and Paul usually cook all the dinners." As Natalie's raised an eyebrow, Lauren raised one of her own. "You didn't know Paul could cook?"

"No," she responded shyly, realizing there was a lot she didn't know about this amazing man.

"Well, don't worry. You'll have plenty of time to get to know all the many facets of my brother. In the meantime, we've only got a few days together, so we're going to let you get to know us, and we're going to get to know you!" Nina responded.

Memories of Christmases long ago popped into Natalie's head as she fell into place beside the sisters, and Mila, chopping, dicing, cutting and cooking. Her heart filled with joy at the sounds of Fiona's laughter, intermingling with all the other children's. Yes, it would definitely be a Christmas to remember.

Paul's family sat outside around a fire roasting marshmallows and making s'mores for the children. They shared Christmas memories of the past over hot chocolate and coffee. When the fight to keep her eyes open began to win out, Paul suggested Natalie turn in for the night.

"I'll be back, guys. Let me get her settled in," he stated, waving a hand at his family bundled around the fire's warmth.

"You're tucking her in, you say?" Rick teased.

"Telling a few bedtime stories, huh?" laughed Jonathan.

Paul shook his head and waved their taunts away.

Inside a beautiful fire crackled, popped and blazed in the fireplace, much like the one outside. Yet, this one was created for two.

"Come here for a moment," Paul said, pulling her away from the direction of the stairs and towards the fireplace.

They sat close together on the couch, as he pulled an afghan Mila had hand-knitted over their laps.

"So, what do you think of my family?" he asked in a husky voice.

"They're wonderful. I wish I had such a large family to share the holidays with. I don't understand why you all don't come together more often," Natalie expressed.

"We just needed a reason to, like Dad said, and Fi provided that. Sometimes, it's the heart of a child that helps us to recognize what's most important."

"You're right about that. She's just glowing under all of the attention your nieces and nephews are lavishing on her."

"That's because she's the baby of the bunch, outside of baby

Angelica. But that's not why I brought you over here…not to discuss my family, or anything. This last year, spending time and bonding with Fiona has been, really special. She's added a light into my life in a way that I hadn't expected," Paul stated, rubbing his hands together and staring into the fire.

Natalie glanced nervously at him and then into the fire, as well.

"See, she's made me realize what I've been missing in my life. I spent years building my dream, which was my business. It's stable now, and I realize I still don't have what I really want."

"What's that?" she asked, looking confused.

"Someone I really care about. I've spent the last year learning all about Fiona, and she's been learning about me. Now, I'd like to spend time getting to know her mother a little better…that is, if she's open to it."

Paul took Natalie's hand in his. Holding his head down and slightly to the side, he watched her closely.

"Paul, I'd like that, too, but…" she looked at him with somber, regretful eyes. "I already don't have enough time for Fiona with the business. I just don't have time to date."

His heart sunk just a little as he continued watching her. He saw the disappointment in her eyes and in that moment, he knew that she didn't want to turn him down. She simply felt as if she didn't have a choice.

"What if I had a solution to that for you? Would you consider dating me then?" He asked playfully, but seriously.

"I don't see how you could," she stated, the hopeful look in her eyes betraying her words.

"I've done a lot of research on this and spoken to Jonathan. GSU has an internship program that'll allow you to exchange services with their students. You can provide them with the experience they need while getting work for free or at a reduced price in your shop. For instance, you can hire on two botany students, or students interested in small business ownership, accounting, or floral design. They will receive credit hours in exchange for the work they do for you."

"Are you serious? Why didn't I know about that?" Natalie asked in astonishment.

"Probably because you're working at capacity and there is only so much one person can do in a day. You are trying to do everything at your shop, and be a full-time mom, and be a functioning human being on top of it. That's too much for any one person to handle. You can do it, as you've clearly proven, but you and I both know the toll it's taking on you. So I'm going to tell you something, and it's an absolute truth. Barely anyone who succeeds in business, or in life for that matter, does it alone. And if you try, you're fighting an uphill battle."

She was looking at him, almost in a trance, trying to take in everything he was saying.

"Nat, Someone gave me a chance once; gave me help and encouragement and support. And I'm here now to give the same to you."

Natalie didn't know how to respond. It was like his words were releasing a deep well of emotion that she'd kept at bay for so long now. "It sounds so good, but I'm not sure how it'll work," Natalie finally replied, shaking her head from side-to-side, .

"Trust me on this, Nat. It can work. Nina's a skilled web developer, that's what she does for a living. She wants to give you the gift of customizing a website for you, where your customers can place orders online. Lauren's brother, Max, owns his own delivery service. He's offered to provide free delivery of your flowers within a fifty mile radius for the first year, and then at a discounted rate for the second and third year. If it's further than that, you can get the service for a small fee, or hire UPS or FedEx."

Natalie sat back against the couch in astonishment, moisture starting to glimmer at the corner of her eyes. "You seem like you've got this all figured out."

"I do. That's part three of your Christmas present. When I saw the struggle you and Fiona were having spending time together, I drew up a plan and presented it to my family. They all agreed it's a win-win situation, and they've come on board to support you on this. It was Jonathan's idea for me to start my business, but the one thing we've all learned is that I'm an astute businessman. I won't steer you wrong, Natalie."

She pulled her bottom lip into her mouth and worked it back and forth with her teeth. She wanted to say yes, but the other problem was her heart. She wasn't sure she was over losing Dan. The thought of growing close to another person and losing them was devastating. Natalie didn't think she could do that to herself, or Fiona.

"Sleep on it, and we'll talk about it some more in the morning. It's been a long day for you, and I know I've overwhelmed you with all of this. I just want you to know that you do have options, Nat, and I do care about you and that little girl, a lot."

"I know you do, Paul. I just...I just don't know that I can stand to lose another person close to me. Fiona was little when it happened, and she doesn't remember her dad. I don't want her to know that kind of pain...ever," she emphasized, her eyes welling up with tears.

"This season is about love, hope, and faith. All the anxiety and stress you carry can be, and will be, replaced with hope, joy, and peace; all you have to do is believe in the Lord. You'll be healed from that fear, and soon you'll be overflowing with hope through His power. Then you can open your heart up to all that life has to offer. Just consider it, Natalie, that's all I'm asking."

She nodded her head slightly, recognizing the truth in his words.

Paul placed a hand on the side of her face and gently touched his lips to hers. Caressing her face with his thumb, he applied pressure to her lips, causing her to open hers and share a sweet kiss with him.

The chiming of the clock acknowledged midnight had arrived and sealed the moment in their hearts and minds forever. When it finished chiming, Paul was the first to pull away.

"Merry Christmas, Natalie."

"Merry Christmas, Paul."

She stood and walked to the stairwell, before looking back at him.

He stared after her and whispered good night. He was left alone with his thoughts for awhile before the children entered the cabin to go to bed.

CHAPTER 8

*N*atalie awoke feeling well rested and slightly pleased with the world. The smell of bacon frying and fresh coffee brewing drifted up the stairwell. She smiled as she looked at Fiona's little figure curled up close beside her.

With one hand she gently stroked her daughter's long curls. Pressing a kiss to a soft, warm cheek, she smiled when eyes similar to her own opened and stared back at her. Fiona's green-flecked eyes were the only thing she inherited from her mother.

Her long, thick lashes batted a couple of times before recognition dawned in them.

"It's Christmas, Mom!" Fiona bounced up and down in the bed. "Come on, we've gotta wake everyone! It's Christmas," she sang out, beaming.

"First thing's first…go wash your face and brush your teeth, and then we can check on the others."

Fiona hopped up and ran into the adjoining bathroom. Natalie pulled a brush through her long tresses, before tying her bathrobe tightly. She quickly joined Fiona to wash her face and brush her teeth, as well, before applying a light coat of lip gloss and a couple of strokes of mascara.

"Come on, Mom, he already thinks you're beautiful," Fiona giggled, pulling on Natalie's hand. "Let's see what Santa brought."

When they entered the hallway, she collided with Paul.

"Merry Christmas," he greeted, with an instant look of yearning in his eyes.

"Merry Christmas," she and Fiona greeted simultaneously.

Clearing his throat, he stated, "Uh, everyone's downstairs waiting for you two."

"Let's go, we can't hold up Christmas any longer can we?" Natalie asked Fiona, who smiled back and dashed for the stairs.

"Any more thought on our discussion?" Paul asked.

She smiled hesitantly. "Come on, let's not hold up Christmas."

Natalie grinned at all the smiling faces beaming up at her when she entered the living room.

Her jaw dropped at the sight of her father sitting next to Charles.

"Daddy!" she exclaimed, running to his arms.

He squeezed her tight, his white beard tickling her face. "Merry Christmas, baby."

"What are you doing here?" she asked when she finally pulled free from his embrace.

"Oh, this young man here might've had something to do with it. The way I hear tell it had something to do with my granddaughter. Always said she took her smarts from her ol' Grampa Merle," he chuckled, getting a boisterous laugh from the room.

"I called your dad up and invited him for Christmas, and he gladly accepted," Paul announced.

"B…but Dad, you don't celebrate Christmas," she spluttered.

"Nat, I made a lot of mistakes in your life when you were a kid. I have a lot of regrets. One thing I've learned through the years is we can't go back and fix 'em. All we can do is try to be the best we can now, one day at a time. That's all I have to offer. One day at a time. I'm sorry I didn't give you the Christmases you deserved as a kid. I was angry about the divorce, and I took it out on you. And I apologize. It wasn't something you deserved."

Natalie's eyes filled with tears and she struggled to find the right words to say. But Fiona was not lacking any.

"Well, I guess this means you aren't a Scrooge after all, Grampa!" Fiona announced.

The adults grew quiet, while some of the kids snickered. Paul looked between Natalie and her father, waiting to hear his reply.

"Who said I was a Scrooge?" he growled.

"Mom said it."

"Well, you know what? She was right. But Grampa Merle is no longer a Scrooge. I am here to celebrate with you and this family if you'll have me darlin'," he said, looking from Fiona to Natalie.

"Daddy, I wouldn't have it any other way," Natalie said, throwing her arms around her father again.

Family. This was what Christmas was all about. Whether it was your birth family or the one you were just blessed to have around you. Natalie realized there was nothing greater than to share it with a spirit of love.

Fiona was excited about the three dolls she received, one of which was porcelain to add to her growing collection. It had been the first gift she was encouraged to open, sent with love from Aunt Keri.

She received a few board and card games, clothing, jewelry, books, and shoes. She used the new phone Natalie had purchased her to call Dan's parents and wish them a Merry Christmas, as well as Natalie's mom, Angie. Natalie chatted briefly with her own mother, who knew that her father was coming and approved of his visit.

An hour later all the gifts had been exchanged, and one remained under the tree without a tag. She had been given several nice gifts from his family, which she had definitely not expected. The most heartwarming had been the written plan Paul gave her, detailing expansion plans for her business, and his parents' decision to invest in her. She had little reason to believe the remaining gift was hers.

"Whose is that?" Eleven-year-old Jesse asked.

"Let's see," Charles said, reaching underneath the tree. He passed it along to Natalie without a word.

"What's this about?" she asked, turning to Paul who sat smiling at her.

"Open it," he nodded his head at the gift.

Unwrapping the small square box, a deep inhale of breath escaped at the sight of the blue Tiffany & Co. box.

"Open it, Mom!" Fiona exclaimed, clapping her hands together.

Natalie's heart thudded in her chest

She opened the box and removed the little pouch.

Her hand flew to her mouth after she pulled out the sterling silver, heart tag bracelet. The engraving simply read, "Romans 15:13."

She recalled the Scripture and repeated it with Paul from memory. "May the God of hope fill you with all joy and peace as you trust in Him, so that you may overflow with hope by the power of the Holy Spirit."

"Alright everyone!" Mila called. "Let's eat breakfast."

When Paul looked up prepared to get up from his space on the floor, Charles placed a firm but loving hand on his son's shoulder. "Son, enjoy this moment. Join us when you're ready." The entire group filed out of the room, leaving Natalie and Paul alone under the glow of the Christmas tree.

"What else can I do to convince you to take a chance on living, Nat? A chance on us...me, you, and Fi?" he asked after everyone had left them in the room alone.

At that moment her cell phone rang, pulling her attention away from Paul.

"Just a moment," she said, glancing at Emma's name on the caller ID.

"Hello?"

"Merry Christmas! How do you like your Christmas gifts so far?"

"I'm having a beautiful Christmas, Emma. What about you?"

"I'm having a blast with my family. We're snowed in up here in Boston, but I don't care. Being with my family is all that matters."

"Yeah, I'm starting to realize that myself."

"Good, now maybe you'll open your eyes and see the good guy sitting in front of you is the real Christmas gift. It's time to open your heart again, Nat. He's good for you and Fiona both."

"What do you know about all of this?"

"Let's just say that I got a phone call, and this little elf helped some things along. Take a closer look at the name on the bottom of the baskets of all those poinsettias and white roses decorating the place."

Natalie picked up a potted poinsettia and saw The Potted Shed, embossed in the gold foil wrapping on the bottom of the container.

"Emma! You never cease to amaze me," Natalie laughed.

"Merry Christmas, Nat."

"Merry Christmas, Em," Natalie replied, hanging up the phone.

She reached for Paul's hand and took it in her own. "Before this week, I wouldn't have thought many things were possible. I've been so overwhelmed with my business and trying to carve out more time for Fiona and me to spend together. I had no clue how I was going to give her a decent Christmas after Keri canceled our New York trip. I had no time to plan and truthfully I was dreading this day. But you...you," she shook her head and bit her lip, trying to hold back the tears.

Paul reached up and wiped away one lone tear traversing a crooked path down her soft cheek.

"You've shown me the true meaning of Christmas. The one I'd forgotten. It's not about the gifts or the location. Or even this beautiful bracelet. It's in the way you accepted Fiona and me into your heart this season. The way you've allowed us to share this special time with your family. How hard you worked to make this day special for us. It's in the way you all have shown us how important family is, and the way you've given me back hope. And even a sense of peace and joy. This is Christmas to me."

Paul stood up and pulled Natalie alongside him.

"Just one chance, that's all I ask," he said, claiming her mouth passionately with his own.

Natalie's heart blossomed with the possibilities of love, family, and hope. This was the greatest gift any one person could give her.

When he released her from the kiss, she remained holding on to his shoulders to keep her standing. He had literally left her weak in the knees, and she enjoyed it.

"Yes, Paul. Yes, I'll give us a chance," she whispered against his mouth.

"Merry Christmas, Nat."

"Merry Christmas, Paul."

Merry Christmas to all of you from Natalie, Paul, and Fiona!

ACKNOWLEDGMENTS

I want to give a warm thank you to the people who were integral in this project: My dear friends Caroline, Sunny, and Michelle, without whom this story would have never materialized. And of course, my family, who inspire me, support me and love me daily.

SANTA BABY, MAYBE

A Christmas Story of Missed Chances & Silver Linings

Sophie Mays

SANTA BABY, *Maybe*

Sometimes missed chances are just signs
you are headed in the right direction

This book is dedicated to all the people whose lives were touched by the Gatlinburg and Pigeon Forge wildfires. This book was written just prior to the occurrence and is set in a fictional Tennessee town which overlooks the beautiful Great Smoky Mountains. Our hearts and prayers go out to those whose lives were affected.

CHAPTER 1

*L*aid off. Those two words seemed to bounce back and forth inside Colin's head. By themselves, each word was perfectly innocent, innocuous. But together, they became something gut-wrenching and devouring. They'd been eating at him all day, ever since he'd left his now ex-boss's office four hours ago.

Welding school wasn't exactly cheap. He'd made an investment in his own future, and the bottom had fallen out of it. Laid off. What kind of company starts laying people off in November? A week before Thanksgiving? A month before Christmas?

Colin was sitting alone in the Starbucks near his former workplace. He had contemplated getting a drink at the bar that he and his coworkers used to go to, but didn't trust himself getting anything stiffer than coffee to drink, not when his mood was as dark as the cloudy autumn sky outside. One of his closest work-friends used to make fun of him for getting frou-frou coffees, as he called them, but Colin knew that was precisely what he needed today. An icy rain was lashing at the big windows, and Colin sat staring out of them, thinking in circles and not getting anywhere.

What was he going to do now? The thought of troubling his family at this time of year by telling his father or his sister that he'd been let go was too much to contemplate on top of everything else. He took a sip of his caramel latte, rotating the hot cup in his hand as he contemplated his next move.

Jobs were not in abundance this time of year, with most companies waiting until after the holidays to post any new positions. However, with Christmas on the way, there was one market that was booming: retail. He cringed inwardly at the thought. He hadn't worked retail in over fifteen years; not since he was a kid in high school. But, if a company as big as Hawthorne was letting go of welders, the market for his skill couldn't be good. There would be dozens just like him, many more skilled and more experienced, all vying for the same jobs.

The wet afternoon outside looked especially bleak when he thought of that. How long had it been since he had hunted for a job? Six years? Seven? He'd been with Hawthorne since he'd started welding.

Colin took another sip. He'd have to inquire at Frank & Sons, the only other big factory in the area that did any welding. The sad thing was, being laid off when he was as skilled and well-liked as he was, wasn't promising for a long and prosperous career anywhere else. His boss had raked his hands over his thinning hair, audibly racked with guilt over having to let Colin go. They'd let several people go this week, many of them senior welders with excellent reputations.

As he had been told "off the record" today, Hawthorne had new investors who wanted more laborers for less money, and the quickest way to achieve that was by letting go of some of their higher paid employees. Colin rolled his warm cup between his palms. Who knew that working his way up the ladder, working as hard and faithfully as he had, would end with him up being replaced by younger, less experienced, and apparently way less expensive workers. At the moment it boggled his mind.

A woman in a J. Crew skirt suit opened the door, letting a blast of icy air in. Colin's chair was near the door, and he got a face full of November wind, thick with the smell of rain and the cold. He waited for it to close, but she was struggling with her umbrella, which had gotten caught in the corner of the doorway. Other cozy occupants of the coffee shop were turning to look at her now as the seconds ticked, and the chill began whipping through the room.

Colin set down his coffee and crossed the room to help her. "Here, ma'am," he held the door wide so her umbrella could detach. She got it free and smiled gratefully at him.

"Thank you," she said breathlessly. Her light-brown hair was smoothed into a perfect twist at the back of her head, but strands had blown free in the struggle with the umbrella. Her beige and red plaid scarf was askew, around her slender neck.

"It's the worst thing about autumn, I swear," she huffed nodding at the offending instrument. "Umbrellas, that is."

It was his turn to say something, but Colin just stood there, silent as a post, struggling to think of something charming to say to the gorgeous woman in front of him. He was definitely not used to coming face to face with someone as beautiful and refined looking as her on a daily basis.

"No problem," he answered finally. He waved awkwardly and retreated back to his seat by the door.

If his awkwardness bothered her, she didn't show it. Pulling off her scarf and leather gloves, he watched her walk up to the counter to order.

Colin sighed. His thoughts reverting back to his predicament.

His only comfort was the severance pay. After five years, employees at Hawthorne were entitled to ninety days severance benefits. So he had a little time to get a plan together. Of course, if he'd taken the supervisor promotion they'd offered back in May, he'd have six months' severance...

Colin had to clear that thought. He couldn't waste time over what he could have done or should have done. The decisions have already been made. He still had options and some time to act before things got dodgy. His Range Rover was paid off, at least. Thank goodness for small blessings. Three months' pay and he was sure to find something between now and then. It was Friday. He'd take a day or two off to mope, and then he'd bounce back on Monday and be back to work before he knew it.

Better still, he'd already purchased Christmas presents for his family, so really his situation wasn't dire. Colin was that rare breed that stated he would buy Christmas gifts throughout the year for people, and then actually did it. He'd had gifts for his father, sister, brother-in-law, and his sister's two kids bought, wrapped, and stashed in the closet since September. The hardest part of gift giving for Colin was having to wait until December 25th to give them.

The beautiful lady with the umbrella was collecting her coffee now and heading back out the door. She gave Colin a friendly little smile on her way out, opened her umbrella without trouble this time, and walked off into the parking lot. Colin sighed and tried to focus on a plan for his future.

In some backward way, maybe this was a blessing. It certainly didn't feel that way, but it had been proven more than once that sometimes there was a greater plan at work. He battled back and forth as to whether he should apply to Frank & Sons first thing Monday morning.

His eyes roamed back to the wet parking lot. He stared out the hazy window not really looking at anything, but thinking again of the pretty brunette. Maybe he would take a little time before jumping right back into welding. He hadn't taken a day off in who knows how long. He had a few friends around town who might have some leads on odd jobs. Brandon worked building luxury homes up in the hills. Jack worked for a repair company. Jack's wife, Sarah, was helping put up a new apartment complex across town. Surely somebody had extra work that he could do for them. Surely, someone in Evanswood, Tennessee was hiring, and Colin figured he could track them down one way or the other. He took a sip of his latte.

But first, he was going to take a day to let himself be properly angry.

CHAPTER 2

*I*t had been a long, intense day even before her umbrella got stuck in the door at Starbucks. By the time Nora got home, she was ready to kick off her heels, put on her favorite pajamas and never get out from under the fuzzy blanket on her couch ever again. She hung up her umbrella, took off her scarf, coat, and gloves, and walked past her neat kitchen into the living area. With a flip of a switch, the lights flickered on.

She loved the condo that she owned, a luxury unit settled on the banks of the Little River. Smoky Mountain National Park reared up in the dark distance outside her windows, with the twinkling lights of Evanswood shining below. In the low-hanging rain clouds and relentless downpour, even the mountains' shapes were gone in a wash of murky black. When the sun came up tomorrow, the brilliant fall colors would radiate brightly against the dawn sky. The view was one of Nora's favorite things about her condo.

Her day had been a little hectic and she hadn't even managed to finish her coffee, and now she poured the remainder down the sink before tossing the cup in the recycling bin and heading to her bedroom in search of pajamas. She slung off her black pumps tossing them into the corner of her room with the good intention of putting them back on her shoe rack later. She placed her dry-clean-only suit on the back of her chair. She had a few things to be taken to the cleaners and would add it to the pile. It would probably have to be this weekend, unfortunately.

With a sigh, Nora realized that she'd left her briefcase in her car. If she'd realized earlier, Nora might have gone out to get it, but by now she was standing around her bedroom in her bra and panties. That ship had sailed she resigned. She didn't have any urgent cases pending, and if her firm really needed something, they could call her cell phone. The briefcase could wait out in the car until tomorrow.

Nora rifled through her purse to make sure that she'd at least brought her phone in. She found it buried beneath her wallet and lipgloss. She dropped her purse on the bed and opened her dresser drawer to find a pair of pajamas.

With a tiny meow, a bundle of black fur squeezed out from under the bed.

"Oh, hello, Arty!" Nora scooped the cat up and into her arms. Artemis had only lived with her for two weeks, but he was already making himself at home in her quiet condo. It had only taken six months of living here alone before Nora had caved in and took a little visit to the local Humane Society. It turns out, November is a big month for black cats..

She sat Artemis on the bed while she pulled on a set of warm flannel pajamas. She'd picked the red ones with leaping reindeer— Christmas was more than a month away, but the cold fall weather put her in the holiday mood. The black cat followed her out into the living room where she plopped down on the couch and pulled up the fuzzy blanket she'd been dreaming of since the rain had started that afternoon.

A replay of the incident with the Starbucks door and the good-looking stranger replayed in her mind, and Nora smiled. Well, rain was good for some things, at least.

It had been a long week. Nora worked with personal rights and domestic lawsuit cases, and it seemed like she was always exhausted by the time Friday rolled around. At this very moment, she needed badly to relax and forget her work week for a little while. She rubbed at the headache starting to throb at her temples. As her fingers kneaded into her hair, it dawned on her that she'd forgotten to take it down. Artemis was disturbed by the movement, but Nora climbed off the couch and went into the bathroom to take the bobby pins out of her light brown bun. As her hair fell in soft waves, the release of tension brought a happy sigh to her lips.

"What should we watch, Artemis?" she asked as she walked back into the living room. The little black tomcat had claimed a corner of the fuzzy blanket for himself and folded all his legs under his body. His yellow eyes were already closed as if he were already asleep. But, Nora knew better. He ignored her as she picked up the remote off the shelf and selected a movie without his input. "I think you're right. I've been in the mood to watch *Love, Actually*, too."

CHAPTER 3

*C*olin helped set the Thanksgiving table at his sister's house, setting out dishes and carefully stepping over children and dogs. Carol had a son and daughter who were barely a year apart and so similar in appearance and temperament that it was hard to tell them apart, especially when they were wrestling around the house. To anyone not knowing better, the assumption would be that they were twins. Colin told the rowdy duo for the hundredth time not to trip him. They responded in unison, each clinging to one of his legs and laughing madly.

"Hey! Your mom isn't going to like it when I throw you both out in the rain with the dogs!" Colin told them. With exaggerated effort, he walked around the table, setting out plates and silverware, dragging the kids along and driving the two of them wild.

"Colin! Stop getting them worked up!"

"Yeah, Colin," Andrew agreed, chuckling. It had taken a couple years to warm up to each other, but Colin finally liked Carol's husband Andrew. Andrew reached down and pulled one of the giggling children off Colin—it turned out to be the boy, five years old and with his mother and sister's bright red hair. "Ben! Come on, now. Uncle Colin's trying to help, unlike you and your sister."

Once it was one-to-one, Colin had the upper hand and managed to pry his niece Jenny off his leg. Benny and Jenny. Colin couldn't believe his sister hadn't noticed that the short forms of Benjamin and Jennifer rhymed.

"Any luck with the job hunt?" Andrew asked, as Ben wriggled away and six-year-old Jenny raced after him.

Colin shook his head. "Not yet. I thought I might find something through a buddy of mine, but at the moment nothing's really out there. Construction usually slows down in the winter, but this year something is definitely up. I'm down to looking at seasonal work."

"Did you try Frank's yet?"

Colin winced. Of course, Andrew would say that first. Truthfully, Colin hadn't applied at Frank & Sons just yet. If nothing else came up, he'd go to them, but Colin was going to exhaust his other options first. He ran a hand through his thick hair and twisted his mouth in a frown.

"I haven't heard about any openings with them," Colin replied. It wasn't a lie. "But, I'll probably give them a call in the next couple weeks."

"I still can't believe it," Carol muttered, carrying dishes in from the kitchen. They were covered with tin foil, but Colin smelled sweet potatoes and gravy. "After you've worked at Hawthorne's for what, seven years? Happy Thanksgiving, here's a severance package. Nice."

It was exactly how Colin felt, but Carol always had a way of being angrier at other people's problems for them. She liked to champion the underdog. He followed her into the kitchen to help carry out dishes. "Here, let me help you with that. Where's Dad?"

"He's with Abby," Carol sighed, brushing hair off her forehead with the back of her wrist. "You should probably tell him dinner's about ready."

"Hey," Colin nudged her with his elbow. Carol looked up at him with her mouth pressed into a line. Colin made the same face back at her, and she laughed reluctantly. "I'll be fine. There's something in this town for me. I'm set for a couple months, either way."

She elbowed him back and nodded. "Yeah, I know. At least you don't have kids or anything."

Colin looked around at the chaos of Carol's household; the children rolling around on the floor and the dogs yipping and wagging their tails and knocking things off the coffee table. Colin chuckled.

"Yeah, at least."

Their father was cloistered upstairs in the nursery with Carol and Andrew's last and youngest child. Baby Abigail was not really a baby anymore, she was turning two in January. She and her grandfather were putting together building blocks on the carpeted floor, enjoying the relative quiet in the safe zone where the other children and dogs were segregated by the stair guards.

George looked up and grinned when he saw his grown son in the doorway. "Is it that time already?"

Colin nodded, and George stood with Abby following suit. She toddled to the gated doorway then tuned to her grandfather and sweetly demanded, "Up!" He lifted her into his arms and followed Colin back downstairs. George McCullough had black hair once. It seemed like a long time ago to Colin. Back before Colin and Carol had grown up, and before their mom had passed away. Now, George's hair was all gray, but he looked young again as he dodged around the shrieking children as he headed toward the table. He settled Abby in her high chair and pulled out a chair of his own.

Ever since Evelyn McCullough had succumbed to congestive heart failure two years ago, the family had holidays at Carol's house. CHF had an even more lethal ring to it than being laid off, but sitting here with his dad and his sister and the kids, Colin had to concede that things weren't so bad. For the first time since leaving his former boss' office, Colin felt calm.

George led them in a prayer over the meal. Benny and Jenny managed to sit still for the whole two minutes, and then the symphony of clanging plates and passing dishes began. Carol made one heck of a feast, and it took up nearly every inch of the tabletop. She sat now with Abby's highchair between herself and her husband, coaxing mashed potatoes and cranberry sauce into the toddler's mouth with mixed success. The dogs got more of her food than Abby did.

After his first bite, Colin's phone started to ring. He yanked it out of his pocket and silenced it quickly. Whoever was calling, he wasn't interested right that minute.

As he made his way home that evening, he remembered the mid-dinner call and pulled out his phone and hit redial.

"Hello?"

"Hi, I got a call from this number," Colin explained. The sleet was really coming down now. It was stupid to be on the phone, but no one else was out driving on Thanksgiving thankfully.

"Hey! Colin! It's me, Jim."

"Jim? Why didn't your number come up on my phone?"

"Ah, well, I had to get a new one." Now that Colin had a name, he could recognize the voice. It had been a couple years since Jim had quit working for Hawthorne. "The wife finally split. I had to change the phone plan."

After getting to enjoy such a nice time with his own family, Colin tried to sound properly sorry. "That's too bad, Jim. Sorry to hear it."

"It's fine, it's fine. But, I heard from Brandon that you had an eye out for work. You available in a couple hours?"

"What?" Colin eased to a stop at a red light; there was no one else at the intersection. "What kind of job needs guys last minute on Thanksgiving?"

"I've been picking up a lot of odd jobs lately, and I'm working at the mall tonight putting up Christmas decorations. You know, the trees out in the parking lot, and the Santa meeting set-up thing. We need an extra guy, do you want to help out?"

"Um, yeah," Colin couldn't really say no. "Is this... you know... legitimate? Are we getting paid in cash, or what?"

"Paid in cash," Jim agreed with a shrug.

The light was stuck on red. Colin inched forward a little, trying to trip the sensor. "I guess. Can you send me a text with the place and time?"

"Yeah, sure thing. I'll see you in a couple hours. Hey, do you have any tools you can bring?"

Colin started to creep through the intersection. How long did he have to wait if the light was stuck? Surely, there was a legal time limit. Was five minutes long enough?

"Yeah, what should I bring?"

"Just bring the whole toolbox. You never know what we might need."

His whole toolbox? Colin frowned. That was several hundred dollars' worth of equipment, just in his main box. It's seemed a little disconcerting that he was the last guy being called and he was bringing all the tools. He was already wondering if he was going to regret saying yes to this. Colin envisioned the rag-tag crew of tool-less workers. He decided his basic kit, which would be more than enough to put up Christmas decorations.

"I'll bring some—whoa!"

He hit the brakes as a car came cruising through the intersection. To be fair, they had the green light, and they'd had to brake and veer to avoid getting scraped along Colin's grill. The little sedan laid on the horn and zoomed off.

That had been too close. Carol would strangle him if he ever got in a wreck from doing something stupid like that, over-protective as she was. "Hey, Jim, I've got to go. I'm driving. Send me that info." Finally, the light turned green on his side. Colin eased into the intersection, checking both ways twice after the close call. "I'll see you in a couple hours."

"You'll bring your tools?"

"Yeah, I'll bring some. Bye."

CHAPTER 4

"Sorry I'm late," Nora called through the entryway of her parents' traditional two-story house. "It's raining like mad out there. And I almost hit some crazy person creeping through that stop light that never changes over on Maple Street."

"He would have been sorry," Nora's younger sister Becka replied smugly. Becka was just visible in a sweater and apron through the doorway, standing behind the kitchen island. She was slicing up the turkey and stacking the steaming, juicy layers of meat on one of their mother's ornate platters. Nora caught a nose full of the smell and felt her stomach growl. "Bad luck to get in a car accident with a lawyer," Becka continued.

"I don't even do motor vehicle collisions," Nora scoffed as she got her shoes off. She hung up her coat as her grandmother met her in the hall. "Hi, Grandma. How was your flight? Not too terrible?"

"Never too terrible to come visit for the holidays," Grandma Mullen answered. She enclosed Nora in a hug despite her diminutive size. Heels or no heels, Nora was easily a half a foot taller. "Besides, the cocktails are cheaper if you're flying on a holiday."

She laughed at the look on Nora's face as they followed the narrow hallway into the den. There, still in her apron, Nora's mother, Viv, sat sourly, watching the Turkey Bowl with her husband.

"Can you believe your sister has kicked me out of the kitchen?" Viv said at once, in obvious disapproval.

"Well, good," Nora replied. "Dad needs someone to watch the Turkey Bowl with since Mikey took that transfer to California."

Her father laughed as her mother pursed her lips, and Nora leaned over and gave each of them a hug and kiss on the cheek.

"Speaking of that, I cannot believe they wouldn't let your brother off for Thanksgiving," Viv huffed. "What kind of company does that?"

"Nora! Help me set the table!" Becka called from the kitchen, attempting to save her sister from their mother's impending rant.

"Nora just got here," Viv insisted.

"I'll help. It's no problem." Nora was already headed into the kitchen, where plates of food were stacked. "Where's Margaret? Off for Thanksgiving?"

"Yeah, she needed a couple days off." Becka had been loading squash, green-bean casserole, turkey, and boiled pearl onions onto plates and into bowls. She may not have been a professional chef, but it looked like she had outdone herself cooking for everyone. "Margaret offered to help out the first half of the day since Grandma arrived this morning and all. But, we all felt that she should have the weekend off with her kids." Becka scraped the last of the carrots into a glass serving bowl before looking up accusingly at her sister. "Hey, I thought I told you to bring a boyfriend."

"I don't see you filling an extra seat at the table," Nora poked back. She had a dish in each hand, carrying them out to the big dining room table in the next room.

"I thought you were thinking of bringing that guy from your firm?" Becka ignored her comment, not letting the subject drop.

Becka sure had a good memory, Nora marveled, although she wasn't too pleased to admit it. She couldn't have mentioned that guy more than once or twice and that was quite a while ago too.

"Married."

"That sucks," Becka muttered. Five years younger than Nora, she still lived with their parents while she went to pharmacy school. Not that she was about to say it out loud, but Nora was secretly glad that Becka hadn't brought anyone. She knew that part of it was the threat of being upstaged by her little sister yet again. Becka was already notoriously better at finding men than her overworked older sister. Worse still, every time Becka came home with a new boyfriend, it triggered their mother to start making less than subtle comments about grandkids while looking longingly at Nora.

"Yeah. Though, I did have a handsome stranger save me from the doorway at Starbucks last week," Nora chuckled. "Think I should have brought him?"

"Maybe. Was he cute?"

"He was...manly." Nora walked back into the kitchen, thinking back to the encounter. "Definitely didn't look like any of the lawyers I'm usually around. He had this dirty blond hair, and he was just... striking. You know?"

"No, I don't know."

"Like, his nose had probably been broken at some point, and his jaw was really square. His features were almost rugged. Like a sexy lumberjack or something."

Becka squinted at her sister's awkward description.

"Like, you know how Daniel Craig really doesn't have a classically handsome face, but it still works?"

Becka looked scandalized; she was digging stuffing out of the turkey, now, and stopped to put her hands on her hips, the large scooping spoon pointing accusingly in Nora's direction. "Daniel Craig *is* handsome, thank you very much." An exaggerated huff slipped out as she turned back to the stuffing.

"*Whatever,*" Nora mouthed.

By the time the family had gathered to say a prayer over their Thanksgiving meal, the smell of roast turkey, gravy, and the sharp tang of cranberry had everyone ready to eat. It was a fairly quiet dinner— after all, this was the first Thanksgiving without their animated brother here to dominate the conversation as he usually did.

Hours later, while she was dozing on the couch to the background noise of *A Christmas Story*, Nora tried to remember if there was anything that she really needed to wake up for tomorrow.

She groaned as she remembered the charity event. She was going to be up early in the morning; her charity outreach to the children of the Evanswood Boys and Girls Club had an event tomorrow. She had signed up to take the children out for some Christmas shopping. Nora had been looking forward to it all month, but now, falling asleep on her parents' couch, she wondered what on Earth she'd been thinking.

CHAPTER 5

$\mathcal{A}$t one in the morning, Colin showed up in the Northtown Mall parking lot to help put up Christmas decorations. He'd packed his small tool chest in the back of the Range Rover, but he turned out to have worried for nothing. The only guy who hadn't brought his own equipment was Jim, who, of course, helped himself to everything Colin had brought. Still, Colin kept a sharp eye out. Jim was nice enough, but Colin still didn't know him all that well. He definitely gave off the impression that he wasn't a by-the-book kind of guy, and back when they worked together Jim had a reputation for not being particularly reliable.

Not long after Colin arrived at the mall, the Black Friday shoppers starting to form their drowsy lines. Even the earliest stores weren't open for business until four a.m., but the diligent bargain hunters were camped out in increasing droves while Colin worked. By the time the crew finished up the next afternoon, Colin emerged from the mall to find the parking lot swamped with cars, and his Range Rover hidden in the sea of vehicles. He began to wander up the isles in the vicinity of where he thought he remembered parking.

The rising sound of children's voices sounded from the next aisle over. Colin stood tall to look over the row of SUVs in the way. A school bus with the words 'Evanswood Boys and Girls Club', had pulled into a block of open spaces near the back of the lot. A cadre of laughing grade-school kids hopped out, in matching shirts, herded by a pair of matching-shirted counselors and two—no, three—harried-looking volunteers.

The youngest volunteer caught his eye. Her light brown hair caught the gentle autumn sun, and Colin recognized her instantly as the woman from Starbucks. She wasn't wearing a suit today, but her smoothly-styled hair was the same as it had been the day he first saw her. Today, she was sporting dark, snug jeans and a soft-looking, white cardigan. Even as she ran back and forth like cattle herder trying to keep the excited children in line, her movements were graceful and precise.

Colin clicked his car key fob again, hoping he was close enough to hear the beeping sound.

The Rover honked from the next aisle over, and Colin headed toward the sound. Opening the back, he threw in his gear, closed it up and got in.

He watched the woman for another minute while the car warmed up. At a different time in his life he may have struck up a conversation with her back at the coffee shop. He glanced in the rearview mirror at his tired eyes. No, he couldn't imagine someone with her polish and refinement looking twice at him nowadays. Plus, saying you were an unemployed welder wasn't quite the type of pickup line known to make the ladies swoon.

He put the car in reverse. It was another beautiful November day. He'd been up all night, so Colin was only able to appreciate it in a hazy, sleep-deprived sort of way. The Smoky Mountains were rising lazily over the edge of town. They burned with the vibrant orange-red of fall leaves; streaks of golden birches and red maples covering every inch. The sky above was the azure blue of pure lapis.

For Colin, the most he wanted out of the rest of the afternoon was to get home and collapse into bed. If his momentum held out, maybe he could manage a shower first, but that was about the extent of his ambition until he caught up on sleep.

Of course, when he parked in the drive that cozied up against the side of his little house, Colin diligently unpacked his tools before the call of his sheets and warm quilt grew too great to ignore. He wanted to bring everything inside before he forgot. Colin balanced his tool chest on his thigh and unlocked the garage. The garage was the whole reason he'd bought this house. It was almost as big as the house itself, and he'd customized it into a workshop for his projects.

He dropped the box on the counter that ran along one entire wall of the workshop and turned to look at his most recent project in the light from the open door. He exhaled with sheer exhaustion and set his hands on his hips. He scanned the workshop. Without work at Hawthorne, he'd had more time to tinker, and that wasn't the worst thing. His eyes landed on his current pre-occupation. A sculpture out of welded metal scraps, about waist height when it wasn't on a worktable. It had started out without purpose, but a mighty sturgeon with a hundred glimmering, mismatched scales had come to life, leaping out of metallic splashes of water.

Colin had no idea how he'd done it, but the one completed eye of the fish was intensely focused and seemed alive, no matter how you looked at it. The metal he'd fashioned it out of was a glimmering blue-silver, the color you imagined ice water must be, and shone with a stubborn brilliance. The rest of the sturgeon was made of metal that had been tarnished to varying degrees and colors.

The impulse to cobble together scraps of metal had started years ago. At first, he just wanted to practice his new craft. Then he found himself sitting down and creating things to wind down from a long week or to blow off steam. Colin had never been the artsy type, not in childhood, nor in school. He couldn't remember ever creating a thing in any medium, not even scribbles in his notebooks as a kid. But the metal seemed pliant under his hands, willing to work with him to become something elegant, something remarkable even.

Colin sighed again, sleep tugging at his eyelids. Welding sculptures was well and good, but working on something to help pay his mortgage would have been preferable. He turned and headed out the workshop door, visions of his pillows taunting him all the way into the house.

CHAPTER 6

*A*s Black Friday wound to a close, Nora climbed into her car exhausted. She waved out the window to the children climbing on the playground equipment out in the yard at the Boys and Girls Club. She started up her engine and carefully reversed out of her parking spot. It was time for coffee and home, in that precise order.

It wasn't as if she had expected a field trip to the mall with two dozen grade school kids to be easy, but—having little experience with children, herself—Nora had underestimated the challenge of running twenty directions at once. The kids were supposed to be helping shop for the local church's toy drive; this was the first year the Boys and Girls Club had attempted this particular feat. Although the kids were surprisingly eager to think up ideas that other children might enjoy, their excitement over their mission made Nora's job feel like trying to control a herd of wayward goats.

The sun was getting low in the sky, melting over the fiery mountains to the east. Autumn in Tennessee was long and gentle, but it was coming to an end in the next few weeks. The Smoky Mountains kept their intense colors for a good long run, but once December rolled in even the most stubborn trees had to let their leaves fall. The rainstorms of the last couple weeks had already begun stripping the colors from trees around town.

Nora decided to hit the drive-thru at Starbucks, and ordered her coffee black, as always. She tacked on decaf at the last minute, since she didn't want to be up the entire night, though she did need to read through some case files. There was an unholy line, but she sat patiently in her car. The muscles in her body slowly began to relax. It was nice to not be chasing children at the moment.

She glanced in the rearview mirror. Her briefcase was still sitting in the back. She'd left it in the car again last night in her rush to get from work to her parents' house. It was turning into a habit. For a second, Nora thought about bringing it up front and poking through a case file while she waited, but when she reached back, the line moved, and she quickly dismissed the idea. There would be plenty enough time when she got home to review her deposition and the case details for when she met her client on Monday.

The cars inched forward again, and Nora slowly idled forward with them. Her client on Monday afternoon was a custody battle. She'd been involved with the case since last February, and she looked forward to the day it was filed away for good. It had begun with abuse allegations against the husband, which was something that no empathetic person ever looked forward to looking into. The wife had hired Nora to represent her in the divorce and was always eternally grateful when they spoke. But pouring over the details of their sad, dysfunctional relationship always had a way of putting a damper on an otherwise good mood.

Nora pushed those thoughts aside. She'd been having a perfectly pleasant day until that popped into her head, and she was determined to go back to her happy place. At least until she got home and had to open the case file.

When she got to the window, Nora accepted her coffee, paid, and began her drive home. There were many advantages to being a lawyer, but there were plenty of times when a day full of herding rowdy children and helping the kids at the Boys and Girls Club's was much more appealing.

She volunteered at the club every week, reading to the kids, helping the staff, and just trying to give back in some way.

Of course, her out-of-office hours took an upshot at this time of year. There were work events and charity auctions, plus about a million other things that the Boys and Girls Club needed an extra hand with. In fact, next week she was helping with another field trip to the mall. The children were going to meet Santa.

CHAPTER 7

*C*olin sat in his SUV, the engine idling and smoke steaming up around the car. The temperature had taken a dip last night and today was a frigid one. The sun shone down on the frozen ground, kicking up the haze. In the distance was the main office of Frank & Sons. He saw a young man in Carhartt overalls and a thick hoody pulled up over his head making his way from the front door out to a white F150 parked in the lot.

The guy looked exactly how Colin imagined he looked just a few years back. Not quite ready to move, he continued his survey of the generic manila colored building. If he walked in that door, Colin was certain he would come out with a new job. He had a flawless reputation, gleaming references, and a ton of experience. His fingers pinched his lips in thought.

As he stared, he saw his entire life laid out before him. Where he'd been and where he would be heading, were exactly the same place. If he got the job, he'd have a good job with a steady paycheck. But, as he'd just witnessed at Hawthorne, it was also naïve to think that he wasn't expendable. Any good person with the proper training could weld a pipe. When he had signed on a Hawthorne he had loved being part of a team, being loyal to a company; but when it came down to it, the loyalty in return was dictated by a lot more than mutual admiration. His supervisors loved him and in a perfect world would have never let him go, but they weren't the final word.

Another thought crossed Colin's mind as he watched the smoke puff out of the vents on the building. Was this all he was meant for? He wasn't providing for a family, he didn't need to clock in first thing in the morning and out in the evening day in and day out to please anyone. He had chosen this job, but he was a small part of a large machine, with no particular importance.

If he took a job at Frank & Sons, there was nothing to say that as soon as the economic tides turned again, he wouldn't find himself a little older, in another parking lot just like this one, having this same conversation. *Maybe it's worth gambling on himself.* The foreign words ran through his head. What did that mean exactly? He didn't really know, but the phrase replayed in his head. He sat for several more minutes, looking at the building, then to the grey-blue sky skimming over the mountains in the distance.

For the first time in his life, the excitement of the unknown washed over him. He really didn't understand the words completely, but the idea of gambling on himself outweighed the lure of stability and a steady paycheck. Colin had always prided himself on being responsible and level-headed, but he couldn't help the feeling of adrenaline rushing through him. He took a breath and tried to think as clearly as he could. He decided to give himself until the New Year to see if he still felt the same way on January 1st. It would be enough time to figure out if he was being crazy right now, and he knew perfectly well that he could get some sort of a job on January 2nd at Frank & Sons if he so desired.

Colin felt a sudden burst of freedom and it was all he could do to keep himself from tearing out of the parking lot in an epic cloud of dust. With the rest of the day free, he decided he would beeline to his favorite drive-through, get the froufiest frou-frou coffee and drive through the mountains, just enjoying the nature and mull over his newfound path.

CHAPTER 8

*W*as that his alarm going off? Colin blinked awake, expecting to see sunlight seeping in around the curtains. But it was still dark outside, and it wasn't his alarm going off. It was his cell phone on the bedside table.

He flailed around for the phone, knocking it onto the floor before he managed to follow the charging cable to its end. As quickly as he could, he hit 'answer.'

"Hey, Colin!"

With a groan, Colin collapsed backward onto the bed. "Hi, Jim."

"Hey—so I have another job you might want. Are you still looking?"

Where was Jim coming up with this work? Over the past week since the Black Friday job, he'd called twice, both with odds and ends of work that brought in a hundred or so bucks a turn. Colin had been eyeing Craigslist and the classifieds in the paper, and these odd jobs weren't listed in either place. Who did Jim know to get this insider info?

But so far, the police hadn't shown up to bust any illegal operations, so Colin kept taking the work Jim rustled up. Besides, his Evanswood contacts hadn't yet turned up any other work for him.

"What's the job?" Colin managed to get the question out before a huge yawn cracked his jaw. He looked at the clock. It was four AM. Didn't Jim ever sleep?

"Well, you know the Northtown Mall does that Santa thing for the kids, right?"

"Yeah... do they need something else put up for it?"

"Not exactly. I guess their guy that usually wears the suit on Tuesday through Friday backed out. You doing anything those days?"

Colin lay on his back, staring at the dark ceiling. At six-foot-something and two hundred pounds of muscle, Colin didn't really fit the typical Santa prototype. "Are you asking me if I want to be Santa?"

"Yeah."

Well, no beating around the bush there. Colin was about to ask where the heck he'd heard about this job, and why didn't he take it himself, but stopped. It was regular work, of a sort. At least through the month of December.

"Why not? When do they want me there?"

"Great! Just go to the mall office tomorrow by ten and tell them you're the guy Jim sent."

Colin sighed and agreed, and Jim hung up with a cheerful goodbye. This sounded so sketchy. When the phone was back on the bedside table, Colin turned over and tried to go back to sleep. The image of himself in a Santa outfit made him laugh out loud. He tried to imagine what sort of looks he'd get from the mall staff tomorrow when he showed up for work. He was tall and muscular and relatively young, with hands like sandpaper. If they'd needed someone to dress up as a Viking or a lumberjack, he'd have been a better fit.

He couldn't have been asleep more than a few minutes before the phone rang again. Colin scrambled for it blindly and picked up.

"Hello?"

"Hey, it's Andrew. Did I wake you?"

It was brighter in the room now. Colin looked at the clock. Six twenty-two. Six twenty-two and his brother-in-law was calling to chat. "Yeah. What?"

"Sorry about the time. I'm headed to work, and I wanted to call you before I forgot again. I was talking to a friend last night about your sculptures and welding work."

"What about it?"

"My buddy's brother is getting married in January, and they're having some big engagement party in a couple weeks. He wanted to know if you could make something for an engagement present."

"In a couple weeks?"

"I know it's short notice. I told him so, but he wanted to talk to you. Is it okay if I give him your number?" To his credit, Andrew at least sounded apologetic, as if he was aware of how strange a time it was to be having this conversation.

Colin lay back again, thinking of the metal piece he had been working on and the mass of metal scrap pieces he already had in his workshop. Surely, he could come up with something.

Taking a leap of faith, he heard himself say, "Sure. Go ahead and tell him to call me."

CHAPTER 9

*T*he Northtown Mall was bursting with shoppers as Nora and Becka weaved from store to store. Nora always forgot to plan ahead, although every Christmas she swore to herself that she would buy gifts far in advance of the holiday. It hadn't happened yet, and this year was no exception.

Nora was about to ask in desperation if their mother needed another candle for the bathroom, but Becka dragged her away from the Yankee Candle store before she could get it out.

"And how are you paying for these gifts, anyway?" Nora asked suspiciously. She threw a pointed look at the new high-heeled boots Becka was wearing. They were cute, all right, but clearly fresh out of the box and very expensive looking.

If Becka was even a little embarrassed, she didn't show it. "I've been saving up."

"Hmm." Nora tilted her head and raised an eyebrow as if thinking. "Saving up what? The money you've begged off Dad? It seems a little backward to be buying them gifts with their own money."

Becka pursed her lips in disapproval. "They don't mind, and you know that."

They passed Victoria's Secret. The Northtown Mall actually had two, and Nora had never been able to fully understand why. She had never even really looked to see if they offered different apparel, although Becka paused by the entrance. It wasn't as if she didn't have the money, but Nora didn't really see why she was supposed to have underwear that rivaled her clothes for attention. Maybe one day when she was married, but as it stood now, Artemis the cat wasn't really that picky about what she wore around the house.

"You could run up a two-thousand dollar shopping bill every month, and they'd tell you they didn't mind," Nora jokingly chided as they moved along. "Now that I've moved out and Mike moved to California, you know they'll do anything to keep you in the house as long as possible."

Nora was shocked. Becka didn't even bother trying to deny it. But, it wasn't worth arguing with her over it. Instead, she nodded to the Santa meet-and-greet set up in the central atrium of the mall. A big winter cottage had been set up with a fake gold and velvet chair next to it and a big camera ready and aimed.

"I'm bringing the kids here tomorrow," Nora said, watching the next child in line approach the big Santa-suited man. The helper elves were hanging back, probably trying not to make the girl feel cornered. Nora couldn't imagine having a hundred strange children sitting on your lap all day—what a box of chocolates that must be. Not to mention the parents to deal with. "I wonder how you keep your wits about you, doing that all day long," she wondered.

"He's cute," Becka commented under her breath. Nora rolled her eyes.

"Into older men, now?"

"He can't be much older than you, really. He doesn't look old, under the beard. I wonder if he'd let me sit on his lap and take a picture?" Becka gave her sister a scandalous wink.

"You are out of your mind. I think college life is warping you" Nora reddened at the thought of the sexy Santa. Then she giggled. "That is so wrong."

"Uh-oh," Becka grimaced. But, her face beamed with unadulterated fascination. "This next group brought their dogs!"

Nora saw it too. "We'd better go before this gets ugly."

"But that's my favorite part," Becka protested as Nora dragged her away.

"You're terrible."

"Oh, we have to think of something for Jennifer Sharper's engagement party, too," Becka said suddenly as they walked away. "I guess she's getting married in January, and they're having a big affair at her dad's house." She shivered in excitement. "I can't wait!"

"I thought you didn't even like Jennifer that much."

"I like her well enough to go eat, drink, and dance in her honor," Becka replied with a grin.

"Her dream come true, I'm sure," Nora replied dryly. "Thanks for inviting yourself, by the way."

Becka waved her off and led the way into a small boutique so quickly that Nora didn't even get a glimpse of the name. All it sold were bags; big ugly leather ones that were obviously meant to be chic, or so the crisp black-and-white décor was meant to convince you. Some of the bags were large enough to fit a small child, but Nora couldn't see herself spending sixteen hundred dollars on a glorified duffle bag. She was more of a shoe girl.

"It's not like you were going to bring a date to the engagement," Becka told her as she picked up and examined a slightly-less-ginormous shoulder bag from its display. "I'm saving you from showing up alone."

Nora wished she had an argument to that, but Becka was frustratingly right. She thought she'd been flirting with a fellow at her office, but it turned out he'd just been very friendly. He was married, and Nora was the one who'd been reading too much into it. She sighed. *If you're married, you should wear your wedding ring.* Who cared if it was the twenty-first century? It was a courtesy to everyone else to just take yourself off the market and not give any lonely lawyers false hopes.

Annoyed, Nora took the bag from Becka's hands and put it back. "If you want to buy something to carry your entire course load of books in, I can get you one of those roller bags." Becka rolled her eyes but chuckled and followed Nora out of the store.

They made their way along the row of shops, taking in the holiday decorations. The Christmas lights were up inside Northtown, strung along the balcony of the second level and wrapping around the banisters of the staircases. Christmas trees stood at intervals, glittering with tinsel, and big LED-lit stars hung along the ceiling high overhead.

Christmas was in the air, and Nora was trying not to think too heavily about the emptiness of her condo when she went home in the evening. She was an adult for goodness' sake. She didn't need someone with her all the time, checking up on her, sending her texts to see if the firm had kept her working late. She didn't need somebody surprising her with dinner or sending her flowers at work.

And she certainly didn't need someone surprising her with coffee partway through her workday, when the paperwork got so tedious she wanted to curl up in a ball under her desk. Nope, she was fine. It was enough to have her family, to have a good job and a comfortable life. That was enough.

All those other things? The Hallmark love story moments; Nora didn't need them.

And if she could keep herself from thinking too hard about it, she could convince herself that she didn't want them either.

CHAPTER 10

*L*aughing and joking with kids all day definitely wasn't what Colin was used to, but it had grown on him after a single hour at the Santa meet-and-greet. He'd been a little nervous when he showed up and asked to speak to 'the Santa people.' The phrase had slipped out, unintended, and Colin had been painfully aware of how insane he sounded.

But the lady in the mall office had understood what he meant, and within a half hour, Colin was dressed up in the suit, padded as much as possible to make him slightly less lean. He still made a bit of a ripped Santa Claus, but so far, none of the mothers had complained. With the beard, the wig, and a bit of white makeup over his eyebrows, Colin could make it work.

Sure, there was the occasional parent who underestimated how frightened their child was of strangers. Some that still tried to get a picture taken of the poor kid, regardless. In fact, the amused, laughing father who was standing behind the photographer right now was probably finding his two-year-old's desperate struggle to roll off Colin's lap mighty entertaining. This picture would most likely come out of the woodworks in another sixteen years when the kid's graduation came around.

The boy's mother was not as entertained, however, and fretfully collected her toddler from Colin just as soon as the photograph was snapped. Colin quietly apologized for everything he could think of, and then for his very existence as a Santa impersonator as the woman hurried her child back to his stroller.

"Well that was fun," the girl elf at his left muttered. She looked fifteen. Supposedly, you had to be eighteen or older to work at this display, or so Colin had been told by the manager. Given his own slapdash employment here, he got the feeling they weren't sticklers for the rules.

"Fun for you maybe," he muttered back. "All you have to do is smile and act tipsy."

The supposedly eighteen-year-old chuckled. "Who says I'm acting?"

"You better be acting. I'm making a list. *And checking it twice.*"

The other elf was talking to the next family, trying to settle down the children in line. Unlike some of the other employees, she acted like she'd met a child at some point in her life and seemed to be quite comfortable with them. She talked to them with reassurance and engaged with them to help make the situation less intimidating.

A couple with a screaming child walked away, obviously in the midst of a heated argument.

Colin murmured to his elf, "She looked like she was about to deck his halls." The elf rolled her eyes and snickered while Colin suppressed a laugh at the stupidity of her Santa-humor. The effect at least made him jiggle properly like the jolly fat man he was supposed to be. He put on a smile and pushed up the fake glasses he'd been given as the next child approached. This one was blessedly happier.

"Oh, great," the elf sighed. "There's a whole busload of kids coming. A youth group or something. They're with a couple teachers and some church moms."

But Colin didn't get a chance to look up. He was in his Santa mode as the next little girl wandered up and introduced herself shyly.

In fact, Colin got no more than a hazy glimpse at the group of waiting kids. For one thing, there were intense lights pointed at him to help the photographer capture sellable pictures. It wasn't until the first child from the large group paused like a frightened deer six feet from Colin's chair that he got a look at the chaperones.

Colin felt the blood drain from his face as the beautiful woman from the coffee shop—the same one who'd been with the group of kids he'd seen out in the parking lot on Black Friday—stepped up to take the boy's hand.

"Come on, Luke," she said gently. "Don't be scared. He's nice, I promise." She smiled up at him, her eyes twinkling in a silent adult conspiracy. Colin thought he must have swallowed his tongue. She was in a baby blue cashmere sweater this time, with her hair pulled into her signature bun.

The woman managed to coax the boy, who was maybe five or six, up to where Colin sat, sweating through the Santa suit. All he could think was that she was way too close. Surely, this close she'd recognize him. Surely.

Clinging to normalcy, Colin launched into his Santa act and managed to forget the lovely woman beside him. He and Luke had a friendly conversation about the Boys and Girls Club, whose logo was emblazoned on the little boy's shirt. However, when Colin glanced back up, she was looking at him intently.

At that moment, the photographer asked her to step out of the picture for a moment, and she obliged quickly, stepping over to join the group of waiting kids. Colin thought that maybe she was still trying to get a good look at him, even from twelve feet off.

The next few kids were not nearly so afraid, and there proved to be no need for her to approach again. Colin was more than a little thankful for that. The last thing he needed was for the cute Starbucks lady to think he worked full-time as a mall Santa.

———

It wasn't until later when he was working on the engagement gift he'd been commissioned to create, that Colin gave the Starbucks lady another thought. Maybe, he should have said something to her, or even asked her out. Something about her made him feel like there was more to her than met the eye. Maybe he unfairly judged her, and she would have been interested in dating an unemployed welder.

Nah, he decided and dropped his facemask back in place.

CHAPTER 11

*J*ennifer Sharper hadn't been the sweetest girl when the two of them had gone to high school together. Nora recalled many unfavorable memories with Jennifer, although they'd lingered in the same general friend circle for the four years leading up to graduation. Their parents, however, had been in the same social circles for much of their lives, hence her inclusion on the invite list.

The house that Nora and Becka pulled up to looked more like a country club than a private residence. A valet took their car, sparing them a walk from the parking area through the gathering snowdrifts.

"Not bad," Becka muttered.

The front foyer was like walking into the White House. A grand double staircase wound up two opposite walls, leading to rooms on the upper floors. Hundreds of soft yellow lights were strung up for the holidays, casting the entire interior of the house in a fairytale glow. It all looked so pristine as if it was straight from the pages of a magazine rather than where the Sharper's actually lived.

Nora and Becka had dressed as the invitation told them, Black Tie Optional. Both girls were in evening gowns as were most of the other female attendees. Becka's A-line was navy blue with a light shimmer, while Nora wore a graceful sheath in pure black offset with a gorgeous chunky statement bracelet and draping earrings. The elegant black dress had a slit leading up one side—higher than she would have preferred normally, but her tempestuous sister insisted her legs were long enough to get away with it. There wasn't a man in sight who wasn't in a suit, most with ties, but a few rising to the occasion in a proper tux. Everyone had drinks in hand, so after the hosts of the party greeted the girls, they set off in pursuit of their own. Nora hardly recognized Jennifer, who fluttered by without recognition. She had slimmed down considerably for the occasion.

There was a live band playing soft jazzy background music, and a ballroom with an enormous wall of windows looking out into an ethereal, snow-frosted garden under strings of outdoor fairy lights. Nora was spellbound. A moment later she was jostled back to consciousness when Becka caught sight of the bar and pulled Nora over.

"What'll it be?"

"An Old Fashioned and a vodka cranberry, please," Becka told him without asking Nora. Over the last few years, they'd gone to an event or two together, and Becka knew what Nora always ordered. She liked her Old-Fashioned's.

With a few shakes of the sleek metal cocktail shaker, two glasses were poured and pushed across the bar with precise execution. Nora thanked the clean-shaven bartender as she picked up her Waterford glass. She took a sip off the top of the dark amber drink and pushed the cherry to the bottom. Becka followed Nora as she slowly weaved through the crowd.

"This is cool," Becka whispered loudly. Nora had to agree that the swanky soiree was pretty impressive. They made their way through the crowd, doing a circle of the main room.

The two of them were running into a blockage at the edge of the ballroom. Some sort of crowd had clogged up the edge of the dance floor, ogling something. Nora could barely see something metallic gleaming near the back wall.

"It's like an exhibit or something," she told Becka, who was definitely the shorter sister.

"Well, cool. Let's look closer."

And then Becka began gently elbowing her way through the crowd, proving that although Nora was the tall sister, Becka was the bossy one.

"Oh, my," Nora gasped.

The art that everyone was so enraptured with was a glorious wall-size landscape, made entirely of metal. The sheets were all in burnished bronze and shades of copper. It shimmered in the warm light. It depicted a mountain rising over a serene metal lake, surrounded by metal pine trees. A welded elk stood peacefully, a tiny shape in the shadow of the rising mountain. A full moon peered over the mountain's shoulder, wrought in some metal that shone pale gold.

Becka was saying something, but Nora was staring, bewitched.

"Nora!"

Nora shook her head and looked down at her sister.

"I guess this is an engagement gift," Becka told her. "Someone from the groom's side had it made from some local artist. It's quite good."

That was an understatement. The metal landscape was impossible to look away from. It was hypnotizing. No wonder a crowd was standing around it, silent with awe.

Becka moved on after some cute man in a suit caught her attention. With a chuckle, Nora let her go. Her eyes were glued to the piece. It was so... elegantly simple and expressive at the same time. Nora wasn't a fine art buff, and she didn't know a thing about metalworking. All she knew is that it ignited a feeling in her chest, a fascinating contentment. Transcendent, like the pull of a full moon.

After a long while, Nora moved back and let someone else get close enough for a good look. She'd been impressed by the house and the atmosphere. But that art piece was something else altogether.

She turned to go look for Becka and nearly bowled right over one of her fellow guests. The remains of her Old Fashioned splashed over his suit jacket.

"I'm so sorry!" she cried. Nora swiped at his jacket. "I am *so* sorry!"

"It's fine," he said, waving her off. "Don't even worry about it. I stole this jacket off some guy in the parking lot."

Nora looked up and saw the humor in his eye. She relaxed and tried to smile. He smiled back, and suddenly, the memory clicked into place. "Hey! I saw you at Starbucks once!"

He chuckled nervously and nodded. "Yeah. The doors here didn't give you any trouble, did they? I wasn't there to... you know... hold it..."

He laughed nervously again and then clamped his lips shut. Nora let a giggle escape. "No, no trouble tonight. I guess the door saw you come in and it was too afraid to give me any grief."

She tried not to be too obvious as she looked him up and down. He'd been wearing jeans and a flannel jacket when they had met in the doorway at Starbucks. She'd noticed his dirty blond hair and handsome face, but now she could see the rest of him matched perfectly. Broad shoulders held up the suit jacket. His tapered frame was visible as his crisp white shirt, which he wore unbuttoned to the collarbone, followed the V shape. The dress slacks bulged over muscular thighs. He wore a deep purple pocket square that complimented his green eyes.

"Nora," she said, extending her hand.

"Colin," he replied. He shook her hand and then as if were an afterthought, he lifted her knuckles to his lips in a brief kiss. She thought she saw a quick flush pass over his cheeks with the gesture.

"So," Nora said quickly, afraid he might run off. "Are you here with the bride or the groom?"

It seemed like a straightforward question, but he thought about it longer than she expected. Finally, he chuckled and shrugged. "The groom, I guess. Sort of both."

Sort of both? Nora didn't know what to make of his cryptic answer, but he didn't explain further. "I'm with the bride, but I have to admit, I'm not sure how I earned an invitation." Conspiratorially, Nora leaned in to whisper. "We haven't spoken in years. Social obligation, I imagine."

Colin laughed. "I was surprised to get an invite, myself. But, it looks like a pretty diverse crowd. I guess you don't get this successful without befriending a few people along the way. I'm not even sure I know this many people on a first name basis."

Nora looked around and examined her fellow guests. They were all dressed to the nines. Evening dresses and suits and flawless make-up.

"I'm pretty sure I don't, either," Nora admitted. She looked down at her empty glass and smiled. "Would you like to join me for a drink?"

Colin agreed with a smile, and they threaded back through the crowded ballroom to the lounge with the open bar. When they squeezed in, Colin tried to wave the bartender down.

At that moment, Nora saw Becka headed her way, looking at the tall stranger with interest. Frantically, Nora waved her away. Becka gave her a devious grin, and Nora motioned for her to make herself scarce. With a silent snicker, Becka gave Nora the gesture for *I'm watching you*, but thankfully relented and headed back into the crowd.

Nora turned back to see the man behind the bar waiting, and Colin watching her with a raised eyebrow.

"Oh, an old fashioned, please," Nora told the bartender sweetly.

With a glass apiece, Nora and Colin found an empty table and sat down to talk.

"Did you see that landscape?" Nora asked him, the unique piece still on her mind. After all, she'd nearly spilled her drink on him not twenty feet from the artwork, but he might not have gotten the chance to see.

His grin turned secretive. "You mean the engagement gift? Yeah, I saw it."

"I've never seen anything like it," Nora gushed. The drink was helping to loosen her up a bit, but she'd figured out that Colin was a little shy as well. But, she got the feeling that he was someone who opened up once he had warmed up to a person. He was handsome enough that the effort was worth it.

"Really?" he asked. His secretive smile opened in excitement. "It's a… a really unique gift, I guess."

"I'll say," Nora agreed. "I forgot to ask who the artist is. Someone local, I think."

"The artist's name isn't on it," Colin told her. "It's a secret."

Nora laughed. "We have a secret artist on the loose."

Colin took a sip of his drink and sighed. "Time to make up the wanted posters."

His hands had caught Nora's eye at the bar, and she looked at them closely, now. They were big, which matched the rest of him, from his broad shoulders to his towering height. The nails were short and uneven, and if she wasn't mistaken, still with a bit of dirt under them.

Slyly, she looked back up at his face. "So what do you do?"

"I'm a welder," he admitted with a shrug. Just then an upbeat holiday song began playing, causing the dance floor to populate.

"Do welders dance?" she asked cautiously, feeling bold with her second drink and the warmth of their close bodies.

"Welders have been known to a cut a rug or two," Colin returned. He almost followed that up with a relatively lame carpenter joke, but thankfully stopped himself.

Colin stood, tipped back the remainder of his glass and offered her his hand. "Shall we?"

Nora wasn't a huge dancer at these kinds of parties. She typically preferred to blend in, but she loved to just cut loose and have fun when she was with the right people. There were so many people at the engagement party that it was easy to feel hidden in plain sight, leaving them free to dance without anyone paying much attention.

They danced for the next five songs, which fluctuated between up-tempo dance numbers and smooth jazz. Colin twirled her around, and they made up the moves as they went. Nora's smile felt huge across her face as she was twirled and swirled under his arm and around the dance floor. They made funny conversation between songs and several times as they danced. After the band's rendition of *It's The Most Wonderful Time of the Year* came to an end, Colin dipped her deeply in a melodramatic move.

When he pulled her up, a slow, romantic song began to play softly in the background. Still breathing hard from giggling, Nora found a comforting relief as Colin pulled her to him, their hands intertwined, her face resting gently in the sway underneath his shoulder. She could feel the top of her head brush lightly against his jaw. He smelled like Christmas pine and cinnamon, and the dance was a slow, swaying dream. When the final notes hit, they lingered for a minute before pulling back to look at one another.

"Do you want to go outside for a little fresh air?" Colin suggested.

Nora nodded quickly. That was exactly what she wanted to do. He took her hand in his and led her through the crowd. This must be what it's like to have a bodyguard, she thought to her own amusement. As the crowd was thick, she had a few minutes to savor the strength of his hand, gently covering hers. She could feel the callouses from where he must hold his tools. These were definitely not hands used for punching computer keys or flipping through long legal documents.

For a fleeting second, she thought of what it would feel like if he were to slip his hand around her bare back and pull her close. The image flustered her, and she had to shake it from her mind. She needed that cold outdoor air stat! Colin pushed the door open, and Nora entered the enchanting courtyard. It felt like a scene out of a movie, a regal winter wonderland. Nora began to walk toward some seating placed next to a roaring outdoor fireplace when suddenly a shrill voice cut through the air. "Nora! There you are! I haven't seen you in forever!"

It was Jennifer Sharper, of course, and Nora tried to smile as she turned and accepted the half-drunk hug from the blonde bride-to-be. A gaggle of high-heeled and unsteady women had followed behind Jennifer, and it was clear that they were heading back inside, and now meant to take Nora with them. She looked over her shoulder at Colin in dismay as she was herded away.

"Don't worry," Jennifer told him with exaggerated certainty. "We'll bring her right back."

That was a lie. It was time for the party to really begin, and a slew of wedding-themed games and dances were in full swing in the ballroom. Nora was dragged into it and didn't have the heart to excuse herself and try to track down her handsome welder again.

By the time she and Becka were exhaustedly staggering towards the door at the end of the night, half of the party guests were asleep in chairs or muttering to each other over mostly-empty bottles of champagne. It was still dark outside, but dawn would be approaching soon. The clock on the dash in Nora's car read four forty-nine as she eased out of the parking area and found her way back to Evanswood.

"Let me know if Jenny invites you to any more parties," Becka murmured sleepily, leaning against the window.

Nora didn't answer. Colin had disappeared after Jennifer dragged her away. Nora was convinced that they would have enjoyed the remainder of the evening together if he'd stayed at the party. She sighed in disappointment. Another few minutes, and she would have asked for his number. Now, she didn't even know his last name, and unless she found a way to talk to Jennifer Sharper again, there was no way to find out. It had been made known last night that Jennifer, her fiancé, and her family were to be on a plane first thing in the morning to celebrate Christmas in Zurich. Finding out the name of a random Prince Charming probably didn't count as enough of an emergency to go through the rigmarole of tracking down the Sharper clan.

Colin hadn't been wearing a wedding ring. Nora had looked at his hands long enough to be sure of that. His hands looked worn and rough, but strong, and Nora shivered to imagine what sorts of things they were capable of. No wedding ring…

Of course, it was the twenty-first century, and some people just didn't wear wedding bands. Nora fervently hoped that Colin wasn't among them.

CHAPTER 12

"*C*olin? You out here?"

He could hardly hear over the hiss of the torch in his hand. Colin looked up to see his sister Carol in the doorway of his workshop. He cut the heat on his welding torch and flipped his eye protector up. The weather was seasonally cold, with a week left until Christmas, but he was still sweating in his coveralls, gloves, and face shield. He swiped an arm across his forehead.

"Hey! What's up?"

Carol jabbed a thumb towards the house. "I just brought some leftovers over. Dad thinks you're going to starve to death."

Colin rolled his eyes. "I know how to cook."

"You know how to use a microwave." Carol came closer to look at the sculpture he was working on. It wasn't his sturgeon leaping from the water this time. His sister loosened her scarf; his workshop was fairly toasty with all the welding. "Is this a new commission?"

The shape was becoming clear; it was an ornate metal cross, delicately scaled in a thousand tiny pieces of scrap metal to create an effervescent effect. Colin nodded.

"Yeah. Your church asked me to make it, actually. St. Joseph's.

They want to auction it off as part of some partnership with the Heart Association's annual charity fundraiser. Obviously, I couldn't say no to that."

"Wow." Carol examined the intricate metal bands. Even half-done, Colin could still tell she found it impressive. He rarely saw his sister impressed. Most days she just looked exhausted. These days, she was usually running after her brood of offspring or yelling at the dogs. A spear of guilt hit him in the gut. Maybe he should take her out to a movie or something. He'd let Carol take care of their dad. Really, he'd let her take care of everything after their mom passed away. If she was exhausted and overworked, he felt that at least part of it was his fault.

"Is Andrew working tonight?"

Carol nodded. "He picked up all the overtime he could so that we can afford for him to take some time off."

With a yawn, Colin looked at his watch and realized he'd been out here for six hours. The time had flown by.

Carol leaned against his worktable and crossed her arms. "I meant to ask, how'd that party go? Did they like that sculpture you made?"

"They loved it," Colin answered, leaning against the table next to her. "That's actually how St. Joseph's got a hold of me. I guess someone at the party goes to their church, and they asked Andrew's friend who made it."

"Through the grapevine," Carol agreed, smiling. "Well, I'm glad you're making some money from this. I think you like it a lot." That last part was a sisterly intuition. Colin chuckled, thinking of Nora.

"I think I do, too," he admitted. "It was really nice, having people admire my work. But, I think it'll be better when I get a welding job again."

Carol looked at him in surprise. "Really? Why?"

"You know why," he said. "The same reason why Mom never stopped working to write full-time. It's just not steady enough, you know? I mean, I'm doing this piece as a donation."

With a sigh, Carol wrapped an arm around his waist. "But, Mom also never got to finish her book, don't forget. Everything she wrote, we printed out and put in a binder... just to keep..." Carol's voice hitched, and Colin put his arm around her shoulders. Carol pushed on, her voice a little hoarse. "We'll never know how she meant to end it because she would never spend the time on it."

Colin put his other arm around his sister and kissed the top of her head. "She wanted to spend her time with us."

Carol nodded and wiped at her eyes. "I know. I just... all those half-written pages really get to me, you know? I go, and I look through them sometimes, and I—I just wish she'd gotten to—to finish it."

His eyes were welling up with tears now too, and Colin swallowed a lump in his throat. "Come on, Carol. I'm not Mom. I'm not going anywhere anytime soon."

Carol laughed through her tears. "Of course you aren't. You have award-winning sculptures to create."

Relieved that their conversation was returning to a more light tack, Colin laughed. "Exactly. And don't you worry about me starving; the Denny's up the road has a table with my name on it."

Carol shoved him playfully.

"Oh hey! This is kinda just an experiment, but I wanted to show you something." Colin walked over to a small box sitting on his workbench. He grabbed a polishing rag and opened the box. As Carol came over to see, Colin took the delicate ring out of its resting place and ran the cloth around it.

"Here, see if it fits." Colin handed the ring to Carol, whose mouth was agape. She took the smooth metal ring between her fingers and held it up to the light. Tiny detailed etchings were intricately woven onto the surface, leading up to and encircling a gleaming aquamarine stone.

"Colin, this is-" Carol continued to take in the ring, still unable to wrap her head around the fact that her brother had created something so delicate and beautiful.

"It's your birthstone. Like I said, it was just an experiment," he looked a little bashful about it and shrugged. "I was going to give it to you for Christmas, for always taking such good care of me. But, I don't know. Tonight seemed good too."

"Colin, I...this is the most beautiful ring I've ever seen." She slipped it on her finger and inspected it. "I can't believe you made this. It's really mine to keep?"

Colin laughed, "Yeah, of course. I mean, it's not an everyday ring, it was just something I wanted to try, and I thought who better to make it for." He smiled at his sister who still couldn't break her gaze from the ring adorning her finger.

"I guess I better call it a night," Colin sighed. He unplugged the torch and doubled-checked that everything was cooling. "If I'm not careful I forget to eat, I forget to sleep. It's a wonder I've made it this far."

Carol opened his workshop door, and they walked out into the falling snow. "I already have three kids. Don't add yourself to the list of people I have to watch over twenty-four seven."

The night was serene, a crisp mid-December night. Colin didn't have Christmas lights on his house, but his neighbors did, and a shimmering tinsel tree hung from the streetlight. A light snow was falling. The yellow lamplight made the snow look like flakes of gold as it drifted, settling on the road in a thick blanket.

"You better head home. It's getting too deep for your car, and the plows don't come through my street first."

Carol agreed and leaned up to give her brother a hug and a kiss on the cheek. "Thank you for this." She wiggled her fingers in the air, showing off her new jewelry. "I left the food in your fridge. It's probably not too cold yet, if you eat it now."

She climbed into her car. "Oh! Hey Colin, have you called Frank & Sons yet?"

Guiltily, Colin shrunk into his big shoulders. "No."

Carol glared over the frame of her car door. "Good." She cracked a sisterly smile, "I think something better is just around the corner."

He looked up at her surprised, and Carol shut the car door. Her reverse lights flared, and she backed out onto the street. Colin watched until she was out of sight, and then retreated out of the cold, back into his house.

He found the leftovers she'd brought: pot roast with boiled

vegetables. Colin put the whole thing in the microwave eagerly. He hadn't eaten since the morning, and home cooked food was exactly what he needed.

CHAPTER 13

*T*he Monday before Christmas, Nora was at the Northtown Mall again. The only person left to shop for was Becka; Nora was beginning to think that it would be much easier to just buy her sister a gift card. Nora loved her sister, but it was hard to buy a gift for someone who rarely waited to be given what they wanted.

Outside Macy's, Nora stopped and leaned on the rail, looking around at the shoppers. A lot of people saw Becka as selfish. There were times when Nora agreed. But, at least her little sister never had to wonder if she'd ever get the things she needed in her life. If there was ever a change to make or a chance to pursue, Becka just did it and got things done.

Nora had always tended to take the long way around. The scenic route always held surprises, things you didn't even think of. For her, law school had been a slow, steady process. She took challenges one at a time, and never rushed faster than her comfort zone wanted to allow. And because of that, Nora had a comfortable life. Up until now, she'd thought this was the life she had wanted.

But maybe Becka was onto something because Nora knew that if it had been her sitting at that table with Colin the other night, Becka would have gotten more than his number. Nora had played it safe again, trying to take the long way around, and before she knew it, she was hijacked off to dance the Macarena and play engagement bingo with people she barely knew. All while missing the chance to spend time with someone that she wanted to know better.

Of course, Nora reminded herself, he was probably married. Good looking, with a good job, and an adorable shy smile. He was definitely married, he had to be. But, now Nora would never know.

With a sigh, she turned and thought about going through Macy's. Even from here, she could see it was a madhouse inside. The line at the cash registers wound to the back of the store, and the displays were a frantic mess. Sometimes Nora stumbled across pretty outfits in Macy's. But, unless they'd decided to open a department dedicated to shopping for impulsive younger sisters, there really wasn't a good reason to go there today.

Nora walked away from Macy's and wandered down the line of smaller stores. She passed the oversized bag boutique, but even though she loved her sister, she couldn't bring herself to venture in. But when she was past the boutique, another thought came to mind. There was a store on the other side of the mall that was perfect, she thought excitedly.

Excited, now, Nora scanned over the mall directory and mapped in her head which way to go.

On the way, Nora passed by the Santa meet-and-greet again. It looked like a different Santa on duty today, which was a shame. Becka had been right, after all. That other actor had been one hunky Santa.

Nora stopped again as a second revelation hit her. The madness of it was overwhelming. She looked at the Santa in the red and gold chair; it definitely wasn't the same guy, because she knew, now, what he looked like under the hair and beard.

She inched closer to the elf lingering near the fence; there were three today.

"Excuse me?" she said hesitantly.

The elf looked over. She had to still be in high school. "Hello! Merry Christmas, ma'am, what can I do for you?"

"Hey, do you know the other Santa that works here?" Nora asked.

The girl looked at her suspiciously. Nora felt strange for someone in fake ears and jingle-bell shoes to be giving her the side eye. "We aren't supposed to give out personal information… Why?"

Nora bit back the excitement of discovery. "His name is Colin, right?"

The elf nodded again. "Well, yeah. What about him?"

"Do you know his last name?"

The girl looked over at her co-workers; it was hard to tell if she was silently asking for help or checking to see if anyone was watching. It seemed as though the two of them were unobserved, so she turned back to Nora.

"It's McCullough," she admitted. "Colin McCullough."

"Sounds very Scottish."

"He *looks* pretty Scottish. Or Irish. I don't really know the difference, honestly," the elf shrugged.

"Is he…" Nora chewed her lip, trying to frame her question. She wasn't really sure whether she wanted to know the answer to her question. But she was channeling her impulsive, grab-life-by-the-collar sister, and she figured that she might as well ask. "Do you know if he's married? Or with anyone?"

She held her breath while the elf girl thought about it. Finally, the girl twisted her mouth in a frown. "You know… I don't think so. I tried to flirt with him like a million times and he refuses to flirt back with me. But I think he thinks I'm in high school."

Nora was tempted to ask if the girl was in high school, but she was too eager to move on. She thanked the elf helper and waved goodbye.

There was just a little bit of shopping left to do, and then it was time to see if she could track down Colin McCullough.

CHAPTER 14

$\mathcal{A}$t St. Joseph's Church, Colin was lingering in a tiny annex room with the finished project that he'd delivered. Tonight was the night it was supposed to be auctioned off for charity. It had turned out beautifully, but Colin was still nervous.

For the moment, he was alone with his thoughts, for which Colin was thankful. He'd taken a job to make something, and it had turned out well. Then he'd been contacted to make something else, and it had turned out just as good, if not better. Strangely, it felt as if his life was shifting around him. Maybe his luck had changed?

Luck, or Carol's words. No one was more surprised than Colin when he actually decided not to call Frank & Sons the day after talking to Carol in the garage. Maybe there was something magical in the air, but from that moment on, Colin had made the decision that he wasn't going back to his old life. He could always get a welding job. He was skilled, and a hard worker. There would always be something out there for him.

But, what he wasn't sure of was whether he would always have the opportunities that he suddenly found himself with. These last few days, he had fielded phone calls about other commissions, metal sculptures, and even some jewelry pieces. It seemed that Carol had been flashing her new ring around and people had taken notice.

Colin sighed and ran a hand over the metal-worked cross. He was proud he'd been entrusted to make something that would do some good in the world. The idea of it was pretty powerful. His simple act of plying metal into something he thought was beautiful would possibly be bought by someone who actually wanted to display the thing that *he* had made in their home. And the money they spent would go directly to help families dealing with overwhelming medical needs and expenses. The nervousness in his heart reared up again. He hoped someone bought it.

Maybe he was an artist after all. He crinkled his nose and laughed to himself at the idea. He may have to get used to that a bit more before he said it out loud.

"Mr. McCullough?"

One of the auction staff came in, followed by two church volunteers to move the auction piece up into the viewing area for the guests to take a closer look at before the bidding began. Colin lent a hand moving the piece, as he knew how heavy and awkward it was.

Up in the gallery, a circle of art pieces waited for the auction to start. There was an obvious open display stand for the cross, and Colin let the other two volunteers steer it in that direction. They managed to get the sculpture on the stand without incident. The spotlights created a halo effect on the placid piece.

A group of admirers flocked to it at once, and Colin backed away quickly. He straightened his suit jacket and quietly allowed the audience to ogle his work. He'd carried it in with the other volunteers, so no one seemed to credit him with it.

"This one's nice."

Colin jumped. There she was again, Nora, the woman from Starbucks, and the mall, and the women he had held in his arms on the dancefloor at the engagement party. She just kept popping up, and it was hard to tell whether this was a good or bad thing.

Tonight, her straight hair was in a shimmering sheet down around her shoulders, and she was wearing a lovely green sweater-dress that was modest enough for a church, but just clingy enough to make an imaginative man wonder. For all intents and purposes, Colin chalked this meeting up to the 'good' column.

And right now, she was admiring his art. He tried to look casual, which was difficult when he was nervous. Colin didn't like to play poker for precisely this reason.

"I was wondering what this piece was going to be," Nora commented casually. "I heard it's by the same artist as the one at the engagement party."

Colin looked at her out of the corner of his eye. Was she hinting? He felt himself start to sweat, an irrational reaction, but a powerful one all the same.

"Do you go to this church?" he asked.

She leaned closer. "No. I'm actually on the Heart Association Fundraising Committee. But, we were running short on volunteers so I said I would help with guarding the doors during the actual auction."

"So you're guarding the doors in case anyone tried to make a mad dash with any of the auction items, eh?" he chuckled.

"Oh, don't be deceived; I'm much bigger than I look. There will be no thefts tonight. Not through my door," she replied impishly.

"So are you bidding tonight?"

"Me?" he laughed. "I'm a welder. I don't make enough money to bid on these things."

"You did say that," Nora nodded. "Would I have heard of where you work?"

Not sure how to answer, he shoved his hands in his suit pockets. "I doubt it. But I'm currently getting a chance to enjoy the holidays, so not too much focus on working for once."

"That's good. I hear Christmas is Santa's busiest night of the year."

At first, her comment didn't make a bit of sense. Colin was watching the crowd around his art, and puzzled for a minute about what on Earth she meant.

And then, like a brick, it hit him. Colin's entire body froze, and he looked down at Nora to see she was smiling like a cat with a mouse. The blood rushed to his face, and he felt his cheeks reddening wildly.

"If everyone could please take their seats, now." A prim, stern-faced woman appeared at the open door of the large room where the auction was being held. "We're ready to begin the auction, ladies and gentleman."

Another staffer appeared at his elbow. "Mr. McCullough, if you could come with me," she said kindly, nodding at Nora.

Colin had never been so happy to escape in his life. With a red-faced nod, he fled, following after the woman as she led him inside.

CHAPTER 15

*N*ora stood in the back of the hall with the other volunteer who was attending the door. She'd been so excited to see Colin again. Was the entire world determined to interrupt?

She tried to spot him in the audience, but he wasn't sitting among the guests. He'd said that he wasn't bidding, tonight, so Nora wasn't expecting to find him there anyway. With his height, even if he'd been in the seats, she would have seen him.

To her surprise, Nora saw Colin sooner than expected. When the metalwork cross came up for bidding, it was introduced as belonging to him, crafted in full by Mr. Colin McCullough.

Standing there in the spotlight next to his sculpture, he'd never looked so handsome, or so shy. His suit fit him just perfectly, and Nora could swear that every woman in the room let out a collective, admiring sigh.

But Nora could hardly believe her eyes. Did this mean that he'd made the landscape, too? He'd said that he was a welder. Where did he learn to make such stunning art?

Looking at him now, Nora suspected that if she tried to ask him, he'd be too embarrassed to answer.

She couldn't help but grin. He was too much. Built like a college football player, and as sweet as a teddy bear.

The bidding started for his artwork, but Nora's attention was fixed on him. She saw his every expression, and when his sculpture was auctioned away for $50,000, she thought she could tell he was barely able to keep his own jaw from dropping.

As the piece was wheeled off the stage, Colin was escorted off. She saw him gracefully slip into the shadows and from the look he gave her when she outed him as Santa, she imagined he was about to make a hasty exit.

She turned to her fellow volunteer. "Do you think you could watch the door?"

The woman smiled and winked. "Yep. Go get him."

Nora felt herself redden, though not as badly as Colin did. "You saw him leave, too?"

The other volunteer, an older mom who Nora knew for a fact had been happily married for over twenty years, fanned herself theatrically. "Everybody saw him leave honey, believe me."

Hesitant, Nora grimaced. "I hate to leave just for that."

The woman waved her through the meeting room door. "Let me put it to you this way: I can't chase him myself, but I'm not getting in the way of you finding a guy like that under *your* Christmas tree. Go catch that man!"

Nora intended to do just that, and left with a hasty thank-you. He wasn't in the hall when she left the meeting room, and he wasn't in the entryway of the church. She grabbed her coat and hurried carefully out into the icy parking lot, but she didn't see anyone's car running.

And then she realized—if he'd brought in his artwork, he'd probably parked in the back!

Nora got there too late. His taillights were swinging out of the church parking lot by the time she managed to navigate the snowy walkway to the rear of St. Joseph's. And once again, Nora found herself standing there wondering: *Why do I always go the long way?*

CHAPTER 16

*I*t was Christmas Eve, and the Starbucks was closing down until December 26th. Colin sat in an empty chair by the door, waiting for his coffee. Considering it was Christmas Eve, the place was pretty busy. A group of high school Christmas carolers was parked in the center of the place, laughing and singing snippets of holiday songs. It seemed they'd already been out around the neighborhood for a few hours. There was a decidedly cheery, festive feeling in the little coffee shop, and Colin was in no rush to leave.

A little over a month ago he'd sat in this same seat, in almost the same clothes, and brooded over losing what he thought was his livelihood. At the time, he never would have guessed at the odd turns his life was going to take, and the bizarre chances he'd be thrown. He certainly never expected to be working in a Santa outfit.

Colin leaned his head back with a smile. He was going to Carol's house next. They'd watch *Jingle All the Way* in front of a roaring fire. They'd listen to Christmas music and tell the kids that if they didn't go to sleep quick, Santa was going to pass over the house.

In fact, Colin had even tried to borrow the Santa outfit from the mall. It turned out he wasn't allowed to take it home, but Carol had assured him that if anyone showed up to the house in costume, the overexcited children and animals would tear the whole place down.

In about two weeks, he was going to start on the next phase of his life, and Colin was happy with that. He had taken a residency at the prestigious Art Museum, where they wanted him to basically work on new pieces all day long for the next few months. They would supply the workshop, any tools he needed, as well as a pretty decent stipend. He also had several more commissions lined up for both sculptural pieces, as well as some jewelry pieces that he was really excited to work on.

Between the residency and the high-end clientele that seemed to be passing his name around, he had the sense that his work was going to have some good exposure in the upcoming year. He found absolute peace with leaving the life of supervised manual labor behind. He was free to make whatever life he wanted for himself, and every day that he was away from the routine of his old life, he saw more and more opportunities unfold before him.

He had spent years living and dreaming within the confines of what he thought of as achievable. Those things were good and fine, but Colin had started to see the world and his opportunities differently. And things that he had never thought possible for himself suddenly seemed attainable. It was empowering in a way which he could never have imagined. He felt renewed and excited about life. He felt truly blessed; with many new beginnings just around the corner.

Snow was falling calmly outside the big wall of windows. Colin watched it sleepily. He'd sleep over at Carol and Andrew's on the couch tonight, and wake up with children jumping on him in the morning. It was a fate he was resigned to and loved. They would have breakfast and open presents, and Colin wouldn't worry about how he was going to make a living next year. The world, for just a fragile moment, was all in one piece, and he savored it.

His hot peppermint mocha was called out, and Colin got to his feet. The baristas were running to keep up with the orders coming in from both the store and the drive-thru. Just as he reached for his mocha, a standard cup of black coffee was set beside it and called out. A woman's gloved hand reached out to take it, and Colin found himself suddenly face-to-face with Nora.

"Oh." That was all that came out of his mouth. Colin coughed and tried again. "Hey! Merry Christmas."

"Merry Christmas!" Nora replied with a smile. She took his arm and led him away from the counter, where the next order was already steaming.

Colin dutifully followed, coffee in hand. He took a sip, giving himself a chance to think of something intelligent to say. Usually, he felt fine talking to people, even beautiful women. But with all their missed encounters and all the time he'd spent thinking about her, he had built up a total block of nerves.

"So," Nora started with a smile. "You're the mysterious artist, huh?"

Colin could already feel the heat on his face. "Yeah," he agreed.

Nora elbowed him. "And the Santa at Northtown."

His eyebrows rose sharply. Now, he was definitely blushing. "Uh... yep."

"And a welder, too," Nora nodded. He dared a glance at her face; she was still smiling. That was a good sign. "A man of many talents."

"That's what I put on my business cards, anyway," Colin answered with a chuckle. Nora laughed.

"It's really warm in here, with coats and all," she said, indicating her thick peacoat and gloves. "Want to go outside?"

Colin did. Now that she had his heart pounding in his ears, some cool air would be a blessing. She was dressed sleek and elegant again, while he found himself looking just as rough and tumble as the first time he'd seen. Even so, as they stood outside the door to Starbucks, Nora's eyes were on him, and he'd have to be completely dense to misunderstand her thoughts.

"So," she started slowly. "I wanted to ask how you'd feel about going out together sometime."

Had she just said that? Colin forced his mouth to start moving before he froze like a deer.

"Yeah, that would be great. I... I didn't know if you'd be interested."

Nora took out her phone, handling it awkwardly in gloves and with one hand still on her coffee cup. "Now, I'm going to get your number this time. People keep interrupting before I can ask."

Colin gave it to her, hardly daring to believe this was happening. She sent him a text, and Colin heard the tone go off through his pocket. He had her phone number. And here he thought he didn't believe in Christmas miracles.

"Thanks." It sounded silly the moment he heard himself say it, but Nora didn't seem to mind. She giggled, and looked absolutely stunning there in the light from the window, with crystal snowflakes catching in her brown hair.

"Have you ever been to London?" she asked suddenly.

Colin stared, and shook his head. "Nope."

Nora smiled. "I haven't either, but I'm taking my sister next week before she goes back to school. So if you call, and I don't answer it's most likely because of the time difference. But don't think I ignored your call because I'll be waiting to hear from you. And I have your number, too, now. I'd like to see you again, Colin."

To his surprise, Nora reached up and kissed him on the cheek. And Colin surprised himself—apparently, he wasn't as shy around beautiful women as he thought because he caught Nora's chin lightly and kissed her on the lips. Her eyes opened in surprise, but she didn't pull away.

When they separated Nora's cheeks were a little red, perhaps from more than cold. Then she realized that she was in a complete daze, staring up at Colin's lips.

She blinked her eyes clear, then smiled up at him. This taking life by the reigns was fun already! Colin was smiling down at her, too. For some strange reason, she felt that if they both played their cards right, there could be many more holiday kisses in their future.

"If I didn't have to make this Christmas Eve delivery before going to my parents' house, I would say we should go for a walk, but..." Nora let out a sigh and shrugged her shoulders.

"That would be nice, but you're right, we should both get going.

Walk you to your car?" he offered. Nora nodded; suppressing the giddy smile she felt bubbling up.

She got in the driver's seat and pulled the door shut. Colin stood beside the car, holding his peppermint mocha and grinning like an idiot. She began to pull out of the spot and then stopped for just one more moment. A question popped into her head, and however silly, she felt compelled to ask.

She rolled down the window. "Strange question. But do you believe in Christmas miracles?"

Colin's grin grew wider, then took a second before he shook his head subtly. "Before this month, if you'd asked me that, I don't know what I would have said. But right this moment? I can tell you that without a doubt, yes. Yes, I do." Their eyes couldn't break from one another.

"I'm going to call you tomorrow and wish you a merry Christmas, okay?"

Still awestruck, she just nodded, then managed out, "Okay."

Nora slowly moved her foot off the brake pedal, and the car eased forward. Her heart was fluttering a thousand beats a minute, and her face felt flush. As she looked in her rearview mirror, she no longer saw Colin standing there, but through the air came the low, booming sound
- *Ho, Ho, Ho*

Nora laughed out loud, then pressed the gas.

ACKNOWLEDGMENTS

Thank you to my wonderful family and friends. You make my world go 'round.

To Drake: Brainstorming with you is always the highlight of any evening. Thank you for being my partner in crime...even when you're overworked and overtired.

To my parents: Thank you for teaching me to always look ahead at what can be, instead of getting bogged down by the difficult things that life presents. I owe my silver-lining outlook and crisis management skills to you, and couldn't be more thankful.

To Emily: Thank you so much for your help and contribution!

To my mother-in-law Julia: Thank you for always being my #1 beta reader. It wouldn't be nearly as fun to do what I do without you.

SCOTTISH HOLIDAY

A Wee, Lovely Holiday Escape

A Sophie Mays Novelette

Scottish Holiday

To my mother,

For all your tireless efforts to complete our family genealogy. I am so appreciative of all the hard work you have put in. I promise one day I will read and learn it all.

Love You

FOREWORD

I don't normally write short stories, so when my publisher came to me with the fun challenge of writing some shorter holiday stories, I jumped at the chance to grow and explore. This project was especially fun because I find genealogy fascinating (even though I have to admit that I've left most of the heavy lifting up to my mother and grandmother as far as my family tree goes). We have a wee little bit of Scottish in our way back history, so learning about the country, and in particular the Isle of Lewis, was beyond interesting. I know that I'm now itching for a trans-Atlantic visit to the British Isles, and I hope that after reading Scottish Holiday, you are, too! Enjoy!

CHAPTER 1

a surge of nausea swept through Jillian. Even though it was a bright, sunny day, the ferry rolled and dipped in the waves. This stretch of water was called, 'The Minch', whatever that meant, but Jillian couldn't wait until the journey was over.

"Try sitting outside, dear." Another passenger tapped her on the shoulder, giving her some advice. "Don't eat anything else and know where the toilets are, just in case!" With a knowing smile, the kindly lady wandered off, leaving Jillian envious of her ability to walk in a straight line. Struggling to her feet, she made her way to the outer deck, the smell of salt and oil filling her nostrils. Finding her way to a cold, damp seat, she slumped into it, leaning her head back to gaze at the blue sky. What a journey this had been! She had left her cosy apartment in New York, taken three flights to arrive in the Scottish capital of Edinburgh, a train up to Inverness, a rental car to Ullapool and finally, a ferry to the Isle of Lewis. When she looked at the map, it seemed like she couldn't have found a farther outer island to travel to in the British Isles. Jillian was beyond exhausted, the hours and hours of travel taking its toll. She'd been planning this trip for years; her search for her family's ancestors leading her to the tiny island in the

Scottish Hebrides. Although, right now, her stomach rolling, she wondered if it was going to be worth it.

Thankfully, the announcement soon came that the ferry would be docking in the next few minutes and they could expect to be disembarking very soon. Car drivers were asked to go down to the lower level and sit in their vehicles, so Jillian followed the other passengers down three flights of narrow stairs. It took her a few minutes to find her rental car, climbing into the wrong side of front seat with a sigh of relief, all ready to start the engine. Regardless of how nervous she still felt about driving on the opposite side of the street, she could not wait to get off this ferry and into her holiday home!

Half an hour later, Jillian was standing in a small, picturesque house, surrounded by beautiful scenery. Her bags were still packed, dropped by her feet as she stared out of the window at the view. It was simply stunning. Fields surrounded the house, whilst, a little further away, she could see the sea. Sheep grazed nearby, one staring at her nonchalantly as it chewed the rich grass. It was idyllic. Jillian took a deep breath, smiling for the first time in as many hours. Her months of saving up, organizing flights, finding a holiday house and the many, many hours of sitting in plane, bus or car seats had all been worth it. Her next task was to unpack her bags and get the tea kettle on.

Not too much longer, a steaming cup of Earl Grey tea in hand, Jillian found her way down to the water. Hoping that the charges wouldn't be too bad, she speed dialed her friend.

"Kasey? Hi!"

"Jillian! Did you make it? Are you there?"

Jillian grinned. "I'm here and it's gorgeous! I wish you could see it!"

"Tell me about it!" Kasey exclaimed. "What are you looking at, right now?"

Jillian looked out at the view, the sand tickling her feet. She wished her best friend could have joined her on this trip but Kasey couldn't afford the time away from work. Besides, this was a journey Jillian needed to finish on her own.

"I'm looking out at the blue sea," Jillian began. "The sand is freezing but I took my boots off anyway!"

"You did?" Kasey laughed. "Even the Scots will think you're crazy!"

"It is cold," Jillian admitted, walking back to where she'd left her boots. "But they told me to expect that. It's like 40 degrees here or something!" She held the phone in one hand while pulling back on her boots. "There's a river that runs into the sea, and I found some caves round the other side of some rocks."

Kasey sighed into the phone, clearly jealous. "It sounds beautiful. What's the house like?"

"It's lovely," Jillian replied, meandering slowly back up the beach towards her holiday home. "There's a couple of sheep that seem to live in the garden. I don't know if they're supposed to be there or not but they won't leave!"

Kasey laughed at the image. "Well, just make sure you don't fall in love with the place and decide to stay, I want you right back here with me on December 23rd!"

"That's a week away Kasey, don't worry about it! I'll find out what I can about my family and be back on that plane before you know it. I'm guessing these five days will go fast!"

"Well, enjoy yourself," Kasey replied. "Take lots of photos and make sure to bring me back one of those famous chessmen, will you?"

"I have no idea what you're talking about Kasey, but I definitely will!"

She heard Kasey laughing before she hung up. She'd have to look into those chessmen.

Returning to her house, Jillian found the sheep still hanging around the front door. Maybe they intended to spend the night, she mused. It was definitely getting colder now, with Jillian's fingers and toes beginning to tingle. Darkness was falling, even though it was only just passed 3pm and Jillian suddenly realized that she had forgotten to buy any food or supplies! Grabbing her welcome pack, she skimmed through it to find where the nearest takeout place was. Okay, there weren't as many options as back home, but there seemed be a decent

Chinese takeout and quite a few 'Fish and Chip' places, which sounded interesting. She knew of a British-themed fish and chips place in Manhattan, but she'd never tried it. She'd probably give that a whirl, as well as driving to the nearest grocery store. From where she was, in a place called 'Back', she'd have to drive to Stornoway to get what she needed. Glad she hadn't taken her thick coat off and making sure to leave a light on, Jillian made her way to her car, making sure not to hit any stray sheep as she drove cautiously to the bottom of the road and turned right. Stornoway was only a few miles away and she couldn't wait to try her first ever 'fish and chips'!

CHAPTER 2

"What can I get for you, dear?"

Jillian thought for a moment, an array of choices laid before her. "Ummm....I'm not sure. What would you recommend?"

"The fish," came a deep voice behind her. "Definitely the fish."

Turning, Jillian smiled at the tall, sandy-haired man, who grinned in response. "Thank you, I've never had fish and chips before."

"I wouldn't have thought so," he replied, his accent clearly placing him as an islander. "Not too many fish and chip shops in America!"

Jillian laughed, ordering a fish supper with a can of Coca-Cola. She listened to the stranger order the same – except he chose a can of Irn Bru.

"I can't tempt you to try Scotland's favorite fizzy drink?" He held up the orange and blue can. Jillian made a face.

"I've been told it tastes disgusting," she replied. "I'll stick to what I know!" She pointed to her can of Coke.

"Fair enough!" There was a pause as they both received their meals, each wrapped in old newspaper. He handed her a small wooden fork and began to make his way out of the door, waiting for her to catch up.

Oh. Jillian hadn't realized there was nowhere to sit to eat. Her confusion must have shown on her face as the stranger laughed, pointing to a small shop a little ways up the street.

"You're welcome to come and eat in my bookshop if you like. It's warm at least!"

Jillian hesitated. She'd heard that everyone around here was friendly but the idea of going with a complete stranger had her alarm bells ringing. On the other hand, it was freezing already and the only other place she'd have to eat was her car, and that didn't sound too appealing.

"I'm James, if that's any help," the man said, aware of her pause. "I promise I won't lock the door and you can sit right next to it, if it helps you feel better!"

Jillian nodded, her stomach growling and forcing her decision. James smiled and they walked together up the street towards his bookshop.

"So, where are you from?" The bell jangled as James pushed the door open, the lights already on.

"New York," Jillian replied, looking around the little shop. Books covered almost every surface and there was some light music playing in the background. Three comfortable chairs surrounded a small table in the corner, with a coffee machine on the nearby shelf. James waved his hand towards the table.

"Sit wherever you want and help yourself to a coffee," he began. "I've just got to sort out a couple of things over here first."

Over at his desk, James shut down the register and turned the music down. He loved meeting new people and Jillian looked like someone interesting. It didn't hurt that she had a pretty smile, her dark auburn hair tied back in a neat ponytail and big blue eyes looking all around.

Jillian sat in an old-looking armchair, surprised at how comfortable it was. Opening her coke and unwrapping her food, she began to dig in with relish, enjoying every bite. James came over to join her.

"New York then, huh? So, what's brought you to our tiny island, if you don't mind my asking?"

"Not at all," Jillian replied, through a mouthful of food. "I've spent years building up my family tree, you know, looking at my grandparents and great-grandparents and things. Apparently, a few generations ago, my relatives on my mother's side, came from the Hebrides."

A look of understanding came over James's face. "Oh I see, so they were one of the many families that emigrated over to the States?"

"Yes, that's right," Jillian replied. "They were MacDonalds. From what I've learned, they emigrated in the late 1800s and I'm here to see what records I can find for them."

"You'll need to start at the library, then," James replied thoughtfully. "My grandpa used to go there a lot, he was interested in finding out all the lines of our family."

Jillian, wiping her greasy fingers on a paper napkin, studied James for a moment. His chestnut brown hair flopped over his forehead, his dusky blue eyes intense but kind. "Your family's always been on the Isle of Lewis?"

James nodded. "I come from a long line of crofters – you know, working the fields, keeping the sheep and cows."

"There's two sheep in my garden!" Jillian exclaimed. "Are they meant to be there?"

James laughed. "Where are you staying?"

"A place called 'Back'."

"Oh yes." James nodded knowingly. "They're probably Kenny's sheep, just out for a wander. He'll know where to find them. They'll be gone in the morning."

For a moment, Jillian stared at James. This was such a different world compared to New York. Here, everyone seemed to know everyone else; it was such a small community. In New York, she didn't even know her next door neighbor's name! It blew her mind.

"What?" James asked, his eyes lighting with humor.

"N- Nothing," Jillian stammered, wondering how to explain herself without sounding like a tourist. "This place is just very different from home."

James leaning back in his chair, his smile making her tingle a bit.

"It's different if you're not used to it," he said. "But everyone's very friendly. You'll probably have someone at your door in the morning, with a cup of tea or some cakes or something. Everybody knows when there's someone new in the community!"

Jillian frowned for a moment. "You said you come from a crofting family, but you own a bookshop?"

"I love books!" James replied, getting up to turn on the coffee machine. "My grandpa loved sheep, my father loved sheep but I love books….much to his disappointment, I might add."

"Really?" Jillian replied, frowning slightly. "I'm sorry to hear that."

James shrugged, a flicker of sadness crossing his face so quickly that Jillian couldn't be sure she'd actually seen it.

"It doesn't matter, my younger brother loves the land so he'll take over the croft one day. I help out where I can but I bought this bookshop a couple of years ago and have never looked back."

"I see," Jillian said quietly, enjoying the cozy atmosphere. "I think it's a lovely place."

"Thank you," James replied, handing her a coffee. "Sorry this won't be up to your usual standards, it's the best I can do!"

Laughing, Jillian took it from him gratefully, taking a small sip. It was nowhere near her usual strength but it would do.

"So," James began, flopping down into the seat opposite her. "Would you like some help?"

Frowning slightly, Jillian looked puzzled for a moment. "Help with what?"

"Help with your family tree," James replied. "I can help you at the library and with the archives, if you like. It'll be faster with two of us looking and I guarantee there'll be a lot of information!"

Jillian's heart beat a little faster. He seemed genuine and she had to admit he was good-looking. A few days with him sounded like fun and it would be nice to have company.

"That would be lovely," she replied. "But I don't want to take you away from your work."

"Don't worry about that," James said, yawning. "I've got a friend who helps me out at the shop now and again, I'm sure he won't mind helping out for a few days. How long are you on the island for?"

"Just for five days," Jillian replied. "I catch the early ferry on the 22nd."

"Wanting to be back home for Christmas then?"

Jillian smiled, not willing to talk about her family situation at the moment. "Something like that."

"Sounds like we'll have plenty of time to do some exploring then." James's voice was warm and deep. "There's loads of places on this island that you have to see before you go. I'll be your guide to the Isle of Lewis!"

Jillian laughed, a warm glow spreading through her as she thought of spending more time with James. He would make the perfect tour guide.

CHAPTER 3

*J*ames had not been wrong. After staying up late chatting to James and taking at least three wrong turns on the way back to her holiday home, Jillian had been woken by a knock on the door.

Still in her pajamas, she opened the door to find a cheerful looking woman on the front step, holding a basket.

"Good morning! I'm Jessie, I live in the house just up the road. My husband owns this place, I think he met you yesterday."

Still groggy and struggling to make sense of what the very loud and very awake woman was saying, Jillian merely nodded, wondering if answering the door in her pajamas would become a common occurrence.

"I just wanted to say hello and to let you know that you're welcome to pop in anytime, the kettle's always on!"

"Thank you," Jillian managed, her voice a croaky whisper.

"Not at all, dear, not at all. Here you go, I hope you like scones! Enjoy your day and I'll see you tomorrow, if not before." Handing Jillian the basket, the woman patted her hand and walked away, leaving her standing in the doorway, still slightly bewildered. Shivering from the chilly wind that wrapped around her ankles, Jillian shut the door quickly and stumbled into the kitchen, dumping the basket on the kitchen table. She'd only just filled the kettle with water when there came another knock on the door.

"Who is it now?" she groaned, rubbing her eyes as she went to answer it once more. To her utter horror, there stood James who, on seeing her appearance, tried hard to cover his amusement.

"Slept late, did we?"

Closing her eyes briefly in embarrassment, Jillian stepped aside and asked James to come in, seeing no other choice.

"I thought we were meeting at 9am?" she mumbled, hastily tying her mussed hair back as best she could manage.

"It's gone 9am," James said gently, regarding her with a mixture of amusement and exasperation. "At 9:30am, I thought I'd drive by and see if everything was okay!"

"Oh no," Jillian rubbed her eyes, wishing James hadn't seen her in her pajamas. "I must have slept through my alarm…jet lag is a killer."

James merely smiled at her, hoping she couldn't see the way his thoughts were turning.

"I'll go get changed, I'll be right back," Jillian replied, making her way back to the bedroom.

"I'll get the kettle on and some of these scones on the go. Were they from Jessie?" he shouted through the open door.

"Yes," came her faint reply. "She came to the door, just like you said."

Chuckling to himself, James put the kettle on and began buttering some still-warm scones. Jillian certainly made a fetching picture first thing in the morning. Waiting for her at the Stornoway library, he'd been concerned, then a little frustrated but all that had melted away the moment she'd rubbed her eyes and he'd seen the vulnerable side push through. She'd looked so endearing, her eyes still wistful as though she'd just woken from a lovely dream. James shook his head, reminding himself that she would be leaving in a few days. Now was not a time to be chasing anything romantic, they'd just be friends for a while and he'd enjoy showing her around the island. That was all there was to it.

"Ouch!" Jillian winced, gingerly turning her neck from side to side. She'd been in the same position for far too long, poring over old and dusty books that held the promise of finding her family line. James smiled sympathetically, coming over from a set of bookshelves to stand behind her.

"Want me to help?"

Without a word from her, he swept her long, silken hair over her shoulder and began to gently knead her neck and shoulders. Jillian tensed immediately at his touch, initially feeling slightly awkward before relaxing, the pain and tension rolling away as he worked the sore muscles. There was silence for a few moments and Jillian caught herself closing her eyes. There was something very intimate about his touch and she was glad there was nobody else around in the library to see her reaction to him.

"Is that better?"

"Yes, thank you." Despite herself, Jillian felt a warm blush heat her cheeks and bent over the book again to hide her rose-hued face. James was just a friend, she reminded herself. Nothing else. Best keep it uncomplicated.

James moved to a seat across from her, noticing her red face and smiling to himself as she tried her best to hide it from him. His reaction to her sore neck had been nothing more than impulse, but he had enjoyed getting a bit closer to her. Her hair was a gorgeous shade of auburn that shimmered in the light and her skin soft and smooth. He had been tempted to lower his mouth to her neck but hadn't done so, although the pull had been a strong one. He didn't mind admitting he was attracted to her but stopped himself from taking things further. Friendship was the best he should hope for.

"Did you get anywhere with your search?"

Getting his mind firmly back on track, James was surprised to see unhappiness cross her face.

"No," she replied, glancing at him. "There's nothing so far."

James smiled at her, trying to cheer her up. "There's lots more to go through," he replied. "Try not to worry, we'll find a record of them soon."

"Do you really think so?"

He nodded, wanting to reassure her. "Of course we will. There're at least six more logs to go through, they all look like pretty hefty ones too! They're bound to be in there somewhere." He indicated a pile of six stacks of books, accounting births, deaths, and marriages from 1855 onwards. Jillian looked at them, sighing heavily. They really were thick books, it would take her all of her time to go through them! All she had were two names to go on, as well as the approximate year of marriage. As though he was able to read her thoughts, James stood up and reached for one of the tomes.

"Tell you what, why don't we go for a coffee break and then come back and start again. I reckon, if we really went for it, we'd be able to find the records by this evening."

"By tonight?" Jillian replied, disbelief in her voice. "Really?"

"Really!" James looked at her with a gleam in his eye. "I've even got a wager for you. If we don't find them by tonight, then I'll buy us dinner. If we do, then you do."

Jillian studied him for a moment, unsure as to whether he was truly being serious. James held out his hand and Jillian, after one more moment's hesitation, shook it firmly. She was certain of her win.

CHAPTER 4

*I*t was pitch black outside and Jillian and James had been
working steadily for most of the day. The librarian had very
kindly said she would wait until 6pm for them, instead of the usual
5pm closing time. It was now just past 5pm and Jillian's stomach began
to rumble. She smiled a little sadly. At least James paying for dinner
would be a small consolation.

"Ah ha!" James cried out.

Jillian leaped to her feet, all thoughts of food dissipating. "What?
What? Did you find something?"

Without a word, James pointed to a place in the book he'd been
studying, a grin on his face. Jillian bent down to read the tiny writing,
throwing her hair back and out of her face. She could hardly believe it.
There it was. The record of her great, great, grandparents' marriage.

"Oh my goodness," she whispered. "Oh my goodness! I can't
believe it!" She stood up, turning to James in a bit of a daze. "I can't
believe you found it!"

James smiled at her, feeling genuine delight over her happiness.
This clearly meant a lot to her.

"I guess dinner's on you," he replied, his voice barely above a
whisper.

Her eyes filling with sudden tears, Jillian flung her arms around him, feeling him respond in kind and hold her tightly. Trying to hold back her tears, she eventually gave into sobs that shook her frame, so great was her relief and joy. James simply held her, his arms around her waist, waiting for her tears to subside. Eventually, she stopped, burying her face into his neck in embarrassment. She'd barely known James more than a day and here she was crying into his shirt! For some curious reason, he didn't feel like a stranger; it was as though they'd been friends for a long time and, even more inexplicably, his arms around her felt just right. It was as though she fit just perfectly.

Easing back slightly, she smiled into James's face, pushing down the urge to kiss him right there in the back of Stornoway library. "Thank you, James. I can't tell you how much this means to me."

James wiped away the one remaining tear from Jillian's cheek, aware of her closeness. Her eyes were bright and her vulnerability with him was a gift he felt he didn't deserve to receive. Everything about Jillian drew him to her – if she hadn't been leaving in a few days, James would certainly have done something about his attraction. Perhaps he should anyway and just forget about the fact she'd be leaving soon. He began to lower his head but at that precise moment, the librarian interrupted them.

"Did you get what you were looking for?"

"Not quite," James replied under his breath, as Jillian scrambled out of his embrace.

"Yes, yes, thank you!" Jillian scooped up the log and practically ran to the photocopier. "I just need a copy of this and then we can get out of your hair!"

"Oh, I am glad," the librarian replied, photocopying the page for them. "Is it your family history you're interested in?"

"Yes," Jillian replied excitedly. "I just found a record of my great, great grandparents' marriage! I can hardly believe it!"

"Really?" the librarian replied, studying the place that Jillian pointed out. "You know, if you want more details about them, I suggest you go to the church where they were married."

Jillian spun around to face James, a question on her face. James nodded in response, knowing that she was asking him to help her. It wasn't as though he was going to pass up on the opportunity to spend more time with her!

"What will the church records have?" he asked, wondering how much information they would get.

"Well, the church would have been the family's local one, so they should have a record of your great, great, grandmother's birth at least, and possibly her death."

"Oh...," Jillian said, sinking slowly into a seat. "What about my great, great, grandfather?"

"Again," the librarian said, "most people met and married from within the same community back in those days so it's probable that he was also from the same village."

"Are you serious?" Jillian breathed, hardly daring to believe her luck. "The church records will have details of them both?"

"Yes, most likely!" The librarian laughed at Jillian's amazement. "Everything should be there. Just ask the minister and I'm sure they'll be happy to help you."

"Thank you!" Jillian replied, giving the bemused librarian a brief hug. "Thank you so much!"

The photocopied document now safely in her bag, Jillian left the library, James in tow. "So, dinner's on me then?" she smiled, not caring in the slightest that she'd have to pay. "Where will we go?"

"Well, round here, there's not much choice," James laughed. "I'd suggest the Digby Chick. It's nothing like your posh, fancy, New York restaurants, but over here it's the best of the best!"

"Sounds great," Jillian responded, the cold wind whipping her hair over her face. Tying it back quickly, she took James's arm, planting a quick kiss on his cheek. "Let's go! It's freezing out here!"

CHAPTER 5

*J*illian lay in her bed, snuggling under the duvet as she heard the wind whip around the house outside. It was morning, not that you would have guessed it from the gloom. She was surprised she'd woken early but put it down to the excitement of yesterday. Smiling to herself, her thoughts turned to James. He'd been the perfect gentleman, making her smile and laugh all through dinner. What was worse, she found herself deeply attracted to him, wanting more than just the friendship she'd promised herself she'd stick to. She thought back to when he'd held her the library, his strong arms holding her tightly. Her breath caught as she thought of the way he'd leaned forward as though he had been about to kiss her, knowing that she would have responded by kissing him back. Did it really matter if they started something that had to finish? She only had three full days left on the island and she intended to spend every moment with him. The thought of leaving him sent a sudden stab of pain through her heart as she came to realize how much she cared about him. Yes, he was a handsome guy, but his character was what attracted her the most. He had been caring and considerate, helpful and kind – everything she wanted in a man. It was just her luck to find the man of her dreams and then have to leave him behind! There was no way she'd ask him to move to New York, he'd never survive in the big city. What if she were to move here? Jillian sat bolt upright in bed. Could she move here? Would she miss the city? She hadn't so far. Instead, she loved the open space, the beautiful views. Sure it was cold and the gloomy days were miserable, but the cozy fires and warm stoves made up for that. Getting out of bed, she threw her thoughts away, ridiculing herself for having such a vivid imagination. Whilst she could tell that James had wanted to kiss her, she didn't know if it was anywhere near the depths of feeling she was starting to have for him. Maybe he just wanted a casual fling, knowing that he'd never see her again. Reminding herself that she didn't know him that well at all, Jillian got up to dress, anticipating the return of Jessie with more scones.

"Ah, I see we've managed to get dressed today!"

"Very funny," Jillian responded, fairly proud of herself for having scones buttered and coffee already made before James arrived. "Jessie came round again this morning so I made sure I was ready this time!"

"Well done," James replied, feeling a twinge of regret that he hadn't seen her in her pajamas again. This woman stirred up feelings in him that he wasn't quite sure what to do with.

"So where are we going today?"

"Well," James began, munching on a scone. "We're going to go to the church your great, great grandparents' were married in and then, after we find their records, I'm going to take to the Callanish Stones."

"What's the Callanish Stones?" Jillian asked, taking a sip of her hot tea.

"They're standing stones that were probably erected around 3000 B.C," James replied. "They're pretty amazing, plus there're some incredible views. Although it might be quite misty by the time we get there!" He looked regretfully out of the window at the low lying clouds.

"Sounds great!" Jillian replied, thinking that no matter what they did, she would enjoy being with James. "But you said we'd go to the church first?"

Nodding, James took another bite of his scone. "Mmm-hmm."

"Which church?"

Coughing as he accidentally inhaled a few crumbs of scone, it took a few moments for James to recover his composure. "Sorry, sorry, eating too fast! Yes, I forgot to tell you!" His face was wreathed in smiles. "The church your great, great grandparents were married in was this one!"

Jillian sat back for a moment, not understanding. "This one?"

"Yes! This village's church is called Back Free Church, it's the one they were married in!"

Barely able to comprehend what James was saying, Jillian sat in her chair with her mouth agape.

"That means that they were probably born in this village, most likely lived here too," James continued. "In those days, people didn't move around much."

Jillian opened and closed her mouth, not able to speak, her mind was working so fast. This village, this little place where she'd chosen to stay, was the very one her ancestors had lived in? She could hardly believe it.

"Say something, Jillian!" James laughed, seeing her reaction. "I didn't quite realize how important this was to you!"

Knowing he wouldn't understand unless she told him everything, Jillian decided to be honest. She wanted to be. Getting to her feet, she refilled her mug, James refusing a top up. Sitting back down, she gazed out of the window before speaking, not quite able to meet his eye.

"I know lots of people are interested in their family tree, but I'm probably one of the few that have traveled over 4,000 miles to find out more!" She smiled as James chuckled. "There's a reason that I've been so desperate to find out more – I was abandoned as a baby." She swallowed hard, pushing down the lump in her throat. "Obviously I was adopted and my adopted parents were two of the most loving people on this earth!"

"Were?" James asked, leaning a little forward. His face was lined with sympathy.

"They died," she said, bluntly. "Quite a few years ago now. The details don't matter. What does matter is that I didn't find out I was adopted until afterwards." She glanced at his face, seeing his surprise. "I know, how many people don't find out they were adopted until they're an adult!"

"That must have been quite traumatic," James said quietly, reaching for her hand. She gave it willingly, the contact reassuring her.

"It was." She'd promised herself she wouldn't cry but the tears were already threatening. "Since then, I've been desperate to find out anything I can about my real family – and that's what's brought me here."

There was a long silence as Jillian tried to hold back her tears and James just held her hand.

"I'm sorry," he said, after a few moments. "I'm sorry you had to go through that. Do you have any brothers or sisters?"

Jillian shook her head no. "My adopted parents couldn't have any children of their own and my real mother was only a teenager when she had me. She left me on the street for someone else to find. Not that I'm angry with her for doing that, she had a lot of problems."

James said nothing, trying his best to keep his opinions to himself. Jillian needed him to listen right now and that was what he was going to do.

"She died quite young," Jillian continued, her voice a little unsteady. "Like I said, she had a lot of problems."

Without a word, James pulled Jillian to her feet and wrapped his arms around her. Trying to hold back the emotion while being in his arms was a battle she was never going to win. Eventually, Jillian let it flood her, crying great, heaving sobs as she let it all pour out: the pain, the sadness, the loneliness. She gave it all to James and he took it willingly.

James cradled Jillian in his arms, wishing he could take the pain away. He couldn't imagine what it would be like to have no family. Here he was surrounded by relatives everywhere he looked, there was always some third cousin or something introducing themselves! He knew Jillian was hurting and finally understood why this journey had meant so much to her. She needed to know who her family was and who she was. It all made sense.

"I'm sorry," Jillian said, her voice muffled against his sweatshirt. "I've cried all over you." With one last big sniff, she pulled herself free, looking at him with a wobbly grin. "At least you know now."

He smiled at her, wiping away the tears from her cheeks. "I'm so glad you did tell me, Jillian. It's good to know that you trust me."

"I do," she replied, sitting back down at the table. "Of course I do."

James, feeling a little bereft, joined her at the table, tucking into another still-warm scone.

"Well," he began, through a mouthful of food. "I guess we should go to the church then. I phoned the minister earlier, so he'll know we're coming."

"Thank you," Jillian replied, feeling a weight leave her shoulders. "I really appreciate that." She was touched that he would take care of such a thing, going out of his way to help her. She wasn't in the least bit embarrassed to have wept so much, talking about her family was a painful subject and she didn't want to hide that part of herself. Looking at James, she was grateful that he understood, and hadn't run away when she'd turned on the waterworks! He really was something else.

CHAPTER 6

"*Y*ou're quiet," James commented, glancing at Jillian as they drove towards the Callanish Stones. "Everything okay?"

"Yes," Jillian replied, staring down at the paper she held in her hand. "I just can't quite believe it, that's all."

Their trip to the church had been a huge success. She had found records of her great, great grandparents in one of the huge, dusty books held in the back of the church. Having a date of their marriage had helped them to narrow down the timeline and it hadn't been long before Jillian had found both her great, great grandmother and her great, great grandfather's record of birth. Even more exciting, she now had the names of their parents – giving her more family history than she'd ever hoped for.

"Do you think you'll keep looking into it?" James queried. "After a point, it's bound to get more difficult."

Jillian looked out of the window for a moment, taking in the beauty that surrounded her. "No," she said quietly. "I think my journey stops here. I know now that my family is descended from those who made their lives here on this island and that's enough. I feel a part of them, just by being here. I know that sounds a bit bizarre, but I really do feel it!"

"It doesn't sound weird at all," James replied.

"Bizarre," Jillian countered, a grin on her face. "I said bizarre, not weird."

She saw an unrepentant smile on James's face, and, laughing, continued their playful exchange for the rest of the journey.

"These are the Callanish Stones." James spread his arms wide, as though trying to encompass the entire circle.

"They are incredible," Jillian breathed, completely overawed at the sight. "What were they for?"

Taking her hand in his own, James began to walk around the stones, giving Jillian a brief history. Mesmerized by the sight, Jillian listened carefully, all the while thinking how natural it felt to have her hand in his.

"And this is the burial chamber," James finished proudly, hoping she was impressed with his local knowledge. "Didn't I tell you I'd be the best island tour guide?"

Jillian laughed, running a hand down the smooth, silvery stone. "Yes, I'm very impressed James, well done." She paused for a moment, taking in the view. "It's all so beautiful, almost magical if I'm honest. I'm so glad you took me here. Thank you, James."

"Don't mention it," he replied, giving her one of his cheeky grins, his hair blown about by the wind. "Are you getting cold yet? They do a lovely soup inside!"

"Sounds good," Jillian replied, walking alongside him back down to the little shop, hoping the soup would warm her frozen limbs.

A short time later, James and Jillian were back in the car, James expertly driving down the narrow roads, avoiding the odd sheep that strayed across his path.

"Where are we going now?" Jillian asked, yawning as she did so.

"I'm not telling," James replied, grinning at her in delight. "I've got to stop at the store on the way, but you just close your eyes right now. I'll wake you when we're there."

Too tired to argue, Jillian leaned her head back and closed her eyes, falling asleep in a matter of seconds.

❄

"We're here!" James's insistent voice called, and he poked Jillian in the ribs. "Come on, sleepyhead, before it gets too dark!"

Taking a moment to get her bearings, Jillian reached for her jacket and got out of the car, shivering at the cold.

"We're at the beach?"

"Yup!" James replied, seemingly oblivious by the biting wind. "Come on, we've got a long way to go!"

Shaking her head, Jillian followed James down the sandy wooden steps that led to the longest beach she'd ever seen. She could barely see the end of it in the growing darkness. "Is that where we're going?" she asked, stamping her feet to keep out the cold. "It's miles away!"

"Just one mile," James replied, laughing at the look on her face. "Come on, it'll be worth it, I promise!" Without waiting for her answer, he began to walk and Jillian had no choice but to follow him.

A little while later, James slung an arm around Jillian's shoulders. "Well done," he laughed. "You made it!"

Feeling rather warm, despite the freezing wind, Jillian gave him a weary look. "Do you want to tell me why you brought me all the way down here in the freezing wind and in the dark?" she asked, trying to keep the tiredness from her voice.

James looked at her, seeing she was tired. It had been a long walk but this place was special to him and he didn't share it with many people. "Come on," he said gently. "I want to show you something."

Following him, Jillian found herself walking beside a series of caves, the utter darkness making her shiver. James led her a little further away from the sea, right up to the cliffside where he climbed up a steep incline before disappearing from view.

"James? James? Where are you?"

"Here!" He popped back into view. "Come on, it's not much further."

Jillian, her eyes adjusting to the gloom, followed him into a smaller cave, finding it to be completely dry and large enough for them to stand up in. Handing her a torch, James set to work building a small bonfire, and, before long, the cave was lit with an orange glow as the fire eagerly took to the wood. Jillian gazed around her, beginning to feel a little warm from the fire's heat.

"So," James said, throwing down a couple of cushions. "What do you think?"

"It's amazing," Jillian replied, huskily. "Does the sea never reach this part?"

James shrugged. "Not very often, usually only when there's very bad weather. That won't happen tonight," he smiled, seeing the alarm on her face. "I already checked the tides so we're not in any danger. Now, are you hungry?"

Jillian's stomach growled in response, as, elatedly, she sat down next to him. "What have you got?"

"The best winter barbecue you've ever had," James replied, pulling out all kinds of things from the backpack he'd been carrying.

"The only winter barbecue I've ever had," Jillian exclaimed in surprise, seeing the mountain of food James had brought.

"I'm a hungry man," James replied, a twinkle in his eye. For more than just food, he thought to himself, taking in her gorgeous smile. It was just as well she couldn't read his thoughts!

CHAPTER 7

*R*eplete, Jillian sat next to James, her head on his shoulder. "That was amazing, thank you."

"You're welcome."

They sat in silence for a while, listening to the cracks and pops of the fire.

Jillian sighed. "It really is beautiful around here."

"It is," James agreed. "I come here a lot, when I need to think or when I want some time alone."

"What do you think about?" Jillian asked, still leaning against him.

"Life, mostly." James thought for a moment. "The family, crofting, my bookstore – mostly I come here when I have decisions to make."

"Do you ever think about love?"

He didn't answer straight away, making Jillian a little nervous.

"Sometimes," he admitted finally. "I had a girlfriend a while ago, we got engaged, actually."

Jillian sat up, looking at him in surprise. "Really? What happened?"

James shrugged, pain on his face. "We had to break up. It was pretty traumatic."

"I'm sorry," Jillian said, wondering about this mysterious woman. "Did you break it off or did she?"

"She did," he replied, his voice quiet. "Looking back, it was the best thing for both of us. I still see her sometimes but we're not friends. Although she wants to be." He ran a hand through his hair.

"Oh." Jillian wondered whether she should have pried. "Sorry, that was rude of me."

"No, it wasn't," James answered firmly. "We're friends, aren't we? Besides, I feel like I can tell you anything."

Jillian smiled at him, the flames illuminating her features. "Me too," she replied quietly. They sat for a moment, simply looking at one another. Jillian took a deep breath, reminding herself that what he had said was true. They were just friends, nothing more.

"So," she began in a jaunty tone. "What's this place called?"

"The beach?"

"Yes, the beach. Is it called 'the mile long beach' or something?"

James chuckled. "Close, actually. It's called, 'the big beach', although nobody calls it that. It's got a Gaelic name."

"Oh," Jillian said, thinking for a moment. "Would my great, great, grandparents have spoken Gaelic?"

James nodded. "Oh yes, in fact they probably didn't speak any English!"

"Really?" Jillian's eyes grew wide. "I hadn't imagined that! So, I should probably learn some Gaelic while I'm here, then." She laughed at the look of uncertainty on his face. "Come on, you can teach me! What's the name of this beach in Gaelic?"

Getting to his feet, James stretched his tired muscles. "Okay, if you really want to try, this beach is called the 'Tràigh Mhòr'." He heard her attempt it and winced at the mispronunciation.

"Come on, don't laugh at me!" Jillian complained, trying to keep the humor from her voice. "Tell me it again."

"The 'Tràigh Mhòr'," he repeated again, unable to keep from laughing as he heard her attempt. "I'm not sure Gaelic is going to be your thing, Jillian!"

"Fine, I give up, I give up!" Jillian grinned, seeing James almost doubled over with laughter. "Come on, come on, it wasn't that bad!" She swiped at him in a playful attempt to stop him laughing at her. Stopping abruptly, James caught her hand, pulling her against him. Looking for a moment deep into her eyes, he lowered his head and captured her lips as she melted against him. His lips were smooth and warm, her hands reaching up to touch his face, winding her fingers through his hair.

James didn't know where this had come from, it had been an unstoppable desire that had overwhelmed him. She had looked so beautiful in the firelight, her eyes filled with laughter as she tried to get her tongue around the Gaelic language, and he'd had to do what he'd been thinking of almost since the moment he'd met her. He loved how she felt in his arms, fitting so perfectly. He didn't hold back but showed her the depths of his affection.

"Goodnight," Jillian whispered, holding onto James's jacket as they stood in her doorway. She had no idea how late it was, but she didn't care.

"Jillian, I can't leave if you keep holding on to me," James said huskily, seeing her eyes sparkle in the moonlight.

"I guess I'll just have to keep holding on to you then," she replied, standing on her tiptoes and tipping her head back. He met her unspoken request, kissing her once more. He groaned, taking a step back as she dropped her hands. "If I carry on, I won't stop," he said, seeing the look in her eyes. "I don't want to do something we'll both regret. I'll see you tomorrow." Dropping another kiss on her lips, he left her standing in the doorway.

Jillian sighed dreamily, leaning against the doorframe and staring into the star filled sky. She wasn't going to think about leaving, think about what this all meant, she was just going to be in the here and now. The here and now meant James and that was all she cared about.

CHAPTER 8

"**G**ood morning!"

Jillian almost fell over in shock, entering the living room to find James surrounded by Christmas decorations. "James!" she gasped, "you scared me! How did you get in? What's all this?"

"It's Christmas," he said. "Isn't it obvious?" Walking towards her, he dropped a quick kiss on her lips before handing her a cup of freshly brewed coffee. "Jessie gave me the spare key." There was that cheeky grin again. "Come on," he laughed, seeing her bemused expression. "Get dressed and come help me!"

James's enthusiasm won her over, as she spent the morning decorating her holiday home for Christmas, even though she had no intention of staying. They both pretended that she wasn't leaving the following day, laughing together as they prepared the house for the holiday season.

"Mistletoe," Jillian smiled, a little shyly. "Where should we hang it?"

James looked up, dropping the fairy lights he had been sorting out. "I think I know just the place," he said, taking the mistletoe from her. "How about right here?" He held it above her head, waiting for her to lean into him before he kissed her. "I could get used to this," he whispered as she rested her head on his shoulder. "Jillian, do you really have to go?"

"You can't ask me that, James," Jillian exclaimed, stepping away from him. "You know I can't stay."

"Why not?" he countered. "I know you're lonely back in New York, I know you don't have any family to share the holidays with. Doesn't it make sense to stay here with me, even just for a little longer?"

The pleading in his eyes almost won her over but she teetered on the edge of indecision. "It's not like I haven't thought about it," she said, throwing herself down on the sofa. "And not just because of you. I feel at home here. I love looking out over the sea, knowing that my great, great grandparents saw the same view. I might not be able to speak Gaelic," she saw the laughter on his face, "but I feel as though I might belong here, and I haven't felt that for a very long time." She trailed off, feeling completely lost.

James sat down beside her, reaching for her hand. This was an important moment and he didn't want to ruin it. "Jillian," he began quietly. "I think it's obvious that we're both attracted to each other but I need to be honest, I really care about you too." She studied him with uncertain eyes, feeling a pull that she didn't want to ignore. "I would love it if you would stay with me, stay on my island for the holidays, even just to see if this goes anywhere. I know Jessie won't mind. I want to give us a chance, Jillian, don't you?"

There it was. The big question. "I do," she acknowledged eventually. "I really, really do." She could barely believe she was making this decision. "If you really want me to stay, James, then I will. I'll stay with you for the holidays and then, after that...I guess we'll see."

James could hardly believe what she was saying. She was going to stay. She was going to stay with him. "Yes!" He leaped to his feet, pulling her into his arms and swinging her around. "You've made me so happy, Jillian, so happy! You're not going to regret this, I promise!"

Trying to ignore her sudden flood of anxiety, Jillian blushed at his exuberance, beginning to understand how much he felt for her. "I don't think I will," she replied, putting her arms around him and seeking his embrace. "In fact, I'm sure I won't."

Jillian was dressed in her party clothes, feeling slightly out of place as an American in a clearly Scottish gathering. James, his arm around her waist, seemed to sense her nervousness.

"Don't be worried," he whispered in her ear. "Everyone's really friendly and I guarantee you'll be dancing with almost all of them before long!"

Jillian tried to smile, her concern not completely dissipating. The ceilidh was already in full swing, with the fiddler and accordion player filling the hall with music. There were a huge number of dancers on the floor and Jillian watched them a little anxiously from the balcony, not sure that she'd be able to follow any of the steps.

"Come on," James tugged her hand. "Don't worry about getting it all right. I'll teach you. Just enjoy yourself!" Feeling completely lost, Jillian placed her trust completely in James and followed him down the stairs and onto the dance floor, hoping she wasn't about to make a complete fool of herself.

CHAPTER 9

*J*illian flew around the floor, laughing and twirling. She was having the best time, learning each new dance with greater confidence until she was almost as good as anyone else there. She had completely lost sight of James, finding plenty of other dance partners. Everyone was so friendly, greeting her like a long lost friend instead of a stranger. The dance hall was decked with Christmas lights and other festive decorations, with Jillian spotting the occasional Santa hat amongst the dancers. For the first time in a long time, she felt the joy of the festive season bubble up inside her, knowing that it was all due to James.

The musicians played the final chord, signaling the current dance was coming to an end. Jillian thanked her partner, turning down the next dance as she went in search of some refreshments. She was parched, but enjoying thoroughly the evening. Once she'd gotten over her nerves, she'd found her confidence and thrown herself into enjoying the ceilidh, not minding in the least that she was dancing with strangers instead of with James.

Finding herself a large glass of water, she drank it quickly, quenching her thirst. She leaned on the balcony, watching the dancers below as the music played once more. She'd only been a part of this community for a few days and it was already starting to feel like home. She smiled to herself, certain now of her decision to stay through the holidays. She'd phoned Kasey earlier, hoping she wouldn't be disappointed that she wasn't coming back just yet. To her surprise, Kasey had encouraged her to stay, wanting to hear all about James and what had happened between them. Jillian had stopped short of saying that she loved him, which she knew seemed crazy after such a short period of time, but Kasey had only laughed into the phone, telling her not to hold back. 'Men like James come around once in a lifetime,' she'd said, 'so don't lose him!' Jillian thought about that as she watched James dance the waltz with a girl she didn't know. He really was something else. He danced beautifully too, spinning his partner around the floor in time to the music. As the dance came to an end, she thought about going to find him, watching as he bowed to his partner. It was with utter shock that she saw the girl throw her arms around him and kiss him full on the mouth. What was worse, he didn't stop her right away, taking a few seconds before stepping back – but Jillian had seen enough. She backed away from the balcony, turning to race out of the door, only stopping to get her handbag and her coat. Humiliated and alone, she ran along the street, almost miraculously managing to find a taxi to take her straight back to her holiday home.

Arriving back at the little house, Jillian let herself in, immediately letting the tears fall. The Christmas decorations they'd put up together mocked her, the fairy lights becoming blurry as she wept. Curling up on the sofa, she hugged a cushion to herself, crying until she had nothing left. She felt empty and completely alone. The decision she had made only earlier that day now seemed like the worst choice she'd ever made. She'd trusted him and he'd let her down so quickly, tearing away a piece of her heart. Whilst she'd never said she loved him, her foolish heart told her that she did. That's why this hurt so much. Jillian didn't know what to do, didn't know where to go. Was it too late to rebook her flight? When did the ferry leave in the morning? Changing out of her party clothes, she gave up trying to make a plan. Her mind was fuzzy and she found herself weary beyond belief. Sleep beckoned her and she gave it to its comforting embrace, falling asleep the moment her head touched the pillow.

"Shona, what are you doing?"

James pushed her hands away, hating that he'd responded to her.

"What?" she replied, smiling at him coyly. "Haven't you missed me, James?"

"No," James retorted, taking a step away from her. "No, I haven't Shona. We broke up a long time ago, you were very clear in your decision."

"Well, maybe I regret it," she said lightly, moving towards him and running a hand down his arm. "I still think about you, you know."

James let out a frustrated breath. "Shona, you keep trying this and I keep having to tell you no. I'm not interested!" He walked away, searching for Jillian. He hoped she hadn't seen that, or at least if she had, she would give him a chance to explain. Grabbing a quick drink, he searched in earnest, checking both the dance hall and the balcony. Realizing that both her coat and handbag were gone, James worked out what had happened. She'd left. She must have seen Shona kiss him and jumped to the wrong conclusion. Wishing he could kick something to relieve some frustration, James walked out of the dance hall and made his way to his bookshop. He didn't know what to do. He had to see Jillian, had to explain but she wouldn't want to see him tonight. He'd wait until the morning and hope she'd let him explain.

CHAPTER 10

"Jillian? Jillian?"

It was far too early, but James hadn't been able to sleep. He knocked on the door, again and again, hoping to wake her up but there was no answer.

"James, is that you? What on earth are you doing here so early?" It was Kenny, probably out looking for a couple of stray sheep.

"Morning, Kenny. I'm looking for Jillian, the woman that was staying here? I need to see her."

Kenny let out a low whistle. "Like that, is it? Well, you'd best be heading for the ferry terminal, James. Pretty sure I saw her loading up the car this morning."

James felt like kicking himself. He hadn't noticed the car was gone. Sprinting back to his own car, he shouted a word of thanks to Kenny before starting up the engine. He only had thirty minutes until the ferry departed and it was fifteen miles to the ferry terminal. James hoped there weren't any police in the area; he was going to have to drive fast.

"Jillian? Jillian?" James had boarded the ferry, parking his car in the car park and paying for a ticket to Ullapool that he hoped he wouldn't have to use. He only had ten minutes to spare before the ferry closed its doors and he needed to find Jillian and get her back on dry land so he could explain everything.

He hadn't realized how large this ferry was, racing up and down the various aisles and seating areas in search of her. He heard the five-minute warning but ignored it completely. "Jillian? Jillian!" He spotted her at last, seeing her spot him and then turn in the opposite direction. Catching her, he tried to take her hand but she pulled it from his grip.

"Jillian, just let me explain! Please!"

Jillian did not want to listen. She felt as though she'd been put through the wringer these last few hours, her emotions stretched to the breaking point. The two-minute warning sounded and Jillian turned to James, her eyes cold.

"You'd better get going, James. The boat's about to leave and I have no intention of getting off."

"Fine," James responded hotly. "I'll stay. Even if it takes the whole journey for me to convince you that nothing happened, I'm not going to give up."

"Just leave me alone, James," Jillian pleaded, her eyes once more filling with tears. "I can't do this. I trusted you and then –"

"Then you saw me kissing another woman," James concluded, finality in his voice. "I know. I can't imagine how much that must have hurt you."

Lurching suddenly, Jillian fell into James's waiting arms as the ferry began to leave the Isle of Lewis. Struggling to free herself, she stood tall, raising her chin. "Yes, I saw you James and yes, you hurt me. Do you know what else I saw? I saw you kiss her back, James. You feel something for her! What was I supposed to do? Stay because you asked me to? After seeing that, I want to get as far away from you – and from her – as possible."

A single tear fell down her cheek as she spoke, giving James a glimpse of the pain she was trying desperately to cover.

"It's not like that," James muttered, hating that he couldn't deny that he'd responded to Shona. "Please, Jillian. Even if it won't change your mind, won't you please just hear me out? I promise that if you still want to leave after you've heard what I have to say, I won't bother you again. I'll accept your decision without question."

Jillian sighed heavily, supposing that this was the easiest way out of it. "Okay," she whispered. "Okay, James, I'll listen to you."

Sheer relief washed over James, thanking her as they walked towards the cafeteria. James got her a coffee and himself a tea, sitting down at a table away from the other customers. He studied her, seeing her gaze out of the window at the rough sea. She couldn't even look at him.

"I won't try and pretend that I didn't respond to Shona kissing me," he began slowly. "I know you saw it and I admit that it happened." He took a deep breath. "But you need to understand something: Shona was my fiancée."

Giving him a sharp look, Jillian dropped her gaze almost immediately. "I don't want to get in the middle of anything," she retorted. "You two look like you've still got something going on."

"We don't," James replied, emphatically. "The reason we broke up was because I found out that she was seeing someone else."

"What?" Jillian gasped, shocked by his sudden revelation. "I thought you said she broke up with you?"

"She did," James replied, a doleful look on his face. "Only because she didn't give me the chance to break up with her, first! She discovered that I had found out about her affair and broke up with me on the spot. If I'd had the chance, I'd have ended things myself."

Jillian didn't know what to say, beginning to feel a sympathy for James that she tried to push away. She tried to remember how much he'd hurt her, but a little voice inside began to niggle away at her thoughts. Would she have reacted any differently if she'd been in his place?

"Like I said to you before," James continued, "it was a pretty traumatic time. When she kissed me, I didn't mean to respond the way that I did, and I immediately regretted it. I'm not perfect, Jillian, I made a mistake."

"I suppose I can understand that," Jillian responded after a few moments, seeing the hope that sprang into his eyes. "I guess I'm worried that she'll keep chasing you and, like I said before, I don't want to be the one in the middle."

"That will never, ever happen," James replied firmly, thrilled that she allowed him to take her hand. "There is nothing between me and Shona now, and there never will be again. I haven't thought of her once since last night, I've been thinking only about you. I can't get you out of my head, Jillian, even though I've tried. I want to spend Christmas with you, I want you to get to know my family and my island, and I want you to know me inside out. There's so much for us to share together, all I'm asking for is a second chance."

Jillian took a breath. He was staring at her so earnestly, his brown hair flopping over his forehead no matter how many times he pushed it away. She thought back over their time together, of everything he'd done for her in her search for her family. He'd become a part of her life and if she turned her back on him now, she knew she'd regret if for the rest of her life.

"James," she said, placing her other hand on top of his. "I can give you that second chance. You mean so much to me and... whether I'd like to admit it or not...I think I'm falling in love with you."

At her words, James leaped off his chair and pulled her to his feet. Holding her steady, despite the rolling of the ship, he bent his head, moving his face closer and closer until their lips were almost touching. Then he paused, waiting for her to close the distance. Jillian smiled softly, knowing that her response was proof that she forgave him. Her desire mounting with every second, she stood on her tiptoes and touched his lips with her own. They clung to each other for a long time, professing their love and enjoying being in each other's arms once more.

CHAPTER 11

"*Merry* Christmas!"

Jillian smiled as James held mistletoe above her head, giving him a thorough kiss. Christmas Day on the island had been one of the best days of her life. James had introduced her to his parents and his brother, and she'd been welcomed in as one of the family, with his mother giving her a long hug.

"You're very welcome here, Jillian," she'd said, smiling. "James is clearly taken with you!" Jillian had blushed a little, seeing the knowing look his mother gave James before walking back to the kitchen to check on the turkey. Christmas dinner had been delicious, filled with laughter and fun as they pulled crackers, told silly jokes and stuffed themselves full with four separate courses.

Now it was evening. Jillian sat on the sofa, looking out into the dark night. She hadn't regretted her decision since returning to the island, feeling more at home on this small Scottish island than she'd ever felt in New York.

"I have a gift for you," James said, sitting down beside her. "Here." He handed her a large rectangular gift, wrapped haphazardly with various bits of tape. "I'm not the best at wrapping!"

Jillian was taken aback. "I didn't get you anything," she replied.

"Don't worry," James said, kissing her on the cheek. "You being here with me is the only gift I wanted. Anyway, go on. Open it!"

Tearing off the paper, Jillian felt her breath hitch. It was a her family tree. Hand-drawn on thick paper and framed in exquisite antique silver.

"How….when….when did you do this?" she breathed, touching the glass almost reverently.

"I called in a last minute favor," James replied. "Your friend Kasey was very helpful."

Jillian could barely believe what she was holding. Her family tree, stretching back to her great, great grandparents, was finally complete, written out in beautiful calligraphy. It was the most precious gift she'd ever received.

"Thank you, James," she whispered, turning to him with eyes filled with tears. "I can't believe you did this for me! Thank you, thank you." Placing the frame down carefully, she threw her arms around him, filled with a love for him that she didn't know how to express.

"You're very welcome, Jillian," she heard him reply as he held her tightly. "Maybe one day, I'll be able to add my name to your family tree."

Pulling out of his embrace a little, Jillian looked into his eyes, a hope growing within her. "I hope so too," she answered, smiling. "I love you, James.

"I love you too, Jillian," he replied, once more holding her close. "You're my best Christmas present, ever."

ACKNOWLEDGMENTS

I have so much love and appreciation for my amazing family and friends. My most broguish thanks to Drake, Caroline, My-my, Cristi, Ani and my dad. I could not imagine life without each and every one of you!

To my mom: You are the life force that makes our family shine! You are not only an incredible mother, but an exceptional human being on all levels. I know that I don't tell you often enough how much I appreciate all the genealogy research that you've done, but I truly do. It is so exciting and interesting to learn the history of our family, and I hope that one day I can join you on one of your infamous research trips!

To my mother-in-law Julia: Thank you for being my sounding board! Even with the crazy hours I keep, you manage to help me, listen to me and give me indispensable feedback.

To the incredible Isabel: This book would not be here without you. Your contribution and knowledge of all things Scotland were indispensable and I can't thank you enough for all that you did! You are endlessly appreciated!

AFTERWORD

If you enjoyed any of these books, please consider leaving a Review on Amazon or Goodreads.

It is not only helpful to your fellow readers, but even one little review can make a life-changing difference to an author.

Thank You!

Made in the USA
Columbia, SC
11 December 2018